THE
FLORENCE KING
READER

THE

FLORENCE KING

READER

FLORENCE KING

St. Martin's Griffin ❧ New York

Library of Congress Cataloging-in-Publication Data

King, Florence.
The Florence King reader / Florence King.
p.   cm.
ISBN 0-312-14337-0
1. United States—Social life and customs—Humor.   2. Humorous stories, American.
I. Title.
PS3561.I4754A6   1996
818'.5409—dc20   96-7131   CIP

First St. Martin's Griffin Edition: July 1996

10 9 8 7 6 5 4 3 2 1

For "Salvo Calvo"—my editor, Cal Morgan

CONTENTS

FLORENCE KING'S LITERARY OFFENSES

Calvert Morgan

When Florence King asked me, as her editor of four years, to write an introduction to *The Florence King Reader,* I hesitated the way a Jersey nightclub piano player might balk at the chance to open for Horowitz. But Florence insisted, flattering my youthful grandiosity with talk of Maxwell Perkins; more enticing, she made it sound like fun: "I mention you in several places, so if you wrote the intro it would be like us talking back and forth, kidding each other, telling funny stories on each other—proving to the disenchanted that there's still more to this business than the bottom line and the power lunch." And so I accept—she tells me I'm one of the few people she still likes, after all, and it seems smart not to do anything to jeopardize such an exclusive franchise.

Because today's literary climate is so sensitive, I begin with a warning to more sensitive readers. In one of the great American essays (and one of the few truly funny ones), "Fenimore Cooper's Literary Offenses," Mark Twain advised readers to beware the celebrated *Deerslayer* author James Fenimore Cooper, whose adventure novels lay criminal waste to every known rule of good writing. Florence isn't bad at breaking rules herself, though the ones she smashes generally deserve it. In the spirit of Twain, then. . . .

In the twenty years she has been writing, Florence King has scored 114 offenses against political correctness out of a possible 115. It breaks the record.

There are nineteen rules governing propriety in the domain of modern discourse—by the end of the year we're expecting twenty-two. Florence has broken eighteen of them. These eighteen require:

1. That individuals never be referred to as part of a group. Among Florence's book titles: *Southern Ladies and Gentlemen. Confessions of a Failed Southern Lady. Wasp, Where Is Thy Sting? He: An Irreverent Look at the American Male.* . . .

2. That generalizations never be made as to the characteristics of such a group. Florence on the Good Ole Boy: ''He is a consummate womanizer and would, as the saying goes, hump a rock pile if he thought there was a snake under it.''

3. That women never be described in terms that suggest hysteria, instability, or lack of control. ''The woman who is constantly flouncing in and out of rooms in a furious temper, throwing things, and slamming doors is so dear to the Southern heart that it matters not at all that she is also hard on Southern nerves.''

4. That no sexual advance be made without explicit request and consent. Florence's initiation: ''I failed to 'draw the line,' i.e., I let him touch me 'up top.' Covered tit was for the fifth date and bare tit was for the sixth date, so when I let him unhook my bra, I was two tits too early.''

5. That humor never be used with regard to sexual orientation. Florence on being part of the Lesbian community: ''I was invited to speak at a weekend retreat in the Blue Ridge mountains put on by a gang of muff-diving Druids whose flyer said: 'Corn-worshipping Festival, Witchcraft Workshop, Automatic Writing Demonstration, Logic-Is-Dead Bonfire, Nude Dancing, Vegetarian Cafeteria, Non-Smokers.' I returned the flyer with a note across the top: 'It's time you knew I'm a Republican.' ''

6. That children be protected from hostile or threatening expression. Florence's advice for America: ''If we want to regain the respect of the world, we should begin by announcing that children have no business expressing opinions on anything except 'Do you have enough room in the toes?' ''

7. That no statement be made that violates the broadest tenets of multiculturalism. ''America,'' she writes, ''is the only country in the world where you can suffer culture shock without leaving home.''

8. That no statement of disrespect toward any profession be publicly aired. In *Lump It or Leave It:* ''The academic male is a wart hog with the personality traits of a harem eunuch.''

9. That all speech and writing be purged of any content directly reflecting on racial differences. "Fear of committing a racial Pop-Out [slur] is, I submit, one reason why few people speak in complete sentences nowadays. Pop-Outphobia is so widespread that it has thrust white Americans into a perpetual state of tongue-tied incoherence regardless of what subject they are discussing."

10. That the rights of non-smokers everywhere not be infringed. "Smokers are the new greenhorns in the land of sweetness and light, scapegoats for a quintessentially American need, rooted in our fabled Great Diversity, to identify and punish the undesirables among us."

11. That hate-speech be banned from all public discourse. In *With Charity Toward None,* Florence is asked, "How can you hate *people?*"

Her response: "Who else is there to hate?"

In addition to these large rules there are some little ones. These require that the author shall

12. Eschew clarity.
13. Eschew commitment.
14. Never say in short words what can be said in long hyphenations.
15. Suffer fools gladly, in the name of world peace.
16. Pull punches.
17. Judge not.
18. Hug.

Even these seven are coldly and persistently violated in the work of Florence King, the Venus de Milo of the compassionate embrace.

When America produces geniuses, it produces iconoclasts. When it produces genius writers, often as not they're misunderstood by the many, cherished by the few. Mark Twain? He's either a purveyor of juvenalia or a force of moral corruption, his words to be scoured from our school-library shelves at all costs. William Faulkner? If not an emotionally stunted racist, at least a muddle-headed drunkard who couldn't tell a story straight. Mencken? Parker? Ambrose Bierce? People hated them.

King? Florence King? That's simple. She's an unreconstructed Southerner, gun-toting right-wing feminist, high-church Episcopal atheist, post-menopausal misanthropic monarchist. To paraphrase what P. J. O'Rourke said about one of her books, Miss King has made a career out of hating people—and we love her for it.

I've worked with Florence—at first over the phone and by mail, now mostly by fax—for four years now. I'm still in possession of all my limbs, but thanks for asking; it's easy to understand how one might get the impression this is a difficult job. In best ghoulish oral tradition, campfire tales are still told of editors stretched on the rack for insufficient adherence to the King standard. As she herself glee-fully recalls, the very name *Florence* can provoke twitches and quiv-ers in the New York copyediting community; one poor soul was found a few years ago, huddled in a forgotten corner office, suckling a blue pencil as if at a pacifier, every now and then hurling forth the curdling Poeian cry: *"Stet!"*

Florence King now copyedits her own books. I may not be the brightest deer in the forest, but I know how to keep out of sights.

Editors, copyeditors, and proofreaders notwithstanding, of all the departments at St. Martin's with strong opinions about Miss King none beats our publicity team for pure fortitude. After all, Florence is a misanthrope; she just can't stand people. And the only thing a mis-anthrope hates more than the pure fact of *people* is the horrific notion of entreating them, *Get to know me! C'mon, you'll love me!* For publi-cists, contact is the stuff of life; for Florence, in contrast, life on a desert island would be a day at the beach.

In the time I've worked with her, Florence has grown ever more, well, *reluctant* to undertake publicity for her books. In the years before I came aboard, I'm given to understand, she was a trouper; in 1975 she even appeared on national television, heaven forfend, to pro-mote her first book. (And, as she notes in "Everybody's Gotta Right to Be Famous," she's ceaselessly diligent in answering her fan mail—sometimes with disastrous results.) But publicity became a kind of process of self-discovery for Florence: Spend enough time with peo-ple, she learned, and you'll find out exactly what you think of them.

For years she swallowed her bile for the human race, placing herself again and again in the hands of talking heads and phonies until one day, unable to stand it any longer, she issued her own personal *"desiste!"* and retreated to her home in Fredericksburg—from which she emerges now only in self-defense should anyone from the media get too close. At first, we tried to turn the red tide of Florentian anti-flack rage: When one former St. Martin's marketing director reached Miss King directly by phone with seductive cooings of promised fame if only she'd come to New York to do TV, she shot back a letter to the head of the company: "That man is your in-house Mephistopheles." We quit before the shot she shot back got any more literal.

In fact, those of us at St. Martin's who haven't been scared witless by Florence have come to think of her as a rare bastion of old-fashioned integrity in a world where moral fiber is more commonly measured by the frequency and "frankness" of one's Oprah appearances. Publicity's favorite Florence story is one she told on herself in *Charity,* but she left out a few of my favorite parts, so I'll tell it again here:

When *Reflections in a Jaundiced Eye* came out, *The New York Times Book Review* gave it a favorable notice, written by a reviewer whose name I won't do him the unkindness of recalling here. It looked to us like a fine review—just about the right length, not brilliant in its writing but certainly celebratory of the joys of Kingdom. But Florence, after all, is herself a book reviewer, and to her the *TBR* piece was lousy—not because of what it said, but for its stylistic and structural shortcomings. She wrote the sad soul a letter (care of the *Times,* natch) that put the matter in, well, Kingian terms: "You do not know how to write a review. I do. Here are your faults. . . ." In *Charity* she quotes a few of the individual tips she gave him, but she left out my favorite, Fault #7: "You concentrated on too many minor points and in general farted around without ever stating fully the two things that must be in every review: what the book is about, and what the reviewer thinks of it." When she received her response ("Dear Ms. King, Thank you for your recent letter. It was good to know you were thinking of me. How can you ever forgive me?"), she sent a copy to the head of the *TBR* with a friendly little covering note: "Isn't it fun to slice off a pair of balls every once in a while? It really sets you up for the day, like aerobics."

Now, don't get the idea she didn't know this was the country's most important reviewing venue she was calling on the royal carpet. That was just icing on Florence's cake.

But to portray Florence King as nothing more than a vamp for venom—as fruitfully comic as that image is for reviewers whenever she publishes a new book—isn't quite just; it only contributes to the kind of misunderstanding I described above, caricature in the service of fun but at the expense of perception. The fact is, in her books, essays, reviews, and columns, the writer we jokingly call the Queen of Spleen has proven herself a unique creature in contemporary American writing: a critic at large, in the grand, old-world, *belles-lettres* tradition, who is beholden to no ideology or interest beyond her own sense of what is smart and what is stupid. With her every penstroke she defies categorization—and, more invigorating, challenges us to keep up with her without ever breaking stride herself. What other writer could cover abortion, birth control, date rape, gun control, incest, Adrienne Rich, Andrea Dworkin, Mae West, pitcher Jim Abbott, William the Conqueror, and the Dauphin Louis Charles all in one essay?

And, blast it all, she's a nice lady. I oughta know; I've *met* her, and she wouldn't hurt a piranha. When I arrived at her home that afternoon a few years back, she looked just as sweet as her photos suggest, the famous and prodigious bun astride her head looking for all the world like a cannonball, or the second segment of a poisonous wasp. She welcomed me with exemplary Southern hospitality, and fixed me a delicious lunch complete with ice-cream sundae. And before I left, several delightful hours later, she made sure to show me her gun collection: hidden away in her closet, all wrapped up in woolen sheaths, except for the adorable little pistol she kept tucked beneath her pillow.

Florence King started writing at just the right moment for a new critic of the American scene: the mid-1970s, when everything from politics to social revolution was taking on the heady overripeness of a peach left too long in the sun. But her first book, *Southern Ladies and Gentlemen,* wasn't aimed at all of America. She chose, rather, to look away to Dixieland, to the one part of the country—full of old maids and frenzied belles and fifty-seven varieties of good ole boy—that clung to a coherent (if lunatic) social order. From *Cosmo* to Chattanooga, critics hailed it as the debut of a master humorist; its dissection-by-sharp-instrument of the Southern psyche even earned the plaudits of the *Journal of American Folklore:* "A remarkable piece of popular anthropology."

She followed that book with two more "anthropological" studies: *Wasp, Where Is Thy Sting?* and *He: An Irreverent Look at the American Male.* Though perhaps not as fully sustained as *Southern Ladies,* each of these books to my eye contains highlights on a par with her best work. (Florence, in her note preceding *He* in this collection, remembers our standing argument about its relative merit; suffice it to say misanthropy and modesty aren't mutually exclusive.) But it wasn't until *When Sisterhood Was in Flower,* her first (and as of this writing only) novel, that Florence really hit her stride; like *Southern Ladies and Gentlemen,* today it's a cult classic, and King partisans crawl the world in search of used copies. The complete novel is included between these covers, back in print for the first time in years.

"Call me Isabel," it begins, and the fictional veneer never gets any thicker; we all know it's just Florence. And she continues with a wholly American tall tale of a book, which comes closer to the truth the more preposterous it gets. Everything from flower power to bad pulp literature catches on the end of Miss King's skewer, but if there's a single reason for the book's devoted following it's her portrait of the exploding bullet Women's Lib had fired into the lives of women in America. Suddenly it was impossible to tell what was sillier or sadder—the old American housewife, meeting husband at the door with pipe and slippers, or the new American woman, emptying herself of time and energy before she could declare herself "fulfilled." It's taken the rest of America two decades to come to terms with the Malaiseful Seventies; Florence took their measure, and found them wanting, long before we were able to reopen that photo album to those pages of bell-bottom philosophy and earth-shoe idealism.

Looking back, though, *Sisterhood* was just a warm-up. Having loaded the bases, Florence waited until the 1980s to hit her grand slam. If you've picked up this book and made it this far into someone else's lengthy intro, it's unlikely that you don't know about *Confessions of a Failed Southern Lady.* Among Southerners both real and aspiring it's a talisman, a cultural touchstone, even a kind of initiation ritual; it's also one of the unforgettable memoirs of our time, largely because in its pages Florence found her true voice. Putting down the constraints of ''objectivity'' and fiction gave her room to tell a story; the great talent that had begun to surface in *Sisterhood* now came into its own. And her characters! Always comic foils before, now they took on flesh-and-blue-blooded humanity; when Florence let her compassion show, she stepped from the rank of ''humorist'' into the company of Sam Clemens and only a small handful of others. Will Granny and her gynecological imperative, once encountered, ever be forgotten by a breathing reader? I can't see how.

With the publication of *Confessions* in 1985, Florence King's loyalist audience, breathing hard with laughter, was ensured. And as her steady presence as an essayist and reviewer continued into the 1990s, the persona of Miss King, as we know and bow to her today, began to take shape. Was she a study in contradictions? Her pair of essay books, *Reflections in a Jaundiced Eye* and *Lump It or Leave It,* suggested as much; her essays, published in columns for venues as diverse as *USA Today,* Fredericksburg's *Free Lance–Star,* and most memorably under the marquee ''The Misanthrope's Corner'' in the *National Review,* seconded the impression. Reflect on the mosaical self-portrait these essays render: she was, or at least had been, bisexual; she thinks of her life as ''a feminist statement.'' But—no surprise to *Sisterhood* readers—to her mind the feminist movement was a circus of factional crazies, rendering her own brand of joyous spinsterhood the only form of liberation she could bear. As she told the nude-dancing Sapphists, she's proudly a pistol-packin' Republican. But she was just as hard on George Bush as she is on poor Billary, and she blew a hole through the NRA in one essay for their namby-pamby fund-raising tactics.

And that essay—''A Nation of Friendly Misanthropes''—was a part of what I think of as Florence's pièce de résistance, and what she called her attempt to ''win one for the Sonofabitch.'' *With Charity Toward None,* her most recent book, is an ode to the art and craft of misanthropy, and it cleared the air about Florence once and for all. There's not a contradictory bone in her body: she hates pretty much everyone. Oh, she does it with great gusto, and the best will in the world; not for her the dry crabbiness of a Mencken, who lost his capacity for joy long before losing the will to write. But she gives off menace like a rattler with an attitude, and *Charity* is pure King, right down to the company she keeps: one by one, she discards other candidates for the Misanthropic Hall of Fame—Garbo, Mencken, Dorothy Parker, Kafka, Swift, Mark Twain, Ring Lardner—as unfit company. What a delicious thing consistency is: She even hates the haters. Turning the old Ambrose Bierce line on its head, Christopher Lehmann-Haupt wrote in the *New York Times Book Review,* "The only trouble with this book is that its covers are too close together."

Well, though the sentiment might obtain, it'll certainly be harder for a reviewer to say the same of *The Florence King Reader,* by far the longest volume on the King shelf; to say it's the best would be cheating, I think, but it may provide the biggest batch of guffaws 'n' outrage of any book this year. Florence chose every piece herself, and— as her interstitial notes point out—in not a few cases she's gone back and sharpened things up where they failed to meet her mature standards. As Florence once wrote me, "revising a book is like altering a dress: change the neckline and it messes up the shoulder seams; fix the shoulder seams and the waist is too high." But here she's become an expert seamstress, invisibly nipping and tucking here and there— even, in the case of *Charity,* taking the new format as an occasion to craft an entirely new rogues' gallery. I mention this only because I had a hard time earning my keep on this book; I fooled around with the sequence a little, but I know my place. You don't mess with the best . . . not when the best gives steel-ball slingshots as birthday gifts.

The first time I read the whole collection, front to back, such was my admiration at the body of work it represented that I wrote Florence a long wind of a letter praising it. "It's an encapsulation that throws into relief all the great King qualities, both obvious and undernoticed: your wit and your keen perception; your entertainer's sense of timing and your philosopher's ability to linger over a question; your distanced critic's willingness to skewer a character type and your personal memoirist's compassionate (gasp!) portraiture. It's a portfolio that will please fans, sure, but it will do more. It will alert many others to a two-decade phenomenon they'll be embarrassed to have missed."

Which brings us to *The Barbarian Princess.*

Included within is Florence King's celebrated heaving-bosom historical—a chapter of it, at any rate, tucked in between *He* and *Sisterhood* like a dirty magazine between the mattress and the box spring. It does not speak to Florence's philosophical mind, nor to her critical objectivity, nor to her unheralded humanity. But it's one of the funniest pieces, in its way, she's ever written, and for its sheer looniness it may be my own favorite entry in the book. I don't know whether "the goddess Frigga" was really the arbiter of fertility back then, but I contend that the passage (which Florence says she wrote straightfaced) between Vitalinus and Thel about the "barbaric drinking horn" beats Xaviera Hollander for suggestiveness:

> "How do you set that vessel down on the table, with that point on the end?" Vitalinus asked.
>
> "You don't," Thel replied, with an amused shrug. "You lay it down each time you empty it."

I don't think you'll be able to lay down *The Florence King Reader* without finishing it, either.

Florencia Suprema:

Long ago you sent me a copy of your first-grade report card. In it, the estimable C. R. Mullenberg advised:

Florence displays a wisdom and humor beyond her six years. She is a delight to have in the classroom—you never know just what she is going to say next. I hope she doesn't become too conscious of the fact and feel she is above the other children.

Thank god that *never happened.*

All best,

AUTHOR'S NOTE

According to her biographer, Ayn Rand's idea of fun was reading *Atlas Shrugged.* I believe it. I also believe that no normal writer wants to read his own published books. We already know them by heart, having read each page over and over while it was in the typewriter, followed by the rough draft, the final draft, the copyedited manuscript, the galleys, and the page proofs. By the time a book comes out we are sick of it.

When I started compiling this anthology I had to go back and read everything I've published over the last twenty years. I worked in chronological order, starting with my first three books, all published in the Seventies: *Southern Ladies and Gentlemen; Wasp, Where Is Thy Sting?* and *He: An Irreverent Look at the American Male.*

Never having "read" them before, I reacted like Claude Rains in *Casablanca*—shocked! yes, shocked! by what I found. The difference being that Rains only pretended to be shocked, but I was honestly so.

The faults that literary critics call "unevenness" and "spreadiness" are absent from my writing now, but they are abundantly present in these early books—the inevitable side effects of years of hackwork and commercial writing, when I perfected the dubious art of putting myself on automatic pilot and writing to order.

In the early days of my career, I wrote everything and anything that would sell. True confessions stories ("I Committed Adultery in a Diabetic Coma"), paperback-original "eroticas," as soft-core porn novels were called in the Sixties, articles for *Playgirl* and *Penthouse,* as well as several even trashier sexual-revolution mags of the Seventies such as the very short-lived *Foxy Lady,* which never paid me. I also served briefly as an advice columnist for *Viva,* ghosted a book for a Carter-era sex goddess, did a "sweet-savage" historical novel under a pen name, and spent two years before the masthead on the good ship *Cosmopolitan,* churning out articles like "Your First Night with a New Man" while religiously following their tip sheets (how to offer him a new toothbrush without seeming like the kind of girl who keeps new toothbrushes on hand).

All of this was valuable training in applying the seat of the pants to the seat of the chair, without which a writer is nothing, but it played havoc with my literary style in *SL&G, Wasp,* and *He.*

In each book I sabotaged my observer status by inserting myself into the text and going off on personal tangents. I had elements in one chapter that should have gone into another, sentences and paragraphs that didn't segue, labored points, loose ends, too many foreign phrases, too many rhetorical questions, too many parenthetical asides, too many "howevers," too many "after alls," too many "not surprisinglys," too many "on the other hands," too many "if worse comes to worsts," and too many "needless to says"—if it's needless to say, why say it?

One of the values of an anthology is supposed to be the opportunity it gives readers to see how a writer has "grown" over the years. Well, tough titty. I refuse to publish anything unless it's the best that I can make it, so I have cut, revised, edited and in general rewritten the excerpts from *SL&G, Wasp,* and *He* to bring them up to my present standards.

You may ask: why didn't the editors of these books catch these faults and call them to my attention? I imagine they did catch most of them, but there was nothing they could do. Editors really are overworked, though not as much as some of them like to claim. But even if they had had time for heavy blue-penciling, it would not have taught me anything. Self-editing is the only kind that really works, and it takes years to develop. Besides, I love it. Some women primp; I rewrite. Polishing and tightening my prose is my idea of good clean narcissistic fun.

My fourth book, *When Sisterhood Was in Flower,* was my turning point, when I began to slough off the effects of hackwork. My abridgment of the complete novel appears here. I'm proud to say that the first hundred pages needed virtually nothing except very minor fine tuning, such as changing "she stared in disbelief" to "she stared," and "for a brief moment" to "a moment." It was so easy that I was able to photocopy the book pages to use as manuscript for this volume, retyping only small sections here and there where hand editing would have been messy and hard to read.

I trimmed a few scenes that went on too long, but I made only one sizable cut. It comes toward the end when I went "off message," as they say in computerese. I prefer the way Horace put it in *Ars Poetica:* "Remember always never to bring a tame in union with a savage thing." That means don't mix your themes, e.g., don't mess up your murder mystery or your western with sex.

The same rule holds true for comic novels like *Sisterhood.* The original version contained a seven-page sexual encounter that simply did not belong in the book. Thematic inconsistencies are easy to spot. They're almost physically jarring, like missing a step while dancing; a seasoned writer can actually "feel" them. When I reread the novel I saw immediately that the sex scene was wrong, so I took it out. Like all extraneous scenes, it lifted off as easily as a scab.

I did not need to make any substantive changes in the rest of the selections except for some spit and polish here and there when I saw something that could be improved. If anything sounds different from the originals it's due to cutting and bridging in the interests of length rather than revision per se.

I did not include any samples of my true confessions or porns. These are "genre" markets, and a salable piece of genre writing never "sounds like" the person who wrote it—if it did, it wouldn't sell. Mine are indistinguishable from everyone else's so there would be no point in including them in an anthology of my work.

In any case, I threw the porns out years ago and kept only the contract letters. It was a matter of pride. Living alone as I do, I started to worry that if I should die suddenly and the authorities had to enter my apartment, they would find the porns and think I read them. I don't care if people know I wrote porn, as long as they don't think I read it. (I also threw out my author's copies of the sex-goddess ghost job.)

Finally, wherever it seemed called for, I have prefaced or followed some selections with brief italicized remarks and explanations that would have been too scattershot to include in this Author's Note.

A common reaction to collections of this sort is, "Oh, that's a piece of cake! All you have to do is gather it up and throw it in." Not so. Anthologizing one's work is a unique form of self-confrontation. This was the hardest book I have ever "written," so I hope you enjoy it.

THE
FLORENCE KING
READER

SOUTHERN LADIES AND GENTLEMEN

✝

1975

I used a "good/bad" scale to decide which chapters to include here. The first, "Big Daddy," was a favorite of nearly all reviewers so I felt it should go in. The second, "The Gay Confederation," upset News-week reviewer Margo Jefferson (not hard to do), who found it to be a "poorly and tastelessly aimed" exercise in homophobia. You be the judge.

BIG DADDY

The South's favorite accolade, "If you're half the man your daddy is you'll be all right," is the locus classicus of the dynastic novel that tempts so many Southern male writers. The halving process fills the author with dark fascination. He must show a long line of men, each of whom was half as good as the daddy before him, until he gets to the autobiographical character who, by definition, has undergone the most complete mathematical reduction of all.

The stern, drawling Agamemnon known as Big Daddy dominates this kind of novel, as we see in the apocryphal bestseller, *Carmichael's Lament.*

Buck Carmichael was coming home from World War II. Home to Carmichael Junction, the town his ancestors founded.

His throat tightened but he forced back his tears, clenching his jaw until a muscle leaped in his lean tan cheek. As the train slowed, he peered out the window and picked out familiar landmarks: Carmichael's Feed & Grain, Carmichael's Hardware, and in the distance, on the corner of Main Street, the Carmichael Building.

The five-story structure had been built by his father, Big Buck Carmichael, and dedicated to the memory of his grandfather, Old Buck Carmichael. The building housed the family law firm. Big Buck had sent him a snapshot of the office door while he was fighting in the Pacific. Many times, as he crouched in foxholes, Buck had taken it out and looked at it, drawing courage from it while he was fighting for his country. Other soldiers had pictures of their wives and sweethearts, but Buck had a picture of his daddy's door.

Now, he took it from his pocket and looked at it once again. What a door! Even though his grandfather had been dead for twenty-five years, the door still bore his name in honor of his memory. How like his father, Buck thought, to keep Granddaddy's name there. Big Buck had worshiped Granddaddy.

CARMICHAEL & CARMICHAEL
Attorneys at Law
Buckley Carmichael, Sr.
Buckley Carmichael, Jr.
Buckley Carmichael III

On the back of the snapshot Big Buck had written: "I added your name so you can come to work as soon as you get back from the war."

Buck frowned. He was not sure if he wanted to be a lawyer. He had always thought he would like to be . . . a writer. The muscle in his lean tan cheek leaped again as he clenched his jaw. In college he had published a few short stories under a pen name, but he had burned them before he went to war in case he got killed and his father should find them. He had never told his father about his literary ambitions—he didn't dare. Big Buck always said writing was women's work, fit only for the likes of Ellen Glasgow, Margaret Mitchell, Lillian Smith, Flannery O'Connor, Eudora Welty, Carson McCullers, and Lillian Hellman.

No, he could not be a writer, but did he want to be a lawyer? He was ashamed of his indecision. A man should know what he wants to do, should have a master plan for his life. His mother had never been able to make up her mind—he wondered if he took after her?

It was a frightening thought, and he prepared to put it out of his mind in the usual way. God, but his jaw muscle hurt! The damn thing had been leaping in his lean tan cheek for years.

He told himself there was nothing of his mother in him. He was a Carmichael through and through, the spit of Big Buck, who was the spit of Old Buck, who was the spit of the Confederate general, "Swamp" Buck, whose portrait hung in the courthouse.

The train pulled into the station. Buck grabbed his duffel bag and stepped out into the hot sunlight, searching the faces on the platform.

Suddenly, Big Buck Carmichael stepped out of the crowd and stood before him. Buck swallowed hard. Daddy! Daddy! his heart cried. He longed to rush forward and throw his arms around his father and kiss him, but of course he could not. Carmichael men didn't do such things. Instead, he forced himself to walk forward calmly and greet the man he adored in a manly fashion.

Big Buck held out his huge square hand. As Buck took it, it closed around his own like a vise.

"Welcome home, boy," said Big Buck.

"Thank you, sir. It's good to be back." Daddy! Daddy! Do you really love me the way I love you? You never said you did. I guess you do, but if only you would say it. . . . Daddy, please stop squeezing my hand. My jaw hurts bad enough without having a broken hand, too.

"I'm sorry your mother can't be here to greet you," Big Buck rumbled in his bass drawl, "but she went to pieces and we had to put her away." He shrugged. "Nerves. You know how women are."

Buck smiled, joy and inexpressible relief coursing through him as it always did whenever his father included him in the fraternity of men.

"Where is she, sir?"

His father's eyes hardened; Buck trembled.

"At Carmichael Memorial Hospital, where else? She's in the new wing I just built."

They got into the car and headed for home. As they approached the road to the estate, Buck gazed up at the tall smokestacks of the Carmichael Mills. His heart skipped a beat at the sight of these symbols of his father's power. It made him feel proud to be a man whenever he looked at the hard, towering cylinders reaching up to the sky.

Soon they came to the stables, and there, frisking in the grass, was Prince Carmichael, the stallion that sired all their colts. A few moments later, Buck saw something graceful and white at the crest of the hill. Leaning forward, he emitted a hoarse cry of joy.

"Yes," said his father, with quiet pride. "Carmichael Hall."

They went immediately to Big Buck's study, a room full of leather sofas and guns. Big Buck went to the sideboard and poured generous glasses of bonded bourbon for them, then sat down in his armchair with a firm, leathery squish.

"You bein' away four years gave me plenny time to plan your life, boy."

Buck swallowed. For one awful moment he almost said "I want to be a writer." The words were on the tip of his tongue, but then he looked up at the life-sized oil portrait of Old Buck that hung over the mantel. As he gazed at the stern old man, he remembered how, as a boy, he had crept into this room and walked up and down in front of the portrait, terrified yet fascinated by the way his grandfather's fierce eyes seemed to follow him.

He could *not* be a writer, he could *not* disgrace the Carmichael name! Never again must he think of it.

He looked at his father. "That's mighty good of you, sir. What do you want me to do?"

"Come to work tomorrow. Your desk is waitin' for you, and I hired you a secretary. Old Miz Anderson. You 'member her, you had her sister for sixth grade. She's one of the few sensible women I ever met, the kind of woman who belongs in an office."

"Thank you, sir."

"And when you have your first son, we'll add Buckley Carmichael IV to the door the day he's born. That'll be my christenin' present to my grandson."

"I don't know what to say, sir. You're more than generous."

Big Buck smiled the grim manly smile that always covered his deepest emotions.

"You're my son, I'd do anything for you, boy. Now," he said briskly, clearing his throat. "Speakin' of Buckley the Fourth. We've got to have a mother for the boy, so I want you to marry Puddyface Castlemaine as soon as possible."

Buck went numb with horror. Puddyface Castlemaine! Oh, no! Not that simpering belle, that spoiled brat, that goddamned apple of Kincaid Castlemaine's eye! He had known Puddyface all his life and hated her every minute of it. When they were children she had stuck to him like a burr, tagging along on his fishing trips, until his friends called him a sissy and teased him brutally for having a girl around all the time.

Worst of all, she had interrupted his precious hours with his father. On Sunday afternoons when he was growing up, Big Buck used to take him into the den for man-talk; guns and politics and crops, and stories about the cavalry charges led by Carmichaels in the War.

It was the only time he could be alone with Big Buck, and Puddyface knew it. It was never long before the door burst open and in she came, switching herself and smiling pertly while his mother watched from her hiding place behind the stairwell. His mother had arranged those interruptions, had connived with Puddyface to drive him and his father apart.

Later on, he had been forced to date her, and serve as one of her marshals at the deb ball. What a hellacious night that was! The only thing that saved him was her total absorption in her father, Kincaid Castlemaine. She had danced practically every dance with her daddy, freeing Buck to get drunk in the parking lot with the other boys whose dates were dancing with their daddies.

As a child, her father had called her ''Prettyface,'' but when she repeated it after him in her baby voice, it came out ''Puddyface.'' From then on, everyone called her Puddyface, until people had a hard time remembering what her real name was. She had even been announced at the deb ball as Miss Puddyface Kincaid Castlemaine.

And now, she was going to be the mother of his son! He wanted to die.

His father's sharp voice interrupted his thoughts.

''Well? Say somethin'. You're gettin' the prettiest girl in the state and the Castlemaine money besides. Aren't you happy?''

Buck jumped. ''Well, sir . . . I just can't believe it, that's all.''

Big Buck rose and poured them more bourbon, then resumed his leathery seat.

''I want this marriage, boy, I want it bad. A union between the Carmichaels and the Castlemaines will mean that my grandson will own the whole state!''

He leaned forward and spoke urgently.

''You see, boy, my daddy and Kincaid's daddy were rivals. I can win that old feud for my daddy if I can arrange for his great-grandson to inherit all the Castlemaine holdings.'' His face sobered. ''I promised Old Buck on his deathbed that a Carmichael would win out over the Castlemaines. It's my duty as his son to do it, and it's your duty as my son to help me. And it will be *your* son's duty to take over the Castlemaine power and keep it intact for *his* son.''

A deep thrill coursed through Buck. He was part of a master plan, a link in the father-son chain. It meant that his father trusted him. That was love, wasn't it?

''I—I don't know what to say, sir. Except, thank you.''

Big Buck smiled his grim manly smile. ''The weddin' is set for the

end of the month. It would've been sooner, but Puddyface got the pip.
You know how women are.''

Big Buck rose and refilled their glasses, then turned and faced the
portrait of Old Buck.

"We'll drink to him now,'' he commanded softly, raising his
glass.

Buck stood and the two of them intoned the old familiar toast.

"He was a man!''

How time flies, Buck thought, as he poured himself a bourbon. His
son, Little Buck, was now three years old. It didn't seem possible that
he and Puddyface had been married for three years and nine months.
He sighed, remembering the fight they had had about the baby's name
the night he was born.

"I'm going to name him after my daddy," Buck said.

"No!'' Puddyface screamed. "I'm going to name him after *my*
daddy, and if you try to stop me I'll set fire to this house!''

As if on cue, Kincaid Castlemaine had rushed into the room.

"Daddy! Daddy! He's bein' mean to me, Daddy!''

Kincaid knelt beside the bed and took Puddyface in his arms.
"Now, Sweet Pea, Daddy's ole Puddyface. Give your daddy a great
big hug. Ummmm-uhhhhh! 'Deed that's the best hug I ever had! Say I
missed my daddy while I was havin' my baby. Say I love my daddy to
the end of the numbers. Say I never want my daddy to leave my side
ever again, not even for a minute!''

She had repeated everything in her babyish voice. Buck shuddered
at the memory.

Glancing at his watch, he decided he had time for another bourbon
before he left for the airport. He drank it down in one swallow, then
poured another, savoring its soothing effect on his raw nerves. Thank
God he was going on a business trip. Anything to get away from Puddyface's screechy voice.

Suddenly, as he drank, his old ambition popped into his head.
Funny, he hadn't thought about writing for years. Looking into the
bronze liquid in his glass, he imagined himself writing a novel. As a
Southern author, he would keep the faith and break up his para-

graphs with bourbon. He knew that much about writing, anyhow. You weren't supposed to let your characters talk or think too long. Readers were put off by big blocks of print, so a good writer always . . .

He poured himself another bourbon.

. . . remembered to indent often. Every time a Southern novelist indented, Buck reflected, his characters moved one step closer to alcoholism.

He finished the drink and picked up his briefcase. Puddyface and the boy were waiting to say goodbye to him. He was only too glad to say goodbye to Puddyface, but his son was another matter. Looking at Buckley Kincaid (he had compromised on the name to keep Puddyface from reducing Carmichael Hall to ashes), he wanted to pick him up and kiss him, but he forced the thought away, clenching his jaw until a muscle leaped in his puffy sallow cheek. Fathers and sons didn't slop all over each other like women. It was his duty to make a man of the boy, just as his father had made a man of him.

He shook Little Buck's hand instead.

"Goodbye, son. You're the man of the house now. Look out for things while I'm gone."

When Buck got back home he found a coy Puddyface and a proud Kincaid Castlemaine seated together on the sofa. She had her arm through her father's and was pressing her breast against him, as usual.

"We've got news for you," Kincaid said. "Puddyface is goin' to have another baby."

Buck staggered. How could she be pregnant? He only slept with her when he was too drunk to know who she was. He walked over to the sideboard and poured himself a bourbon.

Puddyface stuck out her wrist and gave it a shake. "See what Daddy gave me? Another charm for my bracelet. See? Isn't that pretty?"

She rattled the bracelet and waited for Buck to compliment the gift. Christ, he was so sick of that charm bracelet! She refused to take it off—ever—so that it always rattled in his ear when he slept with her. Kincaid had given it to her on her fifth birthday, adding a charm on every special occasion, taking care to match the charm to the event.

She had a little gold tonsil, a little gold appendix, several little gold teeth, a little gold cheerleader, a little gold debutante, a little gold bride, and now . . .

"See?" she squealed. "It's a little gold baby! Isn't my daddy sweet to me?"

Buck downed his drink, then poured another and obediently inspected the charm.

"It's real cute," he mumbled.

"Isn't it sweet?" she persisted. "Did you ever see anything sweeter?"

"No, never in my whole life. It's the sweetest charm I ever did see."

Buck knew the drill by now. Once, when Kincaid had given her a new charm and he had been too drunk to gush over it, she had smashed all the gun cabinets with the fire poker.

Buck had many reasons for wishing Kincaid Castlemaine dead, but leading the list was the charm bracelet. Unfortunately, Kincaid was healthy and vigorous and gave every promise of living to a ripe old age. Buck foresaw some thirty more years of charms: a little gold hot flash, a little gold hysterectomy, a little gold nervous breakdown. . . . By the time she was fifty she would be a human lightning rod—which, come to think of it, wasn't a bad idea at all.

A daughter! Buck could not believe his own happiness. Throughout Puddyface's pregnancy he had told himself he wanted another son, but now . . .

He held the pink-blanketed bundle closer. For the first time in his life he did not feel lonely. At last he had someone he could love freely, someone who would love him back with the same lack of restraint and self-consciousness. You didn't have to make a man out of your daughter, you didn't have to worry about turning your daughter into a sissy. It would be all right now. . . . It would be all right.

His jaw relaxed and he broke into a tender smile.

"Kissypoo," he whispered. "Say I'm my daddy's kissypoo, say I'll never be anybody's kissypoo 'cept my daddy's. Say I'm the sweetest little ole kissypoo in the world."

"That's it!" he said. "That's what we'll call her—Kissypoo Carmichael."

THE GAY
CONFEDERATION

Most homosexual men either leave the South or move to New Orleans or Atlanta, which is why straight men in small towns are always bragging, "We don't have no queers 'round chee-ah." Those who do not emigrate are among the most colorful Southerners of all, often maintaining surprisingly high profiles in our allegedly homophobic region.

Every obscure hamlet has a homosexual nobody could miss, a mauve decade aberration complete with ascot, lisp, falsetto, and flapping wrist. He's Town Fairy, and nobody minds him because denial works in mysterious ways, its wonders to perform. Southerners believe in heredity, not environment, so Town Fairy is neither the town's fault nor the South's fault. As any blue-haired old lady will tell you, there's nothing really wrong with him, it's just that he was a change-of-life baby.

Town Fairy's life is remarkably happy, even idyllic, free from all Southern strain. He never has to worry about not being masculine because he gets all the sex he wants from brawny young rednecks who would commit suicide if he were masculine. Nor does he have to worry about his parents being unable to "hold up their heads." They were already forty-nine and fifty-six when he was born, so their heads have not moved at all for some time now.

He lives all by himself in the "lovely old house" where he was born and raised, and keeps the roses "just the way poor Ethel would have wanted," say the ladies of the Calvert Street Garden Club, who lionize him when he addresses their luncheon meetings.

It is worth noting, in ironic tribute to Southern hierarchy, that Town Fairy is safer in his Baptist backwater than are gay men in big cities; the garden club ladies are the wives and mothers of the local power structure, and his friendship with them does not go unnoticed by the queer-bashing class. If any man makes a contemptuous allusion to him within earshot of a garden club lady, she will snap, "Now don't you badmouth him. He might be a little funny but he's just as nice as he can be."

Town Fairy also benefits from the ladies' determined ignorance of the seamier facts of life. Even the most innocent Dear Old Thing knows what Town Fairy is and what he does, but the blue-rinse set simply refuses to think about it. Their blind spots expand over time until eventually they forget that Town Fairy is Town Fairy. They even stop thinking of him as a change-of-life baby, until finally, in the serene confines of their minds, he is listed simply as "an only child," which explains why he's a little funny.

Uncle Cary is the aesthete who has taught classics for so long that he speaks Alabamese with a Latin accent. A shrewd practitioner of protective coloration, he knows that his silver-haired-orator appearance reminds Southerners of great statesmen, so he heightens the effect by adding a string tie to his ensemble.

Everybody knows he's a brilliant scholar, which explains why he's a little funny. Rather than fight this widespread Southern attitude, Uncle Cary encourages it by subtly emphasizing the difference between Northern intellectuals and Southern intellectuals. The former are bad people who speak sociology; the latter are good people who speak Latin exactly as it was spoken three thousand years ago. Thus, when Uncle Cary takes his cat to the vet to get her vaginal discharge treated, he tells the other pet lovers in the waiting room, "Her *wageena* is inflamed," and just lets it sink in.

Although Uncle Cary is not particularly eager to receive visits from his child-strewn extended family, he nonetheless welcomes the entire clan on major holidays because he knows they are consumed by a need to make everything "look right." After all, they wouldn't come and *bring the children* if there were anything funny about Uncle Cary, so he obligingly issues invitations and everybody comes and brings the children.

Besides saving face, his kinfolk also want to check to see if he's still funny, and if it's starting to "show." On the one hand, they hope to find that Uncle Cary has finally acquired a lady friend; on the other hand, they expect to find him so far gone into perversion that something Dorian Grayish is happening to him. Perhaps the statue of Michelangelo's David, which he hides in the closet for the sake of the children, is starting to shrivel. Perhaps Uncle Cary himself is starting to shrivel. At the very least they want to see if he looks more like Somerset Maugham than he did last Christmas.

If his house contains replicas of classical statues, and if they happen to be of naked men, well . . . the Greeks and Romans were a little funny, too. That's what happens when you mess around with culture.

Gonad Manqué and his mother go everywhere together, just like Violet and Sebastian Venable in *Suddenly, Last Summer*. Mother is a garish Gulf Coast Wasp whose fashion statement falls somewhere between designer-original funkiness and thrift-shop houri. Drenched in morbidly voluptuous perfumes, her earrings grazing her shoulders, her fun furs molting magenta wisps, her ravaged cleavage mashed into accordion pleats above her beaded décolletage, she's so Southern Gothic that she seems about to fade into a flashback before our very eyes, which explains why Gonad Manqué writes.

Reading a Gonad Manqué novel is like listening to "Clair de Lune" played on the bagpipes. Gauzy descriptions abound; everything is ethereal or opaque or inchoate, especially the refractions, and shot through with tendril-y threads of unrelieved creepy eroticism.

The protagonist is a young boy who is so sensitive and introspective that the sight of a fly feasting on a turd hurls him into a Southern version of the Proustean agony where Real Meanings sell for five cents on the dollar. As the jacket copy puts it: "Caldwell McCready loved the woods. It was his secret place, his and his alone, a refuge from the adult world he did not want to enter, the place where he could dream his childhood dreams undisturbed. But things began to happen that summer that thrust Caldwell into the painful world he dreaded."

Too frail and puny to play with the other boys, Caldwell spends his solitary days sitting high up in his favorite tree. There, hidden behind a veil of Spanish moss, he takes from his pocket an old Bull Durham sack in which he keeps the mementos of rural Southern boyhood/sensitive division: a frog's skull, a cameo with half the face sliced off, and the pennies that closed his grandfather's eyes.

Caldwell would be content to spend the rest of the book thumbing through these talismans, and Gonad Manqué, who has no sense of plot, would be equally content to go on writing about them. But it's That Summer, a season unique to the South, when Something Terrible Happens.

Suddenly Caldwell's woodsy retreat is invaded by inhabitants of the outside world. When "they" come, his sensitivity receives a jolt. Perched in his tree, he watches copulating couples, escaped prisoners committing sodomy, a seven-foot black named Raoul staring at a dead fish, an old crone burying a jewelry box containing the other half of the cameo, a weeping stranger castrating himself, and the town idiot masturbating over a crushed flamingo. These episodes are never connected to each other or to any unifying theme, but Gonad Manqué believes in putting in a lot of what jacket-copy writers call "growing awareness."

The climax comes when Caldwell finds a severed human ear at the foot of his tree and all the Real Meanings fall into place. The ear, which he puts in his Bull Durham sack, belonged to Raoul, who was lynched for sleeping with a white mill girl named Linthead Lil. This makes Caldwell realize "in a blinding flash" that no man is an island and that we are all links in the chain of a common humanity . . . or something.

Armed with this new and wonderful knowledge and still toting around the rotten ear, he pays one last visit to his secret place. There he runs into Linthead Lil—Miss Mighty Thighs herself, the moronic earth mother beloved by Gonad Manqué novelists. Seeing her enormous breasts "spill" out of her dress, our little hero's "manhood rises." As Lil's mighty thighs engulf him, he "sinks his member into her hot, throbbing secret place"—now a touchstone of potency because Raoul was in it—and thinks to himself: "They won't call me Deltaville Sissy Balls anymore because I'm a man now!"

Gonad Manqué's dedication pages are cloaked in mystery because his novels are dedicated to heterosexual men who, in his opinion, are really gay. "To L., who understands," is followed by an interminable quotation in classical Greek that nobody understands, including L.

His epigraphs are even more inaccessible: "Forsooth, good Lord Pluckley, the question's naught but sworn 'ere birds do send the stickie nectar of mead to trickle down the gullet of Exeter's postillion by the morrow."—James Hamilton-Crickie, Fourth Viscount of Fenwick, from *My Gleanings.*

The quintessential Gonad Manqué title is *The Gossamer Dulcimer.* Also popular are River Of titles, such as *River of Unseen Echoes;* Home In titles, such as *Home in Loneliness;* and Time Is titles, such as *Time Is a Lost Flute.*

Under the circumstances, he ought to consider *Forever Umber.*

* * *

Southerners are master alchemists. If the intolerable cannot be changed, driven away, or shot, we not only will tolerate it, but find some way to take pride in it as well.

Uncle Cary's erudition segues with our reverence for the past. Thanks to him, every semiliterate redneck with a gun rack in his pickup knows the meaning of the Confederate tombstone inscription, *Dulce et decorum est pro patria mori.* Bubbas like Uncle Cary for this sort of thing and proudly tell their cronies that the "perfesser" translated it for them. Protected by the South's incorrigible romanticism, when Uncle Cary floats down Main Street in his beret and gendarme's cape, the reality of his homosexuality becomes indistinguishable from our dreams of Jeb Stuart's flowing locks, dancing sash, and jaunty plume.

Town Fairy comes off even better. Like the Confederate monument or the new jail, he is pointed out to visitors. "That there's our Town Fairy," people say fondly, conveying the impression that his decal is posted at the entrance to town along with those of the Lions, the Elks, and the Rotary.

As for Gonad Manqué, he might write funny but he's good to his mama.

A certain amount of unconscious empathy comes into play when Southerners confront homosexuals. It could hardly be otherwise: in the eyes of the rest of the country, the entire South has been a little funny for three hundred years. Our historic role as America's designated eccentrics has made us more tolerant of eccentricity generally than we are given credit for, and often, more than we ourselves realize. We may shrink from articulating it, but we know in our hearts that the South is essentially androgynous. Simultaneously a female oasis of gentility and grace and a male wasteland of taverns and guns, both vying for the accolade of the "real South," its conflicts are similar enough to the conflicts of homosexuals to produce some real understanding and a fairly high comfort level for all concerned.

The Gay Confederation benefits most from our attitude toward psychiatry. In *Southern Honor: Ethics and Behavior in the Old South,* historian Bertram Wyatt writes, "Honor, not conscience; shame, not guilt; were the psychological and social underpinnings of Southern culture.'' They still are. Homosexuals who grasp these fine distinctions—Uncle Cary has mastered them—will enjoy more safety and privacy in the South than in any other part of the country.

WASP, WHERE IS THY STING?

✝

1977

When I wrote this book in 1976, political correctness was in its infancy, consisting chiefly of remembering to say "Ms." and not to say "Nee-grow." The war on the Dead White European Male has now unified his descendents, but the Seventies was the decade of "ethnic awareness" and Wasps were getting the worst of it.

"Johnny Carson's face insults the night," wrote Michael Novak in The Rise of the Unmeltable Ethnics. *"Kiss me, I'm Italian" [Greek, Polish] buttons blossomed on lapels, and Judith Rossner took swipes at us in her novels: "Wasps were born toilet-trained."*

It was time for a Wasp book, so I wrote one. Naturally, I did not reply in kind—that would be un-Wasp.

SCHISM IS OUR SPECIALTY

The Anglo-Saxon Protestant is a preppie, a populist, a tennis bum, a workaholic, a Wall Street power broker, a Norman Rockwell sentimentalist, and the hick in the Brooks Brothers suit. This is not surprising: schism is a Protestant specialty.

Our temporal differences grew out of our spiritual differences and the twain have yet to meet. Depending upon which church door you open, you will find the best people, the good people, or the ones Episcopalians call *those* people.

The Episcopal church is the Chivas Regal of Protestantism. The modest version, called Low Church, is a Protestant church with a few extra trimmings and ministers called Reverend. The luscious version, called High Church, features brocaded vestments, candles, incense, optional confession, and priests called Father. It's as far from Protestantism as you can get without going to Rome, which is the whole point. High Churchers want to be as Catholic as possible without being Catholic. Many call themselves Anglican Catholics, and a few even claim membership in the Church of England, especially on private school applications, where they like to toss off a nonchalant "C of E." My favorite name for them, coined by an old beau, is "Piscop."

Ordinary Protestants are wiped out when they hear a Piscop refer to

"Father Chillingsworth." Seeing Father Chillingsworth all gussied up in lace, brocaded vestments, and cloth-of-gold chasuble is affronting, but what really upsets them are his Sunday afternoon cocktail parties in the rectory.

Roman Catholics regard the High Church wistfully, finding in it reminders of what their own church was like before Vatican II wrecked it. They feel at home, except they may miss their padded leather kneeling rails; many Piscop churches have purple velvet cushions. Otherwise it's the same: genuflecting, making the sign of the cross, statues of saints (though you mustn't pray to them), votive lights, and that churchy smell—a blend of starched altar cloths, candle wax and incense that stirs the Romish heart.

They might be a little put off by the sign on the ornately carved structure that looks like a Tudor telephone booth. It says *Confession by Appointment.* This means, as my grandmother explained when I was six: "Well, you can go if you want to, but you don't have to, and you'd better not let me catch you in there because it's Catholic! Still, it's nice to have it there because it looks so High Church."

Looking down on both Catholicism and Protestantism is a favorite activity of many Piscops, who place themselves philosophically just outside the city limits of Rome and sneer, first in one direction and then the other, like spectators at a tennis match. In a toss-up, however, they would rather look down on Protestantism.

Certain aspects of Protestantism are anathema to Piscops. One is the word *sermon,* which conjures up images of ranting and pulpit thumping. The proper word is *talk,* as in "such a good talk, Father Chillingsworth." In the unlikely event that Father Chillingsworth feels the spirit of the Lord upon him, he must cast it off and remain calm and muted so that he can deliver a *talk.*

Another reprehensible act is overly vigorous hymn singing. The best way to avoid it is to avoid overly vigorous hymns. Piscops are appalled by whoop-dee-doo gospel selections like "Jesus Wants Me for a Sunbeam" and "Brighten the Corner Where You Are." After all, someone might get carried away and fall into religious ecstasy, and you mustn't do that sort of thing in church. We prefer "Nearer, My God, to Thee," which makes us think a little about God and a lot about the *Titanic.*

The ideal Piscop calmative is that quintessence of sexlessness, a boy soprano. Another is Anglican chanting. Found in the back of the hymnal, the Canticles have delicious titles like *Te Deum Laudamus* and *Benedictus es, Domine.* They also come with crowd-control instructions, my favorite being "breathe only at the end of a line."

Piscops are not above using holy communion as a status symbol. In the Roman Catholic communion, worshipers receive only the bread, which they believe is the actual body of Christ. Piscops don't believe in transubstantiation, but nevertheless take both the bread and the wine, known in *The Book of Common Prayer* as "the doctrine of both Kinds." Thanks to this arrangement, the Piscop who really wants to show off takes only the bread and refuses the wine; it's the absolute last word in High Churchiness.

High or Low, all Episcopalians drink out of the same chalice. Father Chillingsworth simply wipes the rim with a linen cloth and passes it to the next soul. Nobody worries; we happy few could not possibly be dirty: *l'église, c'est moi.*

Some Episcopalians are born into the church but many more climb into it. The name of the game is "here's the church, here's the steeple-chase." Becoming an Episcopalian is the Wasp version of the American Dream. You can't blame us; how else can we prove we're "somebody" when the rest of the country thinks we already are? The conventional criteria of assimilation do not apply to us; our grandmothers spoke fluent English and the Statue of Liberty wasn't built when our ancestors arrived, so changing our religious denomination each time we gain another rung on the socio-economic ladder is the only exercise in American insecurity available to us.

In this way Wasps are completely different from other socially mobile Americans. Catholics on the up and up change neighborhoods, and therefore parishes, but they remain Catholic. Many successful Jewish families began as Orthodox, moved on to Conservative, and ended up as Reform, but they did not stop being Jewish. But the chameleon Wasp, not content to switch to a richer church of the same denomination, changes the whole church. He may have started life as a hot-gospel Baptist, but when he arrives he wants purple velvet kneeling cushions, vestments, candles, incense, and preachers called Father.

* * *

Reverend Thatcher of Waspville, Indiana is a Baptodistyerian. Being a "real" Protestant, he takes his text from "by the sweat of thy brow" and prefers homilies like "bread that is worked for is sweeter by far than the sweetmeats of sloth in the mouths of the ungodly." His flock sings labor-oriented hymns like "Bringing in the Sheaves." Far from being solemn, Low Wasp hymns are sprightly foot-tappers. Carpenters can pound nails to them, housewives can beat rugs to them, factories can thump to them. They are music to work by.

The old Jonathan Edwards crunch has gone out of Reverend Thatcher. The more he tries to be modern and with-it, the more he falls flat on his earnestness, especially when he delivers that favorite heartland sermon called "How's Business?"

It begins with a worldly anecdote. Reverend Thatcher took his car to be repaired and the mechanic, not knowing he was a man of the cloth, asked, "How's business?"

"And do you know what I told him?" Reverend Thatcher asks the sea of faces before him. "Business is booming!" It goes on in this vein, with Reverend Thatcher teasing the mechanic by withholding the exact nature of his job, until finally the mechanic asks him point-blank what line of work he's in. Now comes the punch line, which is going to get Reverend Thatcher into trouble with some burly mechanic one of these days: "I am a fisher of men."

Reverend Thatcher is like the progressive teacher who believes that mathematics reduced to the mundane level of squabbles with the milkman over the monthly bill is more thrilling to the human spirit than the cold logic of pure mathematics studied for its own sake. He never stops trying to apply religion to everyday life, which gets him into "Jesus Was a Good Businessman," a sermon in which he tries to prove that the miracle of the wedding feast of Cana was tax-deductible.

The masculine content of Protestantism increases as you go down the socio-theological scale. At the top is lace-bedecked Father Chillingsworth rustling down the aisle in the *exeunt omnes*. At the bottom, exuding pugnacious sexuality, is the fundamentalist preacher striding up and down like a caged bull, throwing the Bible on the floor, putting his foot on it, and bellowing, "I stand on the word of God!"

In the middle of these two extremes is dorky Reverend Thatcher, the truth and the light of the locker room, self-consciously lacing his sermons with "Jesus was a star quarterback . . . Jesus slam-dunked sinners to salvation . . . Jesus pitched a shut-out against sin."

He saves his best theological chalk talks for the young men's Bible group. "Jesus," he tells them, "was no pantywaist." To prove it, he recalls the Michelangelos he saw on his trip to Europe with the synod. "Most old paintings show Jesus as a pale, skinny, sickly guy, but Michelangelo told it like it is . . . er, was. He painted Jesus and the disciples as big muscular guys with good builds. He knew they had to be tough to walk all those miles and rough it the way they did. And Peter and Andrew went fishing every day! You better believe they were in shape!"

The point of it all is that muscularity is consistent and follows through; from physical muscles spiritual muscles grow, and vice versa. Or something. It's hard to tell sometimes just what Reverend Thatcher is getting at because he tends to talk like the Bible: "For if a man saith that muscles be not good, saith he not that they be not good for the soul, which is with the body yet of it not?"

Reverend Thatcher's speaking style goeth far to explain the glazed eyes of his flock and the shoulder-sagging crumple of relief when he finally stops and intones, "Let us pray."

Peer into the middle-class Wasp psyche and you will find either Father Chillingsworth or Reverend Thatcher seated at the controls. Being religious has nothing to do with it; many of us are agnostics, but one way or another we are still Cavaliers or Roundheads.

To illustrate, let us examine the Wasp mother.

Mrs. Jonesborough is the High Wasp mother. She may be a big fish in a little pond in the town that her family has always dominated, but most of the time she is a suburban chatelaine married to a commuting executive or professional man.

If Oakland has no *there,* the Jonesboroughs have no *from.* Mr. Jonesborough was born in Iowa but now he commutes to New York from Connecticut. Mrs. Jonesborough was born in Baltimore but raised in Arizona because her mother had asthma. She met Mr. Jonesborough at UCLA, and since then they have been corporate vagabonds. As old-stock Wasps they ought to have roots, but because they are old-stock Wasps they received the education and the jobs that made them rootless.

Mrs. Jonesborough is not much of a churchgoer but her chief problem is a direct outgrowth of her nominal religion. Protestantism invented the conflicted housewife. The Catholic patriarch compartmentalized his life, thrusting different kinds of women into different niches much like the arrangement of plaster saints in his church. He did not particularly want to talk to his wife, he certainly did not want her meddling in his business affairs, and he did not expect her to be good in bed, merely compliant and fertile. Feeling that too many interests spoiled a good wife, he asked only that she keep the house, mind the children, and talk to God.

Spurred by the concepts of individualism and equality that grew out of the Reformation, Protestants replaced the selfless wife and mother with the wife-as-partner while leaving her workload intact. Consequently, Mrs. Jonesborough is not only required to cook, clean, and nurture; she must also be her husband's companion, consultant, accountant, hostess, psychiatrist, and concubine.

Trying to be all things to one man as well as "a person in her own right" keeps Mrs. Jonesborough in a perpetual state of ambivalence. Should she wash the dishes or bone up on current events? Should she vacuum the floor or exercise her vaginal muscles—or try to do both at once? If the children are getting on her nerves, should she have another baby to prove what a good mother she really is? Whatever she decides to do, she will be exhausted from decision making before she ever does it.

The best way to know Mrs. Jonesborough is through her grocery list, where she stands revealed in the glare of her High Wasp priorities.

Alpo
9-Lives
Harper's
tomato juice
Worcestershire
Tabasco
vodka
food

Mrs. Jonesborough is the lady at the stove with a spatula in one hand and a Bloody Mary in the other. Thanks to her habit of cooking while three sheets to the wind, her standard dessert is an upside-down cake. It didn't start out that way, but she dropped it. She picked it up because what the family doesn't know won't hurt them, and besides, the floor isn't *that* dirty. And even if it is, she believes, like Jane Coe in Mary McCarthy's *A Charmed Life,* that "germs build immunities."

Alex Portnoy thought his mother had magical powers because she could suspend fruit in mid-Jello. The Wasp son seldom has to wrestle with that kind of awe. Usually Mrs. Jonesborough forgets to add the fruit to the Jello. If she remembers, the thought strikes her during happy hour. Muttering, "Oh, God," she struggles to her feet, weaves into the kitchen, opens a can of peaches, and throws the whole business, juice and all, into the mold.

She likes recipes that "you don't have to do anything to," meaning one-step dishes that obediently stew in their own juice in a big pot that turns itself on and off while she reads *Jaws.* The automatic crock pot is the bane of the Wasp cook because she has such all-American faith in gadgets. The ethnic mother doesn't trust the pot and keeps checking on it, but Mrs. Jonesborough, believing the pot can do no wrong, throws in a hunk of corned beef, a head of cabbage, and six unpeeled potatoes, then goes to a meeting of the zoning board. By the time she returns the red rubber bands are ready to serve.

She is the foremost exponent of the glop-it-up school, a cuisine that has been thrust upon America by that Waspy outfit, Campbell's Soups. Adding a can of cream of mushroom soup to a can of tuna and calling it Tuna Surprise makes her feel like one of those women that service magazines call "menu planners."

It doesn't take much to make Mrs. Jonesborough feel good about herself. Dumping a quivering can-shaped blob into her skillet means that she is adding something special to what would have been ordinary fare were it not for her culinary talents. Dumping is what invariably occurs. When the directions say "add gradually and stir," she dumps. Listen my children and you shall hear a constant gluck-blick-gloosh-*plop* as yet another tubular mess gathers air, slides out of the can, and hits the pan.

"Dressing up" canned foods is another one of her specialties. It involves buying a cellophane packet of slivered almonds and scattering them on top of her canned cream of shrimp soup. Sometimes she makes a bouquet garni with cheesecloth but it usually comes undone, bringing forth an exasperated cry of "balls of Christ!" (High Wasps have a bawdy streak, with blithe references to shityng, pissyng, and fartyng little changed since Chaucer's time.)

If her bouquet garni stays intact to the end, she fishes it out and swings it lariat-style in the direction of the garbage can, accounting for the spots on her kitchen floor, and even the walls. She hits the can every time thanks to her excellent aim—all that golf and tennis, and the family membership her husband took out in the Fairfield County Gun Club.

Once dinner is on the table she doesn't care what happens to it. She never pushes food on people; she couldn't care less if the carrot on your plate is lonesome for the carrot in your stomach. Her children are lucky if she anthropomorphizes *them,* never mind the carrots. If a child whines that he isn't hungry, she replies with a Waspy canon of inner-directed rugged individualism: "If you don't want it, don't eat it. Why tell me?"

Sniffing food to make sure it hasn't spoiled is a High Wasp family habit, for there is no telling what might emerge from the fridge at full gallop. Guilty over not being able to do magic things with leftovers, Mrs. Jonesborough saves them anyway, until finally somebody opens the fridge and says, "What's that smell?"

Well, there are several soggy paper bags each containing the neck, gizzard, heart, and liver of a chicken. She often forgets to remove the bags from the chicken's cavity before baking, but three months ago she turned over a new leaf and wrote herself a reminder on her kitchen blackboard: TAKE OUT GIBLETS! She did. They've been lying in the vegetable bin ever since, waiting to be transformed into giblet gravy.

A burst of housewifely energy comes over her and she starts dragging things out of the fridge and throwing them away. When it's all over and some fifty dollars has been pulverized in the Disposall, she opens a fresh box of baking soda and proudly tells her family, "I cleaned out the fridge," then waits for them to compliment her on her precision home management.

From time to time she gets really guilty and resolves to start cooking "from scratch." Out goes the Bisquick and in comes a sack of flour. For breakfast there are *real* pancakes, and she just might beat the batter with the flat of her hand in good Wasp pioneer style. She can never get her pancakes round but she feeds the oblong ones to the dog and keeps trying. As the family glues up on *real* oatmeal (she threw out the instant) she announces that there will be *real* clam chowder for dinner. Her children are so used to Campbell's soup that they think you're supposed to add a can of water to everything; they don't even know what *real* clam chowder means, but they insist upon staying home from school to watch the clams spit out sand. When they get bored with that, they watch the beans swell up, for Mother is also making *real* baked beans. It eases her conscience if she can soak something for eight hours before she even cooks it.

Normally a salt-and-pepper woman, she now goes herb-crazy, buying thyme, tarragon, rosemary—even fennel and cumin, though she has no idea what they are. Proudly lining the little bottles up on her kitchen shelf, where she also keeps her stapler and thumb tacks, she proceeds to "dress up" her hamburgers. The first child who says "the hamburgers taste funny" gets a tongue lashing and a royal command: "Eat! I want that plate cleaned." Suddenly Mother cares, and all the self-reliant little Wasps are confused. Sometimes they're worse than confused; rosemary and Swingline staples look remarkably alike after cooking.

Her housewifely enthusiasms burn briefly but while they burn they are incandescent. Her worst seizures involve *real* pea soup and homemade jelly. Pea soup requires a ham bone, so she buys a *real* ham and makes the family eat it for days. "We've got to finish that damn ham! I need the bone!"

When the homemade jelly lust comes over her, she goes tearing out of the house and down to the hardware store and spends a small fortune on the necessary equipment. Naturally she expects to make her own jelly for the rest of her life, so she pooh-poohs the cost, explaining, "Homemade jelly is so much cheaper than store-bought that I'll save money in the long run." Note the devotion to the concept of puritan thrift, and that fine old phrase, "store-bought." She never stops trying to recapture her Wasp roots.

Soon Mrs. Jonesborough's kitchen is festooned with gauzy arrangements of dripping cheesecloth, and the children stay home from school to stand under the "extractions" with their mouths open. It's as close to homemade jelly as they'll get, for when Mrs. Jonesborough is in these moods she likes to think of herself as one of those old-fashioned cooks who never measures anything. So she never measures anything. Something, she knows not what, goes wrong and the jelly won't jell. Her raspberry soup gets shoved to the back of the fridge where it will sit until it ferments, inspiring her to make homemade wine.

As suddenly as her cooking spree began, it ends. The six dozen mason jars are stored in the garage and Mrs. Jonesborough curls up with *Ragtime*. When the children get home from school she is in no mood to stop and fix them snacks. Self-reliance is back and every man, woman, and child is an island. The little Jonesboroughs can get their own milk and cookies, or they can wait until happy hour and fill up on cheese ball, smoked oysters, olives, pearl onions, and maraschino cherries.

Manic or depressive, Mrs. Jonesborough always fixes a good breakfast. As in England, so too in Waspland U.S.A.: breakfast is the meal you can count on.

The Jonesborough home is usually modern and easy to clean, which helps *some*. The stumbling block is Mrs. J's cottage industry, the gratis clipping bureau. No one is ever permitted to throw out a newspaper. They must be carefully saved—in the children's old baby carriage, a cold fireplace, the guest-room bathtub, the dining room table—until Mrs. J gets around to cutting out the articles she marked. After adding her marginal comments, she passes them around her club, encloses them in letters to her old college friends—or saves them.

Newsprint is the only thing she saves. Passionately dedicated to the theory of puritan thrift, she has a hard time with the practice. Thus, when she takes a notion to make a patchwork quilt, she is caught without a scrap bag.

An instant scrap bag is a contradiction in terms, but then so is Mrs. Jonesborough. Soon Dad's favorite Hawaiian shirt disappears and the children can't find their gym shorts. She promises each family member a nice big handmade comforter by winter. She will see to it that her loved ones are toasty warm even if she has to strip the clothes off their backs . . . to make them quilts . . . that they wouldn't need . . . to keep them warm . . . if she hadn't stolen their clothes in the first place.

But after seventeen squares and numerous puncture wounds (she can't manage a thimble) she gives up quilting. The fifty dollars' worth of quilt stuffing that never got stuffed will be thriftily saved in the utility room until Mrs. J gets an irresistible impulse to start chucking things out to prove what a neat housekeeper she is. One day, confronted by what amounts to a bale of cotton sitting in the middle of the utility room, she announces, "I'm going to clean out the utility room!" It's the fridge number all over again. Dragging the quilt stuffing outside and stuffing it into the garbage dumpster makes her feel that she really has accomplished something.

Next she takes up rug hooking. Now her teenage daughters can't find their pantyhose. Soon the house is full of long quivering nylon pigtails waiting for Mrs. J to summon enough patience to sit in front of the fire for an entire winter and hook them into circular shapes. The plaiting stage of rug making is easy; she can do that while she watches *Meet the Press,* but as soon as she has to look at what she's doing, or worse, read the byzantine directions in *Domestic Arts of Appalachia: Vol. I, Rug Hooking* ($45), her spirit wilts.

Next she decides to make her husband a belt. Lacking an attic full of usable junk amassed by three generations of Wasp goodwives, she rushes out to the hobby shop and buys a belt-making kit. Do-it-yourself stirs her self-sufficiency juices, but what awaits her is frustration. She wants to be the wilderness wife who makes do or does without, but the wilderness wife never had to read a glossy brochure on how to insert tab (A) into end seam (B). She learned belt making from her mother, who learned it from her mother, and on back into time. Mrs. Jonesborough must learn it from Wilderness Enterprises, Inc., and it's just not the same.

If some enterprising businessman invented the "Waste Not, Want Not Kit," he would make a fortune off frustrated High Wasps. Mrs. Jonesborough will buy back her puritan heritage no matter what it costs.

She gets out of everyday housework by adopting the protective coloration of a domestic sanitation warden. Her technique for avoiding making beds is to "let them air." She has the airiest beds in town. Instead of drying the dishes she lets them drain in the rack, telling herself and everyone else, "Draining is more sanitary than wiping."

Whether she washes dishes by hand or in a dishwasher, they never make it back into the cabinets. She has figured out that if she leaves them in the rack until it's time to eat again, she can deflect complaints with authoritative quotes from one of her newspaper clippings on union time-and-motion studies.

The family learns to live with her standards. When the children come home from school and fix themselves a sandwich, they bypass the cutlery drawer and automatically head for the sinkside drainer. There, like a quiver of arrows, are all the household knives, points up. As any Wasp will tell you, standing on tiptoe and grabbing a knife by the blade builds character.

Mrs. J's favorite appliance is, of course, the Disposall, the source of what the children call the "funny spoon." It got caught in the Disposall and they fight over who gets to eat with it. Should Mrs. J have three children and only one funny spoon, not to worry. It's only a matter of time before some more silverware drifts down the Disposall during happy hour.

A special cross Mrs. J must bear are ads showing Waspy-looking women standing proudly beside a long row of gleaming copper-bottom pans hung up on the wall. Because the woman in the ad looks like Mrs. J, guilt and enthusiasm churn in her soul. "I'm going to hang up the pans!" she tells the family, then sprints off to the hardware store, returning with a wall rack, a large-economy-size can of copper polish, and three new copper-bottom pans that she doesn't need but bought to fill up the hooks.

Mr. Jonesborough puts the rack up for her and soon she is polishing her heart out. When all the pans are done to a mirror finish and hung up, everyone must admire them. The next morning at breakfast she is still fishing for compliments. Opening the curtains and pulling up the blinds, she lets the sunlight stream in on the pans, demanding, "Look! Aren't they beautiful with the sunlight on them?"

The pans gleam for a week or so, then suddenly, in the midst of scouring, Mrs. J pulls off her rubber gloves, mutters, "Oh, to hell with it," and curls up with *The Reincarnation of Peter Proud*. Soon the pans turn grayish green but she hangs them up anyway, excusing herself with "a pan should look like a pan."

After a while she stops hanging them up at all. Back they go to their usual storage places—the windowsill, the top of the fridge, inside the oven—leaving a nice empty rack for her and the rest of the family to fill up however they please. Some of the items found on High Wasp pan hooks are transistor radios, bicycle chains, extension cords, United flight bags, and Johnny's athletic supporter.

Mrs. Jonesborough's housekeeping standards are made to order for one kitchen item: the cast-iron skillet. Good housekeepers always have rust problems with cast iron because they can't bring themselves to do what you're supposed to do to keep it good and black. Mrs. Jonesborough can. Simply wipe out the grease with a paper towel and never, ever wash it.

Her other talent is "holding dinner." Fond of happy hour herself, she tends to marry a man who would rather drink than eat—not hard to find in High Waspdom. She knows by a kind of Wasp instinct how to keep any kind of food warm for indefinite periods. She can hold dinner for a couple of days if necessary—and it has been known to be necessary.

According to the casting office, the High Wasp mother is a pleasant parent whose relationship with her children begins and ends with an absentminded "hello, dear." There is some truth to this, for like Queen Victoria and Jessie Benton Fremont, she is first and foremost a man's woman.

She does not go in much for conventional maternal sentiment, but she often calls her children "droopy drawers" or "stinkweed" in most loving tones. Nicknames, especially insulting ones, are a Wasp way of showing affection without showing affection.

She enjoys her children most when they graduate from college and take c/o American Express as their mailing address. Instead of bursting into tears when Johnny tells her he wants to live abroad and find himself, she buys him a Eurailpass.

Once he is out of her hair and traversing the wilds of Khartoum, she starts paying attention to him, becoming the most loyal and persistent correspondent any boy ever had. Like Lady Randolph Churchill, she writes and writes and writes, yet despite their length and frequency, her letters are remarkably unmaternal. "He's got to get his sea legs" is her guiding principle, so she consciously reins herself in.

Instead she fills ten or fifteen pages with an analysis of the political situation in his host country. By the time she finishes her arm is sore, so she lapses into her own version of shorthand in a P.S. where she finally says something personal. Remembering that Johnny has contracted dysentery, she adds: ''Yr last ltr v. funny. Don't worry re trots. E'body has them there. Tk cr yrself & rt soon.''

If she misses him dreadfully and her heart is aching with mother love, she will send him a studio card that says, ''What I like about you is your funny-looking face.''

She behaves this way, not only for the sake of Johnny's independence, but for her own image: smother mothers are un-Wasp.

She was appalled by the masturbation scene in *Portnoy's Complaint*, when Sophie banged on the bathroom door, screaming, ''Alex, what are you doing in there?'' Loath to turn her son into a neurotic like Alex Portnoy, Mrs. Jonesborough handled matters in an entirely different way when her Johnny locked himself in the bathroom.

Bringing the terrible burden of Wasp tact to bear, she pretended that he wasn't really there. She pretended that she didn't have a son. She pretended that he didn't have a penis. She pretended that masturbation hadn't been invented yet. She even pretended that she didn't have a bathroom. If he stayed too long, she sent his father to get him and have a man-to-man talk. When the two of them returned, she pretended that they had never left and resumed the conversation without missing a beat, managing to suggest by her flawless performance that male sexuality is of no importance whatsoever.

It never occurs to her that Johnny might absorb her silent message and come to the same conclusion.

We do produce an occasional smother mother but she does everything backwards, which is why we lack a bona fide Wasp Prince. Instead we have Little Lord Alex, who spends the best years of his life lighting cigarettes, holding chairs, opening doors, and mixing martinis as only he knows how (''Your father bruises the gin'').

Lady Jonesborough doesn't wait on her son; he waits on her. A minor scene in *My Friend Flicka* illustrates her knack for getting mileage out of him.

> No one could do Nell's egg to suit her like Howard. She liked it
> lightly fried on one side, then lightly on the other, not broken. It had to
> be flipped. Howard poured a little of the hot bacon grease into a one-

egg skillet and broke an egg in. While it crackled and spat, he salted it carefully and in a moment loosened the curling brown edges, then with a smooth motion of his wrist, gave the pan a lift and a thrust, and the egg rose a few inches into the air, turned a slow somersault, and slid back into the fat.

Lady Jonesborough starts making Little Lord Alex feel indispensable while he is still a toddler: "Mother can't turn unless her big boy sticks his arm out the window. Signal a right, darling." He is never too young to give her advice, and she goes to him with all her problems. In Mary McCarthy's *Birds of America,* Rosamund Brown automatically turns to her son when she discovers that the local hardware store does not carry bean pots: "How extraordinary, Peter! The man says they don't make them any more. Do you think that can be true?"

Peter reflects: "She was always asking him wide-eyed, troubled questions like that one, to which he could not possibly, at his age, know the answer; it was a kind of flattery, applied to the male ego."

At first Lady Jonesborough confines her pleas to male-oriented problems like driving directions. Spending his formative years buried in road maps is good for Little Lord Alex's geography grades, but it is never long before her supplications spill over into non-boy areas. Does he really think that Woolite does what it claims? If he lisps out a yes, he may find himself washing out her sweaters.

He must guard her with his life. When Daddy is away on a business trip and her ladyship hears a noise in the garage, Little Lord Alex is torn from his bed. Armed with his baseball bat and Cub Scout flashlight, he stalks out to the garage, throws open the door, draws himself up to his full three-foot-seven and shouts, "Who's there?"

Our pint-sized Cerberus soon comes to view all men, beginning with his father, as rivals out to rob him of his lady fair. His vision of delight is his mother frantically waving her tattletale-gray cashmeres from the castle window while Daddy-the-Dragon breathes sulphur below.

When Alex is sixteen, Lady Jonesborough buys him a smoking jacket and teaches him to tango. Daddy, arriving home from work, is greeted by the throbbing strains of "Jalousie" and the disarming sight of Little Lord Alex lunging like a panther into his mother's crotch.

By now Daddy realizes that there's something wrong with Alex but he can't put his finger on it. It's not that he's tied to his mother's apron strings—far from it. He has so much initiative, resourcefulness, and self-reliance that he not only shines his own shoes, but all twenty-five pairs of hers.

He has dated every girl at school, though never the same one twice. The phone was always ringing, and it was always a girl asking for Alex, so there was nothing wrong in the sex department. At least as far as Daddy could tell, which wasn't very far. Instead of man-to-man talks with his father, Alex confided in his mother. Each Sunday morning he told her about the girl he took out the night before.

"She has no style."

"She doesn't know how to dress."

"Her conversation is banal."

"She can't tango."

Ever mindful of Wasp fair play and determined not to give Alex an Oedipus complex, Lady Jonesborough always takes the girl's side.

"She's young yet."

"Try to overlook her faults."

"Give her a chance."

"She's trying, Alex, she's trying."

"Don't be unfair, dear, she can't help it."

By the time Alex is out of college he is greeting his mother with "ciao, darling" and calling her Babs. Now Daddy openly loathes his son, but they never fight. Daddy is now out of the running entirely, for the fights at Castle Jonesborough are between Alex and Babs.

Typical is the one that broke out at the country club when her ladyship got a bit tiddly. Alex had been eyeing her with tight-lipped forbearance all evening, but when she ordered her fourth martini he spoke up.

"Do you really think you should, Babs?"

"Oh, darling, just one more? Please? Pretty please?"

"You've had enough!"

"You're mean to me!"

"Oh, come off it, Babs."

They bickered all evening.

"You always get the fish, Babs."

"Well, I don't want it tonight."

"Everyone is looking at you."

"Let them look!"

"Will you please lower your voice, Babs!"

"Don't tell me what to do!"

"Must you always cause a scene?"

"Take me home this instant!"

When they got home, all hell broke loose. Babs stormed and wept, Alex hurled dire threats, and the two of them chased each other through the house while Daddy watched. Finally, Babs slammed into her room and Alex pounded on the door with both fists.

"Stop being a fool, Babs!"

"Leave me alone!"

Little Lord Alex seldom becomes gay. He regards the entire male sex as a collection of doltish father figures incapable of appreciating his finer qualities, whom he must undermine and sabotage so that he can take their place. A consummate woman's man, he makes an ideal husband for the low-sexed socialite whose chief requirement is an outwardly enviable marriage. He flicks the quickest Bic at the club and is charming to his wife's friends, who adore him because he dances with all of them without appearing to go down a list.

His biggest plus is the way he treats his mother-in-law. Provided she is chic, he absolutely adores her and always remembers that she likes a dash of orange bitters in her gin. Her husband, the brute, never remembers.

The High Wasp mother-daughter relationship was pretty well summed up by Alexis de Tocqueville: "Long before the American girl arrives at the age of marriage, her emancipation from maternal control begins."

Mrs. Jonesborough's idea of a curfew is forgetting to leave the night light burning. Privacy is her highest priority, which is why there is always so much stuff on the hall table: she won't even put her daughter's dry cleaning away. Other people's rooms are sacrosanct in High Waspdom unless you happen to be a cat or a dog, in which case you have the run of the house and may sleep on any bed you choose, but Mother walks a self-imposed chalk line.

Her daughter can buy a diary stamped *My Diary* and leave it open at the most interesting page. She can keep her love letters in a box marked *Love Letters.* She can hang her dildo beside her tennis racket.

Her secrets will go with her to the grave, for Mother Jonesborough's motto is, "It's none of my business."

Other High Wasp maternal exit lines:

"It's your life, you have to live it."

"I refuse to interfere."

"You needn't explain, I trust you."

"I know you want to do the right thing."

"It's your decision."

"It's not my place to sit in judgment."

"You're free to choose your own friends."

Legal abortion has cut into Mother Jonesborough's finest hour. "Knowing somebody" being dear to the Wasp heart, her distaff version of the old-boy network was impressive. Just where and how she acquired her contacts she never revealed, nor did her daughter ask—that, after all, was Mother's business. It was all arranged with a muted, confident-sounding phone call in the den, during which she gave her daughter a wink and a curt nod, and afterwards a brisk pat. "All set," she said out of the side of her mouth.

Of course she was sorry her daughter was in a jam, but deep down in the Waspiest reaches of her soul she enjoyed the whole affair because it gave her a chance to show how unflappable she is.

The Low Wasp mother is Mrs. Myrtle Bailey of Waspville, Indiana.

A pillar of the Baptodistyerian church, Mrs. Bailey believes there are only two causes of divorce: the man drinks and the woman doesn't keep house. She, therefore, will never be a divorced woman. Bailey has never touched a drop. Such a good man, they broke the mold when they made him. You could set your clock by Bailey. Home every night right on the dot, except once a year when he went to the VFW convention. He even worked hard then, you could tell by the way he looked when he got home. Pale and trembling and too tired to eat, but bearing gifts just the same. No matter how hard Bailey worked at the convention he always remembered to bring her and Norma Dean a nice present.

No, never a drop passed Bailey's lips, except of course when he was taking cold, but that was different. Indiana winters were fierce, so Mrs. Bailey always kept a medicinal bottle of whiskey in the cupboard. She herself fixed him a hot toddy with her very own hands, just as her mother and grandmother had done for their badly chilled husbands. There was nothing wrong with taking whiskey for medicine as long as you didn't take it for pleasure. And poor Bailey was not a well man. He was always saying, "Myrtle, I feel a cold coming on."

As for keeping house, Mrs. Bailey was the pride of Waspville, famed far and wide as "a real scrubber." The Bailey home was as neat and clean as the Baptodistyerian church. They even smelled the same. As president of the Ladies Circle, Mrs. Bailey bossed the gang that cleaned the church, so chez Bailey or chez God, the odor of sanctity was Lysol.

The bane of her existence was that terrible habit people had of putting their feet on hassocks. Bailey, of course, was an exception; he wouldn't dare put his feet on her hassocks. He did when they were first married, but he stopped.

Another thing that bothered her were all the jokes about Jewish mothers on television. What was wrong with starching your son's undershorts? She didn't have a drop of Jewish blood but she always starched Bailey's, and his pajamas too. She didn't, of course, know any Jews, but she would say one thing for them: they weren't Catholic. Catholics drank and smoked and gambled and danced and cursed and fought. The Baileys drank not, smoked not, gambled not, danced not, cursed not, and fought not. Which just goes to show you.

As bad as the Catholics were, the Episcopalians were worse. Mrs. Bailey couldn't sleep nights for fear Norma Dean was getting too serious with that no-good Episcopal playboy, Keith Jonesborough, whose mother yelled "balls of Christ!" right in the middle of Main Street when somebody scraped her fender. The young people heard her, too. You'd think a woman with all that money would be more ladylike, especially seeing as how her father and father-in-law owned the whole town between them.

Mrs. Bailey would never forget that time at the Interfaith breakfast when Mrs. Jonesborough ate her bacon with her fingers. Goodness gracious, but that shocked the Ladies Circle! You'd think a woman who'd gone East to college at that Vassar place would know to use her knife and fork to cut her bacon up into little pieces. A terrible person, Mrs. Bailey sighed, shaking her head. She *hated* people like the Jonesboroughs! Well . . . no, she didn't *hate* them, that wouldn't be Christian, she just . . . well.

As for the Jonesborough house, the less said the better. All that fuss about that ugly picture Mrs. Jonesborough had framed! Mrs. Bailey had gotten the story from Norma Dean, who went with Keith Jonesborough to Indianapolis to pick it up. A dirty old picture, plain black and white, with a big splotch on it like somebody had spilled water all over it—or, knowing the Jonesboroughs, spirits. It was supposed to be a picture of a bunch of French lawyers all dressed in black. Foreigners, wouldn't you know? And what they said it cost! You could get "Autumn Sunset" at Sears for $14.95 framed, and it was washable.

She herself had never set foot inside the Jonesborough home, but she had heard from Grace Thatcher, the minister's wife, that a book called *My Secret Garden* was sitting on the coffee table just as big as life for all the world to see. At first Grace thought that Mrs. Jonesborough was finally taking an interest in her yard, but then she found out that the book was all about s-e-x-u-a-l f-a-n-t-a-s-i-e-s.

And the worst thing of all was that Norma Dean thought Mrs. Jonesborough was "just wonderful."

Mrs. Bailey was afraid Norma Dean was having things to do with Keith Jonesborough. That very morning when she was polishing Norma Dean's doorknob (it was doorknob day), she saw the marked calendar on the bureau. Norma Dean hadn't come unwell yet this month.

Mrs. Bailey sighed. The only way to stop worrying was to keep busy. There was always work to be done if you looked for it. Looking, she saw that the plastic runners she kept on her carpets needed scrubbing. Goodness gracious, but people could dirty up a house by walking through it!

Nobody could say she wasn't a good wife, never mind all that secret garden business. The beautiful living room suit they bought when they were first married was still like new, she had seen to that. In fact, it was still new. The day the store delivered it she had put hand-sewn slipcovers on it to keep the upholstery nice. Then she had started worrying about the slipcovers. She hated to think of people sitting on them, so she went up to Sears and bought clear plastic covers to fit over the slipcovers. That way, she could wash the furniture with Lysol too. Summers, when Norma Dean wore shorts, she would get stuck to the plastic and they had to peel her off. The Lysol gave her a real bad rash on the backs of her legs, but it served her right for wearing such short shorts.

Time to scour the bathroom. The dirt really got into those cracks around the tiles but Mrs. Bailey knew how to deal with it. Pipe cleaners. She hated for anybody to see her buying them, though, so she went all the way over to Terre Haute to get them at a store where nobody knew her. Otherwise, if she bought them in town, people might think Bailey had taken to vice.

She hid the pipe cleaners in her sewing basket so company wouldn't see them. There wasn't an ashtray in the entire Bailey home, a fact that made Mrs. Bailey very proud. No one had ever used tobacco within these walls except that time they rented the extra room to travelers, when Bailey had the hernia and couldn't work. Well, along came two hussies who smoked like a chimney. When Mrs. Bailey found them tapping ashes into her saucers, she gave them Hail Columbia.

Then one of the hussies went in the bathroom. There was a lot of clattering, then the hussy yelled to the other hussy, "Where the hell is the goddamn toilet paper?" Next to hearing someone take God's name in vain, Mrs. Bailey hated to hear anyone say toilet paper. She always called it bathroom tissue. She also hated to see it sitting right out in the open for all the world to see and *know* what it was, so she had bought a hoopskirted doll to hide it under. All she had to do was cut the legs off the doll, and the skirt made a perfect hiding place, just big enough for one roll. It was just as cute as could be, and you would never guess there was bathroom tissue under it.

Mrs. Bailey loved to cover things up. She hated it when people put down a cake of wet soap on her clean basin; every bar of soap in her bathroom was in a plastic soap box with a lid. Sometimes, when the wet lid slipped out of Bailey's hands, he yelled, "Cheese and crackers got all muddy!" She had taught him that. When they were first married he had a terrible habit of yelling "Jesus Christ God Almighty!" that he had learned in the army. Mrs. Bailey hadn't tried to change him, goodness gracious, no. Never let it be said that she, Myrtle Bailey, was a nag. She just taught him to say the same thing in a Christian way. That was kind of cute, cheese and crackers got all muddy. She didn't mind bad things as long as they were cute. She had always been broadminded, anybody would tell you that.

Goodness gracious, it was duck day! How could she have forgotten that? She was so proud of her six plaster ducks flying across the wall like an air force squadron. She took them down and washed them carefully in Ivory Flakes—Lysol ate the paint. My, the arguments she had with Norma Dean about those ducks! Every time Keith Jonesborough came to call, Norma Dean tried to take the ducks down. Once they nearly broke the biggest, or leader duck, when they were pulling it out of each other's hands.

Norma Dean never could explain what it was about the ducks that bothered her. She just kept saying, "They're so awful!" and Mrs. Bailey just kept saying, "They'll be yours when you marry."

Goodness gracious, it was almost five o'clock. Just goes to show how time flies when the hands are busy. Bailey would be home from the hardware store soon. Time to fix supper. Let's see . . . fried pork chops, creamed corn, macaroni and cheese, baked beans from a can fancied up with brown sugar and molasses, a nice salad of canned pineapple rings with a cherry in the middle, lemon meringue pie, and milk.

Mrs. Bailey smiled to herself. Nobody could say she wasn't a good wife. Kissin' don't last, cookin' do.

Mrs. Bailey calls her menus "something to stick to the ribs." Thanks to her ironclad belief that a man should have his "supper" the moment he walks in the door, Bailey barely has time to catch his breath before she sets his piled plate in front of him. Without a cocktail or two to take the edge off his hunger and calm his workaday nerves, her leaden cooking really does stick to his ribs. Eventually it falls on his heart.

Dinnertime conversation starts with grace and proceeds to snippety-snappety moral absolutes delivered by Mrs. Bailey to her spouse, who says "Nnnnghump." She's not partial to dieting so they both pack it in. When it's all over, Bailey rises and, still chewing, lurches in the direction of the living room sofa. As he collapses for his evening nap, Mrs. Bailey thrusts a newspaper under his feet to protect the plastic slipcovers. He's still there when Keith Jonesborough comes to call on Norma Dean, which is why she is always wailing "Oh, Daddy!"

Many heartland Wasps of the Bailey persuasion go through life thinking that all food tastes like roast beef, mashed potatoes, and peas. This is what they eat thousands of times at home, before escaping to a sprawling midwestern state university whose cafeteria serves up roast beef, mashed potatoes, and peas because the head dietician is named Mrs. York. They graduate from college, join the Rotary, and spend the rest of their lives attending civic luncheons consisting of roast beef, mashed potatoes, and peas. If there's a salad it's usually that Low Wasp pièce de résistance, a canned pear on a lettuce leaf topped with a blob of mayonnaise.

The last word on Wasp cooking is found in James Jones's midwestern epic, *Some Came Running,* when alluring Gwen French invites the hero to dinner and gives him stuffed beef heart, white potatoes, sweet potatoes, and fried apples. Wasp women, High or Low, like to call themselves a "man's cook," a sexier way of saying that they see nothing wrong with serving two kinds of potatoes at the same meal.

Other than such minor similarities, our schism continues. Building bridges of understanding between the Jonesboroughs and the Baileys is a challenge that sociological engineers have yet to meet. Instead of looking at one another and thinking, "These are my people," each sees nothing but the Wasp stereotype for which the other is responsible.

Besides their different levels of education and blood alcohol, they are also hopelessly divided on attitudes toward the mother country. The Jonesboroughs are anglophiles, but the isolationist Baileys see no difference between England and any other foreign country. Many Baileys don't even know they are Wasps. By now they have heard the acronym on television and know what it means, but they have a mental block about applying it to themselves. They're American, by God, and mother countries are for foreigners.

Without doubt, Mrs. Bailey is a heavy cross to bear, but she scores higher in the mother department than Norma Dean is willing to admit. She snoops when she scents serious sinning, but otherwise she practically pushes her daughter out of the house. A lifelong resident of the Booster Belt, she takes it for granted that Norma Dean will join every club in existence. She believes girls should "go out and do things with young people," and that is just what Norma Dean does. Seldom does an evening pass without a meeting of some kind, and Norma Dean goes with her mother's blessing, provided she "stays with the group''—a standard Baileyism that lends itself to elastic interpretation.

Trips away from home do not give Mrs. Bailey the slightest pause. Y-Teens, Girls State, Baptodistyerian Youth all hold annual state conventions and Norma Dean always attends. Thanks to this relentless joinerism, she spends more time making speeches of her own than listening to her mother's. The independence and self-confidence she gains may be parochial and useful only on a small canvas, but independence and self-confidence they are.

It is Mrs. Bailey, not Mrs. Jonesborough, who is the mother of the Wasp Princess. The holder of this title must be sweet and good, which Mrs. Jonesborough's sui generis daughter seldom is, but Mrs. Bailey supervises the sweetness and goodness and the result is Norma Dean: Homecoming Queen, Corn Harvest Queen, cheerleader, drum majorette, Pep Club president, 4-H Club milkmaid with a dairy queen bosom, and maybe, if God wills it, Miss Waspville.

Mrs. Bailey is her lady-in-waiting. Norma Dean's alter ego, the dress form, is permanently set up in her mother's sewing room throughout high school and college, ready for any princessy eventuality. Armed with her Singer, Mrs. Bailey makes the uniforms, double-stitches the webbed crossbelts, polishes the shako, and always finds the money for a new pair of white cowgirl boots.

One need only imagine Mrs. Jonesborough trying to cope with all those brass buttons to know why there will never be a High Wasp Princess.

HE: AN IRREVERENT LOOK AT THE AMERICAN MALE

✟

1978

My editor, Cal Morgan, keeps telling me not to say I dislike this book. We have had a running argument about it for months. I don't know why it bothers him so; every writer has a least-favorite book and He is mine. Still, Cal is a wonderful boy (I'm six years older than his mother), so as a special favor to him I will say something nice about He.

Alistair Cooke loved it. In one of his transatlantic broadcasts, later published in a collection of essays on America, he called it "a little masterpiece." Since then he has praised my work in several speeches and frequently quotes his favorite passage: "Feminists will not be satisfied until every abortion is performed by a gay black doctor under an endangered tree on a reservation for handicapped Indians."

I have recycled this quip numerous times but it first saw the light of print in He.

THE REGULAR GUY

Like Babbitt before him, the American regular guy strikes observers as "prosperous, extremely married, and unromantic." In fact, he has *husband* written all over him, but the name tag eternally pinned to his lapel reads William "Bill" Fletcher. Asian visitors can be forgiven for thinking that the "Hi, I'm" is part of his name. He will soon set them straight; his business cards, as well as the personalized matchbooks and ballpoint pens that he calls "ice breakers" and hands out to seatmates on planes all read William "Bill" Fletcher.

He's from Back Home, U.S.A., but the best place to find him is in Out of Town, where he spends his time conventioneering, paging and being paged, and saying "Hit me again" to bartenders.

Anyone who converses with him soon develops the sensation of being stuck in a hotel room with nothing to read but *The Toastmaster's Handbook.* This heartland vade mecum is William "Bill" Fletcher's bible, the source of the habit he has of interrupting himself with "that reminds me of a story." It also taught him to develop a forceful delivery, which is why his opinions sound as if they ought to be preceded by a bosun's whistle and a voice bellowing "Now hear this!"

He leans heavily on Q.E.D.s, his favorite being "Football builds character." Argue with him and he will say, "Women don't understand what football means to guys." Ask him what football means to guys and he will say, "It builds character."

Next come the maxims. "Only a man can play the violin because it's like getting a response out of a woman's body" (wink-wink). This is his version of the Balzac quotation about an inept lover being like an orangutan with a violin, but don't try to untangle it or he will jab you in the ribs and boom, "Hey, the party's getting serious!" Besides, any mention of Balzac has an excellent chance of turning into a joke about Zach's balls. Never say anything that could launch William "Bill" Fletcher on the road to clever sexual repartee. Once he gets started, he will order a tray of "whore's drawers" to go with your cocktails; define a French breakfast ("a roll in bed with honey"); proffer sex advice by the author of *She* ("ride 'er haggard"); and deconstruct *The Rape of the Lock* ("Here comes the key!").

A woman is wise to shriek with laughter over these bons mots. If she merely smiles wryly she is effectively announcing that she has experienced mild pleasure but not orgasm. In William "Bill" Fletcher's world, "Did I make you laugh?" and "Did I make you come?" are interchangeable questions, so he keeps pumping away, repeating the punch line and elbowing her in the ribs in a symbolic attempt to send her over the top.

Fake the laugh. If you don't, he will put a comforting arm around your shoulders and say, "You'd be a great gal if only you'd develop a sense of humor."

He enjoys talking to women about sex, but if he isn't sure how a particular woman might react, he tests her by steering the conversation around to other bodily functions. His favorites are vomiting and diarrhea, which have the added advantage of making him sound well-traveled. Any woman with a Chaucerian streak is advised to stifle it, else William "Bill" Fletcher will take it as a sign that he can talk about *real* sex. (He creates prudery where none existed.)

He likes to draw charts and maps on cocktail napkins to illustrate his stories. "This is Guadalcanal, and this here's the lagoon. Here's the beach where we landed, and over here is the cave where I found the Jap colonel taking a crap." Now it's philosophy time. "Could you shoot a man while he's taking a crap? I mean, tell me honestly, could you?''

When he's ready to steer the conversation into really intimate waters, he uses a technique he calls ''getting her to open up.''

''What do you want out of life?'' he asks soulfully, his eyes narrowing to pensive slits. If you say you already have what you want, he smiles knowingly and asks, ''Don't you ever get lonely?'' If you say no, he asks, ''What are you so unhappy about?'' Claim that you are perfectly happy and he will shake his head, smile his worldly-wise smile and say, ''Tell me what you're afraid of.''

This plangent third degree is designed to prove that you are a love-starved waif. Any woman thus grilled finds herself trying very hard to sound active and sophisticated, but watch out when he starts comparing lonely life in the big city to the rich communalism of life in Back Home. You will be sorely tempted to deflate his maudlin testimonial, but don't do it. If you say ''Small towns are dull,'' he will come back with, ''You like excitement, huh? Hee-hee-hee,'' accompanied by every gleam and wink in his repertoire. His conversational terrain is full of such land mines.

Self-containment and formality terrify him. Saying ''How do you do?'' instead of ''Hi'' or calling him ''Mr. Fletcher'' wound him to the quick. He also requires lots of smiles. A pensive woman is a sexually unresponsive woman who needs cheering up, as it were. Telling himself that if he can get her to talk, he can get her to smile, and if he can get her to smile, he can get her to bed, he cases every airport lounge and hotel lobby, ever ready to bellow, ''Whatcha lookin' so sad about, honey? It can't be that bad!''

He regards any *no* from a woman as a sexual no. If, like most women, she automatically says ''No, thank you'' instead of just ''No,'' he will take her good manners as encouragement, until he forces her to be rude to him. If he offers his airplane seatmate his little bag of cashews and she declines them, he feels subconsciously that she has refused him sex; his crestfallen look gives him away. Any refusal from a woman, no matter how minor, sets off desperate cajolery. Does she want his copy of *Newsweek?* No. Would she like to change seats with him so she can see the New York skyline? No. Would she like another drink? No. He will press on, burrowing through her negatives like a mole, offering her his pillow, his earphones, his mints, his crossword puzzle, his pencil, his nail file. He must get a *yes* out of her, no matter how meaningless.

It was William ''Bill'' Fletcher who puzzled Alexis de Tocqueville in the early nineteenth century:

> I have often noticed in the United States that it is not easy to make a man understand that his presence may be dispensed with; hints will not always suffice to shake him off. I contradict an American at every word he says, to show him that his conversation bores me; he instantly labors with fresh pertinacity to convince me; I preserve a dogged silence, and he thinks I am meditating deeply on the truths that he is uttering; at last I rush from his company, and he supposes that some urgent business hurries me elsewhere. This man will never understand that he wearies me to death unless I tell him so, and the only way to get rid of him is to make him my enemy for life.

To women my age who started work in the Fifties, William ''Bill'' Fletcher will always be the Boss, a deus ex machina in the most literal sense: the throat-clearing, coughing, rambling, ungrammatical sciolist on the dictaphone whose letters we had to type: ''This is the house by the side of the road with the white picket fence and the green shingles and the hand-carved columns on the front porch that Fletcher Construction built.''

His appalling ignorance makes him seem more uncouth than he actually is. It's not entirely his fault; much of it goes back to his Depression-traumatized father, who kept warning him not to become a jack-of-all-trades. Shaped by the paternal admonition, ''Find one thing to do and keep doing it,'' he knows everything there is to know about copper fittings or actuarial tables but nothing about anything else.

This is what prompts his breezy exhortations not to let the party get serious, as well as his signature line on all matters literary, ''My wife is the reader in the family.'' Compounding his educational shortcomings is the American canon that men must be simple. A complex and enigmatic woman is credited with an air of mystery, inspiring people to say, ''Still waters run deep,'' which is very sexy. But the same metaphor applied to a man makes him sound furtive, so William ''Bill''

Fletcher takes pains to cultivate his shallowness like the rarest of orchids.

Ignorant he may be, yet he is not stupid. However much he tries to hide it, he suffers from an intellectual frustration that periodically manifests itself in abrupt and often bizarre epistemological cravings.

I shared a seat with an especially persistent William "Bill" Fletcher on a five-hour flight from New York to Seattle. He boomed away for a couple of hours, but at last, when dinner came, he fell silent and concentrated on eating. At least, that's what I thought he was concentrating on.

It was a standard American meal of sirloin tips and parsleyed potatoes, but suddenly, à propos of nothing, he said: "You know, talking about lichee nuts . . ."

I looked up with a start.

"You know," he went on, "they say that if you crack open a lichee nut, inside there's another lichee nut. And inside that one there's another one. And on and on and on. Did you ever think of that?"

"You're defining infinity," I said.

"Nah! Hey, the party's getting serious!"

"It *is* infinity that you're talking about."

"Nah! Listen, see, if you took a picture of me, right? Then you took another picture of me holding the first picture, right? Inside the second picture would be a picture of me holding a picture of me, and on and on and on. It would never end, right?"

His dismissive "Nah!" is his warning to himself not to let the conversation get too intellectual, yet intellectual conversation is precisely what he craves. He must turn to strangers for it because cerebral ruminations are not well-received in Back Home. Nobody in these friendly hamlets listens, really listens, to anyone else, and the worst offender is his wife.

Now in her forties, Betty Fletcher is the same girl she was in college—the one who filled the dorm with the ululating shriek of her favorite record, "Love Is a Many-Splendored Thing," played by fifty thousand violins. It was the homing pitch on the dog whistle of her ambition; she was dying to get married then and she is dying to stay married now. Fear of mid-life divorce dominates her life.

When William "Bill" Fletcher says, "My wife doesn't understand me,'' he is telling the truth. She doesn't want to, for fear of what she might discover if she did. Let him exhibit the smallest sign of discontent and all sorts of warning bells go off in her brain. To Betty, ruminative conversations are a sign of discontent, so he has learned not to initiate them. They would only go like this:

"You know, talking about lichee nuts . . . they say if you crack open a lichee nut, inside there's another one. And inside that there's another one. And on and on and on. It would never stop. Did you ever think about that?"

"What's the matter?"

"Nothing. I was just thinking about how things go on and on, back and back. . . .''

"Are you worried about something?"

"No! I'm just thinking about what's *out* there. I just got to thinking about that old Chinese story about the lichee nuts."

"Something *is* bothering you, I know it. Why won't you tell me what it is?"

God forbid that he should try discussing that other favorite, déjà vu. The moment he said, "You know that feeling that you've been somewhere before or met somebody before?" poor Betty's divorce-haunted brain would start spinning like a top with visions of women on planes, women at company parties, newly hired secretaries, and old motels under new management.

Thanks to Betty, William "Bill" Fletcher falls like a ripe plum into the lap of any woman who will talk to him. Once, having a drink with him, I brought up a fine point of grammar gleaned from Mary McCarthy.

"You know, we say *aren't I,* which is a contraction of *are I not,* which is wrong. Shouldn't we really say *amn't I?*"

His eyes lit with the unmistakable sparkle of intellectual zest.

"Hey! Hey, you're right! I never thought about that before, but damn, it's true! Amn't I? By God, I'm gonna say that from now on. Hey, Charlie, amn't I smart?"

It touched me more than any of the extravagant compliments he had been paying me. I could have cried.

Casanova wrote that for men, "Love is three-quarters curiosity," an observation reiterated by Theodore Reik in *The Need to Be Loved:*

"Nothing in the psychology of women can be compared to the sexual inquisitiveness of the male."

William "Bill" Fletcher is America's foremost sexual quidnunc. Every woman is familiar with his speculative gaze across a restaurant or hotel lobby. It's one of the few times that he's quiet and still. Deep in reverie he sits, eyes squinched up and a puckish little smile lifting the corners of his mouth, a man in search of she-ness.

Knowing nothing about women, he has developed an insatiable need to know everything about them. He wants to be a man who understands women, yet at the same time he fears that such an understanding, were he to achieve it, would be evidence of a dangerously large, even homosexually large, feminine component in his own make-up. The fun would be over then; he could no longer go out with the boys and talk about how hard it is to understand women. Worse, the boys might start having trouble understanding *him*. Unwilling to risk this, he puts the lid on his deeper speculations and concentrates on "I wonder what she's like in the sack?"

He knows all the signs of a hot tomato. A woman who wears a red dress is asking for it. A woman who kicks her foot back and forth is signaling him. A woman who slips off her shoes is hot—not just her feet, but all of her. A woman whose eyes slant is hot. A woman with a cleft chin is hot. A woman who is a heavy smoker likes . . . tobacco? Nah! Going down on guys. A woman drinking alone wants to be picked up. Could it be, is it possible, that she simply wants a drink? Nah!

He is also a self-proclaimed expert at spotting arcane lubricious distinctions across a crowded room.

"See that girl over there in the green dress?"

"Yes. What about her?"

"She's not table nooky."

"How do you know? Is she a friend of yours?"

"Never saw her before in my life."

"Then how do you know?"

"I can just tell, that's all. She's good nooky but she's not table nooky."

He lives in a sexual time capsule, still guided by what he heard behind the barn and down at the barbershop in Back Home, where they still carry *The Police Gazette.* His sexual guidelines are so grandfatherly that you can almost hear the cackle:

"Divorced women are easy because once a woman gets used to getting it she can't live without it."

"Working girls are easy because they can't afford dinner."

"Nurses are easy because they can get hold of ergot. Guaranteed to make the monthlies start. One swig and they fall off the roof, Scout's honor."

Like the laws of the Medes and the Persians, William "Bill" Fletcher's seduction line altereth not. You can tell how many times he must have said it by the way it all runs together. His "God you're lovely I've got to have you let's go to bed" sounds like the flight attendant's "Please fasten your seatbelts and place your serving tray in the upright position."

He also may have a special seduction technique that he "swears by," usually something over-complicated involving props and requiring a level of acting ability that he lacks. Convinced that all women are equally gullible, he makes the mistake of using his special technique indiscriminately, without regard for the possible perspicacity of any one particular woman.

This blind spot turns up in James Jones's *Some Came Running,* when Dave Hirsh decides to seduce an English teacher with an original poem that he has used successfully on seven bar flies:

> The more powerful and dramatic method was to seem to write the poem right in front of them; get thoughtful, ask for paper and pencil, and—with proper hesitations every now and then for thinking—pretend to create the poem right there. . . . He had used this method four of the seven times, and it always created a very powerful and emotional effect. . . . The other way was—usually after some evening of particularly heavy lovemaking which ended in frustration—to show up with the poem next day and say he'd written it that night when he got home, had sat up all night writing it.

Dave's seductee listens to his performance with a stunned expression that he completely misinterprets. At last, when she can't hold it in any longer and dissolves in laughter, he is at a loss to understand what went wrong.

Setbacks like this are par for the course in the life of William "Bill" Fletcher. When they happen, he mumbles, "You really know how to hurt a guy," and shuffles off, vowing that from now on he will avoid "serious" girls—his euphemism for intelligent—and find what he calls "a girl who likes to have a good time."

In other words, a female version of himself. A girl who has changed the final *y* in her name to an *i;* a Luci/Patti/Terri who makes a lot of noise, loves big parties, and always has a whale of a good time on those exhausting evenings when everybody runs from nightclub to nightclub "doing the town."

Luci/Patti/Terri and William "Bill" Fletcher would rather do towns than each other. Theirs is the kind of puritanism that compels them to wear themselves out in late-night carousing so they will be too tired to do much of anything in bed. When they finally get there, around four A.M., Luci/Patti/Terri closes her bleary eyes, opens her legs, and pats the back of William "Bill" Fletcher's neck while he labors over her. He talks a lot about hot women but all he really wants is cooperation, the exhausted woman's specialty.

Meanwhile, back in Back Home, Betty Fletcher is cutting out articles on how to make your marriage work. She might as well put her scissors away. Not only is William "Bill" Fletcher never going to leave her—he worries constantly that *she* will leave *him.*

He has never read *Sexual Suicide,* but he shares George Gilder's belief that men without women revert to barbarism and destroy themselves. Gilder labored the point, but William "Bill" Fletcher sums it up with one of his maxims: "Saved by the love of a good woman."

If Betty ever left him, he would react like Frank Hirsh in *Some Came Running,* who comes home to find his wife gone:

> Capless, the whiskey bottle had fallen over and most of its remaining contents had run out on the rug. Staring at it, the deep, unnameable, unbearable panic seized him again. Frantically, he ran out to the kitchen and got the dishrag and wet it and grabbed some dish towels and ran back in to try and clean it up. . . . It was a very poor effort at cleaning, and it did not even assuage his conscience: Here he was, ruining their house, his and Agnes's house, almost before she had even left it. Guilt of a power and strength unknown to him before gripped him as he tried to clean it up. . . . My God! what would he do if she didn't come

back? The whole place would sink into rack and ruin and decay; and he himself would descend into sloth and dirt and stagnation. A bum. She just had to come back! She just had to!

In conclusion, as they say in *The Toastmaster's Handbook,* William "Bill" Fletcher should study Lord Chesterfield's advice to his son.

"Tell stories very seldom, and absolutely never but where they are very apt and very short. Omit every circumstance that is not material, and beware of digressions. To have frequent recourse to narrative betrays great want of imagination."

"Never hold anybody by the button or the hand in order to be heard out; for if people are not willing to hear you, you had much better hold your tongue than them."

"Loud laughter is the mirth of the mob."

If William "Bill" Fletcher, World War II vet and Fifties masher, strikes you as a relic of the past, think again. He lives! Who do you think is doing the sexual harassing in all these sexual-harassment lawsuits? Who else would think it was funny to ask a woman to dig in his pants pocket for a quarter? Who else would decide to grab every woman he met until one of them said yes? I would bet anything that somewhere in Senator Bob Packwood's famous diary you will find William "Bill" Fletcher's deathless observation, "They'll never repeal the law of averages, ha-ha-ha."

THE BARBARIAN PRINCESS

by Laura Buchanan

✝

1 9 7 8

Here it is, you little devils. The breathless bodice ripper, long out of print, that so many of you have told me you tried to find but, to my vast relief, could not. I ought to have my head examined for including one word of this book in an anthology, but you asked for it, so in it goes— an apt phrase, considering what keeps happening to the heroine.

A little background: By the mid-1970s the anti-feminist backlash had produced a demand for lushly romantic historical novels known in the trade as ''sweet savages'' after the genre's first blockbuster, <u>Sweet Savage Love</u>, by Rosemary Rogers. Original paperbacks with titles composed of three emotionally extravagant trigger words, they sold into the millions.

Deciding to get in on the gravy, I contacted a publisher for whom I had done a ghost job.

''Great!'' he said. ''But there's too much Southern Plantation and French Revolution. Can you come up with a different background?''

I came up with the fall of Roman Britain to the Anglo-Saxons in the fifth century A.D. My editor was delighted, seeing helmets with horns and lots of spiked armor for mauling bosoms in the ''he pulled her to him'' scenes. After settling on a pen name, I created my heroine, a red-haired British Celt named Lydda.

''I don't like it,'' said my editor. ''Too many <u>d</u>'s.''

''Double-<u>d</u> in Welsh is pronounced <u>th</u>.''

''Yes, but sweet-savage readers don't know dat.''

I won the name battle. Then came the title battle.

''Something Saxon Splendor,'' I mused.

''Sweet-savage readers don't know what Saxon means unless it's got Anglo with it. Then you've got to hyphenate it, and hyphens scare them.''

''Because of ethnic sensitivity?'' I asked, puzzled.

''No, because hyphens are scary. They remind them of feminists who keep their maiden names. If we use Saxon we've got to do it in a way that won't make them feel insecure.''

''How about Sex and the Saxon Churl?''

''They don't know what churl means. How about <u>The Barbarian Princess</u>?'' he said proudly.

''They don't know the historical meaning of barbarian,'' I protested. ''They'll think it's about a girl with awful table manners. How about <u>The Celtic Princess</u>?''

"They don't know what Celtic means either, but it would remind them of basketball, and their husbands sitting in front of the tube instead of carrying them into the bedroom. We're talking about love-starved women here. Don't worry about historical meanings, barbarian sounds sexy."

He counseled me on the need to strike a balance between erotic titillation and romantic idealism. "Remember, keep the heroine a virgin as long as possible, and never let her have sex <u>willingly</u> with a man she doesn't love."

I began. The story opens in the spring of 409 with Lydda swimming naked in the Bristol Channel. Roman Britons spoke Latin so I decided to toss in a few obvious phrases for the sake of verisimilitude. When she entered the water I had her exclaim "<u>Quam frigida est!</u>" and when she is chased by a boatful of Roman sailors, she cries "<u>Desiste!</u>"

My editor called as soon as he read it. "Go easy on the Latin. Sweet-savage readers can't handle that. You can have her scream <u>desiste</u> when she gets raped, though."

Since time and place were right, I gave Lydda a childhood sweetheart named Patricius who has strange dreams about fighting off snakes in the neighboring island of Hibernia. It brought a delighted call from my editor.

"I told Publicity we're going to be first on the market with the seduction of Saint Patrick!"

I devised a better idea that would save Lydda's virginity and allow me to dramatize a factual incident. She and Patricius are necking in a field, but just as he is about to "take" her, Hibernian pirates burst out of the woods, throw nets over them, and drag them back to the ship to sell as slaves in the Auld Sod. (This is how Ireland got a Brit for her patron saint.)

Screaming "<u>desiste!</u>" Lydda fights off the lecherous captain and jumps overboard. Since I set her up as a strong swimmer in the first chapter, she makes it back to Britannia, only to learn that her father has chosen a husband for her: the evil and corrupt Roman, Vitalinus.

In Londinium for her wedding, Lydda meets the Saxon general Thel, a blond hunk in spiked armor who has come to negotiate a colonization plan with the Roman Britons to save him the trouble of conquering their country.

It's love-hate at first sight. Thel pulls Lydda to him the first chance he gets. "<u>Desiste!</u>" she cries, as well she might—by the time I got through with his armor it looked like Kaiser Bill's helmet.

On their wedding night, Vitalinus doesn't notice the shredded condition of her bosom because he has no interest in her front; just to keep her virginity perking along, I made him a pervert who forces her to submit to unnatural acts that leave her hymen intact.

They go to Rome, where Thel reappears and ravishes Lydda. Not long after their passionate interlude the psychotic Vitalinus commits suicide. Now that she is conveniently widowed, she and Thel are free to live happily ever after, but I was only on page two hundred. The lovers had to be separated somehow so that Lydda could live to scream "<u>desiste!</u>" some more.

History came to my rescue. By now it was August of 410, so I sent Thel out of town on a government mission and left Lydda alone in Rome to be kidnapped by Alaric the Goth when he sacks the city.

Since Alaric died of a stroke three weeks after the sack of Rome, I made it happen while he was raping Lydda. In short order, she is waylaid by an evil Egyptian sea captain and a sexually insatiable Roman prefect; makes friends with the famous female scholar Hypatia, Alexandria's most liberated career woman; is taken hostage by a pair of early Christian hermits; and, finally, is arrested by a Roman centurion, who takes his pleasure with her and then turns her over to his men. Screaming "<u>desistite!</u>" (gang rape takes the plural), she proves to be such a delectable spitfire that the centurion sells her to the keeper of Constantinople's most select brothel.

There she befriends Marcellus the Eunuch (my editor called this her "free time") and together they escape on a ship bound for Britannia.

By now I was drinking heavily, which explains what happens next. During a storm at sea a falling mast crushes Marcellus and the entire crew is washed overboard, leaving Lydda alone on a rudderless ship. Knocked unconscious when it founders on a craggy rock, she comes to in the arms of a craggy man in black robes.

"Where am I?" she asks.

"Caledonia."

"Who are you?"

"Nagar the Druid."

Of course Nagar ravishes her—it's the only way sweet-savage characters can get a conversation going. He does it on a stone altar in the sacred oak grove, injecting her with so much Celtic awareness that she leads an army of wild Caledonians into Britannia to wrest her homeland from the Saxon churls. Borne on a chariot, her face painted blue, she charges the leader of the hated Sassenach, but lo and behold, it's none other than Thel.

He routs her, rapes her, and marries her in short order. The wedding ceremony is performed by Patricius, who is home on leave from a now snake-free Hibernia, and nine months later he baptizes their son.

This hectic mess earned so much money that my editor asked me to write another one, this time using a background of ancient Greece.

"Something Golden Glory," he suggested.

"How about Chaos and Meander?"

"Too mythy."

That did it. "It's time to cease and <u>desiste</u>," I said.

Since I have to reread this manuscript several times during production, I am excerpting only one chapter from <u>The Barbarian Princess</u>. I couldn't stand any more and neither could you. Here then is Chapter V, the account of Lydda's first meeting with Thel.

Mind you, although this novel is from my flawed early period, I didn't change a word. Bodice rippers are supposed to sound this way.

CHAPTER V

Lydda's handmaiden knocked timidly and entered.

"My lady, your lord father wishes to see you in the *bibliotheca* at once."

Lydda rose and went to the room where Marcus transacted his government business. Vitalinus was with him, and he stood up and watched her eagerly as she crossed the room, his handsome face bearing a sharp, vicious cast that reminded her of a fox or a wolf.

The son of a British mother and a Roman father, Vitalinus bore the best features of each. His dark hair had a reddish tint like the color of black cherries. His skin was swarthy, yet his eyes were the rich blue of a morning glory. His profile could well have provided the model for the idealized portraits of less handsome emperors on Roman coins.

"My dear," Marcus began in his most persuasive tones, "Vitalinus has been summoned to Rome on important business. Therefore you will be married here in Londinium the day after tomorrow."

Lydda was shocked into speechlessness. That meant she had very little time to persuade her father. She would have to speak to him as soon as Vitalinus left.

"I have been appointed Prefect of the Imperial Treasury," Vitalinus said proudly. "You will be a lady of the court! And surely the most beautiful of them all."

She smiled coldly. "My congratulations, my lord."

"I have taken a house in the Aventine for us. As you know, that is the most fashionable quarter of Rome."

"I shall be most eager to see my new home, and to take up my duties as your hostess," she said, knowing that she must go through the evening as though nothing were wrong. With a desperate hope, she thought her father might be persuaded when they were alone, but his sense of propriety would never give in to an outburst in front of the man to whom he had pledged her hand.

Marcus, remembering her tearful reaction to her betrothal, looked relieved. "That's my good daughter!" He beamed. "You see?" he added, turning to Vitalinus. "She is now a grown-up young woman, not the spoiled child she used to be."

"Oh, but I think a touch of the child is charming. She must never change completely, must she? Her freshness is her greatest asset. I'm sure it will be most appreciated at court."

"Yes, yes," Marcus muttered, gathering up some papers. "Now we must meet with the Saxon representative."

Lydda stepped back as though she had been struck. "The *what?*"

"His name is Thel, and he is the leader of the Saxons. Wait until you hear his Latin! We were discussing military camps, and it seems he cannot pronounce *castra.* He calls it *chester.*"

Vitalinus laughed. "And he calls the river Tamesis the *Thames.*"

"You would let a Saxon in this house after—"

Marcus waved his daughter down. "Politics makes strange companions, as Julius Caesar said. Thel is going to help us keep Britannia Roman. We are going to cede the Saxons some land in the eastern part of the island. Their population is growing and they're being pushed out of their own homeland by the encroachments of other barbarians. That is why they make these raids on us. In exchange for giving them what Thel calls 'living space,' they will serve as mercenary soldiers, to keep other Saxons out of Britannia.''

"Do you honestly expect Saxons to fight Saxons?'' Lydda demanded.

"But we are giving them Roman citizenship,'' Marcus explained, spreading his hands. "They won't *be* Saxons then.''

"That's like putting a hawk in the chicken coop and telling him he's a chicken.''

"Now, now, dear daughter, don't trouble yourself with these matters. Women don't understand diplomatic negotiations. It's much too complex for the female mind. Just be charming to him, and you'll be aiding your country in a womanly way. I want this Thel to appreciate that the women of Britannia are *worth* protecting.''

Lydda subsided into seething, frustrated silence. Saxon representative indeed! Wild boars did not send out ambassadors.

When Thel the Saxon entered the *atrium,* Lydda was astonished to observe how young he was. She had seen a few Saxon captives before, shaggy members of the churl class whose moth-eaten furs and overgrown beards and hair made them look like hump-backed old men. The blond giant who approached her now could not have been more than twenty-five. His curly hair, yellow as a daisy, had been evenly cut just below his ears; his beard, of a slightly more reddish shade, was shaped to a point at his chin. He wore a mustache, which she hated, but it, too, was neat and closely clipped. His rich clothing identified him as a member of the class of earls. His shining silver helmet was decorated on either side with eagle's wings instead of the dreaded animal horns. A black sealskin cape that any woman might have envied hung over his powerful shoulders, fastened with a brooch of pure gold inlaid with rubies, and a matching buckle held his sword belt. He carried no *seax;* his sidearms were a Roman short sword and a jeweled dagger of Byzantine design. Instead of a tunic he wore a chain net *byrnie,* and those strange garments the Saxons called *hosa* covered his legs.

Like all tall women, Lydda was not used to looking up to men, and she resented having to do so now. Since the age of fourteen she had been nearly as tall as all but a few Roman men, but now she had to tilt her head back to meet the ice-blue gaze of this overpowering foreigner. For the first time in her life she felt insignificant. The bold Saxon dominated the room and everyone in it, so that he seemed to be the host and they the guests. Although Thel's manners were surprisingly polished as he acknowledged her, she sensed a brutality in him that made her stiffen with wariness and instinctive hostility.

"Let us dine," she said stiffly, leading the way to the *triclinium.*

When she took her place at her table near the men, Thel looked at her with a mixture of surprise and disdain.

"Our guest seems to find something amiss," she said to her father.

"Is the food not to your taste?" Marcus asked anxiously.

"No, Lord Marcus, it is not the food," the Saxon replied, in heavily accented Latin. A condescending smile twitched briefly at the corners of his mouth. "It is merely that in my country, women do not dine with men. They stay in the *brydbur*—I beg your pardon, the bride's bower, as you call it."

Lydda returned his smile, putting as much ice into her voice as she could.

"It so happens that we call it the *gynaecium,* but I try to spend as little time in it as possible. I hope you will grow to like our customs, my lord Thel, since you are not in *your* country."

"No—not yet."

Marcus looked from one to the other and hastened to divert the conversation. ". . . Er, speaking of bride's bowers, I have the honor to announce the forthcoming marriage of my daughter to Lord Vitalinus. It will be celebrated the day after tomorrow. You must honor us with your presence."

Thel nodded his acceptance, then gazed across the tables at the prospective bridegroom and said, "I wish you much happiness."

Lydda flushed scarlet. She watched as Thel unhooked a huge drinking horn from his belt and proposed a toast. The servant filled it, pouring for what seemed like a small eternity. Thel made no move to stop him until the horn was full, unperturbed by the curious silence that fell as his hosts and hostess stopped talking to watch the pouring.

He held the horn aloft and turned to Lydda, his eyes appraising slits as they raked her figure. "May the goddess Frigga, bestower of fertility, bless your womb and keep it full. Wassail!"

With that, he upended the horn and began to drink. The company watched as his throat moved rhythmically, not missing a beat. Marcus and Vitalinus took sips from their goblets, never taking their eyes off their guest. Even Lydda, loath to show any interest in him at all, could not refrain from watching the incredible performance. The barbaric horn must have held at least enough to fill two or three flagons.

At last he stopped and upended the horn over the floor. A drop or two of wine splashed out.

"How do you set that vessel down on the table, with that point on the end?" Vitalinus asked.

"You don't," Thel replied, with an amused shrug. "You lay it down each time you empty it."

Lydda could barely contain her rage. He was the most contemptuous man she had ever met! Beneath his thin veneer of politeness, he sneered at one and all, not even troubling to hide his scorn for them, their customs, and their hospitality. Worst of all, there was nothing they could do about his arrogance, for Marcus and Vitalinus wanted something from him, and he knew it. He held the prefects of the two most important cities in Britannia in the palm of his hand.

Marcus and Vitalinus sat like eunuchs, meek and hesitant and anxious to please this brute who had insulted them. Although Vitalinus repelled her, he was still her fiancé and should have asserted himself. She looked sharply at her future husband, but he paid no attention to her. He was gazing at Thel with an almost worshipful expression in his eyes that made her flesh crawl, though she knew not why.

Her repulsion made her all the more desperate for the evening to end so that she could confront her father. When Vitalinus and Thel at last took their leave, Lydda had her chance.

"Well, Lydda," her father said as he turned from the door he had just closed after his guests. "I am most pleased that you have seen the wisdom of my choice. I don't mind telling you that I have often wondered who would ever accept a hellion like you in marriage. But as you heard, Vitalinus even appreciates your . . . ah . . . spirit. The evening went very well indeed."

"Only because I kept that spirit of mine in check, my lord father." Lydda's eyes blazed as she looked her father full in the face, and Marcus's self-satisfied look faded quickly, for he recognized the warning signals only too well.

The composure Lydda had fought to maintain all evening drowned in a torrent of emotion. "Don't you see what Vitalinus is!" she exploded. "He's a fawning, spineless . . . prig! I detest the very thought of him. How could you even think I could be happy with someone like that? The only person I love is Patricius. I know he will come back to me someday. Please! Don't make me marry Vitalinus! He's—"

"Enough!" Marcus roared, shaking with fury. "You will marry Vitalinus because I order it. You need no other reason. And you have no other choice!" With that, he strode out of the room, leaving a dazed Lydda behind him.

Never had her father been so enraged or so inordinately determined to have his way. And never had he refused to hear her out. But the one time it was most important to her, she had not had her way. He was leaving the house on business now, and he would not return until the next afternoon. Should she run away, she wondered desperately? But there was no one with whom she could take refuge. And she sensed that, for some unfathomable reason, this marriage meant more to her father than anything within her memory.

The understaffed house was in an uproar when she arose the next morning, for Bard and the few servants were making ready her wedding feast. Vitalinus had sent some of his slaves to help, and a full-tilt argument greeted her when she marched into the kitchen to demand to know what had happened to her breakfast. Her handmaiden was in tears over something said by Vitalinus's middle-aged bossy cook.

"Oh, never mind!" she snapped at the woman. "Just give me some mead!"

She could not bear being cooped up in the house one more moment. Although she hated all cities, she hated inactivity more. She slipped out the door unnoticed by the squabbling servants and was swiftly caught up in the teeming crowds.

Soon she regretted her decision. She was too well dressed and obviously privileged not to attract attention from people who were not. Inflation and political confusion had created a dangerous mood among the populace of Londinium, and Lydda quickly perceived that she was the target of growing resentment. She was too young for an old world, too beautiful for an ugly world, and too rich for a poor world. "Huh!"

growled a passing man. "Who d' you think you are—the Queen of Sheba?"

Two tawdry and unkempt women expressed their hostility in a more subtle, female way. As they passed Lydda, they began to whisper to each other like mischievous schoolgirls testing a new teacher's endurance. Sensing their challenge, Lydda held her head higher.

"Look at her, going along with her nose in the air."

Suddenly, fury overwhelmed her. Her nostrils flared and her whole body stiffened into a posture that only served to make her look even more haughty and aristocratic.

As the tension swirled around her and radiated back upon the close-packed crowds, a drunkard lying on the ground in the marketplace stumbled to his feet and, growling like an animal, aimed his wineskin at her face and squeezed it with all his might.

The jet of acrid wine struck her in the eyes. She staggered backward and fell blindly against a counter strewn with cheap trinkets, rubbing her stinging eyes with her fists.

Cheers, shouts of approval, and scattered applause broke out, but over them all rose a deep, heavily accented voice.

"Is that all you've got to squirt at ladies, you besotted cur? I knew Britannia was short of men but now I see there is no shortage of cowards!"

Through burning eyes, Lydda saw Thel the Saxon pushing his way through the crowd, rapidly making his way to her. He used his thick-set shoulders like battering rams, charging without mercy or regard for the sex of the people in his way. Men and women tripped over each other and fell to the ground, and he kicked them aside as if he were clearing a path through the weeds. The terrified drunkard clutched his wineskin and tried to crawl under a counter, but Thel caught him on the buttocks with a crashing blow of his bearskin-booted foot. The man squealed like a stuck pig and babbled an apology, but Thel planted a foot on his chest.

"My first inclination is to tear out your tongue, but as a Saxon I believe the punishment should fit the crime." He reached down and grabbed the wineskin from the man's grasp, and held it out to Lydda.

"My lady?"

Lydda took the wineskin and joyfully emptied it on the drunkard's face. The crowd laughed and applauded, their hostility redirected to the man on the ground.

Suddenly Thel's brawny arm encircled her waist and she was jerked painfully against his chain-net *byrnie*. The sharp hooks ground into her breasts and caught in the cloth of her *stola*. She felt his fingers slip down to the curve of her hip and knead her flesh. He grinned down at her and continued his exploratory hold like a man inspecting the haunch of a workhorse.

"How dare you! Let me go!"

"Vitalinus won't have to shake the sheets to find *you*. If I may make so bold, my lady, I judge you to be a good *ficken*."

"Take your hands off me! What are you doing here?"

"I followed you, and a good thing I did, wouldn't you say? You little fool, don't you realize that this city, this whole country, is on the brink of anarchy?"

"Who are you to talk about anarchy?" Lydda cried in fury, remembering the slaughter at the house of Petronius. "It's you Saxons, marauding, killing, stealing—"

"Speaking of stealing, I'm taking you away from here before you get into any more trouble. You could easily start a riot single-handed." He grinned impudently as his eyes caressed her body. "Come, my horse is over here."

He grasped her arm in his huge hand and guided her smoothly through the mob. She did not want to go with him, detested him, yet as the crowds parted before him she felt herself carried along on the crest of his commanding presence. His power became her power, and she felt safe. Yet, at the same time, she was overcome by the same sense of helplessness she had felt when the North African sailor had rudely embraced her. How could she feel powerful and helpless at once? And most of all, how could she hate this man so and still enjoy the tingling warmth that the touch of his hand on her arm spread through her entire body?

Suddenly she felt disgusted with herself and jerked her arm away. "I will go nowhere with you! I am going home."

"If ever there was a woman who needed a beating, it's you. Either you *sit* in this saddle, or I'll throw you across it like a sack of meal! Take your choice."

He grabbed her by the waist and lifted her as easily as if she were a leaf, then vaulted up behind her. His arms reached around her for the reins, imprisoning her in a circle of unbelievably hard muscle. She sat stiffly in his embrace, her back against his chest and her buttocks nestled against his lower torso. She was powerfully aware of every line of his body, and sensed that he was just as aware of hers. She could feel his breath on her neck and ears. Her brain throbbed with cutting remarks and outraged declarations, but she could not seem to transfer them to her tongue.

"You look like the Roman goddess of Indignation. I could put you in a niche in the Temple of Jupiter and all the people who are still pagans would come and burn incense to you. They would never know it was a living woman."

"I don't care to be abducted by barbarians!" she spat out, finding her tongue at last.

"Unless you relax and ride with the gait, you're going to have a blistered bottom to present to your husband on your wedding night."

He put his spurs to the horse and rode off, scattering pedestrians, chickens, and dogs before them.

"Where are you taking me? This isn't the way home."

"Let's ride for awhile on the *strand.*"

"The what?"

"It's Saxon. It means the road that borders on a river."

The horsewoman in Lydda overcame the indignant lady. Matching the rhythm of the ride, her body relaxed, sliding easily against Thel's sturdy form. It was several moments before she realized that her breasts were bouncing freely, just above his hands. Instantly, she went stiff again—just in time to come crashing down on the hard wooden saddle with a sharp slap. Her buttocks stung and she felt for a moment as if her spine had been pushed through her skull.

Thel laughed knowingly and reined the horse in. "Is this what you were afraid I'd feel?"

His hands cupped her breasts and held her fast. He pulled her back against him and buried his lips in her neck. As she struggled to free herself his tongue explored her ear, sending a crawling heat up the side of her head that seemed to pluck at the roots of her hair.

"Oh, you filthy beast! Let me—"

His hand turned her head and his mouth was on hers while he held her face in a viselike grip. His teeth cut her underlip and she tasted her own blood. Dizziness and fear swept through her and she waited for her jawbone to snap under his fingers. She had never been so terrified in her life, not even on the Gaelic ship. Then, her captor had been fatuous and vulnerable, but this man was crafty and powerful, possessed by a lust beyond her wildest imaginings.

Suddenly he raised his head, his mouth red with her blood and his eyes blazing.

"Let me go?" he mocked. "Is that what you were going to say? All right, I'll let you go—back to your betrothed! By the time you get to Rome you'll wish you had surrendered yourself to me! I brought you out here intending to tear off your clothes and take you, but now I think I'll wait until you're ready to tear *my* clothes off. You will, Lydda! That degenerate will make you so hungry for a man you'll *beg* me to take you!"

He jerked the horse around and galloped toward the city. This time he did not hold her tightly. When he came to her house he reined in the horse, half shoved and half helped her slide to the ground, and galloped away without glancing back. Lydda stared after him until he disappeared from sight. Then she went slowly into the house.

WHEN SISTERHOOD WAS IN FLOWER

✝

1982

CHAPTER ONE

Call me Isabel.

The story of how I was shanghaied into the feminist movement begins in Boston in the politically pulsating year of 1971. I was not pulsating. Except for wishing that Nixon would appoint Ayn Rand Secretary of Altruism, my progressive fires remained unlit.

You may as well know, before you get any further into this, that my politics were and still are Royalist; I believe in absolute monarchy and the divine right of kings. One thing I like about Bloody Mary: she never said a word about lung cancer.

I felt out of place, to put it mildly, amid the Harvard-SDS atmosphere, but being from a family that has lived in Virginia since 1672, I had decided to live up North to engage in what writers call "gathering new experiences." I kept waiting for the spirit of liberal enlightenment to benefit me professionally, but it did not. With mind closed and legs open, all I gathered was lovers.

I am a native of Queen Caroline Court House (the Virginia way of designating a county seat), a Tidewater hamlet on lower Chesapeake Bay named for George IV's consort, Caroline of Brunswick, who is best remembered for refusing to change her underdrawers. "She stank," wrote Lord Malmesbury, with admirable aristocratic bluntness, in his diary. One of his extant letters containing the same observation is proudly displayed in our town library as a tribute to the complacency of our patroness.

The Queen's attachment to the tried and true was shared by everyone in town, especially by my grandmother, who refused to use a telephone. She communicated with calling cards, turning down the corners this way or that with such Druidic expertise that she could say *I am at home on Thursday but will be out of town over the weekend attending a funeral* without writing a word.

A firm believer in the theory that if time had any decency it would stand still, she liked to set a good example for it by appearing in historical *tableaux vivants* at Colonial Dames soirées. Dressed in full farthingale to represent the Spirit of Old Virginia, she would march out to a drum roll, strike a suitable pose, and freeze in place.

Freezing in place was the cornerstone of all Granny's thinking, which is undoubtedly why my mind-broadening move North did not work. One of her many definitions of a lady was someone who died in the same house, in the same room, in the same bed in which she had been born—and, though she didn't spell it out, conceived. Her fixation on stay-put living was such that she must have found it grimly fitting when my mother went her one better and died at the table. It happened when I was eight. In an attempt to talk, laugh, and eat all at the same time in the manner of sprightly Southern belles, she swallowed a bone.

My father took little notice of Mama's demise because it had nothing to do with the *Titanic*. Genteelly referred to as his hobby, his interest in the great sea tragedy was actually a monomania of the most degenerative kind; as far as he was concerned, anything that had happened after 2:20 A.M., April 15, 1912, had not really happened. In a steady-on-course progression toward madness, he filled the house with ship models, drawings, and an exact-to-scale diagram of the fatal slit, which several people mistook for a vulva; recited the entire passenger list from memory; and whistled "Nearer, My God, To Thee" while he shaved.

All this left little time for work. Ostensibly, he was president and general manager of the cardboard container manufacturing firm he inherited from his family. A profitable business in anyone else's hands, it started sinking as soon as Daddy took the helm. He insisted on making far more hat boxes than the modern American woman needed, and spent most of his and his secretary's office time corresponding with other *Titanic* freaks, an eerily formal lot who used "Esquire" and "Your obedient servant" and held what has to be the quaintest prejudice of all time: they snubbed the *Lusitania* as an upstart shipwreck because it resulted from an act of man instead of an Act of God.

The other member of our household was Mama's younger sister, Aunt Edna, who worked as secretary to the rector of St. Jude the Impossible, Episcopal, but whose real career was having cramps. The whole town knew about Aunt Edna's female trouble. She recited her complete gynecological history to anyone who would listen, made bets on when her irregular menses would start, and somehow connived to get three paid sick leave days a month from her boss, Father Chillingsworth, who personally interceded with the bishop on the subject of her delicate parts and kept a record of her period on his Canterbury desk calendar with all the other movable feasts. Once, he got it mixed up with Easter and wore the wrong vestments.

After Mama died, Granny took over my raising and the long battle for my mind began. Her chief task, as she saw it, was to break me of all unfeminine habits. The most unfeminine thing a girl could do, in her opinion, was become a ''bluestocking,'' as she called female intellectuals, so when it developed that I loved to read, she set out to separate me from books with every weapon in her arsenal.

First she explained what happened to little girls who read too much.

''Your eyes will fall out. They'll just fall right out and go plop at your feet. You'll end up on a street corner with a white cane and a little tin cup. I can just see you going tap-tap-tap with your cane and rattling your poor little cup. People will say, 'There's that poor little girl who wouldn't listen to her grandmother, and now look at her with those big black glasses over her poor little empty sockets.' ''

When that didn't work, she tried the blood-poisoning argument.

''If you read a book when you have a cut on your finger, the ink will enter your bloodstream and go all through your system, and when it reaches your heart, you'll die. You'll just fall down dead. People will say, 'That was the poor little girl who died while reading. The ink killed her.' ''

Only Granny could reduce the flower of Western culture to the status of an air bubble. The more she nagged, the more I read, the more she nagged. Matters came to a head when I was seventeen; I told her I wanted to be a writer.

''Why can't you be a true Southern woman like Kissypoo Carmichael?'' she cried. ''Mark my words, you'll wind up in the insane asylum if you try to go against nature. Mental exertion ravages the female organs, too. You'll have trouble down below if you don't watch out. You know what they always say: a whistling woman and a crowing hen always come to a tragic end.''

College is supposed to be a time of growth and discovery. Granny, of course, did not want me to go, but I insisted, so in keeping with her definition of compromise, I was enrolled in St. Mary Star of the Sea Episcopal College for Women, a small, select grave of academe located on lower Chesapeake Bay in the town of Queen Caroline Court House. It was three blocks from home, so I kept on walking to school the same as before.

Although I was a student of the Sixties, my only contact with campus turmoil was the evening news. The closest St. Mary Star ever came to a riot was the time a mouse joined us for Evensong, and the nearest thing to a controversy was a hushed argument over whether "Bread of Angels" could be sung as *"Panis Angelicus."* The high-church element prevailed as usual, so we sang it in Latin. Had any days of rage erupted in our Anglican enclave, we would have referred to them as *"dies irae."* The local crab fishermen didn't call us soft-shell Catholics for nothing.

To prepare for a writing career, I majored in literature and took all of the many zero-growth courses that St. Mary Star offered, such as advanced Latin, the Augustan Essay, the English Rural Novel ("Eee, by goom, thart's summat"), and Tragedy 303, an intensive seminar in the plays of Racine in which we were forbidden to speak except in alexandrine verse. It was taught by Miss Dalrymple, who was Kissypoo Carmichael's adopted half-sister, a relationship so fraught with bend sinisters, wrong-sided blankets, and double cousinships that Miss Dalrymple was said to commit incest every time she took a douche.

I graduated from St. Mary Star qualified to do nothing except crossword puzzles in ink and play Rhyming Sam in a traveling carnival, so I took a stenotype course at Queen Caroline Business School. I thought being a court reporter would be a good way to gather experience for writing, but no Lizzie Bordens or Black Dahlias came my way. Instead I took boundary disputes, apocalyptic Southern-style car wrecks, and divorcing good ole boys who broke down on the witness stand and sobbed, "I'll love her till the ocean wears rubber pants to keep its bottom dry!"

When I had been working a few weeks, my father wrote a note saying "I hate this century" and shot himself. The next month, Granny died in the cemetery, felled by a heat stroke as she was trying to read the worn inscription on a seventeenth-century tombstone to see if it belonged to one of her ancestors. "She formed a Cross on the grave," said Father Chillingsworth in his eulogy.

I had the choice of staying home and menstruating with Aunt Edna, or striking out to gather experience, so I left and headed North. I tried New York first, but it affected me the way mention of Eleanor Roosevelt affected Granny, so I pressed on to Boston, where I made the mistake of renting an apartment in Cambridge that turned out to be next door to the Hare Krishna headquarters. It was an experience I preferred not to gather, so I moved out and tried Beacon Hill because I thought people like George Apley still lived there.

I had been living in the new place about a week when I crossed paths with Polly Bradshaw.

What was to be my last day of peace and quiet started with a trip to the post office. I emerged from my apartment on the misnamed Joy Street to mail my latest manuscript, *Beloved Rake,* to Moth and Flame Regency Romances. It was my fifth sale to the brooding-and-riding-crop genre and by now I had a method down pat. I wrote them on the stenotype machine while I was drunk and transcribed them when I was sober. In case you're interested,

```
          K     O     PL
             H     E    R
                         RBGS
                   U
          HR    EU        T
                          L
  TP       AO             L
```

means "Come here, you little fool."

As I walked into the post office at Government Center, my manuscript was scorched by a boy whose flaming draft card had got out of control. He gave me a sign—peace or the finger, I couldn't tell which—and returned to his sleeping bag. On the other side of the plaza, a group of Gay Liberationists chanted "Two, four, six, eight, we don't overpopulate," and a person of uncertain gender wearing a Halloween skeleton costume marched up and down with a sign that read REMEMBER KENT STATE.

I mailed the manuscript and started back home. As I was crossing the plaza, a strange intense girl in tie-died bell bottoms and Mao jacket rushed up and kissed me.

"I love you," she whispered. "Pass it on. If everybody says it to everybody else, we can forge a chain of love to stretch around the world."

I peeled her off me and crossed the street. On the corner I was stopped by a boy wearing a placard that read SAVE A TREE. He held out a flowerpot containing a pathetic pine seedling.

"This is a tree. Do you know what trees do for you? Man, they're the best friends you've got. Like they breathe for you, you know? Like they work their ass off for you! Got any spare change? It's not for me, it's for the trees."

I evaded him and trudged on up the Joy Street hill, picking my way through dog droppings and spacy college students in floppy felt hats decorated with *Richard Nixon Is a Lesbian* buttons. They were just standing there hugging themselves, but as I drew abreast they came to life with a vengeance. Lips curled, and a boy clenched his fist and shook it at me.

"Reactionary!"

How did he know? I wasn't wearing anything expensive, just a plaid skirt and a sweater set with a single strand of cultured pearls. This sort of thing was always happening to me since I had moved North, like the time in New York when I was called for jury duty and the defense attorney took one look at me and said "Challenge." Defiantly, I tossed my head at the students and walked the rest of the way up the hill to my building.

As I mounted the steps, I ran into the landlord, Vittorio Gioppi, known to his tenants as Gioppi the Woppi. The sobriquet had been started by the Martinellis in 2B, who claimed he gave Italians a bad name, and quickly spread through the halls like the recent fire in another one of his buildings.

When he saw me, he tried to conceal the crumpled paper bag he held. It was very full but not at all heavy, which meant that he was on another lightbulb-stealing mission. Whenever the tenants in one of his buildings complained that their hall lights had gone out, he would sneak into another one and rip off the bulbs.

"Hey, you seen any hippies around here?" he asked me.

"They're all over the place."

"Nah, I mean on the premises here."

He waved grandly at the two scabrous row houses that were laughably affixed with little brass plates long gone to green that read *Tradesmen and Servants Enter in Rear.* We had hand-painted carriage blocks, too. One said *fuck* and the other said *suck.*

Gioppi squared his ovoid shoulders proudly. "I'm talkin' about Commie bums that wanna destroy our American Way of Life. Last night at the V.F.W., somebody told me there was a bunch of them Weathermen camped out somewhere on the Hill. If you see 'em, call me right away, hear? We gotta stop them creeps. My buddies and me wanna capture 'em singlehanded so we can go to Washington and get hard hats from President Nixon.''

He laid a hand over his heart, his fingers caressing his rhinestone-studded American flag pin.

''I got *my* Plymouth rock right here. My grandmother, rest her soul, wasn't in no D.A.R., but I love my country more than life.''

He had seen Granny's picture in full battle regalia the day I moved in, so it was meant as a dig. One of these days I was going to tell him that my grandmother wasn't in no D.A.R. either. Like many members of Colonial Dames, she looked down on the Daughters and frequently referred to them as Johnny-come-latelies because they required ancestors who went no further back than 1776.

Gioppi got into his car, which was plastered with flag decals and patriotic bumper stickers, including *Support Your Local Police; Register Communists, Not Firearms; Remember the Pueblo;* and *Put Your Heart in America Or Get Your* [picture of a donkey] *Out.* As I watched him drive off, I thought how comforting patriotism must be.

I entered the building and climbed up to the top-floor studio I had just rented. It was unremarkable in every way except for a pink marble fireplace. Naturally, the fireplace was no longer functional, but it was a shining jewel in Gioppi's otherwise tarnished crown, and a pleasant reminder of the days when Beacon Hill's favorite George had been Apley instead of Jackson.

The room had been part of a huge turn-of-the-century bedroom which Gioppi had divided into two cell-like apartments by tacking up a piece of fiberboard to make a wall. It was only slightly thicker than paper but so far there had been no noise problem. Whoever lived next door was hardly ever home; I heard nothing except an occasional dull thwacking sound.

I took off my good clothes and got into a pair of jeans and a Fork Union Military Academy sweatshirt that had belonged to an old beau. I mixed a strong drink, lowered myself carefully into Gioppi's sprung arm chair, and lit a cigarette. Granny gazed in disapproval from her silver frame. Not because I was smoking and drinking—tobacco and bourbon are Southern vices, after all—but because I was wearing jeans. They had been grounds for expulsion at St. Mary Star, but even that anachronism paled before Granny's standards: she used to put on her hat to go out and get the mail.

I turned on the TV, but there was nothing on except soaps and a local PBS feminist talk show called "Heated Topics." I had never watched it but I had read about it in the papers. It was so controversial that it started with a viewer-discretion warning and ended with a disclaimer. Despite these cautionary measures, they had been thrown off the air a few times. The last show to cause trouble was the one on do-it-yourself gynecological examinations, when they all started looking up each other's twats and turning their Isles of McGillicuddy to the camera.

Having just finished writing a Regency, I couldn't take the soaps, so I decided to watch the feminists.

While all the cautions and warnings and no-nos were on I got up and fixed another drink and returned in time to be greeted by the moderator. She had long red hair parted in the middle and hanging down in the usual feminist style, a bony face full of freckles, and one of those long, lean Yankee builds. She wore a little Mother Bloor number that passed for a dress.

"Hello, I'm Polly Bradshaw," she began, in a chowdery Boston accent. "This afternoon we continue our twenty-part series on alternative choices. On our last show we discussed natural childbirth. Our guest today is going to tell us about a really *super* natural way to have a baby. Would you please welcome Ms. Grace Garrison-Talbot, president of the Birth Bucket League of America."

Ms. Garrison-Talbot came on stage rolling a large clay urn on its rim like a spare tire. She wore her hair in a top-knot stuck with a leather hat pin and a T-shirt inscribed *Get Back on the Can!* She took a chair across from Polly Bradshaw, righted the urn, patted it fondly, and began her spiel.

"This is a birth bucket, used for centuries by women before *male* physicians conspired to make us give birth in a prone position."

The slide toward feminist English had begun.

"When did the birth bucket originate?" asked Polly Bradshaw.

It was a fatal question; feminists can always trace anything back to a dry Atlantis. Ms. Garrison-Talbot launched into a tribute to the good *old* days, when every country was a matriarchy and the world was full

of wonderfully well-adjusted people who chewed on umbilical cords like beef jerky and were so happy that they neglected to leave anything to posterity except the shards of their old birth buckets. Next came the standard tribute to those daredevil Celtic warrior queens with names like Fellatrix, who filled their birth buckets during pit stops at the chariot races. She finished with the tragic tale of somebody named Elspeth of Thuringa, who committed suicide in 1274 after her birth bucket was stolen from under her by a band of monks.

"Our Judo-Christian heritage," Polly Bradshaw malapropped, her voice bleak.

"Now, I know what your first question is," said Ms. Garrison-Talbot. "Everybody always asks it. You must be worried about the baby's soft spot."

I was worried about hers. She turned the birth bucket on its side so the camera could pick up the interior.

"You have to put something soft in the bottom for the baby to land in. Ancient Egyptian women used crocodile dung. It's not available here in Massachusetts, but if you plan to give birth in the Gulf Coast area, your husband or the father of your child can gather it for you as mine did. It's a good way to test his supportiveness. Remember, though, it must be *fresh* dung. The best way to gather it is to wait behind a crocodile who is moving his or her bowels. When the dung emerges, thrust a skate board under the anus to catch it. Do *not* use plastic bags! Their crinkly sound tends to anger the crocodile."

"Is it possible to get the dung from zoos?" asked Polly.

Ms. Garrison-Talbot's eyes hardened. "The zoos have been totally unsupportive."

"What are the chances of setting up a meaningful dialogue with zoo directors?"

"Nonexistent," Ms. Garrison-Talbot said grimly. "We've tried to get our dung through the proper channels but we met with mockery at every turn. My car was even defaced. Someone wrote 'baby sitter' on the windshield and a *male* veterinarian referred to me as the 'ding-dung lady.' "

Polly Bradshaw grimaced in disgust. "We'll never be free until they stop calling us ladies. Grace, what are your plans for the Birth Bucket League now?"

"Polly, we're going to fight for our rights to crocodile dung. We're setting up a letter-writing campaign to put pressure on the zoos, and my husband is chairing the Ad Hoc Dung Now committee from his hospital bed in Everglades Memorial. We're not going to give up until every woman is able to purchase crocodile dung from the zoo of her choice.''

"Beautiful! Right on!" cheered Polly Bradshaw.

"In the meantime, I can recommend some substitutes for crocodile dung. Moldy bread is the best. Crumble it and line the bottom of your birth bucket with it. It's soft, and a natural source of penicillin, which means it's sterile. And best of all, it's easy to obtain—every active, involved woman's kitchen is full of it.''

She turned the birth bucket on its rim and rolled it over to Polly Bradshaw.

"The League would like to present this to you in gratitude for your interest and your work in the Women's Liberation movement.''

Polly received her gift with effusive thanks and signed off.

"That's all for now. Join us Monday when my guest will be Boadicea Vigilant, activist, revolutionary, and member of Women's International Terrorist Conspiracy from Hell, who will discuss her book, *Disarming Rapists: The Surgical Solution.*''

I turned off the TV and poured myself an even stiffer drink and brooded about the big publishing contracts feminists were getting. I wondered if I should try to climb on the Women's Lib bandwagon. First, I would have to change my name—Isabel Fairfax lacked the necessary agitprop crunch. I toyed with Zenobia Alert for a few minutes, and then gave up. I had nothing to say to a feminist readership. I hoped they *all* got raped by a battalion of Turkish cavalry. Not by the Turks—by the horses.

I sat drinking, too tired to bother with dinner. Sometime later, I heard my next door neighbor come home, and soon the dull thwacking sound started up. What was he, she, or it doing in there? I yawned, had yet another drink, and finally called it a day. Stripping down to pants and bra, I crawled into Gioppi's lumpy couch and fell asleep.

Sometime around midnight, I was blown out of bed by the explosion.

It started as a great gulping roar, like a Wagnerian treatment of the belching of the gods, and turned into a blast-off worthy of Cape

Kennedy. Before I had time to be scared, I was on the floor in the middle of a pile of books.

When I got to my feet, the building was quivering. Outside, screaming people poured into the street and dogs barked all over the neighborhood. I stumbled through the book-strewn blackness and turned on the lights, which miraculously worked, and looked around.

The six hundred books I owned, which I had kept in neat piles all over the floor, were now in messy piles. But what really riveted my attention was the fiberboard wall that separated me from my next door neighbor. It was starting to take on all the elements of a Regency novel: a ripping noise like the heroine's bodice, a corner-to-corner slit like the villain's grin, a buckling like the old baronet's knees, and a waft of powder filling the air as though from a dowager's dusted bosom. And of course, since no Regency is complete without the collapse of an olde Englishe sea wall, the two-by-four studs snapped in half and Gioppi's chintzy room-divider gave up the ghost.

Now I no longer had to wonder who my next door neighbor was. All I had to do was look into the other apartment. There, sprawled on the floor, wearing an *I Am a Human Being* nightshirt and clutching the birth bucket, was Polly Bradshaw.

We stared at each other. For a moment I thought I had left the TV on. She was the last person I had seen before falling into bed half drunk; maybe I hadn't really gone to sleep; maybe I was still watching "Heated Topics."

Gradually my mind cleared and I remembered the *P. Bradshaw* next to my *I. Fairfax* on the mailboxes. I had noticed it when I moved in but it had not registered on me while I was watching her show. I was sure I had not met her in the hallway, but that wasn't unusual considering the weird hours I kept. Night people never meet anybody.

"I saw you on television," I said unoriginally. Why not? It's already replaced *E pluribus unum.*

"What happened?"

Hearing sirens, we pulled on our clothes and ran downstairs. The first person we saw was Gioppi in his V.F.W. cap, talking excitedly with a crowd of policemen. He hurried over when he saw me.

"I told you so! They was Weathermen, four of 'em, building bombs in my cellar! The dirty Commies blew theirselves up! How's that for starters?"

He was beside himself with joy. The decorations he had won in World War II were lined up on his lapel; the most prominent one was a Good Conduct medal with a spillover of oak-leaf clusters. He must have been the company brown nose.

Just then we heard a policeman identifying the dead Weathermen for a reporter. Naturally, their names were Farnham, Durham, Denham, and Bingham. Gioppi the Wasp-hater beamed.

A few minutes later, somebody from the coroner's office arrived and matters got ghoulish, to Gioppi's unbridled glee. The coroner's man happened to be Italian, too, so we were singled out for a real treat. He went into the smoking building and emerged momentarily with a container about the size of a dishpan, covered with heavy black plastic. He held it out to Gioppi like a thoughtful neighbor in time of need who says, "I want you to have this."

"Farnham," he intoned, whereupon Gioppi lifted the cover and picked up a finger encircled by a Harvard class ring.

"I went to Boston College night school," Gioppi said proudly.

Over the next couple of hours, Farnham, Durham, Denham, and Bingham were found here and there in the shattered cellar of the house adjoining ours and in the back courtyards of both. Gioppi was like a child on an Easter egg hunt. Knowing that he would never again be in such a good mood, I followed him to the ambulance where he was turning in a foot and told him about our wall.

"What wall?"

He had grasped the situation perfectly. Polly and I took him upstairs and showed him the damage.

"When can you put up a new wall?" we demanded.

His eyes slid off to the side in that familiar Gioppi way. "Soon," he said.

"When?"

"Very soon. Just as soon as I see the insurance people."

"When are you going to see them?"

"Soon."

He beat a hasty retreat. Polly and I looked at each other and then at the mess. In the middle of the now-spacious room, lying half in my section and half in hers, was a Nixon dartboard. That explained the thwacking sound.

We introduced ourselves formally, standing in the rubble exchanging pleasantries like two Londoners after a buzz-bomb attack. She asked me where I worked and seemed surprised by my answer.

"Didn't you hear the typewriter through the . . . wall?"

She shook her head. "I've been doing volunteer work at the Self-Sufficiency Center every night for weeks. They need all the help they can get," she said gravely.

An uncomfortable silence fell, brought on by the discoveries we were making as we glanced into each other's apartment. There was an Angela Davis Defense Fund poster in her kitchen. While I contemplated that, her eyes locked onto my mantel, where I had hung the sampler I embroidered under Granny's tutelage:

> God bless the squire and his relations
> And keep us in our proper stations

She turned to me with an inscrutable expression. "Well, I guess we're going to be roommates for a few days."

"I guess we are." She was staring at my pile of *National Review*.

"Well," we said in unison.

We returned to our beds. Polly fell asleep right away but I lay awake thinking. Gioppi's ha-ha policy was probably with the Ha-Ha Insurance Company. He would never build a new wall, never. I was stuck in this Jericho with a Women's Libber for a roommate. It was almost as bad as sleeping with Ramsey Clark.

CHAPTER TWO

The next day was Saturday. I assumed Polly would want to sleep late after the explosive happening but I was wrong. She was a morning person.

Shortly after sunrise I was awakened by something that sounded like a Gioppi drain fighting a losing battle against corrosion.

"Ushuum! Ushuum!"

I put one eye over the edge of the blanket and saw her. She was folded up on the floor in the lotus position with her fingers circled and her toes sticking out of her knees. I rolled over and went back to sleep. An hour later I was awakened again, this time by a *ta-click, ta-click-*

ta-click. I surfaced again and found her exercising on a walking machine. It looked like a large scale with a revolving conveyor belt. With shoulders back and head held high, she was going purposefully nowhere.

The third time I woke up she was standing beside my bed with a mug of coffee.

"Are you planning to get up soon?" she asked reproachfully. "It's nine o'clock."

"Is it only ni—" My voice failed in mid-sentence. I reached for my cigarettes, lit one, and started hacking.

"Would you like some breakfast? I made a pot of oatmeal."

"Awwhhhrrr!"

"Are you all right? Here, I brought you some coffee. It's decaffeinated. Take a sip."

She glanced disapprovingly at the overflowing ashtray and made several helpless gestures in my direction while I choked and gagged my way into a new day. At last I was able to breathe well enough to finish my cigarette. I sat up, face flushed and eyes streaming, and reached for the coffee.

"Thank you," I croaked.

Just then something large, orange, and alive crawled out from under her bed.

"Oh, there's Quadrupet. Last night scared him so much he went into hiding. I hope you don't mind cats."

Mind cats? My spirits rose. Feminist or not, she couldn't be too bad if she had a cat.

"I love cats," I said.

"Well, I hate them, but I can't get rid of him. He came in one day and refused to leave."

Quadrupet gave me a glance of heartwarming contempt and leaped up on my bed, planting himself just far enough away so that I had to stretch to pet him.

Polly fixed herself a cup of coffee and returned to my bedside. She looked around for an empty chair but all the chairs were piled with books. She gave up and perched on the bottom of the bed.

"Well!" she said with a bright smile. The unspoken words were *here we are.* "What kind of things do you write?"

I had a mouthful of coffee and smoke so I nodded my head at the pile of manuscript carbons on the table. She leaned over and read the title page and frowned.

"It's about a rake?"

"All my books are about rakes." I sighed. "I wanted to start with something simple while I was learning the mechanics of fiction. Someday I'll write about real people."

"They made us read something in school called 'The Man With a Hoe' but I think it was a poem."

We exchanged wary stares: two people in search of a wavelength. I drained the coffee and threw back the covers.

"I think I'll get dressed now."

When I emerged from the bathroom she was picking up pieces of the wall and stacking them neatly beside the door, arranging them according to size and degree of damage.

"For picket signs," she explained.

I felt like saying "It's my wall, too," but I didn't. When she had gotten all the pieces picked up, she started cutting the fiberboard into neat rectangles and tacking them onto the broken studs. While she was thus engaged I got my broom and dustcatcher and started sweeping up. It was a discouraging task; the fiber particles kept rising like strands of hemp from a hangman's rope after the drop.

When we had finished, Polly turned to me with another bright smile.

"Time for lunch."

It was ten-thirty. I had another cup of coffee and joined her at her table. I would have preferred to sit alone at mine but for some reason we couldn't seem to go our separate ways. We were caught up in the psychology of strangers brought together by a disaster.

She opened her refrigerator door and removed a pristine covered icebox jar. I had never seen such a neat, clean refrigerator. She had decanted her tomato juice into a covered pitcher decorated with little red pictures of ripe tomatoes. Mine was still in the can, decorated with two V-shaped indentations encrusted with brownish goo.

The icebox jar contained alfalfa weed. She emptied it onto a plate, sprinkled some lemon juice on it, and poured herself a glass of skim milk. She sat down and began to eat.

"Are you sure you won't have some alfalfa? It's delicious."

I smiled carefully and shook my head.

"How about a glass of milk?"

Awwhhhrrr! "No, thank you."

"You know, my Uncle Ezra writes. I wish you could meet him, but he lives in California now. Have you ever read any of his books?"

She got up and went to the tiny bookcase that Gioppi provided. I had one just like it. It was the size of a night table with two shelves. Polly's was as neat as her refrigerator; in fact, there were only three books in it. She brought them to the table and handed them to me.

They were written by Ezra Standish Bradshaw and bore the imprint of the Spartacus Press in Greenwich Village. The titles were:

Like It or Lump It: The Coming Social Change
Whales Are Human, Too
The Goading of America: A History of the Bradshaw Family

Recognition dawned—horribly. She was one of *those* Bradshaws. . . . I glanced warily at her as she chomped her way through the alfalfa patch. No wonder she was a feminist. Feminism was tame compared with some of the causes the Bradshaws took up. Leaders of Wasp America's loony left for more than two centuries, they ran to anarchistic Unitarian ministers, little old ladies given to missionary uplift, and derailed sociologists who roamed the ghettos telling the poor to sell their valuables and buy guns. Wherever you find a round hole, you'll find a Bradshaw sticking halfway out of it. The first sentence in *The Goading of America* summed them up: "Margaret Fuller accepted the Universe but the Bradshaws do not."

I browsed through the book. It was full of family photos with captions like "Aunt Tabitha after her hunger strike" and "Uncle Soames arrives in Harlan County." Not surprisingly, there were a great many pictures of injured people; the Bradshaws were happiest when they were beating themselves into plowshares and losing fingers to mimeograph machines, pubic hair to hot tar, and shoulders to the common weal. Their masochism resulted in very confusing captions, such as "Rev. Nathan (on stretcher) being aided by wife Abigail (with bandage) waving to Jared Bradshaw in departing police van (not shown)." The only photos that did not need explanatory cutlines were the ones taken at sit-down strikes in the Thirties: all the Bradshaws were standing up and making speeches.

Polly was scooping up the last of her alfalfa. It looked like green hair with nits.

"What are you going to do today?" she asked brightly.

Go back to bed. "Work."

"Well, I'll be out of your way. I'm going to picket a funeral parlor."

"A funeral parlor?"

"Yes. Have you seen their ad in the Yellow Pages?" She fetched the book and opened it to the offending entry: "To Ease Your Mind, We Employ Female Attendants."

She took a picket sign from the closet. It read: MISS GOODY TWO SHOES IS DEAD.

She waved at me with two fingers in a V-for-victory sign and left. I crossed over to my own territory and curled up on my bed beside Quadrupet. Soon we fell asleep in each other's arms.

Since Polly had brought me my morning coffee and offered me lunch, I felt I should cook dinner. When she returned from the funeral parlor she sniffed the air appreciatively and gave me another bright smile.

"What're you cooking?"

"Something that's white and oval and crawls up your leg. Uncle Ben's perverted rice."

She frowned and shook her head. "You mean *con*verted," she corrected. "It's a process that puts back many of the nutrients that are lost when white rice is polished."

I dumped some stroganoff on top of my failed joke and we sat down at my table. I studied her as we ate. Aside from that touch of the games mistress that marks old-stock Yankee females, she was definitely what men called "too pretty to be a feminist." If you can imagine a strawberry blonde with Faye Dunaway cheekbones who picketed an undertaker, that was Polly in a Bradshaw nutshell.

After dinner I offered her coffee and brandy. It mellowed her and she began to talk about herself.

She had majored in economics at Radcliffe so she would be ready to redistribute the world's wealth when the revolution came. Meanwhile, she had worked briefly in the trust department of a bank—two weeks, to be exact—before being fired for circulating petitions demanding the abolition of inheritance rights, and free safety deposit boxes for poor women.

After that she had done some modeling. Most of her jobs had been glove ads—her fingers were almost as long as her legs—and she had done a brief stint as "Problem Elbow" in an ad for cream to make elbows smooth. The same firm wanted her to do "Freckles" but she had refused to countenance products that generated appearance anxiety in women.

Her Hammurabi-like instinct for laying down laws and her refusal to trade on her looks caused one uproar after another. The manufacturer of Boy Hip Jeans begged her to model his product but she would not work for him unless he also hired a woman whom Boy Hip Jeans would not fit. When he balked at that she produced an amputee, bringing forth cries of "meshuggeneh!" and a curse on her house.

Finally the model agency, used to girls who were willing to do anything to get work, gave her the boot and blacklisted her—worldwide, she added proudly. It was a Bradshaw first.

Her job on "Heated Topics" grew out of the publicity surrounding her citizen's arrest of a construction worker who whistled at her. She had marched onto the building site, put her hand on the worker's shoulder, and intoned, "Come with me." The worker, thinking, as he later explained, that she was a hot patooty, followed her all the way to the police station, where she cited an old colonial law still on the books that prohibited "sinfull and lustfull soundyngs." The case turned into such a brouhaha that the public television people offered her a half-hour afternoon talk show.

"It's important work because there's so much that needs to be done for women, but the pay is peanuts," she sighed.

That surprised me. I thought TV personalities made big money. I also thought the Bradshaws were rich. They had been once, back in the heyday of the Bradshaw Shipping Line. The early Bradshaws had been such a notorious pack of slave-trading, rum-running, penny-pinching Yankees that their guilt-ridden descendants had found it necessary to give all their money away to wild-eyed liberal causes. The only one left who was comfortably off was Uncle Ezra, who made a mint on the lecture circuit talking about saving the whales, an obsession with direct links to the New Bedford branch of the family.

"That's the story of my life," Polly finished. "Tell me about you."
I didn't think she was ready for it but she had enough brandy in her
to remain vertical, so I began. When I was through she looked
stunned, but there was a missionary gleam in her eye.

"You need to work out your prejudices," she said flatly.

"I don't have anything against the *Lusitania,* I just wouldn't want
my sister to go down on it."

She frowned. "I thought you said you were an only child?"

Jesus. . . . The girl was unreal. I wondered if she had an *I Am a
Humorless Feminist* nightshirt. I fixed another round of spiked coffee
and the talk turned to men.

"How many lovers have you had?" she asked me.

I hesitated. Would she understand the writer's need to gather experience? "Ten," I replied.

Her hairline moved. "Ten! Are you sure?"

"A lady never loses count."

Now a gleam of grudging admiration joined the missionary gleam.
"I've only had one," she confessed. "We lived together. Here, in
fact," she added, waving into her section of the wreckage. "We had a
viable relationship for a while but his openness was a token meeted-
ness. He wasn't willing to make a serious commitment." A critical,
puzzled note crept into her voice. "He wasn't serious about anything.
He was always laughing. Something would happen that wasn't a bit
funny, but he would double over and grab his stomach and laugh till
the tears rolled down his cheeks." She shook her head. "He was really sick."

"When did you break up with him?"

"Four months ago. I came home one night and told him my consciousness-raising group was forming a masturbation workshop and
he started that crazy laughing again. I got mad and told him I didn't
see the humor in it at all, but that only made him laugh harder. We
discussed him at my CR group and they said it was reactive hysteria
triggered by a perceived threat from my clitoris."

"Did he name Quadrupet?" I asked.

She blinked in surprise. "Why, yes. How did you know?"

"Just a hunch."

*　*　*

The next day, Polly came up with her plan.

"How would you like to institute an open communal environment based on mutual cooperation?"

"You mean live together?"

"Yes! You know Gioppi. He'll never get around to building a new wall. If we rented this place as one apartment we could save money, yet we'd both still have the same space we had before."

She waited for my response with a bright expression of restrained eagerness that I recognized as the Bradshaw missionary gleam, the same look that shone forth from the photos in Uncle Ezra's family history. She was talking thrift but her genes were crying out for a captive audience of the unenlightened, and I was the most unenlightened person she had ever met. She had sighted her Moby-Dick and it was me.

I didn't want to live with anybody, least of all a Women's Libber, but I did want to gather experience. I remembered the resentful envy I felt whenever another feminist writer became a literary lion. Books about feminism *were* hot. Maybe if I lived with Polly I would be able to write one, too, and get in on the best-seller gravy train. After all, she had an ulterior motive for wanting to live together; why couldn't I have one?

"Okay," I said.

"Wonderful! Let's go find Gioppi."

We did not have to look far. He had returned early to help the police look for stray bits of Farnham, Denham, Durham, and Bingham. We found him in the back areaway posing beside a pile of blasting caps and doorbell wire for a photographer from *The Italo-American News*. He was still wearing his V.F.W. cap, to which he now added a snappy salute.

With great reluctance he came upstairs with us. Polly went to her files and extracted a copy of the Tenants' Rights Code. She shoved it under his nose and spoke in her chowdery twang.

"One ap*ah*tment, one rent."

"It ain't one apartment, it's two! You got two kitchens and two bathrooms, right? And two doors!"

"And no wall. One ap*ah*tment, one rent."

Gioppi's eyes slid off to the side in their usual fashion and came to rest on my stenotype machine. It had a startling effect on him. With his history of criminal negligence he had probably seen a lot of them. They say a returning jury will not look at a defendant if they have voted him guilty, but court reporters have even better clues to go by. Perjurers always stare at the stenotype machine the way Gioppi was staring at mine now. He probably thought we had a lawyer in the closet ready to take a deposition.

"One apa*h*tment, one rent," Polly repeated.

I looked at her curiously. Gone for the moment was the idealistic uplifter of humanity. She had turned into the very spit of old Cap'n Nehemiah, the lipless wonder of rapacity who founded the Bradshaw Shipping Line. Gioppi saw it, too, and gave in.

The open communal environment based on mutual cooperation was now underway.

Boiled down, our new arrangement meant that Quadrupet now sprayed my apartment as well as hers, but Polly never boiled anything down. The first thing she did was make a seven-page list of household chores, called *Areas of Responsibility,* that left nothing to chance. Everything was set up like a class schedule; MWF for this, TTh for that, and something else on SSun. FT meant "free time" and there was very little of it.

It was my first experience with an anal-retentive personality. She could not seem to do anything without first checking her list, and each time she went over it she reworked the dots after the numbers, circling, pressing, and stabbing at them with her pencil until the back of the paper was full of black-bordered holes. She made two copies of it and taped one on each icebox. What it actually said was very simple: I would do the cooking, Polly would do the dishes, and we would shop for groceries together.

When you cook for someone else, you make a special effort. When you are a Southerner imbued with a tradition of gracious hospitality, you put yourself out even more. I cooked up a storm: cornbread, smothered chicken, spoon bread, fried apples, hush puppies, and barbecued ribs. Polly gobbled everything and didn't gain an ounce; I gobbled everything and swelled up like a balloon. By the end of our first six weeks together, I looked like her politics and she looked like mine.

Housekeeping was declared an individual responsibility; each of us cleaned what used to be our respective apartments. The line of demarcation was the scarred area of the floor where the wall studs had stood. Given Polly's literal mind, I shouldn't have been so stunned when, finding a piece of discarded manuscript that had drifted across the border, she bent down, tore off her half, and let my half lie there. It stayed there for two weeks because Southern standards of housekeeping had changed drastically after the Emancipation Proclamation. The only thing in my apartment that wasn't dusty was the bourbon bottle.

Polly, on the other hand, was Ms. Clean. Though she scorned the concept of housework as an instrument of women's oppression, her section of our domain could have passed a white-glove inspection. It sounds like an unresolved conflict but it was much simpler than that. Like most spit-and-polish housekeepers, she did not like to read.

Mentally, she was what employers in pre-Lib days dared to call a "sharp gal," the kind they had in mind when they wrote that classic ad: "Seek bright, quick, self-starting miss desiring opportunity for advancement. Must be good at detail."

In common with most math majors she had an astronomical I.Q. but her pool of general culture was Dismal Swamp. Like the magazine editor who wrote "Who he?" in the margin next to "Andromeda," she gloried in militant ignorance.

"Gordian knot? Never heard of it. Needlework is a male conspiracy to keep women passive."

"Mary McCarthy? Never heard of her. You must mean Bernadette Devlin."

"Stonehenge? Never heard of one. Better call a locksmith."

As the list of never-heard-of-its got longer and longer, the temptation to pull her leg became irresistible. I lay in wait for the perfect chance and she handed it to me on a platter.

She belonged to a group called "Feminist Consumers United Against Brand Names," whose members had taken a solemn oath to buy only generic items and report suspicious or recalcitrant retailers to the group's watchdog committee.

Knowing that I had studied Latin, one night she asked me if I knew the generic name for a certain laxative suppository.

"Ultima Thule," I replied.

She didn't bat an eye. Opening her memo book to U, she handed it to me and asked me to write it down. I complied and she left for the drugstore. Half an hour later she returned wearing a smile of grim triumph.

"He said he never heard of it. That proves he's part of the pharmaceutical companies' conspiracy."

She filed a watchdog report. Shortly thereafter the newsletter of the FCUABN came out with banner headlines about the mysterious unavailability of Ultima Thule suppositories. "They've even taken it out of the pharmacopoeia!" wailed the editorial, and issued a call for the usual flood of protest letters to the Food and Drug Administration.

I had struck a blow for liberal arts. I struck another one a week later when I convinced her that every feminist should read *Madame Bovary*. I gave her my copy and waited. And waited. She consigned it to FT, so it took her forever to get through it. She finally finished it one night while I was cooking dinner. I held my breath as she came into the kitchen.

"What did you think of it?" I asked eagerly.

"She needed credit counseling."

I gave up striking blows for liberal arts.

As I got to know her better, I realized that her political stance was rooted in something even deeper than her Bradshaw genes. Like most female reformers, she had a feminine nature and a masculine mind, a fatal blend that produces a knight in petticoats, determined to rescue humanity in distress and carry it off across a sidesaddle. Polly's motivating force was love; she wanted a world in which everybody loved everybody else whether they liked it or not, but she set this overflowing feminine cup in motion with a thoroughly masculine arsenal of charts, graphs, quorums, task forces, ad hocs, tunnel vision, and lists.

Her fondest dream was finding pathetic creatures in desperate need of her help, which was why she hated cats. She was constantly looking around for a worthy cause, and since our new free-form apartment was still small, every time she looked around she saw me.

With the subtlety of a child yelling "Tag, you're it!" she set out to improve my health. Her first assault consisted of taping the "Seven Deadly Signs of Cancer" on my bathroom mirror and delivering a daily lecture on the perils of tobacco during my morning hacking sessions.

"Lung cancer is an equal opportunity disease. Back when smoking was considered unladylike, women didn't get it, which led people to think that it was a man's disease from which women were naturally immune. But now," she said ominously, "women are catching up."

"Awwhhhrrr!"

"It's not *logical* to go on smoking when you *know* it's dangerous. Look, it's right here on the package. Listen. 'Warning: The Surgeon General has determined that cigarette smoking is dangerous to your health.' They've made *studies* on this. The Surgeon General wants to *help* you!"

"The federal government has three duties. Print the money, deliver the mail, and declare war. Give me my cigarettes."

"If you won't get the smoke out of your lungs, at least you could get some fresh air into them. Let's start a jogging program! You never go out. You stay up half the night and then sleep through the most healthful part of the day. Every morning when I do my exercises I have to look at you lying in bed."

"Why do you do all those exercises? You weigh less than me and you're seven inches taller."

"Do you think you need a metabolism test?" she asked hopefully. "The Artemis Clinic for Women has just opened and—"

"I've already had a metabolism test."

"What did it measure?"

"Lizard."

Convinced that women could do anything men could do, she rejected the notion that menstruation is a hindrance, so the first time she found me hunched over the john vomiting she jumped to conclusions.

"Why didn't you tell me? I'll call the Center. You might have to go out of state but don't worry, I'll take care of it. Suction is better than curettage. It's just like vacuuming the floor. Whoosh, and it's all over. I went to a suction seminar and they showed movies. There's nothing to it, just *whoosh!* You can go home the same day and they give you free orange juice."

"UrrrrrAAGGGH!"

"I've got the forms. Do you want me to fill them out for you? It's the first trimester, isn't it? Count. You've got to count. Think back. Try to remember when it happened. Do you want to have it and put it up for adoption or do you want to keep it? Just tell me what you want to do; I've got forms for everything. I've also got some brochures that explain everything legalwise. If you want, you can pick out the adoptive parents now and go live with them. It's a new alternative choice called 'Mom Times Two.' The adoptive mother pretends that you're her sister. When the baby arrives she thinks she's its aunt. If she isn't convinced, they'll send somebody around to hypnotize her. Do you want me to call them? They've got a list of women with liberated husbands. Would you like to talk to a counselor? I know everybody there. I've also got some pamphlets on—my God! You're bleeding!''

"Of course I'm bleeding! I've got the curse!''

She shrank back and leaned against the basin. I rested my clammy cheek on the toilet seat and we contemplated each other.

"The curse?''

"Yes, you know—that wonderful thing that happens every month.''

I reached a shaking hand into the cabinet and took out a Kotex. Polly left and I fixed myself up and hobbled back to bed with my heating pad. She was waiting for me, full of sisterly solicitude.

"Would you like some milk?''

I almost threw up again. "No, some bourbon, if you please.''

She brought me a drink and sat down beside the bed. "I've never seen anyone suffer so much,'' she said.

"It runs in the family.''

"Don't say that! That's an obsolete notion.''

"It is not. Granny had cramps, Mama had them, and Aunt Edna still has them. It's the Upton womb.''

"The what?''

"Upton was Granny's maiden name. Every doctor in Virginia knows about the Upton womb. Granny's grandmother's doctor gave a speech on it to the state A.M.A. meeting way back when. He called it the Gettysburg of womankind. Everything that can go wrong with a womb has gone wrong with one of ours.''

"You mean they actually call it the Upton womb?'' she asked incredulously.

"Of course. Granny's is in a jar at University of Virginia medical school. She donated it when she had her hysterectomy. They needed it to study because there're Uptons all over the state. We were First Families so it's had time to spread.''

"The male-dominated medical profession has conspired for centuries to convince us that we're weak. Your grandmother," she said darkly, "was brainwashed."

"That's like saying Stalin was brainwashed."

"I have an idea," she said brightly. "Why don't you attend the Dysmenorrhea Summer Camp? I had the founder on my show a few months ago. It's a new treatment combining physical therapy, psychological counseling, and group supportiveness. It's up in Maine. You could borrow my car and—"

"I can't drive."

She regarded me with a look of pure horror. I could have bitten off my tongue; it was something I had been planning to keep from her.

"Why not?" she demanded.

I hesitated, loath to tell such a ruthless humanitarian that I was an agoraphobiac. Her old kit bag was packed with centers and clinics for every known affliction ending in *iac* and she would like nothing better than a chance to carry me to one in her arms, explaining to the curious along the way, "She's not heavy, she's my sister." She would also want to have a "dialogue" on Origins of Your Agoraphobia, which would mean another bout with her literal-mindedness. I had never gotten lost as a child—nobody could get lost in Queen Caroline—but she would insist that I was burying a trauma. She would never understand that agoraphobia was my quirky armor against a gregarious America, and a tool that had helped me to acquire the inner resources and private space she wanted for all women. But there was no use trying to explain this to her. Like all reformers, she stood four-square behind individuality because it was the best position from which to give individuals a good hard shove.

I cast around for an excuse she would swallow.

"A girl reaches driver's-license age at the same time she starts to date," I said nonchalantly. "Her boyfriends drive her wherever she wants to go, so she puts off learning."

"I dated when I was sixteen but I had a driver's license," she countered.

"Queen Caroline is such a small town I could walk wherever I needed to go."

"A small town in the middle of *nowhere.*"

She was starting to get suspicious. I got desperate.

"Cars pollute the environment," I said loftily.

"You hate the environment. You've been anti-earth ever since Ayn Rand came out in favor of factory smoke. As soon as you're over your period I'm going to teach you how to drive."

"What?"

It was a rhetorical question but that never bothers a Bradshaw. "I'm going to teach you how to drive," she repeated.

"But I don't want to learn!"

"Yes, you do, and you're going to," said the liberal.

CHAPTER THREE

The driving project started out auspiciously enough when I got a score of one hundred on the written test for the learner's permit. Polly the Helper broke out in I-told-you-so optimism but I knew it meant nothing. I was a test-taker, that's all. In college I knew that *Sartre* went with *existentialism* and now I knew that *octagon* went with stop sign. I hoped I wouldn't hit one, as Aunt Edna did when she took her driving test. Her argument was "Well, I stopped, didn't I?" as though driving *over* a stop sign were the real sin. It was one of many things that haunted me the first day Polly took me out on the road. Maybe this, too, ran in the family.

She had a Karmann Ghia that she kept in the underground parking garage at the TV studio. I looked at it dubiously. It had a stick shift. I knew about gears; I had shifted them for my high-school boyfriend so he wouldn't have to take his hand out of my blouse, but his car had the stick on the steering column. Polly's gear stick was on the floor, enclosed in a little leather bag like a Victorian piano leg in pantalettes, so what little knowledge I had was useless.

She drove us out to Quincy, which she called "Quinzy," and stopped on a quiet residential street. I slipped reluctantly into the driver's seat while she went round to the trunk and took out the sign she had made from a piece of our former wall: CAUTION! SUDDEN STOPS! She taped it on the back of the car and got in beside me.

"Now," she began officiously, "assume the proper driving posture. Both hands on the wheel at two o'clock and ten o'clock and seat belt fastened."

I put both hands on the wheel and then removed them to struggle with the seat belt. There were two, one for the lap and another for across the shoulder. It was like wrapping a mummy. I let go of the wrong piece at the wrong time and hit myself on the nose with the buckle. Polly reached over to do me up and poked me in the ribs. I squealed and went into hysterics from stored-up fright, but she saw nothing funny about assuming the proper driving posture.

She finally finished fixing the belts. "You are now ready to drive," she intoned.

I stretched out my feet but they touched nothing except warm air.

"You have to adjust the seat to your height," she said. "The lever's under the front cushion."

"I can't bend over, the belts are too tight."

She reached behind my legs and pulled. I shot forward against the wheel like a cannonball. The shoulder belt snapped open and covered my left eye like a pirate's patch.

"You are now ready to drive," she said again.

"Oh, yeah?"

She turned and looked at me critically. Then, without cracking a smile: "That's a hazard. Your vision must be unimpeded at all times."

I glared at her with my remaining eye while she readjusted the belt. This time it was too tight.

"Let me take off the top one," I pleaded. "I feel like I'm suffocating."

"It never bothers me."

I refrained from pointing out that she was virtually titless. We argued for a few minutes and finally she gave in and let me wear the lap belt only. I was now ready to drive.

I turned the key and the engine roared into life. Instinctively, I jumped back but went nowhere. At Polly's instruction, I "depressed" the clutch and then concentrated on finding first gear. I found it at last and shifted.

"Now, lift your left foot as you depress your right one on the gas pedal. Gradually! If you do it too fast you'll—"

All sorts of red lights went on and the motor stopped. It happened three more times.

"Why does it keep stalling?" I wailed.

"Because you take your foot off the clutch too fast! Give it a little gas and raise your foot slowly until you feel it engage. Try it again. Feel that little click? That means you've engaged. It's like sex—you have to wait for the exact right moment."

That made me wild, since I had long harbored the suspicion that she was not very good in bed. Now, covered with sweat and shaking all over, I exploded.

"I know how to have an orgasm! What I don't know is how to shift these goddamn gears!"

"Prudence Patience puts up pickles," she singsonged.

In my mind's eye I saw her skinny ancestors in their little white caps, working from dawn to dusk. I wished one of them were in front of me now.

Finally, I managed to proceed down the street in first without stalling. Polly cheered me on.

"Beautiful! Now clutch and shift to second."

"What's that awful noise?"

"Take your foot off the gas!"

"It'll stop going if I do!"

"No, it won't. You can't depress the clutch and the gas at the same time. That's called revving the motor."

"What? I can't hear you!"

"Revving the motor! You're doing it again!"

Two days later, she decided I was good enough to leave the residential areas and take to the traffic. It was in the business district of Quincy that I had my first encounter with a four-way stop. Nothing was more calculated to bring out our respective political personalities. I considered it a democratic horror, but it filled Polly with gulpy we-the-people emotion.

"You take turns," she said happily. "Whoever gets to the intersection first goes first. It's voluntary self-policing."

"That's putting too much trust in human nature," I said darkly. "They ought to have a regular light. It's the only way to *make* people do the right thing."

I was scared to death. I knew *I* would wait my turn, but what about those other drivers? They might not have my internal gyroscope. I lurked at the stop sign and hunched over the wheel, scrutinizing their faces for some indication of their inner worth. The one on my left especially worried me: he had a weak chin.

Just then a chorus of horns sounded.

"Go on!" Polly yelled.

Five days later, she decided I was ready to take my road test.

"I hope you get a woman examiner," she said as she drove me to the Department of Motor Vehicles. We pulled into the test area and waited. A few minutes later, the office door opened. Polly looked up expectantly; then her face fell.

"Oh, shit, it's a man."

"Suppose he says something about my wearing just the lap part of the belt?"

"Don't worry," she said with a crafty wink. "I'll handle it."

Oh-shit-it's-a-man was clearly an Irishman, weighted down with a neck full of religious medals on a chain. The most prominent one, bigger than a silver dollar, featured St. Christopher. When he leaned down and stuck his head in the car window, the medal spun around and I saw the message on the flip side: *I am a Catholic. In case of accident, please call a priest.* I took it personally and started to shake.

He asked me to do the hand signals, then looked dubiously at my seat belt arrangement. "Your shoulder belt is unfastened," he chided.

"There's a medical reason for it," Polly piped up. "She's had a vasectomy."

I closed my eyes and put my head on the wheel. Ms. Malaprop rides again. . . .

Naturally she started babbling. "I mean mastectomy! I always get them confused. It was performed only two weeks ago so she's still sore. The doctor told her under no condition should she use the shoulder strap until everything heals up or else she'll rub a blister."

"All right, all right," said the examiner, holding up his hand in a placatory gesture.

As he got in beside me, he could not resist a furtive glance at my bosom. It was the same kind of look children used to give pregnant women back when pregnancy meant you had done something dirty. The glance, his medals, and Polly's blooper unnerved me so much that I flunked the road test.

Twenty horrible minutes later, we were back. Polly's hopeful face fell when I gave her the thumbs-down signal. She listened while the examiner analyzed my performance.

"Due to deductions, you failed to qualify," he said in toneless, training-manual fashion. "You lost ten points for passing a school bus, five for driving over a fire hose, five for wide backing, five for driving on the sidewalk, five for joining a funeral procession—"

"I turned on my lights."

"We don't give credit for that. Let's see," he went on, continuing down his list. He frowned and gave a puzzled grunt. "This is something I've never come across before. I guess I'll call it 'inventing a new traffic law.' "

"What?" Polly said incredulously.

"She yielded the right of way to an Animal Rescue League truck."

"It reminded me of Quadrupet," I explained. She rolled her eyes.

The examiner went on. "And then we have turning into the wrong lane, driving in the bus lane, driving over an island, jerky stops, and failing to signal."

He totted up his figures and handed me the card. "Your score is two."

"Two?"

"That is correct."

"What did I get that for?"

"Your right turns. They were absolutely perfect." He shook his head. "I can't understand it."

"I can," said Polly.

He walked back to his office making the sign of the cross. I unhooked the seat belt and moved over and Polly got behind the wheel.

"See?" I said in exhausted triumph. "I told you I couldn't drive."

"If at first you don't succeed, try, try again."

"Please close the copybook."

She frowned pensively and looked around in confusion. "Did he leave something?"

"Jesus. . . ."

Although I did everything except break a wheel on a butterfly, Polly would not let me give up. The next morning, she literally dragged me out of bed and took me out on the roads again. We spent the entire session backing around the same corner while she held the door open to check my distance from the curb. Worse, she brought along her carpenter's folding rule to measure it. It was one of the items from her self-sufficiency tool box. She persisted in calling it a "folding carpenter's rule" and I just as persistently pointed out that it was the rule that folded, not the carpenter, but she was too saturated in Femspeak to hear the difference.

After I learned how to make my tires hug the curb, she cured me of my love affair with the brake by making me downshift to second when approaching an intersection and coast to a smooth stop. To test this, she brought along a huge picnic jug of grape juice and poured herself a brimful cup each time she saw a red light coming up. The idea was for me to stop so smoothly that she would not spill a drop.

To me, "not a drop" was a figure of speech. To Polly, it meant *not a drop.*

"Look," she said reproachfully, after she had consumed some seventeen cups. She pointed to a small purple stain on her pants leg. It was one drop.

"Don't you have to pee?" I asked nastily.

She frowned pensively. "No, do you?"

"Jesus. . . ."

She broke my habit of using the clutch as a footrest by yelling "FOOT!" at the top of her lungs whenever I did it. Once, a cop heard her and offered to give us an escort to a hospital where, he said earnestly, they had a bilingual emergency team.

Thanks to her rock-headed persistence, the next time I took my road test I passed with flying colors. To celebrate, I treated her to a seafood dinner in Lynn. I couldn't believe I had a driver's license at last; all through dinner I kept taking it out and looking at it. Polly kept telling me that I was now completely independent, but she said it without her usual feminist intensity, so for the first time, we thoroughly enjoyed each other's company.

Afterward, we walked along the shorefront and bought some clams to take home. It had been a perfect day, so of course it couldn't last. Something about the combination of Polly and me seemed to inspire Fate to surpass herself.

When we came to the dumpy part of the beach, we found an abandoned cement mixer lying on the sand. Childlike, we peered into the ball, but instead of the nothing we expected, we found the something nobody ever expects: a dead body.

It was a white female, approximately twenty-five years old. My fingers automatically tapped out the familiar words on an imaginary stenotype machine. Polly misinterpreted my gesture.

"Stay calm. You must stay calm; otherwise the newspapers will say 'the hysterical women who discovered the body.' They always say that, just like they always say 'the women passengers screamed' when they write about a skyjacking. Do some breathing exercises and then we'll go for the police. Ready? And one, and two, and thr—''

We both screamed. The corpse moved.

As we clutched each other and backed away, the woman stuck her head out over the lip of the cement mixer and inched forward in a wormlike motion, but the effort was too much for her. Her head lolled and her arms fell out of the ball and dangled over the sand. Their color hinted at an interrupted embalming.

"She needs help!" Polly cried.

We pulled her out of her lair and tried to stand her on her feet but she kept buckling. She had Radical hair, long, frizzy, and dirty blond under a Navy surplus bosun's cap. That much was par for the course around Boston, but the rest of her would have attracted attention even on Beacon Hill.

She wore a green Marine Corps T-shirt tucked into an Army surplus canvas money belt, and a skirt made from an old pair of draperies that fastened to the money belt by the drapery hooks, which she had apparently never bothered to remove. I imagined her ripping them from someone's window like a hippie Scarlett O'Hara and fashioning a skirt on the spot. They must have been the floor-to-ceiling kind originally; the hem she had fixed up with safety pins of varying sizes and colors was a good ten inches deep. Under it peeked a pair of green rubber mud-boots with bright yellow lacing.

Whoever she was, she was not That Cosmo Girl; her witchiness was the kind that went with the eye of a newt. She looked like a necromancer gone wrong.

Polly tried slapping her lightly to bring her out of her funk. As she swayed to and fro, the marijuana fumes she gave off almost turned us on, too. At last her eyes opened and she gave us a zonked smile.

"What are you doing here?" Polly asked.

"I am here . . . I don't know."

"Where do you come from?"

"Many places."

It sounded like *Pelléas and Mélisande*. There was some more in the same collapsed vein before we finally got a complete sentence out of her.

"My thing is urban despair," she mumbled, then passed out again.

Polly turned to me, aglow with sisterly zeal. "We've got to help her! Let's take her home with us."

I gave her a wild look and opened my mouth to protest, then stopped. On any other day I could have objected, but not this one. I felt my new driver's license burning inside my wallet like a saint's stigmata. I didn't have the nerve to argue against her sisterhood support system after having just benefited from it myself.

Polly put her arm around the girl's waist. "See if she left anything in the cement mixer," she said. It was the sort of sentence I had never expected to hear.

I peered into the ball, certain I would find a pile of picked bones and a bowl of blood, but there was nothing except the usual Army surplus duffel bag painted with peace symbols. When I picked it up, it gave off a muffled twanging sound, so I figured she owned the usual guitar.

"Hold up her other side," Polly instructed. "We'll carry her between us."

Given the difference in our heights, it didn't work, so I went and got the car.

"Where'll we put her?" I said, looking at the tiny sports car in consternation. The back seat was a mere slit.

"I'll hold her in my lap," Polly said fervently.

I dumped the duffel bag in the slit and got behind the wheel. Polly slid in beside me and dragged our unconscious sister on top of her. I wondered if she would indulge her seat-belt compulsion at a time like this. Yes, she would; anal-retentives never give up. While I waited in gear, she pulled and stretched and buckled and clicked until the two of them were trussed and ready to drive. I wanted to buy the car from her just for the pleasure of taking a razor to those goddamn belts.

We headed back to Boston like Franz Josef's flunkies transporting the decomposing corpse of Marie Vetsera from Mayerling. Polly was making comforting sounds and cradling the girl's head.

"For God's sake, stop hugging her, Polly. You don't know what she might have."

"Urban despair! Urban despair!"

"I know . . . I know," Polly crooned.

"Tant pis," I muttered.

Gioppi was fortunately nowhere in sight when we got to the house. I carried the duffel bag and the clams and pushed from behind, while Polly pulled from the front. In this manner we finally got Urban Despair up to our door.

The moment Quadrupet saw her he laid his ears back so far he looked like a weasel. We put her in a chair and Polly started flying around like a ministering angel, fetching water and spirits of ammonia. I went through the duffel bag.

My first surprise was the musical instrument. It wasn't a guitar but a lute. I put it aside and reached into the bag again. This time I found something that contained her name. It was a dog-eared music manuscript.

" 'A Madrigal on the Death of Edward the Second,' " I read aloud. " 'An original composition by Gloria Hammond.' "

The rest of her belongings consisted of a few extra pairs of underpants, a ratty fur jacket that looked like Good Will Surplus, and an electric curling iron. I couldn't imagine why she bothered to curl her hair considering what she looked like from the neck down. I put it down to that vestigial female vanity found in bag ladies who carry a sliver of mirror in their ragged pockets.

Polly glanced at the musical composition. "Edward the Second? Never heard of him. I wonder if I can get her to eat something? Give me one of those clams."

I reached into the bag and pulled out a fried clam. She put it in Gloria's mouth but it just lay there like an extra tongue. She took it out and threw it away.

"Maybe she's a diabetic," Polly said with alarm. "This could be a coma. Look, there's something in her money belt that feels like a medicine bottle! Maybe it's her insulin."

The money belt yielded plenty of medicine bottles but none of them contained insulin—just uppers and downers and lots of sugar cubes.

"She's a dope fiend!"

"Narcotics addict," Polly corrected. "What she needs is a good night's sleep." She started turning down her bed.

"Where are you going to sleep?" I asked.

"On the floor. I'll use the bolsters."

"Why don't you put her on the floor? She wouldn't know the difference. Why do you have to give your bed away?"

"Because she needs it more than I do."

"We don't know who she is or what she might do! She might get up in the middle of the night and find a knife and stab us while we're asleep!"

"That's a chance we'll have to take."

I poured myself a double bourbon and coaxed Quadrupet out from under the stove. I put him in my lap and we brooded together while Polly sat beside the snoring Gloria applying cold cloths.

When it was time for bed, she put the bolsters on the floor and tried to make a mattress out of them but it was impossible. They were wedges. Whichever way she turned them she ended up with geometric lumps. Mine were the same kind so there was only one thing to do.

"For God's sake, sleep with me," I grumbled.

The day beds Gioppi supplied were less than twin size. Polly fell asleep right away but I lay there trying to avoid her sharp bones; it was like being pressed in the Iron Maiden.

The next morning, Polly got up first, bright and chipper and aching to do good. I heard her bustling around in her kitchen making coffee. She brought me a cup.

"Gloria's awake," she said happily. "Come in and see her. She looks so much better."

I went solely out of curiosity. She was sitting up in bed, still wearing her bosun's cap. To the eye of a Non-Helper, she looked worse.

"Gloria, would you like some apple juice?" Polly asked. "It's unfiltered."

"Yump."

She was too weak to hold the glass so Polly put it on the night table and Gloria leaned over and slurped at it.

"Would you like a natural egg?"

"Nmmph."

When the apple juice had sunk below slurping level, the Great Humanitarian held the glass to Gloria's lips and helped her drain it. She smacked her mouth appreciatively and asked for another. Polly ran and got it. When she had drunk off the second one she looked almost normal except for the green rubber boots sticking out of the sheets.

"You were really thirsty, weren't you?" Polly said happily. "Now I'll get you some cof—"

"Whan that Aprille with his shoures soote / The droghte of March hath percéd to the roote."

"Oh, my God, she's hallucinating!" Polly cried.

"No, she isn't. That's *The Canterbury Tales.*"

Even Polly had heard of them. We stood there, she in alarm and I in growing empathy as Gloria went through the entire Prologue without missing a beat. Here was somebody even more deeply mired in irrelevancy than I was. She had struck such a blow for liberal arts that Polly was staggering.

Gloria got out of bed, went into the bathroom to splash a little water on her face, and joined us at the table for coffee. Except for looking a little blurry around the edges, she was completely recovered.

"I'm a medievalist," she explained. "There was no urban despair in the Middle Ages. It was pre-Renaissance, pre-industrial, pre-everything."

We had a Henry Adams in the house. "Did you major in history?" I asked.

"Yes, but I'm really a medieval music historian. I did my thesis on balladry in the reign of Edward the Second. I set his murder to music."

"Who is Edward the Second?" Polly asked.

"King of England 1307–1327," Gloria replied with authority. "He was forced to abdicate by the Welsh barons. They wanted to kill him but they had to find a way to do it without leaving any marks of violence on his body so they could pass it off as a natural death. How," she asked rhetorically, "could they do it? Starvation was out, and so were stabbing, poisoning, drowning, smothering, defenestration, and exsanguination."

Polly jumped as though she had been electrocuted. "What are those last two?"

"Throwing him out of a window and draining off his blood."

"Oh."

"Finally, they figured out a way to do it that would leave no trace." She paused dramatically. "And since he was gay, it was also a symbolic punishment." She leaned forward, surveying us under beetle brows. "Do you know what they did to him?"

"No," I lied. "What?"

"They shoved a hollow reed up his ass, inserted a red-hot poker, and then withdrew the reed."

Polly emitted a squealy grunt and raised her bottom off the chair.

"No trace of foul play appeared on the person of the king," Gloria went on. "The deed wasn't discovered until the embalmer cut the body open to prepare it for burial and saw that there was no work to be done."

Polly listed further to starboard until she was perched on one hip. She hastened to change the subject.

"Wouldn't you like to take a shower, Gloria? And get into some clean clothes? We'll lend you something."

Gloria acquiesced with a blurry smile and went into Polly's bathroom. The Sister of Us All heaved a quavery sigh and changed hips, but her respite was short-lived. The water came on and Gloria started to sing one of her original compositions, called, we learned later, "Poore Ned's Burnyng Bunghole."

> The royale arse did scorch and melte
> Where once Piers Gaveston's pryck was felte
> Where Hugh De Spenser plunged his rod
> And shot full wyll his manly wad
> Was rendered down to fiery suet puddying!

"Oh, God," Polly groaned, flexing her fingers, "I can't make a fist!"

A little later, the water shut off and Gloria emerged from the bathroom sans robe, sans towel, sans everything. She wasn't even wearing pubic hair. Her pudenda had been shaved as bald as an egg and painted with that garish antiseptic poetically known as gentian violet. Polly went all compassionate when she saw it; to her it was the mark of the free clinic. Having labored in different vineyards, all I could think of was *I never saw a purple twat and never hoped to see one.*

I drew the blinds and Polly produced a supportive smile and some fresh underwear. We breakfasted on scrambled eggs and cornbread. As we ate, Gloria told us how she had come to be in the cement mixer. She had lost her job as music teacher at an experimental private school a week before. The post had included faculty housing in addition to salary, and so, finding herself homeless as well as unemployed, she had decided to camp out on the beach with some radicals she knew. But the radicals had stolen her severance pay and, apparently, dumped her in the cement mixer when they mistook her bad drug trip for death. Or maybe she had climbed into the cement mixer by herself. She really couldn't say.

"I was fired for unconventional teaching methods," she confessed.

"If you were a man, they'd have called them 'innovative,' " Polly said darkly. "I'll help you file a discrimination suit!" She went to her file cabinet and took out a folder full of forms. "Now," she said, all businesslike, "tell me exactly what happened."

Gloria wiped her mouth on the back of her hand, medieval style. "I was telling my class about the Black Plague in the fourteenth century. I wanted to make it come alive for them, so I decided to do something creative. I sang a song about a monk who traveled around lancing people's plague boils; then I handed out knives and told the kids to act it out. A little boy got hurt."

Polly put down her pen and closed the folder.

That night, Polly moved her mattress onto the floor for Milburga the Mad Minstrel and slept on her box springs. It was the first fatal step. By the time the droghte of March yielded to Aprille, Gloria had taken roote.

I kept telling myself that I ought to move into a place of my own and try to get some serious work done, but writer's curiosity held me back. Gloria was the sort of person I would have avoided before I met Polly, but now I found myself getting interested in what made her tick.

It was frustrating; we learned almost nothing about her. Like Mélisande, she skirted inquiries about her origins with gauzy non sequiturs, and her habit of breaking into Middle English obscured whatever regional accent she might have had.

There was some talk about getting her a job, but even Polly had to admit that her appearance ruled out any possibility of a nine-to-five life, or even a midnight-to-dawn one. The most ghoulish thing about her was the way she squatted naked on her mattress and curled her hair. It was unlike any grooming operation I had ever seen, including documentaries on baboons. Instead of dividing the hair into sections and working on one at a time the way you're supposed to, she simply shoved the curling rod into her tangled web, captured any old clump, twisted it up into a knot, and pressed the button. When the steam rose, she looked like a troll on a heath.

The only normal thing she did was watch Polly's TV show, if that could be called normal. She never went out, preferring to spend the day sprawled on her mattress with purple labia to the breeze like Cleopatra's sails, strumming her lute or reading Froissart's *Chronicles* while I stenotyped Regencys. About once a week, when her yearning for the Middle Ages got too strong, she would pop some pills and escape into the past. These interludes produced some of our most bizarre conversations, like the time she yelled, ''We need more friars!'' and Polly said, ''Isabel has a Dutch oven.''

Matters remained in limbo until a fateful morning in June when the phone rang during breakfast. Polly got up to answer it. I paid no attention when I heard her say, ''Oh, no!'' because most of her phone calls started that way, but when she returned to the table pale and shaken, I knew something had happened.

''That was a lawyer in California. My Uncle Ezra was harpooned during a Greenpeace mission. He left everything to me in his will. His house, his royalties, and two hundred thousand dollars.''

CHAPTER FOUR

Uncle Ezra's demise triggered an international incident that nearly led to World War III. In true Bradshaw fashion, he had managed to involve not only the Japanese whaling ship whose captain cut him in half, but an Italian merchant vessel, a Dutch underwater exploration team, a Canadian cruise boat full of senior citizens on their way to peaceful Polynesia, and a Russian nuclear sub.

Only the whale escaped unscathed, ''which,'' said Polly in an NBC interview, ''was the way Uncle Ezra would have wanted it.'' Never mind the nine hundred and sixty-three lawsuits that buried The Hague in paper, or all the people at Lloyd's who would have to work until four A.M. for the next ten years. The Bradshaws were happy.

Her network appearance drew a number of very good job offers from television bigwigs who wanted her to do a toned-down version of "Heated Topics" for them, but she refused to have anything to do with what she called the "co-optive Establishment." Fired by Uncle Ezra's example of selfless idealism, she shifted into high Bradshaw and decided to use her inheritance to start a feminist commune in California.

"The house he left me is in Ventura, near Los Angeles. I've never been there but I've seen pictures of it. It's huge! I want to fill it with women! I'm bursting with ideas for exciting projects! We can do so much good! We—" She broke off and looked at me uncertainly. "You'll come, won't you?"

"I wouldn't miss it for the world."

I meant just that and no more. The last thing I wanted to do was join a feminist commune, but I thought there might be a book in it that all the Women's Libbers would buy. I was willing to write it as long as I didn't have to read it.

"Me, neither," said Gloria.

In the excitement of the past week we had almost forgotten she was still with us, but now she was ours for keeps. Any hope of getting rid of her had vanished when Polly decided to embrace the entire female sex.

We decided to drive to California, so Polly turned in her car for a new Ford van. I blanched when I saw it. Having learned to drive on a low-slung sports car, I was now dead set against anything else. Like Queen Caroline, I preferred the drawers I knew to the drawers I didn't.

"It's up too high," I complained. "It doesn't have any fenders to measure by. I can't drive it."

"Yes, you can. Perkin Pritchard proved by practice," said the nattering nabob of positivism. She went on to point out the many advantages of vans.

"It can serve double duty. After we get to California and start the commune, we can use it for a mobile crisis unit. Everybody uses vans for that nowadays. Meanwhile, it'll save us money. We can take all our stuff with us instead of shipping it and paying freight rates." She pursed her thin lips. "You know how dear they are."

She had changed since becoming an heiress. Always thrifty, she was now as tight as a drum. Something about having a lot of money had brought out the Cap'n Nehemiah in her.

To make sure we would not have to ship anything, and to prove that women were as well-organized as men, she took charge of the move down to the last detail. It brought her to such a pitch of obsession-compulsion that I was afraid she was going to crack up.

"We must make lists," she instructed, a muscle in her cheek jumping. "First we need *Inventory of Apartment Contents.* Then each of us will make a preliminary *Must Go* list and check it against a preliminary *Expendable* list. Then we'll compile a final master list of every single item in the van and devise a coded notation to tell us exactly where to find it."

Gloria's list was a model of simplicity. She had added nothing to her net worth since her arrival except a new bottle of gentian violet for her crab condition.

My list was much longer and began with something that was bound to upset Polly: Quadrupet.

"I knew it," she sighed.

"We're bonding."

Since we were taking him, we had to take his belongings, so I listed them: a scratching post the size of a small tree, a bamboo pagoda that he refused to sleep in but loved to hump, and his mobile, all gifts from me. I had made the mobile from a broom handle, a weighted Christmas tree stand, and an umbrella-style plastic clothes dryer. From the clothespins dangled strings of varying lengths tied to crumpled cigarette wrappers, which he batted at for hours on end. This unique contraption stood 4'6¾" high—Polly measured it with her carpenter's rule—and would not fold or bend in any direction. We would have to transport it upright.

When Polly added my list to hers she nearly turned the van in on a truck. It wasn't the usual girlish problem of too many clothes. Neither of us had a big wardrobe, but we did have: six hundred books, Aunt Tabitha's suffragette banners, the Nixon dartboard, the walking machine, the file cabinet, ten reams of writing paper, stenotype machine, three cartons of stenotype tape, tripod, typewriter, picket signs for all occasions, a model of the *Titanic,* and the birth bucket.

As if all of this were not enough, Polly insisted on taking the pieces of the wall.

"Leave them here," I pleaded. "Why drag along something that didn't cost anything in the first place?"

"Use it up, wear it out, make it do, or do without."

When the inventory was finished, the packing began. My method was to have a few drinks first, while I thought about packing. Then, when the thought was no longer painful, I packed. I was feeling no pain at all when I scooped up two teacups, an electric knife, my file on famous English murders, my Latin dictionary, and a bathrobe and tossed them into a cardboard box.

Polly watched with mounting anguish as I stumbled around the room in my state of terminal miscellany.

"Stop it!" she shrieked. "I can't stand it! Never mind, never mind, let me do it."

That's how I got out of packing.

After she got the boxes sealed up she went to the dime store and bought so many tags and labels that I thought we would have to pack *them.* There were red tags for breakables, blue tags for soft goods, and yellow tags shaped like light bulbs with a picture of Mr. Kilowatt for electrical appliances. She bought white labels with OPEN THIS END! written in green, which were not to be confused with the blue labels that had OPEN OTHER END! written in red, nor used when the situation called for buff labels with check blocks to tell us whether the items in the box were for ☐ *Bedroom* ☐ *Dining Room* ☐ *Rec Room* ☐ *Attic.*

"Logic," she said through gritted teeth as she checked away, "is not a male quality but a human quality."

When the packing was finished she measured all the cartons and then crawled around in the back of the van armed with clipboard, slide rule, and her ever-present folding yardstick. The result was *Preliminary Loading Specifications.*

"Look," she said worriedly, pointing to some figures on her clipboard. They were 8⁹/₁₆ and 14⁵/₇. "What are we going to do about that?"

I shrugged. "I never add fractions if they have different bottoms."

She glared at me. "Do you know what this means? We'll have to rent a U-Haul cartop carrier."

That broke her heart but it was still cheaper than the "dear" freight rates. She drove the van down to the U-Haul depot and returned with the carrier affixed. She informed me that it held twenty cubic feet, whatever that was, and then went to work on *Revised Preliminary Loading Specifications.*

By now the apartment was strewn with lists, all decorated with smeary black puncture marks. There was only one thing that had not happened, but I knew it would, and I was right. Around midnight, she made a list of the lists.

The day before our scheduled departure, we loaded the van according to her figures and parked it in the back alley. To make sure nobody stole it during the night, I nominated Gloria to spend the night in it and made her promise to remain vertical so that any potential thieves would be sure to see her. She said, "By my troth," spat three times through her forefinger and pinkie, and left with her lute. I watched from the window to make sure she got settled and then Polly and I went to bed.

A few minutes later, or so it seemed, the alarm went off and it was time to get up. I lurched like a beached seal and tried not to throw up; this was what Polly meant by "getting an early start." The room was pitch black. For a moment I thought I had gone blind from shock, but then Polly switched on her light, swept back her blanket with a d'Artagnan flourish, and rose.

Or tried to. Quadrupet was slung across her neck like a hairy albatross, determined to thwart what he knew was to be a violent uprooting. She tried to push him away but he rolled over on her face and tried to smother her. I waited hopefully, listening to the struggle.

"ZZZZZZZZZTTTTTTTTT!"

"YEEEOOOOWWWWW!"

I peeped over the blanket and saw her sucking her arm. Quadrupet burrowed and went back to sleep.

"Get up," she said to me. "I'm bleeding to death. Where did we put the Mercurochrome?"

"In *Contents of Medicine Chests,* subdivision *Breakable.*"

It was already packed in the van. She said nothing.

According to her departure plan, we were supposed to leap out of bed, strip off the sheets, roll them up, and put them in the still-open box marked *Bed Linens.* This scenario fell apart when she accidentally rolled Quadrupet up in her mattress pad. He lurched manfully and came rolling back out again, then stalked into the kitchen and deliberately knocked over his water bowl.

I staggered into my bathroom and found it plastered with notes from Polly. DO NOT LEAVE TOILET PAPER BEHIND! was stuck on the wall facing the john at such a perfect eye level that I was sure she had measured it. When I went to the basin to brush my teeth, there was another note on the mirror that said REMEMBER YOUR TOOTHBRUSH! with an arrow pointing down to my drinking glass in case I forgot where I kept it. The third note was under the light switch: HAVE YOU FORGOTTEN ANYTHING?

I glanced around and saw a lipstick with about one-eighth of an inch left in the tube. In a burst of predawn madness, I tore off the cap and scrawled STOP ME BEFORE I KILL BRADSHAWS! across the mirror and emitted a high, reedy cackle.

"What?" she called.

"Nothing."

I went into her kitchen for breakfast and found the table laid with those items of New England thrift known as "toots." A toot, she had told me, was a paper twist containing the tag ends of household staples that ordinarily get thrown away. The Yankee goodwife prevented such Babylonian profligacy by dusting the seams of flour and sugar sacks into little squares of waxed paper, which were then secured at both ends.

Thanks to Polly's mathematical calculation of our shopping needs for our last month chez Gioppi, all of our staples had come to an end just in time for our departure. Thus on this last morning there was just enough salt, pepper, sugar, instant coffee, and powdered cream left to make toots.

I sank down in my chair. We could not have a hot breakfast because she had packed all the pots, pans, skillets, and spatulas in the box marked *Kitchen Utensils: Metal.* Instead we were having hard-boiled eggs which she had cooked the night before. She rolled one in my direction and we ate.

Mine was as dry as dust and stuck to the roof of my mouth. I thought some pepper might give it some taste, but as I struggled with my toot it exploded in my face and I had a sneezing fit. Just then Polly unwrapped still another toot containing Quadrupet's odorous Gourmet Kitty tuna. The smell wafted under my nose as I was trying to swallow the egg. It went down the wrong way and my air stopped.

"Do you want some peanut butter?" Polly asked. "It's nonpreservative."

I shook my head violently but she was already opening the toot. She smeared some on my half-eaten egg. The sight of the brown lump nearly finished me off.

"Make sure you eat it. It's a quick-energy food."

She was completely oblivious to my maroon face and my inability to breathe. My windpipe was so full of egg that I couldn't even inhale well enough to cough, and she was trying to plug up the rest of it with peanut butter. When at last I managed an equine wheeze she shook her head and said, "Cigarettes."

After breakfast, she dried the pan in which she had boiled the coffee water, put it in the box marked *Equipment for Refreshments While Traveling,* and picked up the thermos she had prepared for Gloria. I picked up Quadrupet and we were off.

"Good morrow, pilgrims!" Gloria greeted us.

She was wide awake all right. Her pupils were so dilated that her eyes looked black. Alarm coursed through me. She had taken uppers this time and she was in fyne fettyl forsooth.

She jumped down from the front seat and hopped around to the double doors in back, her duffel bag slung over her shoulder like one of those tinkers in fairy tales, the kind there are always three of. She climbed in the back and propped her green rubber feet on a box marked *Writing Materials: I. Fairfax.* I got in front and put Quadrupet's carrying case under my knees.

Polly started the van and pulled out of the alley. I tensed myself for one of her original observations and was not disappointed.

"California, here we come!"

As we drove west on the Massachusetts turnpike, sick Gloria in transit took up her lute and treated us to a frenetic rendition of "The Varlets Set Fyre to the Bowels de Plantagenet."

When she hit the grisly part, Polly tilted up on one hip and groaned. "Gloria, do you have to sing about . . . that?"

She replied with a plinky discord and fell silent. If she couldn't sing about barbecued bungholes she would rather not sing at all.

Even when quiet she attracted a lot of attention. As we waited in line at the tollbooth, family types in Winnebagos stared at her through the window, and the toll-taker muttered "Jesus, Mary, and Joseph" when she stuck out her head and gave him a souped-up smile. It was even worse when we stopped for lunch at Denny's. The hostess took one look at her and led us to a table in the far corner. As we followed, several children pointed and one little girl burst into terrified sobs.

Naturally Gloria was not hungry but she was spitless. She ordered a pitcher of ice water and swilled it down, her eyes dancing about the room like a pair of epileptic fleas.

"Look!" she cried happily. "There's the jakes!" That was medieval for toilet.

"Do you have to go?" asked Polly.

"No! But I balled a Kotex salesman once!"

I suppose there was some tenuous connection between the two remarks but it really didn't matter; we were beyond non sequiturs by then. It was the first time Gloria had ever mentioned her sex life. I was surprised. Not that I thought she hadn't had one; the surprising part was that she remembered it.

"Did you?" I said.

"Yes! And he gave me a key! I've still got it!"

She rose, cackling like the poker-plying varlets of her *chansons,* and gave us a spastic wink. "Wish me luck!"

As she scurried off, Polly and I exchanged puzzled glances.

"Is she going to use a catheter?" she asked.

A few moments later Gloria came bouncing back wearing a triumphant grin. "Listen!" she hissed, jingling her pockets. "Dimes! I've never seen one so full!"

"One what?"

"The Kotex machine! The salesman I balled told me the same key fits every machine in the country! It's the one they issue to ladies'-room matrons! They don't want the matrons to know it because they're afraid they'd get copies made! But the salesman let me in on the secret and gave me one! Whenever I'm short of bread, all I have to do is find a Kotex machine!"

There was nothing to do but eat lunch. Gloria had another pitcher of ice water.

A few hours later we stopped for dinner in Troy, New York. Gloria had come down enough to eat half of a grilled cheese sandwich and her pupils had shrunk back to reasonably normal size so I assumed she was too wrung out to cause any more trouble.

I was wrong. While Polly and I were paying the check she drifted into a souvenir shop attached to the restaurant. When she didn't come out, we left the restaurant and waited for her in the van. Finally we saw her trotting across the parking lot with her pockets bulging.

"Look," she said happily, starting to unload. Her take consisted of a garish ashtray inscribed "Souvenir of Troy," a paperweight with a snowfall scene, a letter opener, a penknife, a slab of wood with scorch marks spelling out "Home Sweet Home," and—something that must have reminded her of the good old days—a plaster statue of a weeping little boy with his bare bottom in the air.

She dumped the whole business in Polly's lap. "I want you to have it," she said plangently.

I wondered if Polly would pack it all in a box marked *Shoplifted Items,* but instead she shoved it haphazardly into the glove compartment and made tracks for the highway.

The problem of where to stop for the night was complicated by Gloria's appearance and Polly's thrift. Any hostelry that had corridors was automatically out because Gloria might wander down them and Polly refused to pay for corridors. Any motel that fell within the category known as "family-style" was also out because Gloria repelled families and Polly refused to pay for toilet seats wrapped in sterilized paper strips.

There was also an ideological problem. Polly had it in for several motel chains because of labor disputes of one kind or another, or because they did convention business with organizations that barred women members. I drove for over an hour in a state of exhaustion while she consulted her many lists and newsletters and said "No, not that one" each time we passed a vacancy sign.

At last we found a place that came up to her standards and down to Gloria's. It was called "Fran's Tourist Cabins."

Polly was too thrilled by the cheap price of a triple to consider the luxury of sleeping apart from Gloria so we all piled in together. The room was the pits: plastic curtains, rubbery doilies, blond Thirties furniture, wall-to-wall linoleum, and a clawfoot tub.

It was my turn for a fix. I took a bottle of bourbon out of my suit-case. "Let's have some hooch. Is there anything to drink out of in this dump?"

"Look," said Gloria, pointing into the bathroom. "I see some hanaps."

I thought it meant "cockroach" but she explained that it was Middle English for cup. These were Dixie hanaps. I fetched three and poured us a round.

"Down the dovecote," Gloria toasted.

We were so tired that we killed the bottle before we knew it. Polly belched gently and passed out. I stretched out beside her on the double bed and Gloria clambered onto the cot. Everything went black until an indeterminate time later when Polly and I awoke to sounds of violent hammering.

We lurched up and grappled drunkenly with each other before one of us managed to find the switch on the sleazy fringed lamp. Its muddy yellow glow revealed the same horrible room, but lacking now one aspect of horror it had contained earlier: Gloria.

Her cot was empty. The hammering began again. Polly ran to the door and flung it open. "Look!" she cried, pointing into the driveway. "She's trying to get in the van!"

We ran outside and found Gloria stark naked, yanking at the double doors and yelling, "Raise the portcullis in the name of the King!"

"Gloria, please come inside!"

"I hear the Plantagenet herald! Make haste to Gloucester!"

Lights were switching on in the other cabins. The manageress emerged from her office-home with her hair in curlers, followed by a burly tattooed man pulling on his pants. A few doors down, a couple who were obviously naked under their raincoats crept from their cabin and surveyed the scene with sleepy grins.

Gloria broke away from us and took off across the driveway, bellowing at the top of her lungs for Roger de Mortimer, Cob O' Northumberland, John of Gaunt, Longshanks, and the Bishop of Ely.

The three of us raced around the driveway. I was afraid she would get violent if we tried to force her back into the cabin, so I decided to use psychology on her.

"Come, fair maid of Kent!" I cried cheerily. "The Black Prince awaits thee in the royal chamber. He is come back from Crécy with a fine French lute!"

"This isn't funny, Isabel!" Polly yelled.

Several of the guests thought differently; a couple were choking. The manageress burst into a hoarse whiskey laugh and caught Gloria by the arm as she rounded the office.

"Okay, kid, okay," she chortled good-naturedly. "You just had one too many, that's all. Happens to the best of us."

"We can't raise the portcullis!"

"Chrissake, kid, you can't get nobody to fix things nowadays. The plumbers charge ten bucks an hour and don't do a goddamn thing."

Her warm, husky maternal voice did the trick. Gloria became docile and allowed herself to be led back to the cabin.

"You gals lay off the sauce now," Fran advised. "If you're hung over tomorrow, just stay in bed, don't worry about checkout time. My maid got shot last night so there won't be nobody around anyhow."

Gloria put her arms around Fran and laid her head on the woman's shoulder. "My liege lord has the pox!"

"That's nothin', you oughta see Harry's piles. Big as baseballs. Now go back to bed and sleep it off. Night-night."

Gloria fell into an exhausted sleep right away. While Polly was giving her teeth their usual one hundred strokes, I had a Coke with ammonia spirits and questioned the wisdom of gathering experience.

The next day the weather turned very hot, giving Polly a perfect excuse for suggesting an even cheaper place to spend the night.

"Let's stay at a campsite and sleep in the van!"

We pulled into a rustic area full of Winnebagos all in a circle like pioneer wagons expecting an Indian attack. After we got settled in our space, we roasted hot dogs for dinner. The sight of Gloria had a predictable effect on the God-and-country set, but other than walking past the horseshoe game in her draperies she did nothing to attract attention. She was back on downers.

When it was time for bed, she collapsed across the front seats and Polly and I went to the community bathhouse for showers. Afterward, we made our way back to the van through the unspoiled wilderness as Polly inhaled deeply and made ecologist noises about how wonderful

it was to be close to the soil and back to nature. Like all agora-
phobiacs, I could not have disagreed more.

To make room to sleep, we unloaded several of the cartons and
Quadrupet's mobile and put them outside on the grass, then spread
quilts and blankets on the floor of the van and climbed in. The camp-
ground was full of dogs, so I attached Quadrupet's leash and wound it
securely around my wrist. He snuggled under my chin and we lay
there in the crickety blackness with the back doors open to the warm
summer air.

"Isn't this wonderful?" said Polly.

"No."

I had to pee. I had done it once in the shower but now I had to go
again. I tried to think of sand and deserts but it didn't help. What to
do? I had no intention of making another trip through the sylvan glade
to the bathhouse. I decided to wait until Ms. Clean fell asleep and pee
beside the van.

When she started snoring, I crept out with Quadrupet and felt my
way in the dark until I made it around to the side facing the woods.
Holding firmly to the leash with one hand, I used the other to unsnap
my pajama bottoms and pull them down to my ankles. It's hard
enough for a woman to pee in a squat in the dark without a cat taking
up one hand, but I didn't dare let go of him. Bracing myself against the
van, I managed to get into position.

Just then a rustling sound came from the woods and the ever-alert
Quadrupet sprang. The sudden movement unraveled the leash from
my wrist and threw me off balance. I tumbled over in a puddle of pee
and let go of him. With a howl of battle, he soared through the air like
a comet and disappeared into the trees.

I panicked.

"HELP! STOP HIM!"

Polly burst out of the van, took one look at my pajama bottoms, and
yelled at the top of her lungs.

"RAPE!"

"HE'S GONE INTO THE WOODS!"

"RAPE!"

It was our wackiest conversation yet. Each time I yelled something
like "We've got to catch him," she thought I meant a man and yelled
"Rape."

Lights were switching on in the surrounding campers. Quickly, I pulled up my pajama bottoms.

"I'm all wet!" I wailed.

"Don't destroy the evidence! You must not wash yourself. Promise me you won't wash yourself. You're experiencing a felt need to counteract perceived self-disgust, but therapy will take care of that. RAPE!"

"Will you shut up!"

"Hand me my shotgun, Mabel," said a voice from the next campsite.

Soon we were surrounded by Middle Americans, all armed to the teeth, and all ears as Polly babbled about blood tests, semen stains, and the morning-after pill. She was so completely beside herself that it was several minutes before I finally got through to her.

"I haven't been raped! It's Quadrupet. He's escaped!"

I threw myself against the man with the shotgun so he would not fire into the woods.

"Don't shoot! You'll hit the Quad!"

While he was figuring that out, a terrible smell filled the air. The underbrush crackled and suddenly Quadrupet was back, hissing, spitting, and snarling with rage.

"Aw, he's been sprayed by a skunk," said the man with the gun. "There's an old hunter's remedy for it, little lady."

Polly gave him a murderous glance when she heard the diminutive but I was all ears as I held the stinking Quadrupet.

"Tomato juice'll do the trick. Takes away the sting and the smell."

Fortunately, we had some in the box marked *Quick Energy Snacks*. Polly opened a can and I put Quadrupet on the ground, where he lurched in place and howled on a high, shrill zitherlike note, the kind of sound the movies use to indicate the entrance of a lunatic. She handed me the can and I tipped it over him, then stopped. I was afraid the shock of coming in contact with liquid would kill him.

"I can't do it," I whispered.

"You've got to," said the hunter. "It's the only way."

It was straight out of James M. Cain. I took a deep breath and poured. Quadrupet exploded in renewed fury and leaped two feet off the ground.

"Wrap him in lots of towels," said the hunter. "Keep 'em tight around him so's he can't lick hisself."

We ripped open *Towels* and I swathed him in three of them and cradled him in my arms. Now he looked like the sheik he wished he were.

"His little heart," I wept. "I can feel it pounding through all these towels." Now that he was safe I lost all control and began sobbing and singing at the same time. "Q-Q-Q-Quad-Quad, sweet little Quad-Quad, him's the only c-c-c-cat that I adore. When the m-m-moon shines over the mousehole, I'll be waiting at the k-k-k-kitchen door. . . ."

It was "our" song. As I strode up and down in my wet pajamas singing to the struggling bundle clutched to my bosom, the hunter looked from Quadrupet's mobile to Polly's *Free Women Now!* bumper sticker and shook his head.

When I caught her eye, there was a most unsisterly look on her face. I could practically see the urge-to-kill dagger of the comic strips hovering over her head.

The stoned Gloria slept through it all.

I was at the wheel when we crossed the California line. Polly gave a cheer and suggested we celebrate by stopping for tacos.

I pulled into a low-slung ultramodern drive-in full of teenagers, station wagons full of children, and carhops in hotpants. The day was a scorcher so I looked for a shady parking space under the roof. Spying one, I made a beeline for it but we never got there. Suddenly, there was a horrible crash that left the van quivering from the impact.

"What did you do?" Polly yelled.

"I don't know!" There was nothing in front of us; no rail, no wall, no other cars, nothing. But I had hit something.

Polly and I got out and inspected the front end, then peered underneath to see if the drive shaft had broken, but all was well.

"Maybe you hit a garbage can and it rolled away," Polly suggested.

I glanced around the lot but there was no garbage can or any other demolished metallic object. I began to feel spooked. Had I hit an electronic eye? Maybe we had won one of those prototypical California contests involving the one-millionth taco.

Just then we noticed that everybody was staring at us. That in itself was not unusual by this time, but these stares were different from the furtive kind we were used to after traveling with Gloria. They were open and unabashed and full of simple-minded admiration. Two carhops had stopped dead in their tracks, trays poised and mouths open; the customers had all stopped eating and some of the kitchen staff had come out of the back door to watch us. Everyone seemed awestruck.

They were all looking up.

"Oh, no! The U-Haul!"

I had forgotten it was on top of the van. Now it almost wasn't. It hung by two screws, its legs twisted like melted hairpins. I had plowed right into the low-slung, ultra-modern California roof.

Just then it emitted a grinding belch and started to slide.

"Catch it!" Polly screamed.

We reached up just in time. As we stood there bracing and heaving, Gloria grabbed her lute, jumped out of the van, and started running round in circles shouting useless directions. A wave of hysteria passed over me. I thought of those photos tourists have taken of themselves pretending to hold up the Leaning Tower of Pisa. I thought of Sisyphus and his rock and the little Dutch boy with his finger in the dyke. A vision formed and I saw us standing there forever like a pair of caryatids, condemned to spend eternity holding up the U-Haul while Gloria danced around us like the strophe of a Dionysian chorus.

"Stop laughing!" Polly yelled.

I was so overcome I dropped my end. The door flew open and, like a piñata, the U-Haul spewed forth gifts. *Published Works: I. Fairfax, Footwear: P. Bradshaw, Glasswear & Misc. Breakables, Rape-Prevention Brochures,* and a ten-pound sack of Kitty Litter that burst like a bomb.

As Polly and I ducked and ran for cover, all of the people who had been watching us broke into applause. A carhop rushed up to us holding out her order pad.

"Can I have your autographs?"

"Autographs?" we said dumbly.

"Aren't you celebrities?"

A teenage boy stood up in a convertible. "Hey, where's the camera? I wanna wave to my girl."

"Are they hiring?" asked the carhop. "My agent is William Morris."

A fat woman in short-shorts leaped out of her station wagon and galloped toward us, bellowing like a sow in rut.

"I got here first! I win! Where's the giveaway?"

"It was real!" I said. "Real!"

The carhop frowned quizzically. "You mean it was a publicity stunt?"

They refused to believe that we hadn't done it on purpose. The carhop kept following us around with her pencil, pleading for an autograph, so to shut her up and get rid of her I scrawled *I. Fairfax* on her order pad.

"I knew you were a famous person," she said happily.

"Listen, I want my giveaway! I'm entitled!"

"Oh, shit," said the teenager. "Nobody got killed."

"What about the weirdo that the U-Haul fell on?" asked the giveaway lady. "She must be dead."

"No, she's the stunt girl," said the carhop knowledgeably. "She knows how to let things fall on her."

That made us remember Gloria. We turned around to the wreckage and saw a pile of boxes with an arm sticking out. At the end of it was a hand holding the lute up to safety like a battleflag.

We hurried over and pulled the stuff off her. It was hard to tell whether she was hurt or not; she looked the same as always.

"Are you okay?"

"Urban despair!"

"Is that the name of the show?" asked the carhop.

"Gimme that guitar! That must be my freebie!"

By the time we got rid of our entourage, called the U-Haul office, and repacked the van we were too exhausted to drive on to Uncle Ezra's house. We decided to stay overnight where we were and finish our pilgrimage in the morning.

"There's a motel right across the street," I said. "They've got a vacancy sign. Come on."

But it was not that simple. Prudence Patience puckered. "They look much too dear. See their sign? Color TV, swimming pool, sauna, banquet rooms. No, that's sinful waste.''

Near tears from strain, I offered to pay for everybody but it did no good. By now she was tight with my money, too. Nothing would do except the YWCA so off we went.

When we finally found it, she even haggled there until they agreed to create a triple room with a wheeled cart that looked as if it had seen service at the morgue. I had to sneak Quadrupet in concealed in my suitcase. I was afraid he would smother before we got upstairs so I had to punch holes in it. This was Polly's idea of saving money.

The Y was too poor to paint but not too proud to whitewash. I had to put on my sunglasses before I could flop down on one of their hard narrow beds and stare at the ceiling.

As I lay there thinking about dark cocktail lounges there was a knock at the door. It was so soft we barely heard it, but when it came again I recognized something that my father had taught me.

The Morse code for S.O.S.

CHAPTER FIVE

The knock came again. I threw a blanket over Quadrupet. "Gloria, you answer it," I said. *That'll fix 'em.*

She opened the door a crack. "Lancaster or York?" she demanded.

"I've got to see Polly Bradshaw right away!" hissed a voice on the other side. "I'm in trouble!"

Gloria and I exchanged a look of shock. In our separate ways we both preferred legends that linger to reputations that precede.

Polly stepped forward and clanged like the firebell in the night. "I'm Polly Bradshaw. How can I help?"

Gloria opened the door all the way. The woman on the threshold looked like a Lufthansa travel poster come to life: the original flaxen-haired zaftig mädchen, except that she was in her late thirties. As tall as Polly and about seventy pounds heavier, she was what grandmothers called "the picture of health" until you got to her eyes. Then she changed from zaftig mädchen to giant panda. I had never seen such a pair of shiners.

She scurried into the room and gazed at Polly as if she were a shrine.

"I saw you on the news when your uncle was harpooned and you said you were going to start a women's commune. I recognized you downstairs in the lobby when you checked in. Are you going to start the commune soon? Because I have no place to go and no money. I ran away from my husband yesterday and I've never had a job in my life because I was married at eighteen and I don't know what to do!"

She broke off and sobbed. Gloria reached into her money belt and took out her traveling drugstore.

"Up or down?"

"Never mind that," Polly said, giving her some coins. "Here. Run down the hall to the soft drink machine and get us some Cokes. Don't put anything in them, just Cokes."

Gloria trotted off and returned a few minutes later with four Cokes and a bulging money belt. She refunded Polly's change and handed the cans around with a grand gesture.

"This is on me. They've got lots of Kotex machines here," she said happily.

Polly turned to her new project. "Now," she began in her officious tone, "what's your name?"

"Agnes Mulligan, but I want to change it so that Boomer—that's my husband—won't be able to find me." Her swollen lids stretched open in painful awe. "He can find anything; he's a survivalist."

That did it. Polly's lips pursed for battle as she contemplated the worst enemy a Bradshaw ever had: the Social Darwinist. If the Boomer Mulligans of America ever got their way, there would be nobody left for her to help.

"He beat me with his divining rod," Agnes went on. "And when I told him I didn't want to spend our vacation in the bomb shelter he built, he shot arrows at me."

"A crossbow?" Gloria asked.

"No, the regular kind. But he's got a crossbow for mountain lions."

"Does it have—"

"Never mind the crossbow," Polly said impatiently. "Did you file an assault charge against him?"

"Oh, mercy, no! He would have killed me for sure."

"Do you have any children?"

"Not with me. Two boys at home. They're survivalists, too. They had their hearts set on vacationing in the bomb shelter. When I said I didn't want to, they zipped me up in a sleeping bag and left me like that for ten hours. I wet myself," she added abashedly.

"How did you get free?"

"The attack dogs accidentally rescued me. They got hysterical—they always get hysterical after a training lesson—and started ripping up everything they could find. They found my bag."

Her blue-black face screwed up for another round of tears. "We had an Irish wolfhound before, but he was too friendly so Boomer shot him."

"How could he hurt an animal?" I said indignantly. Polly gave me a dirty look.

"I would have left him a long time ago," Agnes went on, "but I didn't know how to do it without money. He never let me have a cent."

"He refused to give you a housekeeping allowance?" Polly asked.

"No, it wasn't that. He just went off money. All the survivalists in his group did. They put their wives on the barter system and made us trade with each other. Boomer said it was a good way to practice for *der Tag*—that's his name for when the lights go out and everybody takes to the hills."

"How did you manage to run away?"

"I stole his Raleigh coupons."

The two nonsmokers looked blank. Agnes explained: "They're premium coupons you get with Raleigh cigarettes. Like green stamps. Boomer and all the other survivalists switched to Raleighs so they could save the coupons and redeem them for a year's supply of freeze-dried disaster food for the bunker they're building. Boomer was in charge of the coupons. He kept them in our spare room. So yesterday when he and the boys were out shopping for an elephant gun, I packed up all the coupons and left. I drove all the way from Denver without stopping except to buy gas. I still have a Shell card he forgot to take away from me, and there was some money in the glove compartment that he kept for tolls."

"I don't understand what good the coupons are to you," Polly said. "Are you planning to sell the stuff you get for them?"

"Oh, no. You can redeem them for cash, too. They're worth three-quarters of a cent apiece."

"How many do you have?"

"Six suitcases."

She took us down the hall to her room and showed us her loot. There were Raleigh coupons everywhere. The six huge pieces of manly brown luggage she had also stolen from Boomer were overflowing with them, and so were her various tote bags and make-up kits.

"I haven't had a chance to count them yet," Agnes said.

"We'll help you," Polly volunteered. "It won't take long if we all count together. We've got plenty of cardboard boxes; we'll give you some to pack them in and have them ready for mailing tomorrow!"

"Do you have to lick them and put them in a book?" Gloria asked warily.

"No, just count them."

"All right, let's get to work," Polly said briskly.

"Let's eat first," I countered. "Agnes must be hungry, and we never did get around to tacos, remember?"

She agreed reluctantly. Agnes and I locked up our respective treasures—Raleigh coupons and Quadrupet—and the four of us went downstairs.

Naturally, Polly wanted to eat in the Y cafeteria. "Why go out when there's a perfectly good—"

"Because I need a drink!" I snapped.

"Wait a minute," said Gloria as we moved toward the exit, "there's a jakes in the lobby." She squished off on her green rubber feet and was back a few minutes later with another bulge in her moneybelt.

"Dinner's on me," she said grandly.

We found a steak house with a Happy Hour sign. As we walked in I girded myself for the usual stares but nobody gave us a second glance. We were in southern California now.

"Hi," said the hostess. "You from the Little Theater?" She herself was tattooed. She seated us at a big table in the middle of the room and handed around menus.

Gloria cased the joint quickly and rose. "I'm going to the jakes."

As she squished off, Agnes wrinkled her nose. "I wish she'd call it the little girls' room, don't you?'' she whispered.

"The *women's* room," Polly corrected.

Gloria returned triumphant and we ordered drinks. Since somebody else was buying, Polly ordered a Chivas Regal sour. Agnes chose one of those eggwhite-and-liqueur messes favored by nondrinkers, and I had a double bourbon on the rocks. Gloria had a pitcher of ice water.

Agnes took a sip of her drink and then stared down into its frothy pink depths. It was the "seeking answers" pose of the movie drunk but it didn't work with a Strawberry Cadillac Flip. Not even Ray Milland could have pulled it off.

"I've got to have a new identity before I redeem the Raleigh coupons," she said. "I don't dare send them in under my real name because Boomer knows I have them. I'm afraid he'd contact the Raleigh people and trace me through them." She chewed on her thumbnail and cast a furtive glance over her shoulder. "Do you think it would attract less attention if I packed them in lots of little boxes and mailed them gradually?''

"Agnes," Polly said supportively, "forget the Raleigh coupons for a minute. Now, let's look at your problem logically. One: you have disappeared. Two: you must *stay* disappeared. Three: to effect the above, you need a new name. Therefore, we must deal with three first."

While she was being logical I analyzed the situation along subjective lines. However many aliases Agnes used, her chances of disappearing successfully into anything except the chorus of *Die Walküre* were virtually nil. If she stayed underground long she would become graffiti's newest sensation. *Judge Crater, please call your office, your secretary has found Agnes. . . . Vacationing writer Ambrose Bierce locates runaway housewife. . . . Little Charley Ross laid Big Agnes Mulligan.*

Polly rapped the table authoritatively. "All right, what's Agnes's new name going to be? Everybody will make a suggestion and then we'll vote. Isabel?"

"Ex Parte Mulligan."

Agnes gave me a pensive frown that was hauntingly familiar. "That's nice," she said politely, "but I want to change my last name, too."

"Gloria? What do you think?" Polly asked.

"I balled a draft evader and he said that when you change your name you should stick to your ethnic group because little idiosyncrasies can give you away."

That didn't sit well with the Great Equalizer. She firmly believed that nobody would ever take either of us for a Wasp unless we told them.

"What are you, Agnes?" I asked.

"Welsh. My maiden name was Owen."

"How about Llanfairpwllgwngllgogferychywll?" Gloria suggested.

Another pensive frown. Then: "That's a little too long."

I choked and dribbled bourbon down my front. She was going to make a great feminist.

Polly glared at me. "How about Rhondda?" she said.

Geography was the only interesting subject she knew anything about, thanks to the Bradshaw penchant for international labor movements. Grandfather Lyman, I recalled now, had been thrown down a mine shaft in Wales.

"Double *d* in Welsh is pronounced *th,*" Gloria advised, "but most people don't know dat."

Now we both got a glare. As they weighed the merits of Davies and Morgan, I tried to think of Welsh idiosyncrasies that might give Agnes away. She wasn't going to crack coal or sing in a male chorus, and God knows she didn't lilt.

"Agnes," I said, "why don't you become Swedish?"

"Come to think of it, people have always asked me if I was Swedish," she replied in flattered tones. "Okay, let's pick out a Swedish name."

"The draft evader said you should keep the same initials because capital letters are the most automatic and individual marks of penmanship," Gloria said.

I snapped my fingers. "Astrid Mortensen!"

"I like that," said Polly. "All in favor say aye."

It was unanimous. "Good! It's anonymous." She turned to Agnes. "Well, Astrid, how do you feel?"

Silence fell like a pall as Agnes stared down into her frothy depths. "What?" she said with a start. "Oh. I'm fine, thanks." Her bruised eyes looked furtively around the restaurant. "Suppose some postal worker who smokes Raleighs recognizes the address on the packages and steals them? Just taking that many Raleigh coupons to the post office will attract attention, won't it? They're bound to know it's something valuable. How could I prove they were mine if they get stolen?''

"Insure them," I said.

"Then there'll be a record!''

"Jésu. . . .'' Gloria muttered.

"Agnes, listen," Polly said patiently. "You haven't done anything illegal—''

"If I send the coupons in under Astrid Mortensen, how will I cash the check when it comes? I don't have any I.D. for my new name.''

"Just bring it to me; I'll take care of it. Remember, we're sisters. I wouldn't *let* you go to a bank.''

While the reassurances piled up, Gloria opened her money belt and went to work piling dimes, building an elaborate replica of a medieval castle on the restaurant check. When she finished, she looked up at the astonished waitress and gave her a blurry smile.

"Vegas.''

We returned to the Y and gathered in Agnes's room for the Raleigh coupon count. It soon became obvious that we were in for a long dark night of the soul. Having never done anything remotely wrong in her entire conventional life, she had, in just forty-eight hours, left her husband, stolen his Raleigh coupons, and taken an alias. Awash in guilt, she had to do something right and proper to bring order into her now-disorderly life. This meant knowing *exactly* how many Raleigh coupons she had. The goodness, the purity of being absolutely honest with the Brown and Williamson Tobacco Company had become the touchstone of her sanity.

I started things off on the wrong foot by suggesting a shortcut. "Why don't I go down to the van and get my postage scale? We can figure out how many there are to the ounce and weigh them instead of counting them.''

"Oh, no! We can't do that!'' she cried. "You see,'' she explained, looking at me with desperate eyes, "when you tear the coupons off, sometimes a little paper from the pack sticks to them. That could make them weigh more!''

Nor would she count them fifty or a hundred at a time and then add up the grand total. Anything other than a running consecutive count was also a shortcut, and the very word conjured up unspeakable extra-legal abominations.

So the four of us sat there muttering "twenty-six thousand four hundred thirty-four . . . twenty-six thousand four hundred thirty-five . . ." until well past midnight.

When Polly, Gloria, and I finished our stacks and gave her the totals, her blackened eyes swam with doubt.

"Are you sure?" she whispered hoarsely.

"Positive," we chorused.

"It's not that I don't trust you," she began, talking through her well-gnawed thumbnail. "I'm grateful for your help, but . . . you see, I have to be sure! Sure in my own mind! I can't be at peace with myself unless I know! Please try to understand. I've got to live with myself, to look at myself every morning in the mirror." She screwed up her face and sobbed. "Don't hate me! It's just that I have to *know of my own knowledge!*"

"Jésu. . . ."

So Agnes counted our coupons all over again while we stacked the absolutely-positivelies in the cartons Polly brought up from the van. She, of course, was actually enjoying the countdown, waiting eagerly for the grand total so she could figure out how much X times ¾¢ amounted to. She had her string and masking tape at the ready, aching for the moment when she could start tying and labeling some new boxes.

Around four in the morning, Agnes announced that she had *exactly* 61,345 Raleigh coupons. Polly reached for her Magic Marker and the tying began. Gloria and I staggered forward to contribute our thumbs and then collapsed in the Y's dismal boudoir chairs.

The cartons were no sooner tied up than Agnes started to worry.

"Did I put a slip of paper containing my name and address in each one? You're supposed to do that when you mail packages, in case it rains on the return address and they can't read it. It's in the postal regulations manual."

"I saw you do it, Agnes," I mumbled. "You put a slip of paper in each box with your name and the address of Polly's new house."

"I can't remember doing it! I've got to be *sure!* I can't be at peace unless I'm absolutely sure!''

She reopened all the boxes. Sure enough, there was a slip of paper with all the necessary information in each one. When she had satisfied herself that they were *really* there, Polly retied the boxes and Gloria and I assisted. I had heard of people going to sleep on their feet but we went to sleep on our thumbs.

At last it was finished. Absolutely finished once and for all the final time. We all crashed in Agnes's room. Three hours later, I dreamed that a firm hand was shaking my shoulder and a chowdery voice was saying "Rise and shine.'' I woke up and there she was, fresh and alert and wearing a new denim pants suit. I rubbed the sticky out of my eyes and looked in the mirror. I looked like Mother Goddam. Gloria, who looked dead on normal occasions, now looked exhumed.

"Hurry,'' Polly said. "We have to get Agnes's boxes to the post office as soon as it opens.''

"Stamps cost the same all day long. Let me sleep.''

"You can't. We have a busy day ahead of us. I have to stop by the lawyer's office and get the keys to the house.''

We checked out and lugged the boxes downstairs. When we got out to the parking lot, the question arose of which vehicle to use. The van was too full and Agnes's Impala was too hot.

She wrung her hands and started to cry again. "That's Boomer's car! It's in his name, everything's in his name! He must have reported me missing by now. If we use his car and they catch us in it, they'll impound the Raleigh coupons!''

"I balled a car fence,'' said Gloria. "Switch the plates. Later on, we can paint the Impala a different color and I'll show you how to screw up the registration so you can sell it.''

"Oh mercy! That's illeg—''

"Do it,'' Gloria cut in. I looked at her with new respect.

Polly found her tool chest and handed out shining screwdrivers. We put the Colorado plates on the van and the Massachusetts ones on the Impala and climbed in.

Polly drove. I sat in the buddy seat with Quadrupet, and Gloria and Agnes wedged themselves into the back with the boxes. Agnes looked like a French aristocrat in a tumbril. In a few moments she would have to entrust her Raleigh coupons to strangers. Could she do it? Or would she have a convulsion in the post office?

When we finally found a parking place near the post office, Agnes emitted a piteous wail and clutched her head.

"Did I put Agnes Mulligan or Astrid Mortensen on the slips of paper inside? I can't remember! Oh, wait, I've got to be sure!"

"Agnes!" Gloria yelled. "Don't touch that string! You're going to mail those fucking boxes right now or else!"

Polly's mouth dropped open. Sisters weren't supposed to curse at each other. It worked, though. Agnes became a changed woman at once. Her husband had hollered at her so much it was all she knew. Putting on her sunglasses to hide her black eyes, she hefted a carton and walked into the post office. We followed with the rest and everybody got in line. Absolutely nothing wild 'n' woolly happened. Agnes spoke to the clerk in a cordial, businesslike manner. When he handed her the insurance receipt she tucked it into her wallet and put the wallet back in her purse without checking five times to see if she had *really* put it back.

When the clerk took the cartons to the back room, she did not go around to the alley and peer in the mailroom window to see if he was stealing them. She did not try to hide on a truck, or express a desire to go out to the airport and spy on the cargo loading.

It was, I thought nostalgically, the most normal example of human behavior I had seen for a long time.

Later that afternoon, we were bumping along a winding road with the sound of the sea in our ears. I was at the wheel of Agnes's car, following Polly and Gloria in the van. As we climbed the hill to Uncle Ezra's house, I figured Gloria must be saying "This castle hath a pleasant seat," so I said "Manderley" and Agnes said "Who?" to go with what undoubtedly was Polly's "What?"

It was the biggest house I had ever seen, with all sorts of Queen Anne-ish things dripping and hanging and thrusting all over it. Three full stories, plus an attic, veranda, turret, and widow's walk; the back porch hung out over the sea.

We all got out and said "Well, here we are" several times. Then a silence fell, which Gloria promptly filled.

"It looks like the house in *Psycho*."

CHAPTER SIX

Polly walked through the house inhaling the salty air and exclaiming "Isn't this wonderful?" until she got to the cellar. When she came back upstairs, one look at her ashen face told me that Quadrupet was going to have meaningful work at last.

We unloaded the van and got our room assignments. There were plenty of rooms to choose from and several had private baths, so it was a good start on the road to liberty, equality, and sisterhood. Now I wouldn't have to watch Gloria do her creepy hair-curling act or listen to Polly's mantra.

After we had unpacked, we gathered round the kitchen table for a planning session.

"Now," Polly began, then stopped. From the cellar came a swift, sure thud, followed by a piteous cry of "eek!" that broke off in mid-eek. Polly tried to hide her swallow with her turtleneck, but I saw her throat move. Agnes, ultrafeminine like most big women, gathered in imaginary skirts and looked around at the baseboards for holes. We were all terrified of rodents except Gloria, who liked life best when it included plague. She was smiling her blurry smile, undoubtedly imagining herself driving around in the van singing "Bring Out Your Dead."

"Now," Polly began again. "I want to call us the Don't Tread on Me Women's Commune. All in favor say aye."

It was unanimous. "Now," she went on, "I think we should be completely self-sufficient. I move that we grow our own vegetables and keep poultry. Let's have some discussion. The floor is open."

"Boomer made me put in a garden," said Agnes. "I can do that."

"Can I be the goose girl?" asked Gloria.

"Wonderful!" Polly effused. Things were working out along the selflessly cooperative lines that she cherished. I didn't volunteer for anything because we had already decided that I was to be the commune cook. Not that there was much choice in the matter: Polly considered it a point of honor to be a bad cook, Agnes had forgotten all she knew about cooking from living with males who wanted nothing but roots and berries, and Gloria had barely acquired the knack of eating.

"I wonder," Polly mused, "if we should get a pig?"

"Aye!" Gloria cried, her eyes blazing with ecstasy. Life on a medieval barony.

"What do you want with a pig?" I asked irritably.

"To save on garbage collection. Do you know what they charge to come all the way out here?"

Agnes, who had long since learned to accept any scheme involving rugged individualism, however outlandish, went along with the pig idea, so I was outvoted.

After the strategy session, Polly and I drove to the supermarket to stock up on provisions. Naturally we got into the running argument we always had when we shopped together: my "we must have butter" and her "margarine's good enough." She also bought sixty-watt light bulbs to replace the hundred-watters already in the house. I knew she would have us down to twenty-five watts before too long so I bought some of my own energy-crammed brand when she wasn't looking.

By the time we finished our first dinner at the house we were all so sleepy that we voted to go to bed. As we made the Himalayan trek to our rooms, I decided that the staircase was the kind Olivia de Havilland would mount once, and then never come down again. Giving my best dry cackle, I delivered the signature line from *The Heiress*.

"I can be very cruel. I was taught by masters."

Agnes screamed and shrank against the newel post.

"Stop saying silly things," Polly snapped.

My room was bigger than both Gioppi apartments put together. I was all set to enjoy the first privacy I had known since the wall collapsed when I heard a timid knock at the door. I opened it and found a quavering Agnes hugging her pillow and trailing blankets.

"I'm afraid to sleep by myself," she bleated. "I used to sleep with my sister before I was married, and then I slept with Boomer, so I've never been alone at night before and I'm scared. Would you let me sleep on your couch?"

I bent my head back and gazed up at her tear-stained face. Somewhere inside this 160-pound Juno was a fragile, petite girl who kept coming out. I was too tired to put up a fight so I waved her onto the couch. After spreading her blankets with great care and plumping her pillow for an interminable length of time—an unfailing sign of the insomniac—she crashed down on my couch.

"Do you mind leaving the light on?" she whimpered, as I was

about to turn it off. "It's not that I'm afraid of the dark, I just don't like it." I left it on.

"Talk to me," she pleaded. "My sister and I used to talk each other to sleep."

I suppose if I hadn't been an only child I would have known how to handle the situation, but I was used to entertaining myself in introverted ways. So help me, I didn't mean to do it; I was just casting around for a topic of conversation.

"Look," I said, gazing up at the paint patterns on the ceiling. "There's a man in an Australian bush hat with a big mustache."

"OH, GOD! OH, NO! HELP! HELP MEEEEEEE!"

Polly bounded in. "What's the matter?"

Agnes raised a shaking arm and pointed to the window and the widow's walk beyond. "He's there!"

"Don't move!" Polly ordered. "Stay where you are and pretend there's nothing wrong. Don't show fear! Repeat, *don't show fear!* They always hurt passive women more—that's victimology!"

"Polly—" I began.

"Shh!" She pretended to smile nonchalantly while she talked out of the side of her mouth. "Is he on the widow's walk?"

"There isn't—"

"The best way is to wait until they're about to do it, then pee on them. It's called the disgust factor. We had a lecture on it by a psychologist at the Self-Sufficiency Center during Anti-Rape Week. Crapping is even better. Do you have to go?"

"THERE ISN'T ANY MAN ON THE WIDOW'S WALK!" I yelled. "HE'S ON THE CEILING!"

They both regarded me with expressions of atavistic fear. I felt like the Thing in a Thing movie.

"The ceiling?"

"Yes! In the paint!"

"In the paint?"

"In the marks left by the brush. You can see pictures in them. Didn't you ever lie in bed when you were little and make pictures out of the paint sworls?"

"No," Polly said scornfully.

"I should have known better than to ask. Look, come here. See? He's between the Gainsborough lady and the Indian chief."

Smirking, she humored me with a theatrical display of twisting and bending as she gave the ceiling a mock inspection.

"I don't see a thing. It's all your imagination."

I collapsed in the direction of the bed, missed it, and rolled on the floor.

"What's so funny?" she asked suspiciously.

"It *is* my imagination!"

She frowned pensively. "That's what I said."

"Oh, Jesus!"

She turned and started for the door, then stopped and pursed her lips as she surveyed the ceiling. "But you're right about one thing," she said generously. "That ceiling does need repainting. I'll do it with a roller so you'll stop seeing things."

She looked at Agnes. "Are you all right now?"

"Yes. It's just that I thought she meant Boomer. He has one of those Australian hats. I thought he had come after me."

We finally got to sleep, but the next morning we had another crisis when Agnes found a pile of dead rats outside my door.

"Quadrupet put them there," I said craftily. "He loves me best, so he brings his kill to my room."

That's how I got rid of her. Between men on the ceiling and rats in the doorway, she developed an instant preference for sleeping alone.

After breakfast we drove into town to shop for seeds and the lumber Polly needed to build a pigsty and a chicken yard. She also arranged for a phone. I stood by the door of the pay booth and listened with grudging admiration to the wrangle. I had to hand it to her; like most people I was putty in the hands of a Ma Bell service representative.

"We have eight bedrooms, drawing room, parlor, dining room, cellar, attic, eat-in kitchen, walk-in pantry, wrap-around veranda, three-car garage, and a detached workshop. Yes, that's what I said: *one* desk phone. What? Don't worry, a little walking never hurt anybody. One, repeat *one,* desk phone. How much is the push-button? Never mind, I'll take a circular dial. One *black* desk phone with a circular dial. How much is the extra extension cord? *What?* I can do without it. I'm neither sugar nor salt, I won't melt. Chimes? Nope. A plain ring'll do."

She hung up and emerged from the booth. "They must be ready for nationalization after that," I said.

"It's coming," she said solemnly. "It has to."

Next we went to the public library, where I took out a card so Polly could check out the books she needed, gripping sagas like *How to Build Your Own Chicken Coop* and *Pigs for Profit*. When she had made her selection, I mentioned that *The Egg and I* contained much useful information. I found a copy and handed it to her. She read the jacket flaps and the extracted quotes on the back with a critical air, then looked at me with all systems pursed.

"All right, but I don't want to read the whole book. Can you go through it and mark the serious parts for me?"

The next few days were a nightmare of leveling and beveling as the greatest carpenter since you-know-Who fashioned henhouse, pigsty, and trough. I did a little work on my latest Regency, *Rake of Hearts,* but it was impossible to concentrate while the Liberated Kid was slinging nails. Finally I gave up and went for a walk along the beach.

The solitude was a welcome change from gathering new experiences. I felt as if I had embarked on some mad literary dig without a protective pith helmet. Life with Polly had yielded nothing to write about that feminists would like, though Groucho Marx might. I had a sudden urge to take Quadrupet and flee from California and Don't Tread on Me.

When I returned to the house the livestock had arrived. The pig was black and white with pink showing through, and smaller than I had expected. He looked frightened in his new, sparkling clean surroundings. Would Polly insist on scrubbing the pigpen? Yes, she would. I gave him a sympathetic pat.

"Him is mommy's perfect poo-poo, yes him is! Oh, I see him eyes crinkling. Him smile-smiles, yes him does."

"Isabel—" Polly began.

"Farnsworth!" I exclaimed, the name coming to me out of the blue. "That's what we'll call him! Him is Farnsworth, that him new name-names." He nuzzled my muddy sneaker.

Polly rolled her eyes. "You don't name pigs. Honestly, Isabel, sometimes I think you like animals better than people."

"I do. 'The more I see of Mankind, the more I prefer my dog.' "

Pensive frown. "I don't see what dogs have to do with it."

"That's a quotation from Blaise Pascal."

"Never heard of him. Will you stop hugging that pig?"

"Does him want him own song-songs like Quadrupet? All right, mommy write song-songs for him." I thought a moment, then sang to the tune of Cornell's alma mater: "Hail to thee, O noble Farnsworth, lying in the swill. Though about him flies do gather, mommy loves him still!"

"Isabel, he is not, repeat not, a pet. He's our garbage disposal."

"He's a human being and he has a right to be treated like one." She stalked off, shaking her head. My urge to flee faded in the sunshine of Farnsworth's beady-eyed smile.

At our next meeting, Polly said Agnes needed "retraining to enter the marketplace," so I volunteered to teach her stenotype.

"I think that's *fine*," Polly said stoutly, regarding me with missionary pride. I knew she thought I was turning into a feminist so I let her think it, but my motives were purely selfish.

I was having a writing block. I couldn't bear the thought of doing another Regency, so I figured that if I lent Agnes the stenotype machine I would have a perfect excuse to stop. To clear my conscience still further, I lent Polly my typewriter. With Agnes struggling through beginning fingering and muttering "HR-L," and Polly hammering out incoherent manifestos about rape, I was free.

It was pure blessedness not having to think about men with lowering brows and girls named Edwina. Sheer joy not to have to type "taking the waters" and "ruined himself at the tables." No more walking sticks and reticules, no more coaches in ditches and countesses in sedan chairs. I wondered how I had stood it as long as I had. There was no torture greater than writing the kind of book you don't enjoy reading. Life on a feminist commune was infinitely preferable.

After shoveling up the night's catch of dead rats, I went out to sing to Farnsworth and give him his slop. Next, I took Agnes through her daily stenotype lesson, then retired to my kitchen to try to figure out how to make a cream sauce out of powdered skim milk and "spread," which Polly, in her Prudence Pennypincher lust, had substituted for margarine shortly after she substituted margarine for butter.

I did the best I could with the menus, but everything tasted like what diet books call "zesty." Nobody minded but me. Gloria neither knew nor cared what she ate, and Agnes's experience with bomb-shelter fare had destroyed her palate. As for Polly, she thought good food, like good writing, was counter-revolutionary.

CHAPTER SEVEN

Having vowed to fill the house with women, Polly called another planning session to take a vote on her latest idea.

"The women who need the most help are those age fifty or over," she began. "Unskilled displaced homemakers whose husbands have deserted them. We're all young, so I think our next resident should be someone older. All in favor say aye."

Once again it was unanimous, though not for the selfless reasons Polly supposed. I said aye because I was used to old ladies. Agnes said it because she was too timid to disagree with Polly. As for Gloria, she simply enjoyed saying archaic words.

"Do you have somebody in mind?" I asked.

"Not yet, but I've contacted some Movement women in L.A. and they're going to find someone for us."

A few days later, she announced that a candidate for Don't Tread on Me had been found by none other than the famous feminist lawyer, Samantha Banner, president of Regiment of Women.

ROW was to the left of NOW, and Samantha was so radical that she even objected to "Ms."—she wanted to abolish all honorifics and call everybody "Person," abbreviated "Pn." She had recently filed a lawsuit to force the United States to break off diplomatic relations with all countries having a gender language, and had been arrested in Washington for throwing blood on the embassies of France, Italy, and Spain.

"The woman's name is Martha Bailey," Polly said. "She's one of Samantha's clients. I've invited Samantha to dinner tomorrow night to fill us in on her story."

I spent the next day cooking for Pn. Banner. As six o'clock approached, I put my stroganoff in the warming oven and set up my cocktail bar. When everything was ready we all sat down and waited for our renowned guest. Everyone looked very nice, even Gloria: in honor of the occasion she had refrained from curling her hair.

Soon we heard a car coming up the drive. Polly rose to go outside and do the honors. As she passed my chair, she leaned down and whispered a warning.

"Don't start any sentence with 'what this country needs is. . . .' "

We all peered out the window for our first look at Samantha Banner in the flesh. To my surprise, she looked more like a suburban real estate saleswoman than a blood-throwing radical feminist. Tall, sinewy, and fortyish, she had a gamine haircut and a deep bronze California tan. Instead of the usual pants-and-poncho Lib uniform she wore a skirt and blazer and stacked heels.

"Jésu!" Gloria exclaimed. "She-wolf of France!"

"What's the matter?" I asked.

She answered through clenched teeth. "School spirit!"

Never had those gregarious words been infused with so much venom. Never had Gloria displayed so much emotion either. Gone were the blurry smile and glassy eyes; she was seething. She greeted Samantha stonily and glowered with barely suppressed hatred throughout dinner.

I soon saw her point. Samantha must have been one of those grimly well-rounded coeds who have so many extracurricular activities that they throw off the yearbook layout. The kind who "go out" for everything under the sun, belong to an all-girl honor society with a name like "Valkyries," and use their elbows in basketball games. They served on the girls' honor council and gave unstintingly of themselves, but they were entirely capable of throwing you down and sitting on your face if you crossed them.

After dinner, Samantha opened her attache case and took out a trial transcript.

"This will show you what poor Martha Bailey has been through," she said.

She was the type who handed out literature in living rooms and then sat back and waited for everybody to read it. Gloria folded her arms resolutely and continued to glower, so Polly, Agnes, and I did the honors.

The transcript said:

IN THE COUNTY OF LOS ANGELES

IN THE STATE OF CALIFORNIA

} ss.

Ms. Martha Bailey and "Regiment of Women, Inc."
(a.k.a. "ROW")

Plaintiffs;

vs.

"Inflatable You" Lifesize Rubber Dolls, Inc.

Defendant.

For the Plaintiffs: MS. SAMANTHA BANNER

For the Defendant: MR. MACK LEE SLICK

MS. BANNER: Your Honor, the Plaintiffs contend that the product known as the Inflatable You Lifesize Rubber Doll, contrary to the manufacturer's claim that it is merely a party novelty, is intended solely for sexual use and furthermore, that it is degrading to women. We therefore ask that an injunction against its manufacture and sale be granted.

MS. MARTHA BAILEY, having first been duly sworn, testified as follows:

Q (by Ms. Banner): Ms. Bailey, are you the wife of Ronald Bailey?

A: I was for thirty years but he divorced me last year. He said I wasn't viable. I don't know what he meant by that. I've always washed carefully.

THE COURT: This is not a divorce hearing. Just answer the question.

Q: Ms. Bailey, please tell the court what happened on Saturday, July 27, 1971.

A: I was worried about Mr. Bailey living alone, so I made a batch of homemade scrapple and took it over to his apartment. He always liked my scrapple. I knocked several times but there was no answer, so I tried the door and it opened. I went in. And then I saw him. (Witness paused) On the bed.

Q: What was he doing?

A: He was having things to do with the rubber woman.

Q: Do you mean he was simulating sexual intercourse with the Inflatable You doll?

A: Yes.

Q: What did you do?

A: I got scared and threw the scrapple at them.

Q: What happened then?

A: The rubber woman blew up.

Q: What did your husband do?

A: He yelled for help. He was in pain. The rubber woman was wrapped around his private parts.

Q: Did you offer him assistance?

A: Yes.

Q: What did you do?

A: I pulled on it.

THE COURT: Order in the court.

Q: Were you able to get it off?

THE COURT: Order. Order. Order.

A: No.

Q: What happened then?

A: He had a heart attack.

Q: Ms. Bailey, I show you the remains of the rubber doll that was removed from your husband at the morgue. Is this what you saw on him?

A: Yes.

MS. BANNER: Your Honor, I request that this be marked and entered as Plaintiffs' Exhibit 1.

(The Exhibit, being a torn and shredded piece of flesh-colored latex and bearing two sections of what appeared to be hair or hair substitute on the head and pubic regions, and containing a facsimile of facial features as well as a partially dislodged mouthpiece and ripped air valve in the lumbar region, was marked and entered as Plaintiffs' Exhibit 1.)

Q: (by Ms. Banner): Ms. Bailey, I show you an advertisement from the magazine *Hung*, describing the item known as the Inflatable You Lifesize Rubber Doll, and ask you to read it into the record.

A: I can't, it's too dirty.

THE COURT: The Clerk will read it.

THE CLERK: Are you lonely? Do you want a girl who will obey your every wish and command? Then get acquainted with Dalilah, who never says no. Dalilah is five-feet-two inches tall and measures 44-23-35 from the top down, and Dalilah's top is always down.

THE COURT: Order in the court. If the spectators can't be serious they can leave. Bailiff, clear the courtroom.

(Whereupon, the courtroom was cleared)

THE COURT: The Clerk will continue the reading.

THE CLERK: Dalilah has real, authentic, lifelike features exact in every detail to a real live girl. Nothing is missing, and we mean nothing.

THE COURT: Bailiff, pull yourself together or get out. I'm warning you, Bailiff. All right, get out. We'll recess for fifteen minutes while I find a new bailiff.

(Whereupon, a fifteen-minute recess was called)

RESUMED

THE COURT: All right, Mr. Clerk, let's hear the rest of it.

THE CLERK: Dalilah loves to be dominated and will roll over at the snap of your fingers to try something new and different. She can take anything you can give, and best of all, she never stops smiling. Order her today. California residents please add five percent—

THE COURT: All right, never mind the rest.

MS. BANNER: We request that the ad be marked and entered, Your Honor.

(The Exhibit, being a piece of paper of the type known as pulp, bearing a black-and-white representation of said product and also reproduced photographs of said product lying on a bed beside a human male clad in a towel, and containing a perforated coupon, was marked and entered as Plaintiffs' Exhibit 2.)

MS. BANNER: Your Honor, I have here a new doll exactly like the one owned and used by Ms. Bailey's late husband. I ask the Court's permission to inflate it.

THE COURT: What is your purpose?

MS. BANNER: I would like to enter it, Your Honor.

THE COURT: Mr. Clerk, I will not tolerate levity from officials of this court. You are in contempt. Get out. I said get out. Bailiff, help him up and get him out of here.

(Whereupon the Clerk and the Bailiff left the courtroom)

THE COURT: There is no need to blow it up, Ms. Banner, I grasp the principle. I'm going to dismiss this case. Leave this courtroom, Ms. Banner, and take that latex love goddess with you. Case dismissed.

(Whereupon, the Court was adjourned)

"So you see," said Samantha, when we had finished reading, "we met with mockery. I've filed an appeal but it will take a very long time. Meanwhile, Martha Bailey is terribly upset and very short of funds. Her husband named the doll, Dalilah, in his will, and now several real women named Dalilah have popped up to claim they knew him. Lies, of course, but it'll take forever to unsnarl."

"Martha Bailey needs all the supportiveness we can give her," said Polly, looking around at the rest of us. We nodded solemnly.

"Good," Samantha said briskly. "I'll bring her over tomorrow." With that, she picked up her transcript and left.

There was nothing to do but clear the table. Gloria, who had drawn K.P. duty on that week's Responsibility Schedule, got up and helped me, muttering imprecations as we made the long trek to the kitchen.

"Homecoming . . . student council . . . dormitory board . . . class picnic . . . we want to help you come out of your shell . . . I'd love to get my hands on your hair . . . rah-rah, siss-boom-bah, *shit, fuck, damn!*"

"Gloria," I said when she had finished, "where are you from? You never told us."

"Iowa," she sighed. "I went to Iowa State." She snatched a dish-towel from the rack. "Those well-adjusted campus-leader types were always making fun of me. I hate well-adjusted people! That's why I decided to stick around with you and Polly. I could tell you were okay."

"I see."

The next morning Samantha delivered Martha Bailey. Stout and frumpish, with blue-rinsed hair crimped into fingerwaves, her self-effacement was almost tangible. When she said "How do?" in a mountain twang I asked her if she was from Virginia. She wasn't, but I was close; she named a region of east Tennessee famous for whiskey stills and sudden death.

She relaxed a little after Samantha left, but when she found out I was a writer she gave me a look of dread and launched into a disjointed warning.

"I don't see how you can stand it. Your nerves, I mean. All that mental work would make me nervous. Don't it make you nervous? I have to do somethin' with my hands. It gentles me, don't you know? Seems to me like writin' would be mighty bad on the nerves. It's best to keep busy. It don't do to think too hard. Keep the mind free and the hands busy, I always say.''

It was the gospel according to True Southern Womanhood that I had heard all my life. When she went upstairs to her room, I took Polly aside for a private word.

"She's having the change.''

"The *menopause,*" she corrected.

"But don't you see what she's doing? She's afraid of having a nervous breakdown, so she pinned the rose on me.''

Pensive frown. "What rose?''

"I'm talking about projection, Polly,'' I sighed.

"Never heard of it. The menopause,'' she said authoritatively, "is a natural phase in woman's cycle of growth. We need to throw off these annotated fears and think of it as a new and exciting adventure. If Martha is afraid of the menopause it's because she's been culturally conditioned to fear it. It's not her fault.''

"I didn't say it was.''

"No, but you tend to see everything in terms of the *individual.*'' Her nose quivered on certain words and that was one of them. "You have to look for the root societal cause.''

Martha's warning about the dangers of writing sounded so much like Granny that I took it as a challenge to go back to work. This time I decided to try my hand at a gothic in hopes that Uncle Ezra's windswept house would inspire me.

Starting a new genre is bound to be slow going. I did more thinking than writing. Whenever my typewriter fell silent for any length of time, I would hear a little scuffle and look up to see Martha's worried bifocaled eyes peering at me from the doorway. She always asked the same question.

"You aw-right, honey?''

It was a bed check; she was coming to see if I had committed suicide. Now I changed from a blocked writer to the Thompson gun of literature, writing anything I could think of as fast as I could type it just to keep Martha away from me.

Sir Giles hid the missing Will in Farmer Tankard's well as Lady Henrietta was returning from a mysterious visit to the vicarage when lightning struck her landaulet as Mrs. Braithewaite, the evil housekeeper, watched from the tower with a menacing laugh which sent a chill up my spine while Hawkins lit the tapers that made the dog howl and scurry under the settee where he ate the crumpled letter dropped by the gamekeeper before I could read it.

This is another version of writer's block called "putting words on paper." My fingers were numb and tingling and I felt strangely hot, but when I opened the window, I found Martha on the widow's walk. Naturally I jumped out of my skin, which was just the reaction she was looking for.

"I heard you goin' lickety-split just now," she said worriedly. "You know, honey, it don't do to hurry. It can get you all worked up. I knew somebody back home who was always hurryin' and she just up and went to pieces one day." Her voice dropped to a dramatic whisper. "They had to put her away."

She gave me a solicitous pat and left. I sank down at my desk and put my head in my hands. Now I was damned if I typed and damned if I didn't.

A few days later, Polly got a call from Samantha.

"I've just had an idea," she said. "Those Stop ERA women bake bread for their state legislators. I want to beat them at their own game and appeal to ours through their stomachs, too. Martha's pièce de résistance is scrapple. If she would bake a small scrapple loaf for each member of the legislature, I could hit them with my anti-porn petition, which would help Martha win her rubber doll case. ROW will pay for the scrapple ingredients and we'll use your van to deliver the gifts to Sacramento. What do you say?"

"Beautiful!" said Polly.

The scrapple campaign began with the usual feminist pow-wow about what to call it.

"Loafs for Legislators!" Polly suggested brightly.

"Loaves," I corrected with a sigh. "As in fishes."

After settling on the name, our next task was driving miles out in the country to a farm where we bought ears, snouts, hocks, lungs, sow belly, and other cheap porcine parts. These would be boiled together with livers, kidneys, brains, and a ham bone until they reached the consistency of an acid-bath murder victim, then ground up and mixed with cornmeal and formed into loaves.

The trip upset me because of Farnsworth. That night I had a terrible dream in which Polly, to save money, slaughtered him and served him to me in a pudding, and I, like Queen Tamora in *Titus Andronicus,* ate it without knowing it was my child. I woke up moaning "O detestable maw. . . ."

Scrapple Day arrived and we all gathered in the kitchen. Martha, explaining that men got mad if they found hair in their food, issued each of us a thick black triangular hairnet and showed us how to tie them on. The style emphasized Polly's chiseled facial bones and made her look like the Hollywood version of a young nun. Agnes simply looked like Agnes in a hairnet, and Gloria actually looked better. I looked like the torpedo in *The Enemy Below.*

The production began, and with it Polly's hoof-in-mouth disease.

"Tell us what you want us to do, Martha," she said timidly. "You're in charge here."

Her attempt at flattery came through loud and thick. Instant dominance was too much for Martha. Thus far she had been relaxed and ready to have some girlish fun, but now she grew red and flustered under the staggering blow of Polly's tact.

She reached nervously for her apron, a frilly affair with a bib, and put it on over the tank top and jeans she had been wearing since falling into ROW's hands. The contrast had all the melancholy of Emily Dickinson's certain slant of light. I glanced at Polly to see if she had noticed it, but she was standing nobly at parade rest awaiting orders.

"You three can chop," Martha said, handing cleavers to Polly, Agnes, and Gloria. Naturally she would not let me near such a dangerous tool. I was given the elevating task of denuding snouts of stray hairs.

When the meat was chopped and ready, the boiling began. We used Martha's preserving kettle, which she had brought with her when she moved in with us, and the biggest pots and pans in the house. Soon there was no more room on the stove, so we hunted up some old hotplates. A small state with a unicameral legislature would have been hard enough to seduce, but we were cooking for California.

The whole house reeked of swine, and as the official stirrer—I had been issued a harmless wooden spoon—I got the worst of it. Martha's scrapple was delicious in finished form but in the deliquescing stage it was unbearable. Worse than the smell was the way it looked. Every time I gave it a stir I brought up something that reminded me of Farnsworth: his little cloven hooves, his retroussé snout, his fatty but loving heart.

When the first batch was melted, I gave it to the other three helpers, who cut out the gristle and gave it to Martha.

"Now comes the hard part," she said proudly. "You have to push it through a sieve. You girls watch and I'll show you how to do it."

That's when Polly opened her big mouth.

"You don't have to go to all that trouble," she said airily. "There's no point in doing it the old-fashioned way when we have two blenders and a food mill."

Martha's face crumpled. She wept soundlessly at first, her tears indistinguishable from the sweat drops on her cheeks. Then she gave a loud choking sob and ran from the kitchen. It was an old lady's run, indescribably heartbreaking.

"What did I say?" asked Polly, dumbfounded.

"Oh, nothing," I hissed. "You merely made light of the only ability she has."

Martha ran, shrieking, from room to room. We all ran after her, with Polly babbling as only Polly could.

"I'll drive you to the Crisis Center. You'll feel better there, everybody's upset at the Crisis Center. You can have a dialogue with somebody who's in same-stage restructuring. They have a new group called the Feisty Fifties for displaced homemakers. You can get everything out of your system in an atmosphere of sharing. They've just instituted a lecture series on aspects of transitional—"

"SHUT UP!" Gloria bellowed.

Agnes jumped and said, "Oh, mercy!" Polly shut up. Ignoring us, Gloria pressed Martha into a chair, sat down in her lap and huddled against her, crooning wordlessly. It was hard to tell who was comforting whom, but it worked; Martha quieted. After a while, Gloria pulled her teeshirt out of her valance line and dried Martha's tears with the hem, then helped her upstairs to her room.

She returned a few moments later. "I gave her a Valium," she said. "It'll knock her out."

"Gloria," Polly said reproachfully, "unprescribed drugs are very dangerous. Martha needs professional hel—"

"EEEEEEOOOOOOWWWWWWWWWWWWWWWWWW!"

It was the most bloodcurdling ululation I had ever heard, in or out of movies. Rolling her eyes back until nothing showed but the whites, Gloria squatted on the floor in front of Polly, stuck her thumbs in her ears, and waggled her fingers.

"Sanity, sanity, all is sanity! Fuck professional help! Fuck centers! Fuck clinics!"

Before Polly could reply, we heard a loud sizzle from the kitchen.

"Oh, mercy!" Agnes cried. "The scrapple!"

We ran to the rescue but it was too late. The pots were boiling over and giving off a malodorous stench. I peered into the big preserving kettle and recoiled. An ear was floating on the surface and swelling up with rhythmic whooshes. By now I had heard Gloria sing so many ballads about plague boils that I automatically grabbed a knife and lanced it. It blew up with a deafening bang, bringing forth screams of fright and sending us all racing for cover. Polly and I collided and I lost my balance and fell back against the kidney kettle, knocking the lid off. As the reek of steaming urine filled the room, Agnes gave a mighty gag and threw up in the sink.

"What are we going to do?" I wailed. "We can't manage without Martha."

"All we have to do is follow the recipe," Polly said officiously.

"There isn't any recipe," I said acidly. "Martha cooks without them. It's one of those old-fashioned talents that gives her what little self-confidence she has."

I grabbed a wooden paddle and pulled it through the thickening mixture. "We've got to do something before this shit turns to soap!"

I said it in a spirit of hysterical masochism, knowing that it would be just like Polly to pick this moment to point out that soap requires ashes. If she did, I planned to hit her with the paddle, providing I could get it out of the pot.

"Cornmeal!" she said brightly. "I remember now! She said you're supposed to mix the meat with cornmeal."

Before anyone could stop her, she grabbed a huge sack of cornmeal and dumped its contents into the pots. Now the pig mixture began to swell and heave and give off a silvery scum like snail droppings. We panicked and added water to cool it down, but we added too much, so we had to pour in some more cornmeal to thicken it. When it threatened to harden into cement, we added more water, promptly causing what Polly called "a lack of consistency," a situation we corrected by adding more cornmeal.

We ended up with something that would have turned even a politician's stomach. Everybody collapsed at the kitchen table and tried to figure out what to do.

"Now I know what the Bible means by a mess of pottage." Agnes sighed.

"It's inedible," I said. "It looks like an oil slick with lumps. We'll have to throw it out."

Polly's eyes nearly popped out of her head. "We can't! We'd be out of pocket! We'd have to pay ROW back if we threw it away, so we'll have to find a use for it." She pursed her lips. "Waste not, want not."

"The Lord giveth and the Lord taketh away. Tell him to come and get it." I put my head down on the table and burped.

"It's perfectly good food with lots of nutritious ingredients," she argued. "Somebody would be thankful for it."

"We could donate it to that church we saw in town," Agnes suggested. "You know—the one without a steeple?"

"That's a synagogue."

"Oh. . . ." She thought a moment, then brightened. "I know! We can give it to Farnsworth!"

"He wouldn't eat himself!" I cried, horrified.

We argued over the old adage that pigs will eat anything but none of us knew the answer. Punch-drunk from strain and fatigue, Gloria and I got knottily philosophical, with me defending Farnsworth's ethics like an early church father clinging to a point of doctrine while she played the devil's advocate, trying to destroy me via the Socratic method.

It was too much for Polly. "Never mind that stuff! *I* know what we can do. We'll donate it to the battered-wife shelter in Ventura. That way," she said happily, "ROW will still be willing to foot the bill and we won't have to reimburse them."

"Okay," I sighed, too tired to argue with her. "Internal injuries are internal injuries."

"You can tell them it's blood pudding," Gloria said dryly.

Having decided how to get rid of it, we promptly got into another argument about how to transport it.

"We can't take it in the pots; we won't have anything left to cook in," I said. "We'll have to put it all in one big container."

"We don't have anything that big," Polly countered.

"Yes, we do. The birth bucket."

"No!" she cried, the tigress protecting her young.

"We don't have any choice."

She finally relented and we committed the sacrilege. I held my breath as the porcine glue hit the bottom of the bucket with a splat. Agnes elected to stay behind in case Gloria needed help with Martha, so Polly and I lugged the necrotic donation out to the van and shoved it in.

"One of us will have to sit in back and steady it so it won't tip over," Polly said.

I was too tired either to drive or prop up the birth bucket, but at least the latter offered solitude. Before she could say anything further, I crawled into the stygian gloom of the cargo section and put my arms around our vat of witches' brew.

The battered-wife shelter was on top of a steep hill in an old clapboard house in the center of town. Polly, who knew the keeper, bounced in and announced in cheery tones, "We have a special treat for you!" Then she returned to help move the birth bucket inside.

It was like trying to move the Rock of Behistun. The situation demanded what worried generals call "upper body strength," but we didn't have any after stirring porcine concrete for hours. Moreover, despite my efforts to hold it steady during the drive, some of the contents had slopped over and formed a greasy residue on the handles, so does it come as any surprise that we dropped it?

If only it had broken . . . but it didn't. Instead, as we watched in horror, it tipped over on its side and started rolling down the hill.

"Catch it!" Polly yelled, and off we went behind it.

A rolling birth bucket gathers no moss. People saw it coming and jumped clear, giving it a perfect unobstructed path. It looked like a

giant bowling ball spinning down Hell's own alley, spewing glistening bones and lumpy slime from its toilet-like mouth and leaving a
trail of pig muck the length of the sidewalk.

Have you ever tried to run in melted scrapple? Slipping and sliding
we went, a pair of Sisyphuses in reverse with some Tantalus thrown in
for good measure, our slimy prize going in the wrong direction and
forever out of reach.

We arrived, breathless and screaming, at the bottom of the hill just
as the birth bucket glanced off a fire hydrant and smashed to bits
against a car. We ducked and covered our heads; when we dared look
up again we saw that the car had a blue light on its roof. It didn't have
much else; the aerial was snapped off, the windshield was shattered,
and the hood looked like a cafeteria steam table.

The cops rose from their hunched positions, surveyed the muck-
filled dents in their hood, then looked out the window at us. We were
both dressed in our oldest work clothes; I in ragged jeans and sweatshirt and Polly in the latest thing in feminist uniforms: railroad engi-
neer's striped overalls with a big ERA button on the bib.

The cops got out and walked toward us in that slow, ponderous gait
of cops getting ready to be cops. One of them reached for his notebook
and spoke.

"Well, girls, what've we got here?"

"*Women!*" Polly barked. I closed my eyes.

He pushed back his cap and chewed on the side of his lip, his glance
flickering over her button.

"Uh-huh," he said. He must have had the best *uh-huh* in the law
enforcement business; there was nothing on television to match it.
Looking down at his shoe, he studied the glob of grease on his toe as
though it were a priceless objet d'art and he a collector who never
hurried.

At last he bent down and picked up a gleaming white object. "What
kinda bone is this?" he demanded.

"I refuse to answer!"

"It's a ham bone," I said placatingly.

She snapped her head around to me. "Don't weaken!"

Next he picked up something that looked like a transparent rubber
handkerchief. It was the ear.

"What kinda skin is this?"

Suddenly I remembered from my detective story reading that human flesh looks almost exactly like fresh pork.

"It's a pig's ear," I said helpfully. "We were making scrapple and—"

"We refuse to answer any questions until you read us our Miranda!"

"Miranda, huh?" said the cop, smiling an enigmatic smile. "*Ho*-kay. If the *women* want their Miranda, they'll get their Miranda. One for each." He reached into his pocket and handed us plastic cards.

"That's very nice," I said hurriedly, handing mine back.

"Wait," said Polly. "You have to *read* it to us."

I tried to jab her in the ribs but all I did was hurt my elbow. She had gone stiff with righteous wrath. The cop cleared his throat theatrically and rattled off the caution from memory, then signaled his partner.

"We gotta have this *alleged* pork substance analyzed by the lab. If you *women* will be good enough to accompany us to headquarters—"

"COSSACK!"

"That does it! In the car, *women!*"

"The effin' car won't start," said the driver. "They must've busted somethin' with that depth charge."

"No problem," the first cop said airily. "It's such a lovely day, we'll walk. That'll give us the pleasure of escorting two lovely *women*. Right this way, *women*."

We walked two blocks to the police station, Polly in front with her cop and I behind with mine. It looked like a double date; both of them were swinging plastic sample bags full of scrapple as if we were on our way to a picnic, except that Polly was singing "We Shall Overcome."

When we reached the station house, she suddenly collapsed. Innocent that I was in the techniques of protest, I thought she had fainted until she started yelling at me.

"GO LIMP! GO LIMP!"

When the cops picked her up she was so limp that her arms and legs dangled from their shoulders like sleeping pythons. Ignored by all, I held my head high and walked unaided into the station house.

We were released an hour later after an obviously mock laboratory analysis of our scrapple.

"Fascists!" Polly ground out, as we left the building. "I'll sue them for false arrest!"

"It was your fault."

"*My* fault! You didn't say a word! I did all the talking! *I* was the one who defended our rights!"

"Is that the way you see it? Do you actually think that's what happened?"

"Think? I don't think, I *know!*"

"Your mouth ought to be bronzed!" I exploded. "Then we could put it up on a shelf and everybody could look at it and say, 'There was a mouth! Shall we ever see another?' This whole *day* happened because of your mouth! It started when you delivered the coup de grace to Martha!"

She frowned pensively. "The what?"

"Oh, *God!*"

We maintained a stony silence on the drive back. When we got home, I fed Farnsworth, took a shower, and went to bed with Quadrupet snuggled under my chin.

To my astonishment, a contrite Polly brought me a cup of coffee the next morning.

"Would you like a natural egg?" she asked nervously.

"No. Leave me alone."

It went on like that for several more days. I had never known her to be so anxious to make amends. Until now, her guilt had manifested itself along grandiose liberal lines like worrying about entire countries, but now she was dumping ashes on her head in honor of one, single, solitary individual whom she actually knew.

She even went so far as to *buy* a paperback called *How to Develop a Sense of Humor,* with worksheets in the back. She saw nothing remotely funny about that—to Polly it was evidence of a serious program of study—but she chuckled mightily over the author's examples of his own wit, such as: "When my son said his English class was reading *David Copperfield,* I said, 'what the dickens!' and we all had a good laugh."

When I told her that the son probably went around in a perpetual cringe saying, "Jeez, Dad, cut it out, will you?" she glared at me and told me I was an elitist.

We were back to normal.

CHAPTER EIGHT

By some mysterious therapeutic method known only to her, Gloria put Martha back together again.

Everybody had a different theory about it. Polly said it was inborn sisterhood, which she believed was spontaneous, like combustion. Sentimental Agnes decided that Martha must have had a daughter who died, and now Gloria had taken her place and given her someone to live for.

I felt that Gloria's Middle English drivelations, which drove everybody else crazy, had driven Martha sane. Hailing from the linguistically frozen Smoky Mountains, where people still used words like "gainsay," meeting a girl of twenty-three who called epilepsy the "fallyng sickness" had put her menopause in perspective and made age relative.

"I don't see what that has to do with anything," said Polly after I had finished theorizing.

"Oh, never mind," I sighed.

L'affaire scrapple was a turning point for the Don't Tread on Me Women's Commune. We entered one of those curious limbos of pleasant dullness that men have in mind when they say, "All I want is a little peace and quiet." Agnes and Martha did each other's hair, Gloria spent her time constructing a dulcimer, and I practiced my specialty, doing crossword puzzles in ink.

Polly, of course, kept stoking the flame, but nothing penetrated our complacency. She tried to turn dinner into a consciousness-raising session, but when she said, "The vagina is a hated Other," Martha doused it with, "I don't think we should talk about our private parts at the table."

After-dinner discussions on "Wholeness in the Restructured Workplace" sank in a sea of pink-collar hysteria when Agnes swallowed a bobby pin. The air was pungent with permanent-waving lotion and despairing cries of "I can't get this even!" from Gloria. She meant her F-sharp hammer, but it sounded like home sewing. We had turned into a sorority house.

Naturally it couldn't last. The spell was broken by Samantha Banner, who dropped by one day to see, of all people, me.

"ROW needs some help with our literary quarterly. How would

you like to be editor of *The Enchanted Clitoris*?''

I glanced at Polly, wondering if she had put her up to it.

"It would only take you two or three days' work every three months," she pleaded prettily. "You could pick any days that suit you, or simply come in with Polly when she does her volunteer work for us. That way you wouldn't have to make a special trip. I hope you can help us, Isabel. *The Enchanted Clitoris* needs your touch."

She had no idea what my touch was—it had been carefully kept from her—but in one sense she was right. I was powerless to stop the promulgation of ROW's madcap theories, but at least I could stop them from gang-raping the English language.

ROW's house organ was the *cloaca maxima* of the written word, a jargon-soaked collection of philippics by fulminating feminists whose first rule was: "Don't worry about grammar or spelling, just let it come." What spewed forth were loonynyms like "the clink in Sam Erwin's armor," dummynyms like "I see a cataract in the desert," and the most glorious homonyms since *"tante pis."*

Reading any feminist prose made me weep for Shakespeare and Austen; when I read *The Enchanted Clitoris* I wept for Zane Grey and Olive Higgins Prouty.

"Okay, I'll do it."

"I think that's *fine*," Polly said stoutly.

ROW's storefront headquarters was full of women in rimless glasses who all looked as if they were saving a seat for Madame de Farge. The atmosphere was sweetened only by the aroma of freshly sawed lumber that emanated from the endless rows of makeshift pamphlet shelves that lined every wall.

Polly led the way down a long corridor past the assertiveness-training class, from which bloodcurdling screams of "This steak is tough!" and "I demand to see the manager!" poured forth like a perpetual litany from a demented abbey.

We entered Samantha's office and found her on the phone. She motioned us to sit down and put her hand over the mouthpiece. "It's our New York office!" she hissed importantly, and then returned to her conversation.

"I believe we can hit them with a child-abuse suit. I've read everything they've published in the child-possession line: *Damon the*

Demon, Owen the Omen, and *The Bergering*—that's the one about the bar mitzvah boy. They're definitely in a conspiracy to denigrate children. I'll write the brief tonight. Meanwhile, you take your group down there and throw blood on them.''

She hung up and gave us a triumphant smile. ''I've directed our Free Speech Committee to invade the editorial offices of Alger House. They've just come out with a novel called *Umbilicus Rex* about a fetus who chews up his father's penis during intercourse.''

''That's good for a six-figure paperback sale,'' I said.

Samantha's eyes stretched open so wide I experienced an overpowering need to squeeze mine shut. It was the visual counterpart to hearing fingernails rake down a blackboard.

''You're so right!'' she said intensely, giving me a look of new respect. ''I'm glad to hear a professional writer condemn it.''

Misunderstood as usual.

Polly went off to her committee and Samantha led me to my desk. A towering stack of submissions in brown manuscript envelopes covered most of the working surface.

''Polly said you worked on your college literary magazine, so you know what a dummy is.''

''Yes.''

''Well, then, you won't have any trouble. All you have to do is type up any handwritten submissions, paste up the dummy, and send it to the All About Lilith Press. Here's their address,'' she said, pulling a business card from the Rolodex.

I went through the drawers and found the necessary tools of the editorial trade: ruler, blue pencils, and cropping wheel. There was only one thing missing.

''Where are the rejection slips?''

Samantha's eyes stretched open again. I turned my head and relieved myself with a quick blink.

''We don't have any,'' she replied. ''We never reject anything. That would imply that some people can write and others can't.''

''But suppose it's no good?''

''That's a value judgment,'' she said reprovingly.

''But suppose it makes no sense? Like the ramblings of a demented mind, for instance?''

"Dementia is relative. Besides, our readers could learn much from the inner thoughts of the mentally disturbed."

I couldn't argue with that, but neither could I take in the idea of a magazine that accepted the entire slush pile. I tried another angle.

"Suppose somebody submits something that has nothing to do with feminism?"

She gave me a sublime smile. "Everything has something to do with feminism."

I wondered how she felt about the War of Jenkins' Ear. After she returned to her office I skimmed through a copy of the latest issue. The logo of *The Enchanted Clitoris* was exactly what you would expect it to be; there was a big one on the cover and lots of little ones scattered through the text. They were used after each page number and at the end of each article to signify *The End,* like *Cosmopolitan*'s pussycat.

Most of the text consisted of the letters column called "Vent-a-Spleen," which took up twelve pages. In addition, there was a poetry section, a female rage section, a fiction section for children, called "Freewheelers," and a regular feature called "My Most Unforgettable Bisexual."

There were even a few carefully chosen ads. No vibrator shaped like a penis could be shown, but shower attachments were acceptable, and so were ads for an oval hand vibrator that ran on transistor batteries and looked like a horse groomer's curry comb. Polly had one but she used it to wax furniture.

I found my favorite ad, which appeared in every issue in the same place of honor on the inside front cover.

Do you have trouble getting through to people? Do people have trouble getting through to you? If so, you need PERCEPTOPHONE! A record a day will help you develop insight in 12 easy lessons! Only $16.95! Order now! (stereo console not included).

I looked with dismay at the mountain of copy on my desk. Given ROW's editorial policy, it would take five years to use it all. I opened the biggest envelope first, figuring somebody had sent us a novel, but it turned out to be a sample marriage contract worthy of a Wittelsbach princess and a Hohenzollern margrave. I hid it in the bottom drawer and started on the letters.

Most of them were some version of "I'm proud to be a Lesbian! (Name withheld)." I finally found one that was signed, but the signature was the only thing that made any sense. The body of the letter was a vertiginous shower of ellipses interspersed with words—an attempted simulation of the Sapphic fragment by a Lesbian who Grecianized her girlfriend's name: "The night we . . . oneness . . . wetness . . . Bettyis."

I found an article called "Pistol Packin' Prostate" that was suitable for the female rage section as far as the content was concerned. As far as the syntax was concerned it was a pluperfect mess. The writer had failed to start her narrative far enough back in time, causing the entire piece to read like a double flashback:

"I had had an orgasm when I had slept with him the second time, but I had not known it had happened, since I had had no experience other than the affair I had had during the summer I had spent in Nepal."

I picked up a pencil and started to fix it, but just then Samantha appeared in the doorway and stopped me.

"Wait. You mustn't change anything."

"But it's an awkward sentence."

"That's a value judgment. *The Enchanted Clitoris* is a journal of individual expression."

"Can't I even correct bad grammar?"

"There's no such thing. Everyone has a right to his or her own English. To insist upon rules is elitist," she ruled. "Underprivileged people, for example, do marvelous things with nontraditional grammar."

She was wrong. Only the horsey set can make bad grammar attractive. It takes generations of money and breeding to infuse "he don't" with élan.

"If you correct someone else's writing, you set up a structured relationship," she went on. "Remember ROW's motto: Nobody on Top."

Suddenly she snapped her fingers and hit herself on the forehead. "Oh, I almost forgot! There's something terribly important that has to get in this issue."

She hurried back to her office and returned with a sheet of paper. She handed it to me with a flourish.

"It's my report on publishers of pornographic books in Los Angeles," she said proudly. "I'm going to expose them. See? I've listed their names, addresses, phone numbers, and pay scales."

"I see."

"None of this information is available in *Writer's Market*."

"I know."

"I interviewed one of the authors. Do you know what he told me? The books have no plots and no characterization, so it's possible to write one in a week. He did two a week and made a fortune. Isn't it awful that they pay so much for such anti-woman filth?"

"Yes." I wished she'd shut up; I was trying to read.

"I can't imagine how anyone could write it, can you?"

"No."

"Make sure you run it in a prominent place."

I looked up and gave her a dedicated smile. "I'll mark it *Must Go*."

When she left, I made a copy of the list. When lunchtime came, I invented a trip to the public library and grabbed a taxi.

The highest-paying porn publisher on Samantha's list was Sword & Scabbard, located in a small office building on Sunset Boulevard between a massage parlor and the United Gnostic Church of the People.

I entered the lobby and looked at the neat, glassed-in bulletin board. Except for Sword & Scabbard, the tenants sounded eminently conventional. There were a PR outfit, an insurance salesman, a draftsman, and the representative of a crop-dusting company. The only one that worried me was a man who called himself an oral surgeon, but when I got upstairs and smelled Lavoris I knew he was a real dentist.

I found Sword & Scabbard's office and opened the door. A girl who appeared to be a receptionist looked up from her desk. She was putting something into her mouth but it was only a doughnut. I relaxed a little and returned her lumpy smile.

I told her I was a writer and asked if I could have a word with one of the editors.

"You mean Amy? Just a minute, I'll call and see."

While she was on the intercom, I tried to imagine a porn editor named Amy. It made me think of girls who cried on their wedding nights. I decided she must be one of the new breed of soybean Amys who take natural names along with natural food. Those people had a lot of Mauds, too.

In a moment, Amy emerged from the inner office. I couldn't believe my eyes; she was a natural honey blonde who didn't look a day over eighteen. When she came closer I saw that she was in her late twenties, but otherwise she was the incarnation of State Fair.

"Hi," she said with a pleasant smile. "I'm Amy Chandler. Come on back to my office."

She wore a pair of burgundy slacks with a matching tunic. No chains, no American flags in unpatriotic places, and no buttons except the ones that held her clothes together. It was too good to be true; the place must be a front for something even worse than a porn publisher.

Her office looked like every editor's office I had ever seen: manuscripts in brown envelopes piled in a corner, galleys trailing over the desk like giant tapeworms, and an unfinished letter in the typewriter. The girlish touches recommended by *Cosmopolitan* were also in evidence: plants, a big brandy snifter full of hard candy, a piggy bank, and a quill ballpoint stuck in a Styrofoam snowball.

The most incredible touch of all was a white rabbit in a hutch.

"This is Mac," Amy said, poking a finger through his cage to give him a scratch. "He's our mascot."

He looked like a herbivorous Quadrupet. I sat down and told Amy about my writing experience.

"Oh, gee!" she exclaimed. "You've written *real* books."

"Regencys?" I said, stunned.

"It's all in what you're used to," she said philosophically. "To me, a Regency is a real book after this." She picked up one of the galleys with the tips of her finger and immediately dropped it with a shudder.

"How long have you worked here?"

"Almost a year." She put an index finger to her temple and pulled an imaginary trigger. "I came to California to start a boutique but it went broke. I had to do something so. . . ." She gestured at the four walls of her office.

"Where are you from?"

"Terre Haute, Indiana."

A porn editor from the banks of the Wabash.

Suddenly the door opened and a man came in. I whirled around, expecting to die. *He had something in his hand!*

It was a Thom McAn shoebox full of cookies.

"Hi," he said, offering the box. "Have one. My wife made them." The medieval world had Everyman; America has Everyhusband. He was it. I took a cookie and Amy introduced us.

"Isabel, this is our editor in chief, Bill Wheeler. Isabel wants to write for us."

"Oh, gosh, that's great. Glad to have you aboard."

What was going on? Amy, gosh, gee, Indiana, rabbits, homemade cookies, and a Navy vet named Bill who shopped at Thom McAn. Instead of a den of iniquity, it was Waspville, U.S.A.

"Who owns Sword and Scabbard?" I asked suddenly.

"God only knows," Bill said. "I can't afford to care. I came out here from Joplin, Missouri to work for a big ad agency. Everything was hunky-dory for about a year; then they played musical chairs and I lost. I had to do something, so. . . ." He gestured at the walls the way Amy had.

We got down to business—that wonderful editorial subject known as "needs." Writers never ask editors questions, we "query" them, and instead of saying "What do you want?" we always say "What are your needs?" With magazine editors, it's "current needs."

"Dirt," said Amy. "Two hundred double-spaced pages of it. Here are some samples of the kind of thing we publish." She handed me two Sword & Scabbard paperbacks. One was called *Dipstick* and the other *Swallowing It.*

"And here," she continued, rummaging in her desk, "is a copy of our editorial guidelines. I don't know if it'll do you any good or not. It was written by a guy who used to work here and he was pretty weird, but you might as well take it along."

"The most important thing to remember is not to try anything fancy, like telling a story," Bill advised. He pointed to a framed quotation on the wall above Mac's cage. "Remember what Sir Francis Bacon said."

I got up and read it. It was from the *Essays.* "Some books are to be tasted, others are to be swallowed, and some few to be chewed and digested." Beneath the quotation someone had written: "Ours are to be jerked off."

"Just keep that in mind and you'll be all right," said Bill. "Let's see . . . what are some of our other taboos?"

"Humor," said Amy. "For gosh sakes, don't write anything funny, whatever you do. Humor destroys eroticism. Besides, a lot of our readers are real psychos—they might think you were laughing at *them*." She fanned herself with her fingers.

"Marriage is another taboo," Bill said. "Nobody's ever married in our books."

"Pregnancy is out, too," Amy said. "Let the reader assume that all the women characters are on the Pill, but don't *mention* the Pill or any other form of birth control. Porn readers don't like women who think ahead."

"And don't give any of the characters ethnic names," Bill cautioned. "Make everybody a Wasp. That way, nobody will get insulted."

I stuffed the guidelines and the sample copies into my tote bag and rose. Like the well-brought-up people they were, Amy and Bill walked me to the door. When we got to the outer office they introduced me to the receptionist.

"Isabel, meet Mary Beth Cartwright. Isabel's going to write for us."

"Oh, golly, that's terrific!" exclaimed Mary Beth, and then she, too, got up to walk me to the door. I noticed that she had a limp.

"I used to be a ballet student," she explained, "but then I lost two toes in a snowmobile accident when I went home to Wisconsin last Christmas. That was the end of my ballet career. I had to do something, so. . . ."

She made the Sword & Scabbard gesture and took a cookie from Bill's box. "Ummm, these are even better than my mom's."

We lingered at the door and talked some more in good small-town fashion. When I finally left, Bill called out a last-minute piece of encouragement.

"Just keep it simple and you'll have it in the barn before you know it."

Whoever owned Sword & Scabbard, at least there was one corner of a foreign field that would forever be the North 40.

*   *   *

In the cab back to ROW, I studied *Guidelines for Our Authors*. They sounded as if they had been written by a vice-squad detective who was taking a course in the elegiac couplet at an unaccredited night school.

1. To lessen readers' confusion, kindly avoid such figures of speech as *Pandora's box, right up his or her alley, a lick and a promise, blowhard, prickly heat,* and the interrogatory *Come again?*

2. When referring to characters who are or have been in prison, watch your spelling of *penal.* It is NOT *penile!*

3. Flights of metaphorical prose are not desirable. The phrase *her oleaginous Mountain of Venus* only perplexes many of our readers. We were distressed recently to receive a letter that angrily asked: "What's that statue doing up on a hill with butter all over it?" *Wet cunt* is much better.

4. The following have been declared obsolete by *The Dictionary of American Slang:* quiff, quim, hair pie, muff (noun and verb), knockers, and wink.

5. To avoid alliteration, onomatopoeia, and unintentional rhyme, do not name any characters Peter, Dick, Rod, or Regina.

6. The word *vector* is a physics term pertaining to a straight line and is not generally known. Call your penis something else.

7. As you know, printing errors cost money. Using the British expression *John Thomas* for penis recently resulted in a regrettable incident in final page proofs when we discovered this example of anthropomorphization: *"Gimme a cigarette, baby," said John Thomas.* Remember we are all Americans here.

8. When writing Lesbian sex scenes, chaos often results from the plethora of female pronouns that must be employed. To wit: *"She tickled her clitoris, and with a scream she threw her legs around her hips and dragged her down on top of her."* We suggest that Lesbian lovers be of different coloring, so that one has blond pubic hair and the other brunet. That should help keep your characters straight.

9. Our proofreader is required to read the galleys and page proofs of twelve books a month. Please do not make her burden heavier with tricky sentences. We refer to a recent description of a musician hero who had learned "to master Beethoven." The proofreader automatically changed it to read: "to masturbate often." Remember that we think along certain lines here.

10. Although we require young characters and contemporary settings, please remember to supply your women with garter belts. THIS IS VERY IMPORTANT!

11. Areola is the pink area around the nipple; *aureola* is a synonym for halo. Kindly learn the difference.

12. Get right into the action on page one. Leisurely descriptions of scenery and setting are always fatal. Our readers don't care where anybody is.

That evening, after Polly and I got back from ROW, I locked myself in my room to begin my career as a professional pornographer. For the first time in months I didn't feel blocked—what was there to be blocked about? No plot, no characterization, no dialogue except grunts and groans and four-letter words. I would write a book a week and save my money until I had enough to quit and write a *real* book.

My first task was choosing a pen name. I entertained a fleeting temptation to call myself Brad Shaw, then reluctantly cast it aside. Samantha was monitoring Sword & Scabbard's list so I had to pick a name that gave no hint of my identity. The bylines on the two books Amy had given me were I. M. Pigg and Kandy Kuntz, so I decided to be Pussy Slick.

The associations came readily after that. I decided to write about a girl who goes on a picnic with six men and ends up as the entrée. I rolled a sheet of paper into my typewriter and composed the title page.

BOX LUNCH
by
Pussy Slick

The next page was harder. I was used to Regencys, where women never got anything kissed except their hands. Gothics were equally pristine: the hero never touched the heroine except to pull her out of an abandoned well.

Nor were the sex scenes in my favorite novels any help, chiefly because there weren't any sex scenes in my favorite novels. *Ethan*

Frome is about a man who never got a piece and *On the Eve* is about a man who got a piece and died.

Then there was the Ayn Rand sex scene in which the characters hump because they both love the gold standard. An Ayn Rand romp could get pretty steamy but there was always an air of I-wouldn't-do-this-with-just-anybody that was bound to offend the porn reader's fragile ego.

There was nothing to do but forget my own preferences and begin. My fingers found the keys and I wrote my first sentence:

"She pushed her cunt against his face and he licked it with a loud slurp."

Style, said Flaubert, is everything.

Two hours later, I had done thirty pages. I was rolling number thirty-one into the typewriter when I heard the faint, faraway sound of our telephone, followed by the usual jogging noises as Polly started on her sprint. She caught it on the ninth ring.

"ISABEL!"

I went out onto the landing and leaned over the banister.

"WHAT?"

She waited until my echo faded and yelled again.

"IT'S FOR YOU! IT'S YOUR AUNT!"

I raced down the steps, across the dim foyer, through the pitch-black dining room, and into the kitchen. Polly handed me the receiver and I collapsed panting, in a chair.

"Hello, Aunt Edna? Is anything wrong?"

"Law, no, honey! Everything's *right!* I'm calling to tell you the wonderful news. I'm with child by Virginius!"

I made a strangling sound. She meant the Reverend Virginius Madison Chillingsworth, rector of St. Jude the Impossible, whose secretary she had been for almost as long as I could remember. I didn't know she had been anything else.

"Father Chillingsworth?" I croaked.

"Yes! And he's so happy!"

He was so married, too. "Are you going to have an abortion?"

"'Deed not! I'm going to have a baby!"

"But Aunt Edna, you're forty-one."

"Better late than never."

"Are you sure you're pregnant?"

"Course, I'm sure. I haven't had the Vex of Venus for three months. I've been to seven doctors, just to get a second opinion, and they all said the same thing. I've had the rabbit test and the frog test and every other kind of test and they all came out positive. Isn't that grand? Oh, I just can't wait to see you!"

"See me?"

"Yes, I'll be in Los Angeles tomorrow morning. When I read your last letter I thought it sounded like a right good bunch you've got out there, so being that I'm liberated and all, I've decided to throw in my lot with the Don't Tread on Me Commune!"

"Give me your flight number; we'll meet you at the airport."

When I hung up, Polly's ears looked like pitcher handles. I told her the incredible news.

"Beautiful!"

The missionary glow was back.

CHAPTER NINE

"Flight four-oh-one from Dulles now arriving at Gate Fifteen!"

"That's it!" Polly said eagerly, jumping up from the bench.

I followed her in something of a daze, still unable to cope with this latest and most bizarre turn of events. Try as I might, I could not imagine a pregnant Aunt Edna. It wasn't just that pregnancy interferes with menstruation and I couldn't imagine a nonmenstruating Aunt Edna. It was something else: she simply wasn't the intercourse type. Not that she was one of those pathetic creatures the South calls a "poor thing." She was very pretty and had always had lots of beaux, but they were *beaux*, never heavy love affairs. She used to go out with several men at a time—i.e., the same evening—on group dates to square dances or ball games, as though seeking safety in numbers. She also had a knack for remaining friends with them long after they had married other women, and then she even made friends with their wives. Never once in these odd arrangements had jealousy reared its head. Sensuous women never behaved this way, so I had taken it all to mean that she was either a virgin or something very close to it.

And now she was pregnant by Father Chillingsworth. . . . I wondered if he had seduced her in that smooth satanic way of Episcopal men of the cloth. Or had he used techniques acquired earlier in life, when he played tackle for William and Mary? And what of Mrs. Chillingsworth, a holy terror if ever there was one, the classic hunt matron who was perfectly capable of kicking the dogs out of the way and killing the fox with her bare hands?

"Do you see her?" Polly asked, as the passengers started coming down the ramp.

Like me, she was looking for the woman she had seen in my family photos: the Southern woman who strove for prettiness rather than chic. A bow here, a ribbon there, a bunch of artificial flowers pinned to a belt—all the busy touches of traditional femininity.

We were not looking for someone in a poncho with Gloria Steinem hair, so Aunt Edna was upon us before we saw her.

"Heah I am—both of us!"

We fell on each other and went completely regional, greeting one another in full throat. Aunt Edna screamed "Oh, Law!" and I screamed "I just can't believe it!" and then we both screamed something pert along the lines of "Yeeeeeeeeee!" which means: *Look, y'all, we're high-spirited!*

Everyone in the airport looked, including Polly, who seemed rather overwhelmed, like all Yankees at such times. I introduced her and Aunt Edna promptly screamed again.

"I knew it! I just knew it! The minute I saw you I said to myself I said that's Polly! 'Deed I've just heard so much about you! Why, Isabel's letters are so full of Polly-this and Polly-that, I feel like I know you already!"

"I'm glad to meet you," Polly said inadequately. "Did you have a good flight?"

She was expecting the conventional "yes, fine," but she didn't get it.

"Law, no! I thought I was going to miscarry, 'deed I did! It was bump-bump-bump all the way! Just bump-bump-bump! That's no way to treat a *bearing* woman! I'm going to get Isabel to write that old airline a letter—she's such a good letter-writer, don't you think? I always did say she had a special touch—and tell them they almost brought on my baby!"

By now the whole airport knew she was pregnant. It was just like back home when she roamed all over town announcing the onset of her menses. Passengers hurrying by kept staring at her stomach.

"Give us your baggage check, Aunt Edna. We'll get your things for you."

She calmed down at once and gave me a limpid look and laid her hand on my arm.

"There's something about my baggage you should know," she began in a tremulous voice. "I hope it doesn't upset you or bring back memories, but I thought I might as well go ahead and do it. After all, they were just sitting there in that old place all this time, so I figured that since we pay the storage on all that old stuff, and since it belongs *rightfully* to you by law, I just might as well do it. So, to make a long story short, I did."

Polly was leaning forward in a tilt of curiosity, straining for the end of the long story made short. It was just the response Aunt Edna wanted. She paused dramatically and sucked in her lower lip.

Polly took the bait. "Did what?"

Yankee directness only encourages the Southern woman's thespian instincts. Aunt Edna now laid her hand on Polly's arm.

"Do you know about Isabel's father . . . I mean, how he went?"

"Yes," Polly said uncomfortably.

"That's good. I believe in clearing the air and coming right out with things, instead of keeping it all secret. There's no sense in hiding it because it always comes out eventually, don't you think?"

So far, we hadn't moved from the spot where we first sighted each other. People were swarming and churning impatiently around us but it had no effect whatsoever on Aunt Edna's narrative style; like all Southern women, she was a *succès fou* as an oral historian.

"Besides," she went on, "I thought it would be a nice way to honor poor Fax. It would please him more if I were traveling by ship, but nobody does anymore. So anyway, to make a long story short, I *used* them. As I say, they belong to Isabel when you come right down to it, and there wasn't any point in just letting them sit there in that old place, so I decided to do it."

"Why don't we get your baggage," Polly suggested. "Then you can tell us about . . . whatever it is you want to tell us."

"But that's what I'm talking about, honey! My baggage! I wanted to warn Isabel about it first so as not to upset her or bring back bad memories. You see, I packed everything in poor Fax's hatboxes."

Polly nearly collapsed with relief when the denouement finally emerged. We went to the baggage circle and there, coming through the rubber straps, were Daddy's greatest business disaster, clogging up the flow of all the smart new Touristers and Guccis and Val-A-Paks and causing no end of curiosity among the many California swingers who had never laid eyes on a flowered hatbox in their lives.

"How many do you have, Aunt Edna?"

"Thirty-seven. I needed a lot because I brought a whole layette for the baby besides my own clothes."

Three exorbitantly tipped skycaps later, we had all the hatboxes in the back of the van. The long drive home was made to order for Aunt Edna's story of her ecclesiastical love affair, but wanting the largest possible audience for it, she chose to save it until we got to the commune. To fill up the road time, she regaled us with a long-drawn-out story about something else. Since the longest-drawn-out stories in Queen Caroline are invariably about Kissypoo Carmichael, she told one. Polly almost sideswiped a truck when she heard the name.

"Why on earth do they call her that?" she asked.

"That's what her *daddy* called her," Aunt Edna explained with heavy sarcasm, "so she won't answer to anything else. She was under her daddy's thumb like I was under my mother's!"

I looked at her with curiosity. This was a new Aunt Edna; some change that went deeper than her Gloria Steinem look had taken place.

We arrived at the house. She greeted Agnes, Martha, and Gloria with another cascade of I've-heard-so-much-about-you's; then we all gathered around the table for coffee and an unabridged account of the romance of the century.

"Virginius and I have been intimate for many years," she began. "It started when Isabel was twelve. Of course, we were always discreet. I believe in being discreet. That's why we never went to motels or anything trashy like that. It always happened on church property. In the robing room. To make sure we weren't caught *flagrante delicto*, we did it in the vestment closet."

"With all those heavy brocaded chasubles?" I asked.

"The curtains of charity, honey. We just made a space between Epiphany and Pentecost and fell into each other's arms!"

Agnes's eyes widened. "Did his wife find out?"

Aunt Edna let out a delighted hoot. "Law, no, darlin'! Babe Beaufort was always up in Warrenton ridin' her horses.''

''Who is Babe Beaufort?'' asked a thoroughly confused Polly.

''Father Chillingsworth's wife. Her maiden name was Beaufort,'' I explained, making a mental note to tell her about the Southern custom of referring to married women by their maiden names. She'd love it.

''Her Christian name is Charlotte,'' Aunt Edna went on, ''but she's always insisted on being called Babe.'' She engineered a trenchant pause and rolled her eyes.

''You're pregnant with meaning, Aunt Edna. What are you trying to tell us?''

''Babe Beaufort's a dyke.''

I was so stunned that for a moment I couldn't remember what a dyke was, except that it was something Aunt Edna didn't talk about. Or know about. I couldn't believe she had actually said the word. As I struggled with my thoughts, she went on with the story in standard Queen Caroline style.

''Well, you know how Babe always stamped around in those boots, and wore britches in church, and carried on like a hussar. Everybody knew Virginius married her for her money, but nobody thought a thing of it—Episcopal priests always marry money. Of course, she would have stuck out like a sore thumb any place else but Virginia, but we're so used to those crazy women runnin' around yellin' and wavin' whips that we didn't know there was anything wrong with her. Course, Virginius knew that all wasn't well in the boudoir. He said she went stiff as a board every time he touched her, so finally, he just stopped touchin' her. That's where I came in—I *melted* when he touched me!'' She sighed happily. ''Meanwhile, while *I* was meltin' in the vestment closet, *Babe* was meltin' up in Warrenton.''

She broke off and turned to me. ''Isabel, you 'member that other horsey woman, the one that shot the lawyer from the Anti-Blood Sports Society? Her name is Josepha but she likes to be called Dutch.'' Here she lowered her eyes and sucked in her lower lip.

''She and Babe are lovers,'' Polly guessed.

''For years!'' Aunt Edna caroled happily. ''That's how come everything's worked out so beautifully for all four of us! See, when I told Virginius I was pregnant, he decided to ask Babe for a divorce, money or no, but before he could do it, *she* came to *him* and confessed the whole story about how she and Dutch have been in love all this time.

She said they went to a consciousness-raising meeting and talked about Lesbianism and all, and decided it was time for them to come out of the closet and live together openly. So that means that Virginius and I can come out of *our* closet and get married! Isn't that just grand? Hooray for Women's Lib!''

Polly's triumphant grin spread slowly over her face and locked practically behind her ears.

"The divorce is in the works now," Aunt Edna went on. "It'll be final in time for us to be married before the baby's born."

"Will there be any problem for Virginius in the church?" I asked.

"Oh, that reminds me! I forgot to tell you about his interview with the bishop!" She turned to the others in explanation. "You've got to know what the bishop is like before you can appreciate this. You know the Pope? Well, imagine somebody who's more Catholic than the Pope, only he can't admit it because he's an Episcopalian. Frankly, I think he should go ahead and convert before he loses his mind. That happens, you know, in the higher Anglican circles. The theological doubts just build up and build up until finally they go kaflooey.''

Martha, used to clergymen who never had theological doubts, was starting to look a little confused.

Aunt Edna continued, "Anyway, to make a long story short, His Grace called Virginius in and said: 'Do you think a priest of the Anglican Communion should be a divorced man with two wives living?' That's the way he talks. And do you know what Virginius said? He said: 'Your Grace, if it weren't for divorce, there wouldn't *be* an Anglican Communion.' ''

Now Gloria grinned—the first really alive expression I had ever seen on her face.

"He sounds cool," she said. "I'd like to meet him."

"He'll be here in about three months. He's getting a leave of absence so he can be with me when the baby comes. That'll give things time to blow over in Queen Caroline, too." She looked around at us brightly. "I hope y'all don't mind if I have the baby here?"

"Not at all," I said. "You couldn't be in better hands. Polly knows everything about birthing babies."

Aunt Edna's arrival was a dream come true for Polly; at last she had somebody to fill out forms with. No clinic, center, or workshop was too avant garde for my newly liberated kinswoman. The two of them huddled for hours talking knowledgeably about amniocentesis, the pros and cons of the ultra-sound test, and which Lamaze Method group was better than some other Lamaze Method group. I gave thanks that we had broken the birth bucket; Aunt Edna probably would have given that a try, too.

The house was strewn with what Polly called literature: brochures on the papaya-seeds-for-heartburn movement, pamphlets on how to breathe, folders on how to pant, flyers announcing the formation of a Fluids Seminar, and a prospectus ominously entitled "Beyond Lamaze." It made me think of Ariadne running through the labyrinth with Polly running behind her saving the string.

The changes in Aunt Edna's vocabulary continued to amaze me. Now the language of liberated whelping poured from her lips. Gone were the Southern idioms she used to favor; "afterbirth" and "nursing" were replaced by "placenta" and "breast-feeding," and once she even said "lactation." Inevitably, she also picked up Polly's fractured English. When I heard her talking about "birth-defected" babies, I got homesick for "simple-minded."

While Aunt Edna and Polly concentrated on what comes out, I shut myself in my room and concentrated on what goes in.

My career as a pornographer blossomed. I finished my first book, *Box Lunch,* in nine days. Amy and Bill loved it and promptly issued me a check for fifteen hundred dollars. They wanted another book right away, so I produced *Ripe for Plucking,* about a girl in a migrant labor camp.

"I never thought there was such a thing as the poor man's Erskine Caldwell," said Bill when he had read it, "but you're it."

I got another fifteen hundred for *Ripe.* I put most of it in the bank to replenish my dwindling balance and used the rest to buy a new electric typewriter with an automatic underline key for all the screams and moans that required italics.

Next came *Two Thighs to the Wind,* written in five days. Amy and Bill were so delighted with it that they asked me if I thought I could do a gay boy book.

"We're always short on them," Amy said. "The straight male authors are afraid to write them, the straight women say they don't know how, and our Lesbian authors refuse to write them for some reason I've forgotten.''

I was so intoxicated with my quick success and money I was convinced I could do anything, and since anybody in that mood *can* do anything, I came up with a saga called *Forever Umber.*

''Oh, that's adorable!'' Amy squealed.

No matter what hairy perversions we had to discuss in the line of professional duty, she always sounded like a wholesome midwestern sorority girl whispering in the dorm after lights-out. A fashion designer by training, she took a special interest in the book covers, and did the layouts for mine herself after I inspired her with my next subtle examination of the human spirit, *Knockers.*

''I don't care if the *Dictionary of American Slang* says it's obsolete,'' she said, ''it's a great title and we're going to keep it. I've got the jacket design all figured out. The O and the C are going to have little nipples in them. It's just darling. If you want to do a sequel, I can do the same thing with *Boobs.*''

I did *Boobs* in four days. After I picked up my check, we decided to celebrate with a drink at the cocktail lounge across the street. While we were waiting for the light, the strains of ''Abide with Me'' played on a calliope suddenly filled the air. I looked around at the Gnostic Church of the People but it had no bell tower.

''It's the Born Again Good Humor Man,'' Amy explained, pointing to an ice-cream truck in the intersection. ''He's always around.''

As it passed us, I saw the slogan *Come as a Child* painted on its side, surrounded by a host of popsicles. The associations were instantaneous.

''*Come Truck!*''

''Oh, that's super!'' Amy said. ''Like a Sexmobile, right?''

''Yes. The heroine drives around town and does everybody.''

''Perfect! When can we have it?''

''I'll bring it down next week.''

The editorial conference out of the way, we went into the cocktail lounge and had our drinks.

Amy hoisted her Bloody Mary. ''I have a suggestion to pass on to you,'' she said. ''Bill says you should include some rimming scenes in your books. We were talking about it yesterday and I nearly died!

Mary Beth didn't know what it meant and poor Bill had to *explain* it to her. He didn't go into the gory details, he just said 'analingus' and waited for her to catch on. Finally she did, and said 'ugh.' My sentiments exactly.''

Her eyes grew large with impending confession. She looked around stealthily, then leaned across the table and spoke in a whisper.

"The guy I live with thinks I'm rarin' to go all the time just because I work for a porn company. But I'm not. In fact, I'm frigid, thanks to Sword and Scabbard. I used to have orgasms all the time, but now I can't make it no matter what he does to me.''

"Sex isn't sexy," I maximed, imagining Polly's pensive frown.

"You can say that again! Have you had any trouble coming since you started writing for us?''

"I'm celibate at the moment so I can't say.''

"Have they made you horny?''

"Not yet.''

"Don't worry, they won't. In this business, things get worse instead of better.''

I didn't believe her. Nothing could dim my enthusiasm for writing porns as long as I was making so much money. After all, if I didn't have a sex life to ruin, what else was there to worry about?

The first hint of trouble came three weeks later after I had finished an oral trilogy: *Come Truck, Eating Out,* and *Getting Head.*

One night, Polly, who never cooked, took a notion to surprise us. She came home with something—she would not say what—in a huge corrugated bag and made us all stay out of the kitchen while she took over.

Finally, she called to us that dinner was ready and we went in to see what she had concocted. I couldn't imagine what on earth she could have cooked; there were no aromas and no heat coming from the stove. In fact, the whole kitchen felt oddly chilly.

"Look!" she said, pointing proudly with an icepick. "Raw oysters!''

I clapped my hand over my mouth and ran for the bathroom.

After that, the porns started getting on my nerves and the inevitable happened: I began to indulge in what the trade calls "Fucky Fudging.''

If you will look closely at a paperback porn, you will find that it has an inordinate number of end pages front and back. End pages are the blank sheets on which you write your name or paste your book plates; authors of decent books autograph them on the end pages. Most books have only one set of them, but porns have something approaching a ream in order to make the book look thicker than it actually is.

In the back, you will also find a complete list of the company's titles, along with an order blank so that you can buy directly from the publisher. These ads take up several more pages and add to the thickness.

Now turn to the end of any chapter and you will find that it is followed by a blank page. There are anywhere from ten to twelve chapters in the average porn, so that many blank pages can be inserted.

Finally, investigate the dropped chapter heads. These are the words *Chapter One, Chapter Two,* etc. Chapter heads are always dropped a bit, except in *Gone With the Wind,* where they came right up to the top of the page because the book was so long that the publisher had to save space. Porn publishers have the opposite problem: they have to waste space because their exhausted authors start writing less and less bigger and bigger on more and more paper—Fucky Fudging.

There are many ways to do it. First, you can drop your own chapter heads, saving the editor trouble at the layout stage. Simply roll the paper as far down as your conscience will allow—say five inches from the bottom—and begin.

Next, pepper your story with newspaper headlines, ads, movie marquees, and signs so that you can center them and double space around them. Like this:

BEAVER SHOTS

After you get the sign painted, have your character stare at it for a while, unable to believe what he sees because he's doped up and temporarily afflicted with double vision. Then have him close one eye and reread it so that you can repeat the sign:

BEAVER SHOTS

Fucky Fudging is why porn characters, who show no caution in life's larger moments, always read labels with such meticulous scrutiny:

K-Y JELLY

It is also what makes them staccato, monosyllabic types with that curious tendency to echolalia that runs through the genre. The more they repeat themselves, pause, think, and start over, the more paragraphs you can indent:

> She's a natural blonde, he thought.
> A *real* natural blonde.
> Was she ever!
> "Wow," he breathed, as he stared at her pussy.
> There was no mistaking it.
> No way!
> "Honey," he said, "you're a real natural blonde."

For the same reason, they also interrupt themselves, trail off in the middle of sentences, and drop things:

> Brad wondered if . . .
> No, no, she couldn't possibly want to be bungholed.
> And yet . . .
> She knelt down and spread her cheeks.
> "Margo," he said, "I—"
> The drink slipped out of his hand and crashed to the floor when he saw the jar she had brought from the bathroom:

VASELINE

Then there are the groans, moans, screams, and grunts.

> "I'MMMMMMMMM COMMMMMMMMMING!"
> "YESSSSSSSSSSSSSSSSSSSSSSSSSSSSSSSSSS!"

You can do a lot with "yes." Handled properly, it takes up a whole line.

And then there's "no." Ordinarily an unpopular word in porn, it is acceptable when the heroine is an initially reluctant virgin, which is often.

"NOOOOOOOOOOOOOOOOOOOOOOO!"

"Am I hurting you?" he panted.

"YESSSSSSSSSSSSSSSSSSSSSSSSSSSSSSSSS!"

Normal pain is suggested with "Uh," which, of course, becomes "UHHHHHHHHHHHHHHHHHHHHH!" Abnormal pain, like the kind caused by sodomy, is "Ngh," which . . . . tightly . . . . translates . . . . into . . . .

"NNNNNNNNGGGGGGGGGGGGHHHHHH!"

Do enough of this and you're at the bottom of a page in a trice.

You also turn into a twitch. Most porn hacks cherish the hope of becoming real writers someday, so there comes a point when you start to fight back in obscure little ways. Since plot, characterization, imagery, allusion, tragedy, and comedy were all taboo, I took refuge in maniacally elegant grammar. It made me think I was writing well to have my pimps and sluts and degenerates say things like:

"On whom did you go down?"

"His cock is not so large as Bob's."

"I have fewer rubbers than I thought."

"If this be the clap, I'll kill you."

I was fooling no one but myself; pornography is virtually a synonym for bad writing. The pornographer's first rule—genitals must be described in minute detail—results in cascades of adjectives guaranteed to destroy controlled prose. I realized just how bad matters had become the day I left a note for the electrician that said: "The fuse at the top with the pointy red shiny glass covering that swells into a bulbous mass underneath has emitted sharp, crackling, staccato sparks whenever I turn on the round button with the deeply depressed circular rim on the left side of the heater."

Around this time, I came across an anti-porn essay by Pamela Hansford-Johnson, who claimed that the literary worthlessness of porn can be proved by transposing its style to a description of the boiling and eating of an egg.

I gave it a try and came up with this:

I took the glistening, virginally white oval out of the fiercely bubbling cauldron of hot, hot, hot water and cupped my hand around it, feeling its contours with sensations of shimmering delight. I reached for my long, sturdy, battering egg knife and tapped. The shell slipped off and I touched the tender, moist, protein-swollen membranes of the secret softness. The steamy slice of hot, ready, delectable egg burned my fingers but I thrust firmly with my rigid tool and inserted the erect, serrated blade. The lubricious, golden yellow, ambrosial nectar of the pulsating, quickening core gushed out into my egg cup. I centered my mouth over the slickened surface of the gently curving silver spoon and ate, ate, ate.

When I finished this exercise, I stared at my long, yellow, blue-lined Nixonian legal pad in horror.
    It was perfect.
    Was it ever!
    Really perfect.
    I was going nuts. . . .
    "I'm going nuts," I said.

I guess I had a nervous breakdown. I say *guess* because it did not fit any of the South's nervous breakdown patterns that I had grown up hearing about. I didn't "go to pieces," I didn't "walk up and down the floor wringing my hands and crying," and God knows I didn't "waste away"—my appetite remained as gargantuan as ever, especially now that Martha had taken over as chief cook and was plying us with down-home specialties.
    I did not pull any of those high-strung capers that Southerners like to brag about because they make everybody feel aristocratic. Riding a horse through the house is the all-time favorite in this category, but anything Zelda-ish will do. The trouble is, most such goings-on involve appearing in public without clothes, and that's the last thing a disintegrating pornographer wants to do.
    I was terrified that I had ruined my writing talent, but there was no one to turn to for help. Polly was incapable of grasping abstract agony, and in any case I could not let her know I was writing porn. Aunt Edna was too sunk in self-absorption, and Martha was too prone to projection—if I told her I was having a nervous breakdown, she might have it for me.
    Confiding in Agnes, our weakest vessel, was out of the question. Gloria was the most unshockable, but she could turn any conversation

into a discussion of Edward II's flaming anus and I had written too many sodomy scenes to endure her favorite topic.

So I suffered alone. My nights were worse than my days. I dreamed of broken pencils, stuck typewriter keys, and dictionaries with blank pages. I remained in this state for another couple of weeks, until Father Chillingsworth arrived.

CHAPTER TEN

Father Chillingsworth was driving to California. Aunt Edna stationed herself beside our black desk phone for four days, not daring to leave the house for fear of missing one of his checking-in calls. Very soon he called us from Phoenix—he had a most unecclesiastical habit of driving between ninety and a hundred miles an hour—and told us he would arrive the next day.

All of us assembled on the veranda to wait for him. In honor of his arrival, religious Martha had eschewed Agnes's services and gone to a beauty shop for a professional permanent and her bluest rinse yet. I hoped she wouldn't prostrate herself at his feet; he was a much stronger cup of theological tea than she was used to. I got the feeling she expected something extraterrestrial with an escort of Swiss Guards.

At last we saw his car pull into the drive. Aunt Edna emitted a view halloo and flew down the hill with arms outstretched like the girl in *Kings Row* hurling herself at Robert Cummings. The differences were twenty years and a decided spraddle; she was now "well along" in her Southern vocabulary and "in her third trimester" in her liberated one.

After a warm reunion at the bottom of the hill, they got into the car and rode up to the house. When my uncle-to-be got out and came toward us, Agnes's jaw dropped in frank appreciation.

"Oh, mercy!"

Virginius Madison Chillingsworth was breathtakingly beautiful in the lace and brocades of the Anglican ritual. Out of them, as now, he was merely handsome. At fifty-seven he had silvery temples and the apple-cheeked, carefree look of a man born with a little money who had married a woman with a lot of it. Slightly over six feet, he was massively built, with huge hands and a thick tuft of graying chest hair peeking through the open collar of his sports shirt.

With Aunt Edna clinging to him, he came up the steps, kissed me on the cheek, and shook hands with the communards. Only Polly, who had a number of ministers in her own family, behaved normally. The others reacted visibly to his electrifying presence. Martha dropped the barest of curtsies; Agnes went all girlish in her big-woman way—a kind of twisting, scrunching movement as though she were making room for him in bed. Gloria seemed peculiarly entranced in a nonsexual but nonetheless intense way.

"Well," he said, his glance sweeping around. "Here are all the lovely ladies I've heard so much about, all waiting to greet me. It's indeed a privilege to be so graciously received."

That's when Polly reacted. I never thought I would see her eyelashes flutter, but they did.

While Aunt Edna was showing him their room, Martha heaved a nostalgic sigh and stared off into space with a mesmerized smile on her lips.

"He's just like Roosevelt."

By dinner time, she was calling him Virginius without a trace of embarrassment. He had brought us a huge Smithfield ham, and the two of them discussed country cooking, a subject guaranteed to bring Martha out of her shell.

Next he devoted himself to Gloria, with reminiscences of his trip to her beloved Mont-Saint-Michel, and an obscure little note about the Albigensian heresy. Together they spun it into the finest silk, yet in a way that did not shut the rest of us out.

All of the table talk went the same way. For the first time in nearly a year, we all remained steady on course, with none of the wild lurches into our various monomanias that had characterized our all-female conversations. Polly was actually talking instead of promulgating, and once she even laughed when Virginius told a story about a dogfight that erupted while he was performing the prehunt ritual known as the Blessing of the Hounds.

A week later, he and Aunt Edna were married in a discreet ceremony at the house by a Los Angeles rector who had gone to divinity school with the bridegroom. In view of Aunt Edna's condition, the traditional description, *Spinster,* did not appear on the documents after her name. Farnsworth bellowed throughout the service, but otherwise the occasion was marked by that ineffable civilized touch that Virginius cast forth like incense.

He became the first man to spend his wedding night in a feminist commune. The next day, Aunt Edna enrolled him in Husbands' Class, where he learned how to place pillows, time pains, crank up an articulating bed, and "coach" the whole business when the time came. He even consented to taking part in a seminar Polly turned up called Supportive Panting.

Once again life at Don't Tread on Me settled down. Aunt Edna kept the atmosphere jangling, of course, but that was only the outward physical clamor. An inward spiritual grace started to take hold, whose source was Virginius's fireside chats.

He seemed to know that we all had problems. Without being obvious or overly clerical about it, he managed to find time alone with each of us for long, seemingly casual but intensely probing talks. Wandering into the kitchen ostensibly for a cup of coffee, he would settle himself at the table and talk to Martha while she cooked. Next, he would wander down to the beach and help Agnes carry her clam buckets—manna to a woman who was stronger than many men—and wind up in a tête-à-tête on a rotting log.

Polly was usually collating ROW material in the dining room, so Virginius simply got in line and followed behind, helping her assemble the latest bill of attainder while they talked.

Gloria was the most accessible of all, thanks to her habit of squatting on the cliffside and staring out to sea. One day I looked out my window and saw Virginius squatting beside her. Chaucer only knows what they were talking about but it went on for a couple of hours.

I was the hardest to get to because I worked alone in my room, but one day I heard a tap at my door and found my uncle holding two bourbon highballs.

"I hope I'm not disturbing you, Isabel, but I heard your typewriter stop some time ago, so I decided to see if I could interest you in a break."

We chatted awhile about the latest books—real books—and then he surveyed me with a pensive air.

"You're looking a little strained, Isabel. Edna and I were talking about you last night. We're worried about you."

The drink was very strong; there are no teetotalers in the Episcopal Church, and Southern gentlemen have a heavy hand with the decanter. Suddenly, I found myself pouring out the whole story of my writing career—and the porns.

"Polly worries about what porn does to women and the churches worry about what it does to the American family. Nobody cares about what it does to writers," I said miserably. "I'm afraid I've ruined my talent for good."

His face had not changed as I talked. There was no shock on it, only concern for me. He tapped his front tooth with his thumbnail, nodding slightly, his eyes narrowing.

"Do you think," he began slowly, "that you might be trying deliberately to destroy your talent to please your grandmother?"

"Granny . . . ?"

"As I recall," he said with a wry smile, "intellectuals were at the top of her long list of enemies. I also recall that she had the strongest personality of anyone I have ever met. A remarkable woman, no doubt, one of the last of the great dowagers. But, I fear, a Know-Nothing and a textbook case of megalomania."

He crossed his legs and lit one of his thin, elegant cigarillos.

"It's taken Edna years to get out from under her mother's yoke. She still isn't out completely and she never will be. One moment she's a liberated woman and the next a Southern belle. I think you've been straddling the same fence. You pleased yourself by leaving home and becoming a writer, yet subconsciously you saw to it that you also pleased your grandmother by not writing anything worthwhile. You told yourself, in effect, that it was permissible to write for a living, to treat it as a job, as long as you didn't treat it as an art and derive intellectual satisfaction from it."

He was right, of course. It was so obvious that I had missed it completely.

"Forever feminine was my late mother-in-law's motto," he sighed, blowing out a cloud of blue smoke. He looked at me with a twinkle in his eyes. "Do you remember the time she donated her womb to the University of Virginia?"

"Vaguely."

"That's when I first began to wonder about her. She summoned me to the hospital and demanded that I bless the womb. It was sitting on the bedside table in a jar. I told her that since I had blessed her many times while it was still in her, I felt it was sufficiently sanctified already, and in any case, I did not bless detached organs. She got very put out with me and sent me away, but the next day she summoned me again. This time she wanted me to accompany the womb on its trip to Charlottesville and conduct a ceremony she had spent the previous night choreographing, to be called the 'Dedication of the Womb.' When I told her that I was not empowered to invent new rituals, she called me a pagan and tried to get me barred from the hospital.''

I had never heard any of these details, but that was not surprising; Granny never publicized her defeats.

''But the really intriguing part of the whole affair,'' he went on, ''is that there was nothing wrong with her womb.''

My mouth fell open. Virginius nodded.

''I talked to Rex Montgomery about it a few years after he operated on her. Your grandmother was perfectly healthy in that area. She preferred to believe otherwise, however, so she began persuading herself that she was descended from a long line of fragile flowers who were beset by pelvic demons. Somewhere in the course of all this, she conceived a vision of her womb sitting in a niche at the medical school, the object of a statewide pilgrimage by gynecology students. She decided to donate it to the university, so she started plaguing Rex to perform a hysterectomy. At first he refused, but she kept after him until she wore him down. By then she was past the change, so he went ahead and took it out.''

''She told me the university begged her to give them the womb,'' I said. ''What really happened?''

''Rex connived with somebody he knew at Charlottesville and got them to write her a letter requesting the donation in the name of science. It was the only way they could quiet her down.''

Virginius studied the end of his cigarillo. ''That's why I tried to get Edna as much sick leave as I could manage,'' he said. ''I knew her cramps were psychologically induced, but they were severe just the same.''

Mine, too, I thought. Oh, Granny, what crimes were committed in your name!

* * *

The book in the typewriter was almost finished. I wrapped it up the next day and rode into L.A. with Polly to deliver it and tell Amy that I would not be writing any more.

Polly dropped me at the public library, where I phoned Sword & Scabbard to let them know I was coming and to suggest a farewell celebration before they could make other plans for the evening.

Mary Beth answered the call in a curiously slurred voice.

"This is Isabel. I'm coming in with my latest manuscript. Can you all go out for a drink with me after you close up? There's something I have to tell you."

"Go out?" she giggled. "Don't have to go out. Have a drink right here! C'mon over!"

She had had more than Thom McAn cookies. I couldn't imagine a smashed Mary Beth Cartwright; it was like imagining a smashed Mary Tyler Moore. I hung up and flagged a taxi.

When I arrived, Bill was pouring Mary Beth a Scotch and she was stirring it with her finger. When she saw me, she tried to wave but got confused and stuck her whole hand in the glass. She pulled it out, licked it, and flapped it in my general direction.

"What's going on?" I asked, accepting my glass.

"Folie à trois," Bill said. "Now it's *folie à quatre.*"

"We all caved in at the same time," Amy explained, knocking back her drink. "It started when the typewriter repairman made a pass at me. He said he figured I must be pretty hot since I work in a place like this, so he asked me to meet him at the motel across the street. He promised me a ten-inch joystick. That's when I started laughing, because we had a book by that name last month. I just laughed and laughed—I couldn't stop. Finally he got scared and left, and I kept on laughing. It was contagious and pretty soon we were all having hysterics. Then Bill went out to the liquor store."

"The old Navy remedy for shellshock," he said, patting the Scotch bottle.

"It's this place," Amy said, hiccoughing. "We can't stand it any longer. It's done us in."

"I wonder what's going to happen to us?" Mary Beth mused. "Sexwise, I mean."

"I can't get it up." Bill shrugged.

"Neither can I," said Mary Beth. "Comparably speaking, I mean. God, I used to dig sex but now. . . ." Suddenly she slammed her fist on her desk. "Do you know what my pussy is like? Do you have any idea what my pussy is like? Well, I'll tell you what my pussy is like!"

"Sweetie," Amy said kindly, "you don't have to repeat yourself to take up space. You're not reading galleys now—this is a party. No dropped heads, ha-ha."

"Wait a minute! Wait a minute! I wanna tell you about my pussy. Will you let me tell you about my pussy? About this lubrication busi-ness—I don't lubricate like the women in our books."

"Who does?" Amy said. "If I did, I'd get a Pap test before it was too late."

"Wait a minute! Wait a minute! I wanna ask you something. Do you think my pussy is a passion-drenched, quivering, oleaginous, swollen triangle of lubricious lust? Do you think my coral lips glisten with the burning spray of cunt nectar?"

"I hope not," said Bill. "You've used up all your sick leave."

"Do you have any idea what my hair-fringed cloven oval is like? Well, I'll tell you what my hair-fringed cloven oval is like. IT'S AS DRY AS A GODDAMN BONE!"

We all screamed and poured another round. It started to get very hot in the office so I went to open a window. That's when I saw Saman-tha's car. She was circling the block looking for a parking space; through her hatchback window I saw several cardboard cartons full of mason jars.

"She's coming to throw blood!" I cried. "Lock the doors!"

"Who's coming?" Amy asked blurrily.

"Stop talking dirty!" Mary Beth yelled.

I finally managed to get through to them and explain who Samantha was and what was imminent. Bill recovered first.

"The number," he said. "Call the number."

"What number?"

"The one they gave us to call if there was ever any trouble."

"The police?"

"No, just a number. I don't know whose it is. They just told us to call it."

"Who's they?"

"We don't know that, either," Amy said, reaching for her phone list. She managed to find the number and recite it to Bill, who managed to punch out the right buttons on the phone.

"Trouble at Sword and Scabbard," he said tightly into the mouthpiece. "There's a Honda driving around the block with a radical feminist in it. She's going to attack the office."

He hung up and we all gathered at the window and waited. We didn't have to wait long. In a few moments we heard the strains of a familiar old hymn; then the Born Again Good Humor Man tore around the block on two wheels, aiming his truck straight at Samantha's tiny car.

Glass shattered and steel crunched. Samantha's Honda skidded in a circle in the middle of the street. The Good Humor truck reversed with a squeal of tires and shot forward again, aiming this time for her front end. She kept skidding around and the truck kept going for her like an enraged bull, until all four of her fenders were crumpled like balls of discarded onionskin in a writer's wastebasket. There was blood all over the street; the few Mason jars that hadn't broken were rolling around in the remains of the hatch.

Samantha jumped out and took off down the street on her long, basketball player's legs, her screams drowned out by a church chorus on the truck's tape deck. *"Stand up, stand up for Jesus, ye soldiers of the Cross! Lift high his royal banner, it must not suffer loss. . . ."* The singing rose up for a moment, then faded quickly as the truck spun around and disappeared down an alley.

"That's who owns Sword and Scabbard," Bill said.

The ice-cream truck had no sooner left than a tow truck marked "DeLucia's Garage" appeared. A man jumped out, affixed a hook under the bumper of Samantha's ruined car, and towed it away. Finally, there came a street-cleaning truck to wash away the blood and glass with foamy jets of water. In no time, all traces of the melee were gone, and there wasn't a cop in sight.

Soon a huge black Buick pulled up in front of the building. Two powerfully built men in pastel Western suits got out and hurried into the entrance.

"Here they come," Bill said.

"Are they going to throw acid on our kneecaps?" Amy whispered.

The door burst open and the pair entered. Both were in their thirties, with shiny black hair and alert dark eyes. The shorter and stockier of the two introduced himself as Gino and seemed to be in charge.

"You guys okay?" he asked us, his jaws working over a piece of gum.

"Nobody came upstairs," Bill said. "It was just the one woman in the car."

Gino's dark face split into a wide grin. "Yeah," he said happily. "You know who that broad was? The one we been waiting for. She's president of that ballbreaker outfit—HOW, NOW, POW?" He turned to his partner. "What the hell is it, Dominick?"

"ROW."

"Yeah!" He grinned again and motioned us to sit down. He studied us closely.

"You guys all got that look," he began, then nodded in agreement with his own statement. "Yeah, you got that look. Nothing personal, you know what I mean? Everybody who works here gets it. Nobody ever lasts very long." He clapped his palms over his knees in a gesture of finality. Beside me, Amy whimpered.

"Look, folks, we gotta put in a new set. I'm real sorry but like I said, it don't look like you gonna last much longer anyway. It gets to you, working here. The last guy that ran this place shaved off all his hair and went to Tibet. Said he was gonna be a monk. Swore he never wanted to touch another broad as long as he lived."

He turned to his partner and snapped his fingers. "Dominick, the case."

Dominick handed him a tattered black attaché case. When he opened it, I saw that it was full of cash. He wet his thumb and started peeling off bills.

"Let's see, whatta we pay you guys?"

Amy, Bill, and Mary Beth quoted their weekly salaries and Gino paid them in full without question. Then he turned to me.

"I don't work here, I'm a writer."

"She just turned in her latest manuscript," said Amy, holding up my brown envelope.

"That's fifteen hundred, right?"

We nodded and he counted out fifteen one-hundred-dollar bills and handed them to me. Once again, he studied us shrewdly, an amused smile playing on his lips.

"Now, look," he said softly. "You don't have to declare this on your income tax, so don't, okay?'' He clapped his hands over his knees again and stood up.

''You guys got a consolation prize coming,'' he said. ''Come on over to the restaurant and have a nice dinner on the house.''

''What restaurant?'' we asked.

''My mother's,'' he said reverently.

CHAPTER ELEVEN

Aunt Edna was ready to throw her foal. Virginius reserved a ''birthing room'' for the two of them at the hospital; she was determined to have natural childbirth, but because of her age, her doctor advised her to arrive early for careful monitoring just in case, so they left for the hospital before her pains started. Virginius, who was going to move in with her for the duration, promised to call us with regular reports and let us know when labor began so we could be there for the event.

The house was strangely empty after they left. It was winter, and the wind whistling in from the sea made the old walls creak and groan. We gathered in Martha's warm, redolent kitchen and, to Polly's despair, swapped old wives' tales.

''They say a baby with older parents will have a high I.Q.,'' I said.

''Statistics show—''

''They say having a baby late in life delays the change,'' Martha said.

''Recent research—''

''I hope it comes this weekend. Sunday's child is fair of face,'' said Agnes.

''If the baby comes at night and there's blood on the moon, make sure you look at it through your legs and spit three times.'' This, of course, was Gloria's contribution.

Suddenly Agnes cocked her head and listened.

''What was that?''

''What was what?''

''I heard a noise, kind of like a thumping.''

''It's the house,'' said Polly. ''I got the appraiser's report the other day and you should see—''

She was interrupted by a horrendous bellow of "BANZAI!" and several gunshots. The thumping turned to heavy footsteps, and then the kitchen door burst open.

Agnes screamed. "BOOMER! OH, GOD! OH, NO!"

I looked into the barrel of the shotgun and then up at the man who held it. For a moment I thought it was General Patton come back from the grave: he had all kinds of things hanging on him—straps holding water canteens, binoculars, a walkie-talkie, a bowie knife, a map case, two crossed bandoliers containing extra ammo, and two extra guns, one over each shoulder.

Under all the paraphernalia he wore a camouflage-print battle outfit, boondocker boots, an Australian bush hat like the man on my ceiling, and a gas mask lodged under his chin. He was at least six feet four and looked entirely capable of doing all the things Agnes had told us about. In short, Boomer Mulligan was a paranoid's paranoid.

The first thing he said was "Ack-ack-ack," which quickly grew into "Awwwwggghhhrrr!" and then graduated to "AAAAHHHHHGGG!" It sounded very familiar, a kind of morning sound. I was so terrified that it took me several seconds to realize that he was coughing—with his finger on the trigger. I saw the coroner filling out my certificate. *Cause of death:* 61,345 Raleigh coupons.

At last he recovered and spoke in a hoarse, raspy voice. "You stole my wife," he said accusingly, looking menacingly around the table.

"Boomer, please! Don't shoot!"

"Shut up! You're coming with me, Agnes. I'm gonna—*ack-ack-ack*—make a real woman out of you. Everybody up!" he ordered. "Put your hands on top of your head and walk!"

We rose and paraded in single file out the kitchen door. I was bringing up the rear so I had the gun in my back. Agnes had turned to jelly, but her sobs and pleas moved him not.

"It's no use, Agnes. I'm gonna fuck—*ack-ack-ack*—you. You deserve it."

"How did you find me, Boomer?"

"I got ways."

He herded us into the living room and stopped.

"You," he said, prodding me with the gun. "Pick up that portable TV and bring it."

I did as I was told and he marched us up to the third floor and put us in one of the never-used smaller bedrooms without a bath. He motioned me to put the TV on the bureau and plug it in.

"Turn it on to Channel Seven," he said.

"What's that for, Boomer?" Agnes asked.

"So's you can watch the hostage crisis."

"What hostage crisis?"

"This one, you sap!" The shout caused him to have another hacking seizure. We waited through it until he had stopped wheezing. "I called the TV news people," he went on. "They'll be here any minute."

Still drawing a bead on us, he used his other hand to uncap his water canteen and take a long swig, which he swallowed, and then another, which he gargled and spat out. Clearing his throat, he reached into his cartridge belt and took out a Vicks cough drop and popped it between his grim lips.

He left the room with Agnes in tow and shut the door. I heard him outside, doing something with a chain—apparently he carried one of those, too. When I saw the knob move I realized that he was tying the chain to it and wrapping the other end around the banister.

We heard the two of them going down the stairs to the second floor. From the direction of their footsteps, they were headed for her room.

"That man's crazy as a loon!" Martha sobbed. "What's he gonna do to poor Agnes?"

Before anyone could reply, a commotion sounded from the driveway. Looking out the window, we saw TV trucks pulling up to the house, followed by a police car and an ambulance. Turning to the television set, we saw the same thing, only better. As we watched the screen, we saw some technicians attaching a microphone to a long pole; turning around, we saw it bobbing outside the window.

An on-the-spot reporter kicked off the drama.

"Ladies and gentlemen, we are at the Don't Tread on Me women's commune to bring you complete coverage of the hostage-taking. The terrorist's name is Boomer Mulligan, president of a group that calls itself 'Stop Women's Lip.' I have here a copy of their latest newsletter, *The Wife Beater,* which contains an interview with Mr. Mulligan telling of his plan to capture his runaway wife, Agnes, who fled to the commune. Mr. Mulligan, who is a survivalist, is armed and dangerous and has told WNLA that he has placed explosives around the house and yard.''

That did it. Hurling myself at the window, I screamed into the mike. ''Save the pig! Take him out of the pen! Get him away from here!''

''Ladies and gentlemen, we are getting a statement from one of the hostages. She seems very distraught, but we'll try to interview her. What is your name, please?''

''Never mind me! Get Farnsworth!''

''Ladies and gentlemen, you have just heard the voice of Greta Farnsworth, who's being very courageous about this. You just heard her say 'Never mind me.' ''

''I'm not Greta Farnsworth!'' I yelled, hearing my own echo from the TV behind me. ''I'm Isabel Fairfax and Farnsworth is my pig!''

''We have a correction. The hostage misspoke. Her name is Isabel Fairfax and she just referred to the terrorist as a pig. Standing by in our studio are three members of the National Organization of Women, who are going to discuss female rage.''

While the NOWs were venting about venting, I suddenly remembered Quadrupet and threw myself at the window once more. The microphone danced before me but I pushed it aside so I could see into the big oak tree in the side yard. It was Quadrupet's aerie, and as I expected, he was there.

''There him is! Oh, him didn't get him din-dins!''

''Ladies and gentlemen, we have another statement—''

''Fecal-fecal fart-fart, him is mommy's heart-heart!''

The microphone vanished.

''Ladies and gentlemen, we're experiencing some technical difficulties. We now switch you to Lance Gerard, who has located the Don't Tread on Me milkman for a statement on food supplies.''

I looked at the screen and there, in the glare of a revolving blue police light, was nice, normal Mr. Willard having his fifteen seconds of fame.

''I would assess that there was sufficient quantity of dairy products so as not to impact anybody very much, should the negotiations reach a stalemate at some prior time.''

Next came the two old ladies who lived down the road. We had avoided them after one meeting because they both had total recall of nothing, so they were ideal candidates for the "what were you doing when it happened?" interview.

"I was weeding the garden over by the back fence where the slats are loose when my sister comes out and says, 'I thought I heard shots,' and I says, 'It was probably kids. You know how kids is.' Then my sister says, 'No, it came from that place where they keep the women.' Dinner was ready by then so we set down to the table and my sister says, 'I hear a siren,' and I says, 'It's them kids,' but she was sure it was a siren and started to go out and look, but I says, 'You better not go out,' on account of them kids that stole her pockabook last Halloween. You never know what kids might do."

Suddenly we were switched back to the studio. A puffed-up anchorman announced that they were negotiating with Boomer about installing a direct telephone line so they could negotiate with him some more. Moments later came a second announcement that he had agreed. Soon Ma Bell's crisis team arrived and they, too, were interviewed. It was obvious that they had taken a company-sponsored course in the psychology of terrorism.

"The terrorist has a felt need to feel met," said one earnestly. "The moment of counter-intensity follows when the ego is diverted to a sense of outside-worldness in a technological stress-factor reduction." Here was the man for Polly; it would be a verbiage made in heaven.

The reporter interrupted. "Ladies and gentlemen, we are in contact with the terrorist. He is ready to state his demands. Hello? Go ahead, Boomer."

"Ack-ack-ack."

"Are you there, Boomer?"

"Yeah. Just cigarettes. I'm trying to cut down."

"Can you tell us how your wife is?"

"Dumb as ever. Never mind her, it's the country I'm worried about. It's fulla nuts."

"Boomer, would you describe yourself as a concerned citizen?"

"Yeah."

"Boomer, would you like to describe your beliefs to our viewers?"

"Yeah."

"Boomer, do you think we're headed for an apocalypse?"

"Nah, but I'll tell you one thing: all hell's gonna break loose."

"Boomer, what advice can you give our viewers to help them survive?"

"Shoot to kill."

"Boomer, will you let us speak to your wife?"

Agnes came on the line with a shrill falsetto keen and complicated the situation at once.

"I'm not the one he wants! Nobody wants me, I'm Swedish! My name is Astrid Mortensen!"

Polly, Gloria, and I exchanged stunned looks. The alias we had concocted for Agnes had not lasted past the arrival of the Raleigh-coupon check. After that, everybody had forgotten about it. Apparently, she was now in such a panic that she had snatched it out of the blue in some wild hope that it might save her.

"Ladies and gentlemen! We have a new development—"

"We got no new development," Boomer snarled. "This is my wife and I'm gonna — her."

It was bleeped. "Ladies and gentlemen, Boomer Mulligan has just told us that he's going to have a dialogue with his wife."

"Hey, look!" said Gloria.

We turned and saw her standing in the closet, looking up at a panel in the ceiling.

"There's a crawlspace or egress or something in here. It must lead to the attic."

We crowded in and looked. As she removed the ceiling panel we saw the unfinished timbers of the attic.

"Give me a leg up," she ordered. "I can go down the back steps to Agnes's room."

"Gloria, honey, don't," Martha pleaded.

"Help me up."

"But Boomer's armed and dangerous," Polly protested.

Gloria gave us her best troll's smile. "So am I."

Had she brought a knife from the kitchen? She would not be dissuaded, so we joined hands in a cat's cradle and hoisted her up. She crawled over the edge of the opening and crept soundlessly off across the bare dusty floor of the attic.

She had been gone some twenty minutes when the reporter started announcing a "vigil."

"Ladies and gentlemen, night has fallen here at the Don't Tread on Me women's—"

A scream cut through his words and seemed to shake the house. It was an unearthly sound, agonized and shrill, like something coming out of a misty bog.

"Who was that?" Martha quavered.

Unable to tell what was happening in our own house, we looked at the television screen. The reporter was apoplectic.

"Ladies and gentlemen! Something has happened! We may have reached a turning point—"

Suddenly the front door burst open and there was Gloria on camera.

"Make haste!" she cried. "The deed is done!"

Everyone streamed into the house; cops, ambulance personnel, cameramen, and the jabbering newscaster. A fireman with an ax ran upstairs and broke the chain that held our door; we rushed out and clambered down the stairs to the second floor, our hearts in our throats, dreading what we might find.

The first person we saw was Agnes, stark naked, running up and down the hallway screaming about Swedes, Raleigh coupons, and a ransom of freeze-dried disaster food.

Also naked except for his Australian hat, Boomer lay prone on her bed, groaning and coughing at once, his eyes open in an expression of dumb shock as if he could not believe what had happened to him. Neither could the horrified newsmen; only a seasoned Edward II scholar could remain unaffected by the sight of Gloria's curling iron sticking out of his ass. The ambulance attendants removed it gingerly and wheeled him out on a gurney.

"He raped me!" Agnes screamed.

She was still running naked up and down the hall, to the stunned edification of the sixty or so men present.

"She's a natural blonde," whispered one of the camera crew.

Polly and I finally got a robe on her and one of the doctors gave her a shot to calm her down, but more excitement loomed. Two ominous cars of the type known as "unmarked" careened up the driveway and skidded to a stop just before they went through the veranda railing. Four men jumped out, one of them carrying handcuffs and another a wire-service photo and some other papers. They raced up the steps with a bevy of uniformed troopers behind them and flashed badges at us.

"FBI. We've just received word from the director of the Minnesota Women's Prison. The escaped convict, one Astrid Mortensen, is wanted on five counts of armed robbery and murder of a prison guard." He looked at the photo, then at Agnes. "Come along quietly."

"But she's not Astrid Mortensen!" Polly cried. "We just made that up because of the Raleigh coupons. She's really Welsh but Isabel said she ought to be Swedish, so we picked out a Swedish name for her and used the same initials because Gloria's lover said that—"

"Wait a minute," said the agent. "Are you saying that this woman is not Astrid Mortensen?"

"Yes, of course not!"

"I can prove it," Agnes mumbled sleepily, staggering to her feet. "My driver's license. It's in my bag. I'll get it." She started for her room but the FBI men grabbed her.

I fetched the bag and the men looked at the driver's license. The resemblance between Agnes and the escaped convict was striking, and so were the zaftig vital statistics.

"I'm sorry, but she'll have to come down to the Bureau and have her fingerprints taken."

"But the doctor just gave her a sedative," Polly argued. "She's almost out."

"I'm sorry, we can't let her go until we're sure of her identity. You'll have to get her dressed and come with her. If she's the woman Minnesota says she is, she's a real killer."

So we had to dress Agnes. It was like dressing a corpse. By the time we finished, she was completely unconscious and had to be carried downstairs by four men. The cameras ground away, recording it all while the news reporters got it all wrong. As we made our way through the crush, somebody asked us if Agnes had committed suicide after witnessing her husband's rape.

The FBI would permit only one of us to accompany her in their car. I quickly volunteered for fear Polly would start some sort of political argument. She, Martha, and Gloria followed the government cars in the van.

We arrived at the field office and dragged Agnes in for her finger-printing. She kept collapsing on the ink pad, until she was covered with smudges that looked like the bruises she had the night we met her. They put the prints on a machine and we all waited. Before long, proof that she was not Astrid Mortensen came spinning out and she was cleared.

But of course it was not over yet. Agnes could get drunk on half of a Pink Lady, so whatever the doctor had given her was bound to have an even more startling effect.

It did. When the FBI man leaned over her to apologize, she came to and gave him a groggy leer.

"I'd like to suck your cock."

He blushed, but before anyone could stop her, she opened her mouth and made a lunging dive for his crotch. Her chair turned over and she fell between his feet and started licking the toe of his shoe. He managed to haul her up but she threw herself into his arms and stuck her tongue in his ear. Several other agents came to his rescue but it was like trying to separate someone from a large, amorous seal.

She kept rubbing herself against whichever agent was nearest. She must have had an orgasm at some point in the fray; by the time we got her into the van, she was limp and peaceful and slept all the way back to the house.

"She won't remember any of it," said Martha.

None of us had the strength to haul her in, so we decided to let her sleep it off in the back of the van. Martha covered her with one of her homemade quilts—we must have been the only feminist commune to hold quilting bees—and we dragged ourselves inside.

Just as we got in the house, the phone rang. It was Virginius.

"I just talked to the television people. They said you were safe but had to go with the FBI. Is everything all right?"

"Fine, don't worry about a thing," I said. "How's Aunt Edna?"

"In labor. She was watching TV, and when she saw you singing at the window it brought on the baby."

"We'll be right there."

Virginius met us in front of the birthing room looking like Marcus Welby with a camera slung around his neck. He was scrubbed and sterilized and decked out in operating-room green with a little matching cap.

He had barely greeted us when a familiar view halloo from the birthing room split the air.

"Oh, Law! Here it comes! Virginius, bring the camera or you'll miss the head!"

We heard grunts and pants and Virginius's clicking camera interspersed with "Oh, Law!" and "It's just slidin' like a greased pig!"

A few minutes later there was another sound that made me think of Quadrupet when he had females on his mind. Martha, the only mother among us now that Agnes was conked out in the van, broke into a tremulous smile.

"Oh, Law! I did it! I just did it like I've been doin' it all my life! What is it? Oh, tell me quick." For once she was not interested in dragging out a story.

"A girl!" Virginius cried.

He stuck his head out the door to announce the weight—six pounds, four ounces—and flagged us in.

Aunt Edna was still in position, waiting for either the placenta or the afterbirth, and the baby was lying on her stomach. It would have been embarrassing had it not been for Virginius. Even blood-spattered, he exuded such civilized charm that the slimy baby and Aunt Edna's pudenda seemed like conversation pieces at a rectory sherry party.

The doctor shooed us out so Virginius and Aunt Edna could "experience bonding time." We were all hungry, so we left to have a late supper. Agnes was still out cold in the back and didn't come to until we drove back to the hospital. I waited nervously to see if she had awakened to a new life of nymphomania, but she was her old self again, back to "Oh, mercy." We got her some black coffee and then we all went up to see the baby.

Everyone involved in the birth was now washed and dressed. Aunt Edna, obviously in fine fettle, was sitting up in bed reading a pamphlet on postpartum readjustment.

"I'm going to buy one of those papoose slings called a 'Snuggli,'" she said. "That way, the baby hangs over my front and bumps against my stomach when I walk. That keeps 'em in a fetal position longer and makes 'em think they're back in the womb. It says so right here.''

"What are you going to name her?" Martha asked.

"Virginia Upton Chillingsworth."

Virginius took a purple stole from his pocket. "I'd like to baptize her now, while everyone is here."

It was another of his perfect touches. There was no need for an immediate baptism; the baby was healthy, but he sensed that we all needed a formal ritual after the chaos of our hostage crisis. More practically, it was also a means of keeping Aunt Edna from working herself up and demanding to hear a blow-by-blow account of our siege told in exactly the manner she would have told it.

I was the official godmother, but everyone was a sponsor of sorts. To my surprise, Gloria was much more familiar with the responses than I was, especially the ones that appealed to her the most. When Virginius came to "Dost thou renounce the devil and all his works?" she responded with such a vigorous "I renounce them all!" that everyone jumped.

"Wilt thou be baptized in this Faith?" asked Virginius.

"THAT IS MY DESIRE! IT IS MEET AND RIGHT SO TO DO!"

By the end of the rite, Martha was so carried away by Gloria's fervor that she shouted "Praise the Lord!" in the classic Baptist manner. Agnes added a mainstream Methodist "Amen."

Polly looked very peculiar, but then she was a Unitarian. I put her dull eyes and draggy manner down to theology and fatigue, until she groaned and clutched her stomach.

"Look at that child! She's sick!"

Just as Aunt Edna pointed, Polly fell to the floor and rolled over in agony. It was typical of her efficiency to get sick in a hospital; a passing doctor looked in and saw her and called for a cart. They loaded her on it and pushed her down the hall at a dead heat.

"It must be appendicitis," Martha said. "Has she still got her appendix?"

Everyone looked questioningly at me as the original roommate but I did not know. She had never said anything about it, and despite her Bastille-busting efforts for women's liberation, she was very modest, so I had never seen her naked enough to notice a scar.

We waited nervously for the verdict. In a half hour or so, the doctor returned.

"Nothing serious," he said. "Just acute diarrhea."

My mouth fell open. I had lived with her anal retentiveness too long to believe the doctor's diagnosis. Her mind was like cement and the contents of the other end even harder; she went through Ultima Thule suppositories the way I went through cigarettes. Polly with diarrhea was like Napoleon with modesty.

"Are you sure?" I said.

"Yep. Never saw a case quite like it. But don't worry, she'll be okay after a couple of days here."

CHAPTER TWELVE

Two days later I drove to the hospital to pick up Polly. She was paler and thinner than ever and her marchlike walk was gone, replaced by a scooty creep. Clutched to her breast like a security blanket was a little pillow shaped like a life preserver that the hospital had given her. When we got to the van she put it on the front seat and lowered herself gingerly over the hole. Not to put too fine a point on it, the Bradshaw had gone out of her.

She was unusually quiet on the drive but I put it down to exhaustion. I didn't realize just how purged she was until we were half-way home.

"I'm going to sell the house," she said suddenly.

"Why?"

"Because it's an awful house. Uncle Ezra was too busy with the whales to keep it up the way he should have. And besides, he . . . he—" She broke off with a quavery sigh, her eyes closing in momentary despair before she went on. "I found some papers of his. He was involved with a group from Berkeley that claimed termites are an endangered species and. . . . Well, there're some serious structural problems. I want to get rid of it while I still can. If I wait any longer I'd get arrested for fraud."

"What about the commune?" I asked.

"I don't know, I don't care," she moaned, reaching under herself to rearrange her pillow. "Oh, God! Now I know how Edward the Second felt."

The next day the For Sale sign went up and soon lots of friendly, gung-ho realtors with company insignia on their jackets came swarming around. Polly, who did not believe in ethnic idiosyncrasies, was the honor-bright Wasp, practically *introducing* them to the termites. Her honesty paid off; in a few weeks she got a low but acceptable offer from a condo developer. We had eight weeks to vacate.

My first thought was Farnsworth. Polly wanted to sell him back to the farmer who had sold him to us but I set up an outcry.

"He'll be slaughtered and eaten!"

Once again Virginius came to the rescue. He knew of an interfaith council that operated a children's miniature farm near Los Angeles. They needed an affectionate pig that the little visitors could pet without danger, a job description that suited Farnsworth to a tee, so after an emotional farewell I let them take him.

Now we all had to plan new lives, a task Aunt Edna simplified by inviting everyone back to Virginia.

I seconded the motion. "Oh, please come. We can all live in my old house. Now that Aunt Edna will be living at the rectory, there'll be plenty of room for five of us."

I meant it; I couldn't imagine parting from any of them now—even Polly. They all hated California, so the idea of moving back East appealed to them. The big question was, what would they do when they got there? A few more rap sessions, plus some more fireside chats with Virginius, and the matter was settled.

The most startling solution was Gloria's.

"I'm going to study for the priesthood," she announced. "Virginius is going to sponsor me."

It was mind-boggling only because the idea of women priests was mind-boggling. Once you accepted that, a clerical Gloria made perfect sense. Sweeping across dimly lit stone floors in a cassock was, when you came right down to it, just about the only thing she *could* do for a living.

She now looked respectable enough to get into divinity school. Realizing her Edward II fantasy on Boomer had exorcized her demons sufficiently so that she had let Agnes cut and thin her hair and agreed to dispense with her drapery skirt. The New Gloria was almost normal, except for certain immutable Old Gloria touches, but that was as it should be: Episcopalians have always preferred the flying buttress to the pillar of church.

As far as I could tell, she wasn't the least bit religious, but she was extremely churchy, and that was far more important. To the Episcopal mind, devout believers are an embarrassing annoyance: the point of it all is to be Christian ladies and gentlemen.

Agnes was going to be Virginius's new secretary. Her stenotyping was now a model of speed and accuracy, so she would be a great improvement over Aunt Edna.

"You'll just love Queen Caroline," Aunt Edna assured her. "It's small, but you don't have to worry, I know everybody for miles around. Come to think of it, there are a couple of very interesting single men I can introduce you to. Now that you're going to get divorced, you can start thinking about getting married again."

Agnes shook her head. "Thanks, but I'm through with marriage. I just don't like being married. I guess it's because I never cared for sex."

We all looked at each other and then thoughtfully contemplated the wall.

Polly and Martha were going to start a Southern deli called "Polly Bailey's" whose specialty was to be homemade scrapple. Martha would do the cooking and Polly would do the entrepreneuring. They were very excited about it and already talking of chains and franchises. I offered them my father's old warehouse and the rest of the hatboxes to get them started. At long last, Queen Caroline would have a Yankee industry and Polly would have a practical outlet for all that Yankee energy.

I assumed her political spree was over. Since the night of her momentous purge she had not mentioned ROW, George McGovern, free checking accounts for paupers, IQ tests that discriminated against the retarded, concerts for the deaf, or any committee.

Free at last, I thought to myself. At that precise moment, she looked up from the dinner table and nailed us with the Bradshaw Gleam.

"When we start hiring people, I have a marvelous workers' plan I want to institute. My Grandfather Lyman tried it in Wales but the mine owners weren't ready for it. Basically, the president of the company serves as president of the union. That way, everyone works to-

gether on an equal basis for the betterment of all, and worker-manage-
ment strife is eliminated.''

I turned to Gloria. ''Here we go again. She's going to organize her
own labor.''

''Jésu. . . .''

FINIS

CONFESSIONS OF A FAILED SOUTHERN LADY

1985

It's hard choosing excerpts from your most popular book. I didn't ask for opinions because I knew I would get a different answer from each person. Even harder is excerpting around a storyline. Although the dust jacket of Confessions of a Failed Southern Lady *clearly says "memoir," several reviewers called it a novel because it reads like one.*

I wanted to put together a sampling of one chapter from the beginning, one from the middle, and one from the end, but it would have contained too many unmoored references. That's okay for those of you who already know the book, but it's frustrating for new readers, so I decided to go the straight chronological route and include the Prologue, Chapter One, and Chapter Two. That takes the story up to my birth and establishes the suspense, which is: "The baby—or the grandmother?"

The events surrounding the publication of Confessions *would make one of those story-of-a-book books. I toured it with an abscessed tooth that I had pulled en route and later displayed on a talk show (Cal doesn't believe this but he was a sophomore at Yale when it happened). Even more dramatic was the fracas that erupted in England between the Brit paperback publisher and a feminist bookstore called "The Silver Moon." It started over the cover illustration and grew to monstrous proportions. I had nothing to do with it and wasn't even there, but both sides outdid themselves defending me. That doesn't happen often; I usually end up alienating everybody, but this book is different.*

PROLOGUE

There are ladies everywhere, but they enjoy generic recognition only in the South. There is a New England old maid but not a New England lady. There is a Midwestern farm wife but not a Midwestern lady. There is most assuredly a California girl, but if anyone spoke of a California lady, even Phil Donahue and Alan Alda would laugh.

If you wish to understand the American woman, study the Southern woman. The sweetening process that feminists call "socialization" is simply a less intense version of what goes on in every Southern family. We call it "rearing." If the rearing is successful, it results in that perfection of femininity known as a lady.

I was reared. On the day in 1948 that I got my first period, my grandmother gave me a clipping. I suppose it came from the Daughters' magazine since she never read anything else. It said:

> When God made the Southern woman, He summoned His angel messengers and He commanded them to go through all the star-strewn vicissitudes of space and gather all there was of beauty, of brightness and sweetness, of enchantment and glamour, and when they returned and laid the golden harvest at His feet, He began in their wondering presence the work of fashioning the Southern girl. He wrought with the golden gleam of the stars, with the changing colors of the rainbow's hues and the pallid silver of the moon. He wrought with the crimson that swoons in the rose's ruby heart, and the snow that gleams on the lily's petal. Then, glancing down deep into His own bosom, He took of the love that gleamed there like pearls beneath the sun-kissed waves of a summer sea, and thrilling that love into the form He had fashioned, all heaven veiled its face, for lo, He had wrought the Southern girl.

That my mother referred to this paean as "a crock of shit" goes far to explain why Granny worked so hard at my rearing. She was a frustrated ladysmith and I was her last chance. Mama had defeated her but she kept the anvil hot for me and began hammering and firing with a strength born of desperation from the day I entered the world until the day she left it.

This is the story of my years on her anvil. Whether she succeeded in making a lady out of me is for you to decide, but I will say one thing in my own favor before we begin.

No matter which sex I went to bed with, I never smoked on the street.

CHAPTER ONE

My ladylike adventures have taken me from Seattle to Paris, but last year I was carried back to Tidewater Virginia, which my ancestors helped to unsettle.

A romantic version of my address can be found on the first page of Thackeray's *Henry Esmond,* which kicks off with a description of the Esmond family's royal grant "in Westmoreland County between the Rappahannock and Potomac rivers." It was the only book I ever read that Granny did not tell me to get my nose out of. Though she hated "bluestockings"—her name for female intellectuals, who could never be ladies—she actually read a few pages of it herself, muttering, "Esmond . . . Esmond . . . do I know any Esmonds?"

Being an Englishman, my father was singularly unimpressed by Granny's ancestors, so I knew he was getting ready to enjoy himself. I met his dancing eyes and read the message in them: *Don't tell her it's a novel.* We let her go on until she was saying, "It was Samuel Esmond who married my great-great-grandfather's half-sister." Preening herself, she added, "Our royal grant was next to theirs."

I had heard about our royal grant many times. Granny was always careful to keep it in the same place, but the grantor changed depending upon what monarchical name happened to pop into her head while she was launched on her pipe dreams. Her boasts were believable as long as she stuck to kings and queens from the pre-1776 era, but when she claimed a royal grant from William IV, my father started laughing so hard he had to leave the table.

"William the Fourth reigned from 1830 to 1837, Granny," I said.

"Be that as it may," she replied serenely.

Our ancestors did arrive very early in Virginia—1672—but they were not the kind of people Granny said they were, and they rose very little in the social scale in subsequent generations. I would not be at all surprised if I turned out to be a direct descendant of the Spotsylvania hatchetman who relieved Kunta Kinte of his foot.

I began life by letting down the side. Being the first person in my family who was not born in Virginia made the radio quiz shows of the Forties a painful experience for me. Crouching like Cinderella beside the huge Philco console, I listened to the wild applause that vibrated through its brocaded sound vents when a contestant named Texas as his home state. Texas always got the biggest hand, but any state seemed to arouse the audience; even Rhode Island got a big sympathy vote.

I looked up at the two adults on the sofa. Granny was crocheting and Mama was reading the *Times-Herald* sports page and chainsmoking Luckies. They looked as if nothing was wrong, and of course, nothing was wrong for them. They had a home state; I did not.

"What would I say?" I asked.

"About what?" Mama muttered abstractedly.

"If I was on the show and they asked me my home state?"

"You're a Virginian," Granny said with a sublime smile. "Everyone is."

"But I wasn't born there. Suppose they asked me where I was born?"

Mama lit a new cigarette from the butt in her yellowed fingers.

"Well, tell 'em the truth, what's wrong with that?"

"Because they wouldn't clap. They only clap for states."

"If the District isn't good enough for 'em, tell 'em to take their sixty-four dollars and shove it."

"Oh, Louise!" Granny cried. "That's no expression to use in front of the child! How do you expect her to grow up to be a lady if you cuss like a trooper?"

"Oh, shit."

"I don't have a home state," I mourned.

"Oh, for God's sake! Tell 'em you're from Maryland, then. Washington's really in Maryland anyhow. Washingtonians used to have to put both District and Maryland tags on their cars. Tell 'em *that*."

Like charity, schizophrenia begins at home. Washington would really have been in Virginia, too, if Virginia had not been what Mama called "a bunch of goddamn Indian-givers." In 1789, the Old Dominion donated a section of Fairfax County to make up the South Bank of the District of Columbia; but angered when all the important government buildings were erected on the Maryland side, they took it back. The disputed portion was called Alexandria County until 1920, when it was renamed Arlington County. It was here that Mama was born in 1908.

Arlington is now part of the polyglot Yankee suburb known tactfully as "Northern Virginia," but until the end of World War II there was no such place. It was simply part of Virginia, a rural area dotted with small villages whose names survive today as shopping malls or beltline exits: Rosslyn, Clarendon, Ballston, Cherrydale, Tyson's Corner, and Bailey's Crossroads. The people who lived there were not commuters in the modern sense; they might, like my grandfather, have worked for the "guvment" because the government happened to be close by, but otherwise they looked on the Nation's Capital as a shopping town, the way people in northern Mississippi regard Memphis.

Mama grew up in Ballston on a dirt road in a white frame house bordered by a field of wild strawberries and enhanced by a lacy gazebo in the backyard. She had an older brother, Botetourt (pronounced Bottatot), named for the Virginia Royal Governor from whom Granny claimed descent. Granny, of course, actually called him Botetourt; Mama called him Gottapot and everyone else called him Bud. After my grandfather died in 1921, the worthy Botetourt married and moved to Falls Church, leaving Granny and Mama to fight out alone what was by then a hopeless battle over Mama's image.

She was not pretty but our Indian blood had come out in her and given her face a noble cast. She looked like a blond Duchess of Windsor; the same winglike cheekbones, big tense jaw, and thin clamped mouth. Her stark features and big-boned bonyness were made for devastating compensatory chic, but unlike the Duchess, Mama was not interested in creating illusions.

She started smoking cornsilk at eight. At twelve she taught herself to drive by stealing Botetourt's car and driving all the way to Fairfax Courthouse before they caught her. At fifteen she quit school, applied for a work permit, and got a job as a telephone operator at the Clarendon exchange. With her first pay she bought an infielder's glove and joined the telephone company's softball team as shortstop. Granny tried to put a good face on matters by attending a few games so people would think she approved of girlish sport, but the day she noticed a lump in Mama's cheek and realized it was tobacco, she had to be helped from the bleachers and escorted home.

Scarcely a day passed without an "Oh, Louise—Oh, shit" argument. The worst crisis erupted over the gazebo. Granny kept telling Mama to "use" it, so Mama hung a punching bag from the middle of the roof and got one of her good ole boy pals to give her boxing lessons. Men felt comfortable around her and frequently took her to ball games and races, but no matter how many times Granny told her to keep her dates waiting, my competitive mother would dress early, lie in wait behind the curtains watching for her escort, and then throw open the door before the first ring and say, "I beat you!"

Knowing that she could do nothing with Mama, Granny looked

around the family for a malleable girl who would heed her advice, a surrogate daughter cast in the traditional mold, someone delicate and fragile in both body and spirit, a true exemplar of Southern womanhood. Someone, in other words, either sick or crazy.

One of the joys of growing up Southern is listening to women argue about whether nervous breakdowns are more feminine than female trouble, or vice versa. They never put it quite that bluntly, but it is precisely what they are arguing about. These two afflictions are the sine qua non of female identity and the Southern woman is not happy unless her family history manifests one or the other. Her preference is dictated by her own personality and physical type. Well-upholstered energetic clubwomen usually opt for female trouble, while languid fine-drawn aristocrats choose nervous breakdowns.

Granny's next-door neighbor in Ballston was Aunt Nana Fairbanks, who made a home for her niece, Evelyn Cunningham. Evelyn was the same age as Mama but famed for a very different sort of double play: on the day she was supposed to be taken to the state mental hospital in Staunton, she had such bad cramps that she missed the ambulance.

Here was an ornament to grace any family tree, so the two dowagers started fighting over her. Picture, if you will, Aunt Nana, *née* Cunningham, moving across her yard in her Mandarin glide to meet Granny, *née* Upton, who is moving across her yard in her Roman matron strut. They meet at a hole in the hedge like two opposing generals in a parley ground and discuss the prize booty both of them are determined to claim.

"Evelyn is having a nervous breakdown," Aunt Nana said proudly. "All of the Cunninghams are high-strung."

"Evelyn doesn't take after the Cunninghams," Granny replied. "It's the Upton womb that's causing those spells of hers."

"I was in the middle of my nervous breakdown when I married Mr. Fairbanks," Aunt Nana recalled with a fond smile. "I was so run down I only weighed ninety pounds. He had to carry me around in his arms that whole first year."

"When I married Mr. Ruding, the doctor told him I might never be able to carry a child." Granny smiled. "I had a descending womb—it runs in the family—and it was just hanging by a thread. I couldn't sleep, I cried all the time—just like Evelyn."

"I almost lost my mind," Aunt Nana reminisced. "Evelyn's mind is going, I can see all the signs."

"You can just look at Evelyn and tell she's delicate down below," Granny sighed.

"It's the Cunningham taint."

"It's the Upton womb."

Granny got the prize booty. One morning around four she was awakened by a violent pounding at the door. It was Evelyn, her blond hair in rag curlers and her peaches-and-cream complexion streaked with tears.

"Aunt Lura! Aunt Nana said she's going to send me to the *in*sane asylum again!"

"There's nothing wrong with your mind, it's your parts. Come in and have a glass of warm milk."

Evelyn accepted and stayed two years. During this time Granny had the malleable daughter of her dreams. Clay in the hands of a strong personality, Evelyn did everything she was told. There was no need to teach her to be late; her catatonic seizures, when she stood frozen in the middle of her room with silent tears running down her face, were good for at least half an hour. Nor did she have to be reminded to "make him look for you." Wandering off was one of her specialties. Ballston parties at this time were enlivened by the many girls who pretended to disappear, and Evelyn, who actually did.

No matter when these spells occurred, Granny always blamed them on premenstrual tension, which she called "the pip." Eager to deny Aunt Nana's diagnosis of madness, Evelyn grasped the pelvic straw Granny held out. Soon she forgot all about the Cunningham taint and started talking about the Upton womb, until she convinced herself that being "delicate down below" was part of her charm.

Choreographed by Granny, she became the most popular hysteric in the Virginia Hump. Men came from as far as Leesburg to gaze into her popping eyes and grasp her trembling hands. The intense femininity that seemed to come so naturally to her held them in sexual thrall. They grew hot with desire when she searched frantically through her pocketbook, shrieking, "Oh, what am I looking for?" They sighed like furnace over her habit of breaking into a chorus of "Jada Jada Jing" and being unable to stop. They could not get enough of her berserk sensuality; the more she shook, the more she gasped, the more their spirits rose, for if she was this way on the porch, what must she be like in bed? Even the man whose car she wrecked came back for more; he bought another one and went on giving her driving lessons just to be near her.

The one man in Ballston who was not in love with Evelyn was Preston Hunt, whose heart belonged to Daddy. If the Jewish boy's problem is the umbilical cord, the Southern boy's is the tail of the spermatozoön. Preston's father was a classic Colonel Portnoy whose favorite word was "manly." Preston was not manly enough to suit Daddy. The family hardware store was frequently the scene of screaming debacles whenever Mr. Hunt, who saw himself as a hot-tempered *beau sabreur* of the Old South, lost what little self-control he had and inflicted corporal punishment on his twenty-eight-year-old son.

It was rough-and-ready Mama who met Preston's emotional needs, and so he began courting her. She despised him for being the *garçon manqué* she knew herself to be, but he came along at a time when she needed to show Granny and Evelyn that she, too, could catch a beau. They got together, and to Granny's unanalytical delight, they used the gazebo, where the punching bag swaying gently in the breeze supplied the filip Preston required. He came over every night and sat in the lacy boxing ring talking about his father.

"My daddy whipped me till my nose bled buttermilk," he confided happily. "I was late to work this morning and he took an old harness left over from when we sold them, and he just laid it on me something terrible. But I deserved it. Daddy's right to whip me when I need it, I know that. I don't mean to talk against him." His voice began to tremble. "You know that, don't you? I love Daddy! Did I sound to you like I was finding fault with him? Tell me the truth, Louise. Do you think I badmouthed Daddy just now?"

"You're a sissy, Preston," Mama snarled in the azalea-scented night. "I hate sissies! If I were a man, you wouldn't catch me being a sissy! I hate you, Preston! Get out and don't come back!"

Naturally he obeyed but he always came back. He could not keep away from her. A few nights later he would return and they would sit in the moonlit gazebo and whisper another round of sweet nothings.

"I'd like to kill you, Preston. I'd like to get in my car and run right over you. If I were a man, I'd wipe the floor with you! I'd knock you into the middle of next week! Stop doing your mouth that way. You know what way I mean—twisting it down at the corner and making that squirty noise. Why are you sitting with your feet folded one over the other? You always sit like that! I hate the way you sit! *I hate your feet!''*

"I'm sorry, honey—"

"Shut up! Get out!''

In the summer of 1933, he bought season box seats on the first base line at Griffith Stadium and took her to see the Senators play every weekend. As Mama expertly marked her scorecard and squinted through the smoke from her Lucky Strike Greens, Preston gazed at her with plangent expectancy, but she was so intent on the game that she forgot to bully him. Unable to bear the torments of respite, he devised ways to get on her nerves, like eating his hot dogs from the middle, but it drew nothing more than an absent-minded "Stop that, Preston."

As the season wore on, he developed several new facial tics, squeezed his blackheads, and even tried wearing one black shoe and one brown one, but Mama was too engrossed in Lou Gehrig to notice. At any other time of the year she would have threatened to cut off his feet and throw them in his face, but not in summer.

By the end of the baseball season Preston was in an advanced state of anxiety. The situation came to a head the night he escorted Mama and Granny to a dinner dance given by the Daughters, at which Granny was scheduled to play the Statue of Liberty in a patriotic tableau.

It was a dressy affair that required all the things tomboys hate, like armpit-length white gloves, so Preston was counting on Mama to be in a bad mood. She was, but there was nothing she could do about it. The hall was crammed with Daughters, and like all Southern girls in the presence of formidable dowagers, she was forced completely out of character. She could not very well bellow threats about running over him while all the old ladies were telling her how sweet she looked, so the abasement Preston craved continued to elude him. He lasted through dinner, but finally the specter of a gentle Mama proved too much for him. Murmuring his excuses, he drifted away. Some moments later when the dancing began he was nowhere to be found.

"Where's that nice boy?'' bayed one of the Daughters, and it traveled around the herd. Soon the question was on every wrinkled lip as the dowagers rubbernecked the ballroom, speculating to each other and commiserating with Mama about what a shame it was that she had to miss the grand march.

"I'll split his scalp open!" roared Mr. Hunt. But for once, Preston had anticipated his father's desires and beaten him, as it were, to the punch. He was found unconscious in a men's room stall, a shattered bourbon bottle beside him, his stiff white shirtfront saturated with whiskey and blood. Evidently he had slipped while chugalugging and struck his head on the toilet seat. His scalp was split open.

An ambulance came and took him to the hospital.

"Do you want to go to him, Louise?" asked Granny.

Her question turned on the Daughters. Eyes burning with the morbid eroticism of old ladies, they urged Mama to take up a vigil at Preston's bedside.

"A sick man falls in love mighty fast," one said brightly.

"Men don't care about hugging and kissing," said another. "They just want somebody to take care of them."

"Catch a man when he's flat on his back and he's yours forever," advised a third.

It was the penis-washing school of femininity. As Mama tried to dream up an excuse they would swallow, a strange voice spoke.

"I say, I found this on the men's room floor. It must have fallen out of that chap's pocket."

Turning, she saw a tall wiry man in his early thirties with dark red hair the color of black cherries. There was a trombone mouthpiece sticking out of the breast pocket of his tuxedo. He held a cigarette case.

"Oh, yes," said Granny. "That's Preston's. We'll keep it for him."

He handed it to her and was about to turn away when one of the Daughters gazed intently into his face and clawed at his sleeve with her brown-spotted hand.

"Are you here tonight?" she asked.

"I believe so, madam."

Her egrette danced on her palsied head as she peered closer.

"Have I seen you?"

"That's for you to say, madam."

"But I must know you," she quavered. "I've never met anyone I didn't know."

"I'm in the band, madam, my name is Herbert King."

"Oh, the band! Then you're not *here*." Her head shook harder as she cocked it in the direction of the ballroom and listened carefully. A look of alarm spread over her face.

"But the band isn't playing!" she cried reedily.

"We're on a break, madam."

"What did you break? I declare, this night is star-crossed."

Before it could get worse, they were interrupted by ruffles and flourishes from the Ballston Fife and Drum Corps.

"Oh, Law!" Granny exclaimed. "It's time for the tableau. I've got to get into my costume."

She and the other Daughters bustled off. My parents were alone together. After a stealthy look around, Herb took a flask from his pocket and poured gin into Mama's punch cup, then served himself a straight shot in the little silver cap. They stood sipping together on the edge of the ballroom as the patriotic tableau began.

As the fifes struck up a shrill rendition of "Columbia, the Gem of the Ocean," Granny sailed in, draped in cheesecloth and dignity, a tinfoil-wrapped flashlight in her left hand and a hastily covered 1933 Sears catalogue in the crook of her right arm. Raising the light on high, she began.

"Give me your tard, your poah . . ."

"Who's that old bat?" Herb whispered.

"My mother."

It was a bad start but the gin helped. After the tableau Mama introduced him to Granny and he offered to drive them home. Granny accepted, charmed by his accent and the nationality it proclaimed. Like all Daughters in their secret hearts, she was such an anglophile that she would have accepted a ride from Jack the Ripper.

They piled into Herb's roadster; Mama in front holding the trombone and clarinet and Granny ensconced in the rumble seat looking like Queen Victoria presiding at a durbar.

She got the shock of her life when she invited him to dinner the following Sunday. He knew nothing about his ancestors and seemed less than awestruck when she told him about hers. Alarmed, she showed him my grandfather's framed copy of the Lancashire Assize Rolls of 1246 containing the name "Griffin del Ruding," but all he did was smile politely. Gazing around at the documents and charts that lined the walls of her parlor, he said he felt as if he were in the British Museum, and Granny, whose idea of wit lay somewhere between blackface vaudeville and slippery banana peels, took it as a compliment.

He did, however, expound on the subject of his immediate family because it gave him a golden opportunity to pull Granny's leg. Arranging his face in a deadpan mask, he told her the sad tale of the Kings: his father, a longshoreman on the Limehouse docks, crushed to death under a bale of machine parts; his mother, dying of the drink in Whitechapel Hospital; his brother Harry, fallen at Ypres and buried in Flanders Fields.

This much was true, but when he got to his sister Daisy he gilded the lily.

"She was a good sort, our Daisy was, but she ran afoul of a heartless seducer. Left her in the family way, he did. After that she took to the streets. Every night she walked up and down, up and down, up and down. . . ."

"The poor child!" Granny cried.

"Oh, no mum, she did quite well for herself. She had fifty yards between the station and the church."

Evelyn fell madly in love with him at first sight. Used to effortless conquests, she simply sat down across from him, smiled her *exaltée* smile, and waited for him to turn to jelly. She met with Herbish impassivity. Challenged by his unflagging disinterest, she started chasing him. When she learned that he liked to attend the National Geographic Society's Sunday night lectures, she got one of her devoted beaux to drive her into Washington so she could stalk her elusive prey.

Herb entered the lobby and found her perched like an epileptic hummingbird on a stone flower urn. There was nothing to do but invite her to join him. Unfortunately, that night's offering was a slide lecture called "Insects of South America."

They went into the lecture hall and took seats on folding wooden chairs. Evelyn's poppy eyes widened. "These are the kind of chairs they have in funeral parlors," she whimpered. As the room filled up with entomologists, she looked around warily. "These people depress me. They look like they're a hundred and thirty if they're a day." She fidgeted and kicked her foot back and forth until the first slide came on.

"The Amazon beetle," intoned the lecturer.

"Oh, my Lord! Why didn't somebody step on it instead of taking its picture? They ought to cut that old jungle down! I bet they brought back some bug eggs on those old pictures. I itch. Don't you itch? I swear, something's crawling on me. When people go to those old foreign countries they always find things in their clothes afterwards. I bet something crawled in the camera when they weren't looking—*there's something down the back of my dress!*"

The audience was composed of dusty emeritus professor types whose misogyny was easily stirred. Amid barks of "Get that woman out of here!" Herb led the shaking, sobbing Evelyn outside. As he stood on 16th Street wondering what to do with her, her beau drove up and helped her into the car.

She did not return home that night. Around three A.M. Granny received a phone call from Ellicott City, Maryland, one of the elopement towns of the Upper South. It was Evelyn announcing her marriage to the boy who had helped her stalk Herb. Having caught her in a weak moment, he had begged her to marry him and she, busily scratching, had said yes.

The following week Herb asked Mama out to dinner. I don't know how much his choice was influenced by his bout with Evelyn's full-throttle femininity, but for whatever reason, they started courting. It was a peculiar courtship. They never had a normal Saturday night date like other couples because that was Herb's big work night. They never went dancing; it would have been a busman's holiday for him, and Mama hated to dance. The one baseball game they attended produced a conversation that anticipated Abbott and Costello by ten years, and the bassoon concert left Mama with permanent psychological scars. Herb drank but he didn't smoke; Mama smoked but she didn't drink, so they could not enjoy Repeal. Both liked to take drives in the country but he wouldn't go over thirty and she wouldn't go under sixty, so they could not occupy the same car without giving each other nervous prostration. There was nothing to do except keep on eating dinner, so that's what they did.

What they talked about over their dinner dates is unimaginable because they had absolutely nothing in common. Both had left school at fifteen but Mama quit because she hated school, while Herb's termination was decided for him by the rigid caste system of Edwardian England. Mama never read a book; Herb was a compulsive reader who had educated himself with a library card. Mama hated to be alone; Herb had so many inner resources he could have committed *folie à deux* all by himself. Had he been shipwrecked on a desert island he would have become, like the Birdman of Alcatraz, a self-taught expert in natural history.

They were alike in only one way, and perhaps it was the thing that drew them together. Neither of them had turned out the way they were supposed to. Herb was a product of the East End slums, the son of a slattern who played the piano in a pub for free gin, yet he was a gentleman and a scholar. Mama was a ninth-generation Virginian, the daughter of a relentless memsahib, yet she shrugged off every tenet of Southern womanhood and turned the air blue every time she opened her mouth.

My parents were *sui generis:* they had invented themselves.

Granny was overjoyed by the marriage. Every practicality dear to the hearts of mothers melted in the glow of Herb's sun, which happened to be the one that never set. He was English. It was all she cared about, all she talked about. It dropped, like the quality of mercy, into every conversation she had; the butcher, the baker, the Daughters, the Dames, and the hobo who begged old clothes all heard about "my son-in-law, he's English, you know."

That Herb's free-lance income varied, that he worked in an unstable and sometimes unsavory field, that he occasionally hired out as a bartender, that he would never have a pension, that he was, in fact, technically unemployed, mattered not. An Englishman was Granny's version of a doctor.

CHAPTER TWO

Being a great believer in roots, Granny wanted them to live with her in Ballston, but Herb needed to be near the big downtown hotels and clubs, so they moved to northwest Washington and set up housekeeping in a two-room apartment on Park Road, conveniently located around the corner from the 11th and Monroe streetcar line. The building was a former townhouse whose owner had been ruined in 1929; unable to afford an architect or a contractor, he had converted the place himself, evidently while still in shock. Mama and Herb had a triangular foyer with the front door on the hypotenuse, an L-shaped kitchen with nothing in the windowless short leg, and a Tudor priest's hole in the bathroom that led to a back porch where Mama kept a wringer washer. To do the laundry, she had to get down on all fours and push the basket through ahead of her. The only convenient feature was a hall that ran down one whole side of the unit, making it possible to reach any room without going through any other. When Herb got home from work at two or three in the morning he could get to the bathroom or kitchen without going through the bedroom and disturbing Mama, who was a morning person. He read until sunrise and went to bed around the time she got up.

Her idea of breakfast was coffee and cigarettes, so Herb cooked his own bacon and eggs. Her other specialties, culled in bridal haste from Depression-era newspapers, were mock chicken salad, which involved a can of tuna fish; and mock salmon loaf, which involved a can of tuna fish and a bottle of pink vegetable coloring. When Herb, oblique as always, suggested a mockless Friday, she fixed him a hot dog.

She got pregnant shortly before their first anniversary. The news brought Granny to Park Road on winged Enna Jettick feet.

"I was worried about you being alone at night, what with the hours Mr. King keeps," she said as she sailed in, "so I decided to come and stay with you until the baby is born."

Great believers in roots are seldom great believers in luggage. Granny had never owned a suitcase and looked down on people who did, calling them "gallivanters." Hooked over her wrist was an old Lansburgh's shopping bag containing a couple of extra housedresses, six pairs of pink rayon drawers (XL), six pairs of orangy service-weight stockings, an extra set of Shapely Stout corsets, and a curling iron that had to be heated on the stove.

Herb bought a rollaway bed for the living room and adapted to her presence with awesome nonchalance. Their mutual preference for the formal mode of address elevated the situation to an eerily civilized plane. Going into a kitchen filled with the smell of scorched hair to find a two-hundred-pound mother-in-law in a cloud of steam, he merely said, "Good afternoon, Mrs. Ruding," to which Granny graciously replied, "Good afternoon, Mr. King."

To everyone's benefit she took over the cooking. Ever solicitous of male comfort and well-being, she fixed all of Herb's favorite dishes: boiled cabbage, boiled potatoes, boiled brussels sprouts, and *boeuf à l'anglaise,* or boiled beef. When he happened to mention that he liked grilled kidneys for breakfast, she put on her hat and went immediately to the store to buy some. In exotic moods she fixed her two gourmet specialties, chili and shrimp curry, omitting the chili powder and the curry powder respectively. Her explanation: "We don't need any foreigners around here." Herb agreed: "There's nothing like good plain food."

He gained ten needed pounds and the marriage gained a needed buffer. Being home in the daytime had thrown him together with Mama in a Garden of Eden intimacy that neither was equipped to handle. They had never known what to do with themselves in tandem and now there was the problem of entertaining a pregnant tomboy. Washington was full of interesting things to do and Herb had a nose for finding obscure free exhibits and lectures, but Mama would have none of it. The Smithsonian bored her, the Library of Congress was too quiet, and the National Gallery was full of dumb pictures. It was their courtship all over again, with the sobering addition of an embryonic tie-that-binds, so Granny arrived just in time. Now Herb could go off by himself during the day without feeling guilty. He left the apartment after his noon breakfast and threw himself into the most innocent pastimes in the history of husbands. The time slugs on his reading-room slips were his bond.

Mama spent the day eating for two, smoking for six, and listening to Granny's obstetrical lectures. It was the tiny garments subdivision of "delicate down below." Descriptions of dilating one, two, three, four fingers; the tragedy of poor Alice Langley who dilated four fingers and stayed that way ("Her husband started chasing other women"); stretch marks, varicose veins, calcium deficiency ("a tooth for every baby"), tubal pregnancies, breeched presentations, ten-month babies that never got born, babies strangled by the cord, the woman who delivered placenta previa, and the woman who delivered a watery mole.

The stygian serial acquired another raconteuse when Granny ran into Jensy Custis on 14th Street. Jensy was a black woman who used to work for Granny in Ballston. Now she was living in Washington and doing free-lance cleaning, so Granny hired her to clean the Park Road place one day a week.

When Jensy saw Mama's swollen ankles, she let out her "OOOO-EEEE!" of fright.

"You got de dropsy, babe?" she asked ominously.

Before Mama could reply, Jensy launched into a story about the time her midwife-mother had officiated at the birth of a sixteen-pound monster born with an exposed backbone, webbed feet, and its face on top of its head.

"Jensy, you remember the watery mole, don't you?" asked Granny.

"Oh, yes'm, I sho does," Jensy said with a nostalgic sigh. "I cleaned fo' dat lady's sister fo' years."

"What's a watery mole?" asked Mama.

"It's a baby that never becomes a baby," Granny explained. "The doctor called it a 'human deliquescence.' It's just lumps of slime held together by stringy bands that would have been the bones and muscles." She shook her head in wonder. "It was the only one ever born in Virginia."

"Ain't been one lak it befo' or since."

They were like two good ole boys eulogizing a favorite hunting dog.

Granny and Jensy belonged to the babies-are-women's-business school of obstetrics, whose first rule was "Throw out the men and get to work." When Mama said she was planning to have the baby in a hospital, they recoiled in horror.

Jensy, a font of puritanism, sucked in her lip and gave Mama a look of heartbroken disillusionment.

"Is dis my sweet pure chile I hear talkin' 'bout goin' to a hospittle? Miss Louise, you doan want *mens* messin' wid you at a time lak dat, does you?"

Granny, more devious, used the excuse of our aristocratic heritage.

"Louise, giving birth at home is the only way to be sure of getting the right baby. Suppose you got some trashy woman's baby by mistake? It wouldn't have any blood. Hospitals get the babies mixed up all the time, you know. Of course, they don't dare admit it, but I have it on good authority. Those nurses are so busy having things to do with doctors that they can't think straight."

"Dat de truth. Dem nurses is lak de fleshpots of Babylon."

"Many nurses are insane, you know. They get so jealous from having to take care of other women's babies that their minds go. They get even by deliberately mixing the babies up."

"Dey lips drip honey but dey's strange womens."

"As for those identification bracelets," Granny said scornfully, "they're so cheap and flimsy they just break and fall right off. Did you know that, Louise?"

She did now. She reached for a pack of Luckies, her fourth that day, and tore off the cellophane strip. She had heard every obstetrical caveat known to science and myth except the one about smoking during pregnancy. For all of Granny's strictures on ladylike behavior, no one ever heard her utter a word against smoking: tobacco, after all, comes from Virginia.

"Louise, promise me you'll have the baby at home. We'll get Tessie Satterfield, and Jensy and I will help her." Tessie was a retired obstetrical nurse—but never a fleshpot—who lived in Ballston.

"All right, Mother, I'll have it here. Now leave me alone, I want to listen to the World Series."

Except for taking the sun on the bathroom porch by crawling through the priest's hole, Mama got no fresh air or exercise. Whenever she tried to go out, her keepers set up an outcry. Did she want to miscarry? Suppose she fell down and hit her stomach like Pauline Fairfax when she leaned over to pick up a dime and couldn't stop? Didn't she know that walking during pregnancy put pressure on the bladder? Suppose it burst and the baby drowned? Did she mean to walk past dat firehouse wid all de mens sittin' out front wid dey chairs tilted back an' dem lookin' at her an' *knowin'*?

Her combative instincts dulled by pregnancy, Mama gave in and spent the day lying in bed drinking pot liquor until she was as fat as Granny. Around this time Herb bought another rollaway cot and set it up in the short leg of the kitchen. There, amid his library books and copies of *The National Geographic,* he slept, leaving Mama to her ash-strewn sheets. Granny called his action "considerate" and told everybody in the Daughters until the telephone wires buzzed with that *ne plus ultra* compliment old ladies bestow on sexually restrained men: "He never bothers her."

As the pregnancy neared its end, Granny began casting eager glances at Mama's stomach.

"It's going to be a girl," she said firmly.

"How the hell do you know?"

"Because you're carrying low. Boys are carried high."

"I don't have any high or low left. The goddamn thing's all over the place. You're talking through your hat, Mother."

At the start of the ninth month, she saw a bluish tinge in Mama's navel. From this curio of whelpery she extracted what she wished to believe and manufactured an instant old wives tale.

"The navel vein," she intoned sonorously. "That means it's a girl. You never find a navel vein in a woman who's carrying a boy, but a girl baby always brings one on. You see, when a girl baby turns around inside the mother's stomach, she always pushes up on that vein."

"With *what?*"

"Miss Louise!"

On New Year's Eve, Mama started to feel certain twinges. It was the biggest night of the year for Herb so Granny told him to go on to work. He returned home the next morning expecting to find a baby in the apartment, but Mama was still in a holding pattern. Four days later her labor began in earnest and Granny called Tessie Satterfield.

Rawboned, crop-haired Tessie arrived amid repeated backfires in her ancient Model A. Mama sent Herb to the drugstore for two cartons of Luckies, but by the time he got back the first big pain had hit and she had bitten a cigarette in two. It was to be six hours before she would be able to smoke another one, a hiatus that goes far to explain why I am an only child.

Around ten P.M. her waters broke and Granny put together another legend.

"Look at all that water! That means it's a girl! You never get that much with a boy!"

"Whatever it is, it sure is big," Tessie grunted.

After the horror stories Mama had heard, "whatever" was an unfortunate word. She let out an agonized yell that sent Herb running for the bathroom and me into the world. Nobody who smokes four packs a day can yell very long without coughing. As her gothic ululation changed into a phlegmy rattle, Tessie broke out in triumph.

"I see the head! Keep coughing, Louise!"

"Ack-ack-awwrrrggghhh!"

"Hyeh it come!"

"Ack-ack-awwwrrrggghhh!"

"It's a girl!" Granny cried ecstatically.

"Ack-ack-awwwrrrggghhh!" To some of us, it spells Mother.

Nobody remembered Herb until Jensy ran into the bathroom to get more towels and found him sitting on the edge of the tub with his head between his knees. They scared each other silly.

"OOOOEEEE!"

"Lor' blimey!"

She told him the news and ran back to the bedroom with the towels. It was time for the placenta, a holy relic as far as Granny was concerned. When it came, she gathered it lovingly into a towel.

"Look," she murmured reverently. "Nine perfect little sections of blood, one for each month of the missed lady's time."

"Look at dat."

Herb emerged from the bathroom during this gynophilic litany, and hearing the word "Look," he did.

"Crikey! It's dead!"

"Oh, no, Mr. King, this isn't the baby! It's the afterbirth. See? Nine perfect little—"

"Take it away," he groaned, staggering against the wall. Overcome, he headed for the bathroom again, with Granny and Jensy trailing behind him reciting old wives tales.

"The afterbirth has to be disposed of in a certain way, Mr. King. The husband has to bury it. It's his duty!"

"Flush it down the loo," he gasped, between heaves.

"Oh, no, Mr. King, you can't do that! It's *birth* blood."

"You spoze to bury it unner a dogwood tree so it bloom in de springtime an' bring de chile good luck."

They kept following him around with the bloody towel and chanting hex stories until he gave in and agreed to give the placenta a proper burial. After fortifying himself with a shot of whiskey, he borrowed a shovel from the janitor and went out into the alley. He told Granny and Jensy that he dug a suitable grave, but years later he told me that he had thrown the sacred object into a garbage can.

The next day:

"It's a girl," Granny said tenderly, gazing down at my red wrinkled face.

"Mother, you've said that seven times in the last hour."

Granny got up and stood at the bottom of the bed and gave Mama an appraising stare.

"Louise, how do you feel?"

"My ass hurts."

"That's to be expected. I mean how do you *feel*?"

"All right."

"Well, you don't look all right. You remember Nancy Montgomery? She thought she was all right, too, and then her ankles exploded. I think I'd better stay until the end of January."

At the end of January:

"I'm worried about your varicose veins. You remember Betsy Winchester? She got so she looked like a road map. I think I'd better stay until the end of February."

At the end of February, Mama ignored her protests and went out to the store.

"You remember Fanny Wallingford? She died in the A and P."

"I never heard of Fanny Wallingford and neither did you! I'm sick of being cooped up in this apartment! I feel fine!"

"Be that as it may, I think I'd better stay awhile."

It was a fatal regional vagary. Southern homes are full of people who are just "staying awhile." When Evelyn Cunningham took two years to drink a glass of milk, Granny told everybody that she was just staying awhile. That unparalleled tactile experience of stepping on a human face in the middle of the night lingers like a moist legend on the Southern foot because someone who was just staying awhile was asleep on the floor when you padded slipperless to the bathroom. Sears sells more camp mattresses and foam-rubber pallets in the South than anywhere else in the country. Southerners buy more adhesive tape than anybody else; not to bind our wounds but to make extra name strips for the mailbox so the postman will know who is just staying awhile. The most challenging jobs in America are with the Southeastern Regional Office of the Bureau of the Census, and there's always plenty of overtime.

As Herb would later tell people, the longest-running comedy in the history of the American theater is *The Mother-in-Law Who Came to Dinner*. It opened on Park Road in 1936. Granny never officially moved in with us, she just stayed awhile. Nor did she ever go back to Ballston and pack the rest of her belongings; that would have been an open betrayal of her Virginia roots. Loath to let anyone actually *see* her moving, she announced that she was just staying awhile and asked people to bring things to her.

Each time our relatives and friends visited us they brought over another dress, another pair of Enna Jettick laced oxfords, more rayon drawers, and those crocheted head scarves known in Granny's youth as "fascinators." One week Aunt Charlotte and Uncle Botetourt brought over a hat, the next week Dora Madison produced the veil, and the week after that Evelyn Cunningham showed up with the stuffed bird. It went on for more than a year, but nobody ever suggested that Granny had moved. They simply pulled another size 44 from a Lansburgh's shopping bag and said, "Since you're staying awhile, I thought you might need this."

Thread by thread, button by button, they put Granny together again. The tactful transfer reached its climax the day Dora brought over her one-eyed fox fur piece and Aunt Charlotte appeared an hour or so later with the creature's missing eye.

Everybody knew what she was up to. Expecting Granny to stay away from an unformed blob of female material was like expecting a cobra to stay away from a flute.

BOOK REVIEWS

✝

1984 – 1993

THE DEATH AND LIFE OF SYLVIA PLATH, by
Ronald Hayman. Birch Lane Press: 235 pages

**ROUGH MAGIC: A BIOGRAPHY OF SYLVIA
PLATH,** by Paul Alexander. Viking: 402 pages

When the expatriated American poet Sylvia Plath gassed herself in
her London flat in February 1963, Betty Friedan was anticipating
the publication of *The Feminine Mystique* later that year. The con-
fluence of these two events was the first trickle in that river of no return known as the Women's Movement, for Plath, trying to write
while saddled with two toddlers and estranged from her philandering
husband, died a martyr to Having It All.

She has since become feminism's patron saint. Feminist pilgrims to
her Yorkshire grave have hacked her married name off four tomb-
stones, and Robin Morgan, editor of *MS.,* has devised a sacrificial rite
for Plath's husband, Ted Hughes, now Poet Laureate of England. She
wants to dismember him, stuff "that weapon" in his mouth, sew up
his lips, and then "we women [will] blow out his brains." Bliss it is to
be buried here and there in Westminster Abbey.

Two excellent new biographies bring dispassionate yet sympathetic
masculine points of view to this long-running passion play, but nothing can disguise the fact that Sylvia Plath was the Brat of Endor.

The compulsive erudition that destroyed her nerves seems to have
run in the family. Her German-immigrant father was a forbidding Herr
Doktor figure, an entomologist and authority on bees as well as a lin-
guist who taught modern languages at Boston University. One of his
students was Sylvia's mother, a first-generation German-American
who so worshiped the written word that she later claimed her famous
daughter tried to talk at eight weeks.

As a child Sylvia read, wrote, drew, painted, danced, played the
piano, and kept a maniacally thorough diary, using the entries as goads
to remind herself to read more books, take more courses, get more
A's, win more prizes and medals, write more stories and poems. The
more she excelled, the more she expected of herself; the more she expected of herself, the more she had to excel.

Eight when her father died, she demanded that her mother sign a paper promising never to remarry. Mother signed, and thereafter devoted herself to her precocious daughter's education with uncomplaining self-sacrifice. Wracked by guilt, Sylvia drove herself mercilessly to justify her mother's struggles. While still in high school she sold a story to *Seventeen* and poems to the *Christian Science Monitor,* but she lived in dread of the free-lance writer's rejection slips, the eternal student in her seeing each one as a failing grade.

Her mother had moved to Wellesley so that Sylvia could attend the prestigious girls' college on a town scholarship and live at home, but Sylvia insisted on the even more prestigious Smith. Her tuition there was covered by two scholarships, one endowed by novelist Olive Higgins Prouty, author of *Now, Voyager* and *Stella Dallas,* who was to treat her like a mother. Meanwhile, her real mother took a second job to pay her board bill.

At Smith she sold poems to *Harper's,* won the *Mademoiselle* fiction prize, and in June 1953 received the coveted *Mademoiselle* guest editorship that triggered her first nervous breakdown. Many Plath partisans prefer to believe that her sensitive nerves were shattered by the execution of the Rosenbergs at Sing-Sing while she was in New York, but the real cause of her collapse was less flattering.

A lifelong teacher's pet, she was thrust suddenly into the non-academic working world, a minion at the beck and call of toughminded New York publishing pros concerned with getting out a magazine. Instead of being praised and pampered, she was criticized and made to rewrite one of her pieces four times. She responded like a true intellectual, making supercilious remarks about the ''drudgery'' and ''detail'' of offices and crying when asked to work overtime.

To get even, she threw all her clothes out the window of her hotel. Returning home in a borrowed dress, she learned that she had been turned down for a short-story seminar at Harvard Summer School. Devastated by this fresh diminishment and terrified that she had ''lost her creativity,'' she plunged into a heavy reading program to re-establish her scholarly bona fides. But, unable to finish James Joyce's *Ulysses,* she panicked. Certain she was losing her mind, she devoured the works of Freud and Jung and diagnosed herself as a schizophrenic with an inferiority complex, an Electra complex, and penis envy.

When she sliced at her legs with a razor blade ''to see if I had the nerve,'' her mother took her to a public hospital where she was given electroshock treatments. Shortly thereafter she disappeared. After a three-day manhunt involving Boy Scouts, bloodhounds, American Legionnaires, and confusing headlines—SMITH GIRL MISSING FROM WELLESLEY—she was found in her own home, in the basement crawl space where she had hidden after taking forty sleeping pills that nearly killed her.

Olive Higgins Prouty paid the medical bills and found Sylvia a sympathetic female psychiatrist—just what she didn't need. Having a new teacher figure to impress thrust her back into her frenzied mode. Now she became a shrink's pet, intent on having the best anxieties, the neatest dreams, the sharpest memories; striving for straight A's in penis envy, gold stars in schizophrenia, and the Electra Complex honor roll. The handwriting was on the wall and it said Phi Beta Kaput.

If Plath's story is ever turned into a country music song, it should be called "Mothers, Don't Let Your Daughters Grow Up to Win Fulbrights." After graduating from Smith she went to Cambridge and met Ted Hughes, an unwashed English intellectual in the fullness of his gummy socks, "a big, dark, hunky boy, the only one huge enough for me," the rangy Plath confided to her diary. She loved the "virile, deep, banging poems" he wrote (one was called "Fallgrief's Girlfriends"); he was "a breaker of things and people" with "a voice like the thunder of God." That very night they "made love like giants" even though Hughes lived in a renovated chicken coop, and Plath wrote a sickie poem about being stalked by a panther.

She boasted in a letter to Mrs. Prouty about Hughes's thrilling way of "bashing people around," but her patroness was unimpressed. "He sounds too much like Dylan Thomas for me to think he would make a satisfactory husband and father," Prouty warned, but Plath paid no heed. Hughes, a Yorkshireman, probably reminded her of Heathcliff; reading *Wuthering Heights* has destroyed more women than the cholera.

Once married, she turned her perfectionism on the housewifely arts, struggling to keep their sooty flat clean while the gamey Hughes, who did not bathe for three weeks during their honeymoon, dropped dandruff and nose-pickings along with poetic pearls. When his first book was published the following year, Plath wrote her mother: "I am more happy than if it was my book published! I am so happy *his* book is accepted *first*." She also said she wanted him to be acknowledged as the better poet. That's what female egomaniacs sound like when they're trying to be feminine. For all her insecurities, Plath was the kind of American woman who gets a lock on femininity by saying, in effect: "Listen, buster, I'm giving you five minutes to dominate me, and if I'm not dominated by then, you're toast."

She announced that she intended to have "a batch of brilliant healthy children." Seven, to be exact, since Ted, who dabbled in witchcraft, believed that the seventh child was significant. She had never given any evidence of even liking children, but she insisted that childbirth was "closer to the bone" than sex or marriage, and that being "mountainous-pregnant" was her favorite state.

Why? Hayman and Alexander don't say, and Plath's feminist groupies are too partisan to question any of her motives, but the answer is as obvious as the purloined letter. She loved being pregnant because *the academic year runs nine months.* Having a baby reminded her of school.

She had a daughter and a son in quick succession, both home births aided by Ted, who hypnotized her to ease the pain. He also hypnotized her to cure her insomnia and relax her "razor-shaved" nerves, but her anxiety attacks and rages mounted. "A kind of macabre marathon for all concerned" was the way a hostess described a weekend with her. She burned the contents of Ted's desk in a backyard bonfire, reciting an incantation as she danced around the flames, then wrote a poem called "Burning the Letters." When his mistress called, she ripped the phone out of the wall and then wrote "The Black Telephone's Off at the Root." Meanwhile, she was writing her novel, *The Bell Jar,* about her collegiate nervous breakdown. Instead of writing about what she did, she did what she wanted to write about. Truly creative people don't operate this way, and perhaps, deep down, she knew it.

Ronald Hayman and Paul Alexander tell substantially the same story and both tell it well, though Hayman's attempt to fold summaries of the poems into his ongoing narrative (Ted Hughes holds all the copyrights and refuses permission to quote) occasionally leads him into florid waters, e.g.:

The suggestion of superhuman size—residue from the dream and the earlier poem—emerges in the idea that his toe, as big as a seal, is in San Francisco while his head is in the Atlantic, and, with a fond affectation of contempt, she compares him with the devil by saying he has a cleft in his chin instead of his foot.

Alexander's book is more evocative of time and place and more dramatically effective. His most macabre story concerns Sylvia's final gas bill, which must have been rather large. Ted's mistress forwarded it to a third party, writing on it: "She was your friend. You pay it."

He probes deeper into Ted's occultism, and proffers an ominous theory held by several of Plath's friends:

> After years of being repeatedly hypnotized by Ted and acting on his posthypnotic suggestions, Sylvia was highly sensitive to any signal—conscious or unconscious—that she perceived him to be sending. Several times during the fall she had told her mother that Ted wanted her to kill herself; if she believed this, it might have propelled her on some new and purposeful path of action [the night of her death].

Alexander also includes a highly significant Fifties cameo: the guest speaker at Plath's 1955 Smith graduation was Adlai Stevenson, who told the class that their highest goal should be a "creative marriage."

As contemporaries of Plath can attest, *creative* was the foremost buzzword of the decade, used incessantly by everyone from manufacturers of Paint by the Numbers to employers advertising for female office clerks ("Seek creative miss to file architectural plans"). "Being creative" was a perfect excuse for majoring in English, an airy-fairy way of saying you liked to read, and a rationale for free-floating discontent and unfocused rebellion.

Creative's twin was *intense,* a code word for superiority used by intellectual snobs who wanted to recuse themselves from American egalitarianism without doing anything illiberal. The creative 'n' intense set made a fetish of being high-strung, the theory being that nerves are to aristocrats what splinters are to carpenters. Their favorite reading was Freud in paperback and they never met a complex they didn't like.

When they gathered in their basement apartments to deplore Eisenhower conformity, there was an Oedipus on every rattan rug and an Electra in every butterfly chair. This aspect of the Fifties, rather than the feminine mystique, may have been what really produced Sylvia Plath.

The American Spectator, January 1992

PARACHUTES & KISSES, by Erica Jong. NAL Books: 352 pages

Here is Book Three of Jong's Clitoriad, the continuing adventures of Isadora Wing, Jong's alter ego and the heroine—I use the word loosely—of her first two novels, *Fear of Flying* and *How to Save Your Own Life.*

As Book Three opens, Isadora is the rich and famous author of *Candida Confesses* and the wife of Josh Ace, the younger man she met at the end of Book Two. Josh is a failed writer but he assures her that his ego is strong enough to handle her fame, so they buy a Connecticut farmhouse and the thirty-six-year-old Isadora decides to have a baby (the amniocentesis scene, the Lamaze panting scene, rhapsodies about "peaks and valleys").

But the tie that was supposed to bind comes undone; Josh is not only jealous of his wife but of the baby as well. He moves out and tells Isadora to lead her own life, which is like telling Messalina to lead her own life.

Leaving the baby with a series of nannies, Isadora has affairs with her investment counselor, the rabbi who buried her grandfather, the son of a famous sex therapist (his pillow talk: "Will you assume the female superior position?"), a disc jockey with one blue eye and one brown one, and men she picks up at the Conrail station in her suburban Connecticut town.

Plot is not Jong's long suit but she has a sure hand with incidents, piling them on and faking action by having Isadora jump into her silver Mercedes and drive somewhere. No wonder I keep calling this book "Diaphragms & Seatbelts"; Isadora drives so much that I kept expecting a threesome with Starsky and Hutch. She jumps toll booths on the Merritt Parkway, misses freeway exits from speeding while stoned, rushes her daughter to the hospital and her dog to the vet, picks up and delivers lovers, rolls down an icy driveway, and crashes into a stone wall. When not behind the wheel she flies to San Francisco to address a witches' convention or to Russia for a cultural exchange—anything to trick the reader into thinking that this woman is capable of some other forward movement besides a pelvic thrust.

Jong's sow-in-heat prose style is impossible to quote in a newspaper, but here is her elegant statement on family planning: "She had books to gestate, places to go, men to marry, a whole odyssey to shlep through before she could go home and get knocked up."

Writers who have nothing to say always strain for metaphors to say it in. Jong strains so hard that we need Lamaze panting exercises to get through her sentences. Isadora kicks one of her lovers out of bed and sends him home "before dawn dyed the Connecticut hills the color of fuchsined water in some recollected apothecary jar." Ready for a cerebral episiotomy? Try this: "O sweet sex, Laurentian waterfalls, Joycean rivers, Millerian springs (so black they are blue, too)—it's *you* that Isadora longs for! The whole humid earth opening like the Great Mother's thighs. . . ."

The book is as cluttered as the remainder table where it deserves to end up. There are quotes from Joyce and e.e. cummings, as well as Jong's own . . . well, poems. Sophomoric comparisons ("like Dorian Gray, as if his soul had grown old while his flesh remained young"), bumper-sticker philosophy ("all mothers are working women"), cutesy-poo feminism ("Goddess forbid!"), eighteenth-centuryisms ("Sirrah, anon, Gadzooks"), Joan Crawfordisms ("What is pride compared to motherhood?"), sermonettes ("All the pain one gets in life is somehow for the best"), the vagina as Socrates' cave ("As if all primordial truth and wisdom lay therein"), and an analogy between sex and mortality that Jong probably thought was fresh and original ("her orgasms grasp at the emptiness of certain death").

Writers who take sex this seriously always lay themselves open to unconscious humor. Isadora's feminism is shaky at best, coming and going like a recurrent malarial chill. Dressing for a tryst with the disc jockey, she dons "black T-shirt with rhinestones, black jeans, black cowboy boots with silver studs, black fringed cowboy jacket," and then suddenly cries out in despair, "Will we never be free, never?"

Of her better sentences, two sound suspiciously familiar. "During sex one has a man's undivided attention" rings an Edwardian bell. Much too crisp and epigrammatic to have come from Erica Jong's sledgehammer, wouldn't you say? It sounds more like one of those belle époque courtesans famed for her stiletto wit—my guess is Mrs. Patrick Campbell.

I don't have to guess the author of the other sentence. "Sex is God's joke on the human race" is from *The L-Shaped Room* by Lynne Reid Banks, who attributed it to Irish folk wisdom. Jong doesn't attribute it to anybody.

Except for being dirtier, *Parachutes & Kisses* is just another narcissistic entry in the "Love Story for the Eighties" genre. They are not novels, merely bound collections of beauty-shop chatter. Lynn Reid Banks wrote a "woman's novel" too, but when her pregnant heroine hides in a slum rooming house to have her baby, she finds friendship and support among the raffish tenants she had intended to avoid. *The L-Shaped Room* is about the family of man and the brotherhood of mankind, not day care and amniotic fluids.

Jong has always been lubricious but this time she has gone too far. Four of her scenes should be translated into Latin and relegated to the footnotes of Krafft-Ebing's *Psychopathia Sexualis*. Two involve bestiality, another a perverted use of food, and the worst describes a degrading and unspeakable performance with a tampon.

In the publicity kit that came with my review copy, the publishers boast that this book "reflects the heart and soul of the contemporary woman." Let's hope not. In my book, Erica Jong is a disgrace to womanhood and the publishing world as well.

Newsday, October 14, 1984

FOREIGN AFFAIRS, by Alison Lurie. Random House: 291 pages

K nowing how to begin a novel is one of the lost arts of our time. Desperate authors trying to hook the browsing book buyer use everything from fake journalistic leads to the single, esoteric line of dialogue designed to shock. These trendy openers usually result in a distortion of dramatic time, confusing the reader and making more work later on for the author, who must then write a long tedious flashback that confuses the reader all over again.

In her latest novel, Alison Lurie simply begins at the beginning with an irresistible no-frills paragraph reminiscent of Thomas Hardy's terse kick-off in *Tess of the d'Urbervilles.*

> On a cold blowy February day a woman is boarding the ten A.M. flight to London, followed by an invisible dog. The woman's name is Virginia Miner: she is fifty-four years old, small, plain, and unmarried— the sort of person that no one ever notices, though she is an Ivy League college professor who has published several books and has a well-established reputation in the expanding field of children's literature.

The invisible dog is Vinnie's imaginary companion. Although she was married briefly in her youth and has had numerous affairs (''Plain women often have a sex life. What they lack is a love life''), we soon realize that we are in the presence of a world-class old maid. Lurie makes this clear by taking Vinnie through her picky, gently paranoid routine of getting settled on the plane. The passage is a shining example of another lost literary art, ''showing instead of telling.''

An experienced traveler thanks to her many sabbaticals, Vinnie slips on board ahead of a group of tour rubes. Filching her favorite magazines from the rack before the stewardess can distribute them, raiding the overhead lockers for pillows and blankets, she builds herself a nest with the officious busyness of a selfish little sparrow in a world of eagles.

By the time she finishes her cushy fortress, we have learned the basic principles of female self-preservation without having to slog through a feminist manifesto. Aware that the world does not care what happens to unattractive aging women, Vinnie has resolved to take care of herself—a resolution that includes light-fingered habits like swiping all the soap and perfume samples from the lavatory before the other passengers can get at them.

Life has made Vinnie a realist, and in a spinsterish way a Social Darwinist. She is a survivor and a user in the best sense, a woman who arranges the world around her with a first-strike insistence. The trendy call it "taking control of your life" but Vinnie calls it "making the best of things."

We are only three pages into the novel at this point, but already we are solidly on her side, making her one of the few authentic protagonists in contemporary American fiction.

Only a very brave or very obtuse man would try to strike up a conversation with this plumped-up eccentric, but Vinnie's seatmate on the London flight is both. Fifty-seven-year-old Chuck Mumpson of Tulsa, one of the tour rubes, has "Ugly American" written all over him. On this, his first trip to Europe, he is wearing cowboy boots, a suede suit with patch pockets, a string tie and a Stetson.

The horrified Vinnie classifies him at once as "a person without inner resources who splits infinitives" and tries to ignore him, but Chuck will not take the hint. He regales her with American instant intimacies, including the story of his sister-in-law's operation, and confides that he is going to England to research his ancestor "who wuz an earl."

When her efforts to avoid him in London fail, Vinnie gets drawn into his search, as do all of her rarefied academic friends. They include the troubled young scholar Fred Turner, torn between his feminist wife who believes in total honesty and his feminine mistress who believes in total womanhood. Neither of these women has any concept of true selfhood, and it is against this frantic yuppie triangle that the rock-solid love affair of Vinnie and Chuck is played out.

Lurie carefully keeps herself out of the story and lets her readers draw their own conclusions, but her message is clear. Today's young women are like tourists; "disoriented, ghostly beings; they walk London's streets and enter its buildings in a thin ectoplasmal form, like a double-exposed photograph." Confused by cultural signposts promising seven emotions in three weeks, they go from one identity to another until they no longer know who they are, but inner-directed Vinnie can change without coming out of character.

Despite the novel's serious theme and poignant ending, it never lacks for humor. Running like a bubbly underground stream through the main story is a subplot about Vinnie's private war against the mysterious, malignant book reviewer L.D. Zimmern, who panned her in the *Atlantic*. Who Zimmern turns out to be and how Vinnie discovers the truth while taking part in a Druidic re-enactment is wildly funny.

This novel deserves one of the big literary prizes. Lurie has taken an old locker-room saw, "Homely women are good in bed because they're so grateful," and turned it into a flawless jewel.

Philadelphia Inquirer, October 7, 1984

JENNIFER FEVER: OLDER MEN, YOUNGER WOMEN, by Barbara Gordon. Harper & Row: 288 pages

Here we have an answer to the burning question that presses in on us nightly in TV commercials: How long does a John Deere last?

Barbara Gordon, author of *I'm Dancing As Fast As I Can,* has found that the most common name for young women in America today is Jennifer; hence "Jennifer Fever" is her name for chasing spring chickens. An admitted Jennifer herself in her day and now a woman of a certain age, Gordon examines the phenomenon from its origins in the sands of time to the American pursuit-of-happiness version that flared up in the Me Decade.

The allure of the sweet young thing is the warp and woof-woof of our entire cultural baggage. The Old Testament tells the story of King David, felled by a chill in the winter of his years, whose advisers summoned a virgin named Abishag to sleep beside him and warm his old bones. "The last best hope," Gordon quips dryly, "a kind of human Lourdes." The theme picks up speed in the New Testament, whose whole point, says Gordon, is "the adoration of a young woman who combines fertility and virginity."

Gordon interviewed a host of Jennifer-struck men on why they prefer young women. It's not what you thought—at least so they claim. They're more concerned with things like the "scarring factor," for example.

"Middle-aged women are bleak, pessimistic . . . [have] a down feeling about everything," said one old goat. "Everything is bad—plays are bad, restaurants are bad, music is bad, newspapers are bad, food is bad. You can get killed in airports."

Jennifer, on the other hand, thinks everything is super, like, I mean, totally incredible. You might have to put a bag over her brain because she thinks Pearl Harbor is an actress, but she has a matchless advantage: she can have babies.

"Men are attracted to women of childbearing age," another old goat intoned sonorously, "not because he wants children, but because Darwin said you are going to be attracted to this kind of woman. It's what keeps the species alive."

This kicked off a tribute to the loyalty of males in the animal world, where females do not experience menopause, but go on bearing until they die. If women remained fertile for life, the sanctimonious old goats implied, men would have little incentive for leaving them. Is this true, Gordon wonders? If wives did not have the menopause, would men have no desire for Jennifers? "My guess: it wouldn't change a thing."

Jennifers are progressive only when it comes to their careers. They know their feminist rights even though they are too young to have marched for them; otherwise they are sexual reactionaries who practice old-fashioned flirting, including that time-honored Southern-belle number called "hanging on to his every word."

The wives abandoned by Jennifer hounds are Janets, a fad name of thirty years ago. Two famous Janets who allowed Gordon to use their real names are Dore Previn, put-away wife of André, and Jane Spock, put-away wife of Dr. Benjamin Spock, who liked babies even more than we thought. He jumped the fence at seventy-one to marry a woman forty years his junior.

Jennifer Fever is a decidedly upper-middle-class disease; lumpen-prostate men seldom catch it. Gay men are highly susceptible to Jeffrey Fever, but Gordon found no evidence of Jo Fever. The lesbians she interviewed go to great pains to explain why the sapphic sisterhood is too fine to take the fuzz off the peach—women's greater capacity for commitment, companionship, sharing, etc. The usually cynical Gordon takes them at their word, never suspecting that they might be hiding something under all that lugubrious moral superiority. The joker in the deck of lesbian fidelity is female vanity: no woman of fifty is going to undress in front of a woman of twenty no matter how much she might lust for her.

As tape-recorder books go, this one is better than most thanks to Gordon's dry quips, e.g., on taking estrogen: "Men grow sideburns, women get side effects." She also deserves credit for taking on a subject that required her to listen to men run down women her own age. Said one: "Who wants to make love to a woman who looks like the inside of an overcoat, pockets flapping below her stomach."

That old goat has one foot in the grave and the other in his mouth. I hope he catches Jennifer Crud.

Newsday, June 28, 1988

FEMININITY, by Susan Brownmiller. Linden Press/Simon & Schuster, 270 pages

Mothers of book reviewers are famed for admonishing their young, "If you can't say something nasty, don't say anything at all." Feminist authors bring out the dutiful daughter in me. I confess I approached Susan Brownmiller's new book with the unabashedly prejudiced intention of tearing it to pieces, but I couldn't do it. As they say in the soaps, I tried, God knows I tried, but I kept running into an undeniable fact. Brownmiller has exchanged feminist footnote-in-mouth for satirist tongue-in-check, and displays a decidedly unfeminist gift for demolishing her enemies without raising her voice.

Her thesis is that "femininity fails as a reliable goal," but women are once again pursuing it anyway, as they always do when life and liberty get too much for them. The Eighties woman, she says, is appalled by the harsh realities of economic independence and threatened by the changes that have taken place in the sexual order. As unprecedented numbers of men turn gay or become heterosexual Peter Pans, desperate and disillusioned women are scurrying back to the age-old female solution of pleasing and appeasing the male sex. The two prizes in shortest supply today are men and jobs, and women are out to vamp both.

As one who lived through the Fifties, Brownmiller knows all too well what the vamping arts consist of. With the weary cynicism of a woman who has tried to figure out what color "Where's the Fire?" lipstick is while her ribs ached from the embrace of a waist-cincher (a "Merry Widow," as I recall), she details the batty, nightmarish existence a woman must lead in order to look "nice." That much of this material could be published as-in in *Cosmopolitan* and be read straight is what makes it so funny and so tragic at the same time.

Rarely have I marked a galley as heavily as this one. There is something quotable on almost every page.

The anti-pants Eighties woman: "They need to wear skirts for their careers because it is, after all, still a man's world and they are but feminists in it."

Chic: "To care about feminine fashion, and do it well, is to be obsessively involved in inconsequential details on a serious basis."

The literature of beauty: "Other women manage to grow beautiful nails, why can't you? The feminine competition of nail-growing, woman against herself, woman against nature, and woman against other women, is so absorbing that accounts of the struggle, which read like the triumph over polio, have been written by Shirley MacLaine and Helen Gurley Brown, among others."

Shoes: "To qualify as passably feminine a shoe does not absolutely require a high heel. All it demands is some ingenious handicap to walking more than half a mile. . . . A high-heeled, backless, open-toed mule, which manages to combine all the important impediments to walking, might at first glance appear to win the race for maximum feminine effect, but few women are willing to go this far. The backless mule is tainted by an unsubtle image of kimono-clad whores. . . ."

Perfume: "Perfume is, after all, a gloss that requires little time or effort, that is rarely noticed in its absence, and that does not inhibit the capacity to function. For these reasons its usefulness as a delineator of the feminine may be on the wane."

There are also one-liners ("a sweating woman is a wrecked illusion''), Joan Rivers-style routines (''Who said that clothes make a statement? What an understatement that was. Clothes never shut up''), and a disquisition on the use of the sidesaddle worthy of a Whig lady's diary.

Brownmiller does not recant feminism but she leaves no doubt that she has had it with Having It All. With refreshing bluntness and in-gratiating exasperation she admits that she does not like children, that she refuses to shave her legs, and vows that she will never give up the comfort and convenience of pants—one Fifties decade is enough, thank you. I get the distinct impression that here is a woman who has learned how to say ''like it or lump it.''

I also discern the emergence of a stern, spinsterish attitude toward her own mission in life that is admirably unequivocal: ''Pursuit of achievement in literature, science and the arts is a single-minded am-bition that will never be restructured . . . men are right when they say that the required expenditure of time and effort leaves little room for life's other rewards.''

Certain areas of her thesis are insufficiently explored. Those years of change in the sexual order when men were ''humanized'' into inef-fectualness were, by charming coincidence, the years of feminism, so she paints herself into a George Gilder corner that would be extremely hard to get out of had she chosen to pursue her own argument instead of dropping it.

Another fault is a lingering feminist tendency to go back too far in history and biology to explain how women got the way we are. She occasionally gets bogged down in Elizabeth Gould Davis land, that dry Atlantis of anthropology à go-go where key phrases leap off the page like prehistoric flying fish: Mother Goddess, pantheistic, mono-theistic, patriarchal, primordial, myth, pagan. Except for her descrip-tion of the hyena's clitoris, which has a certain terrible fascination, these excursions create a feeling of spreadiness that spoils the rigorous classical unity of her contemporary monograph.

Brownmiller has always been the best writer among feminists, but unfortunately this has never been a lavish compliment. She emerges here as one of America's best women writers who just happens to be a member of the starry sisterhood. Given feminist fiats like Ellen Wil-lis's ''good writing is counter-revolutionary,'' it's extremely pleasant to report that Brownmiller takes as much trouble with her Latin as she does with her English.

Little things like this warm the cockles of a right-wing heart.

Newsday, January 8, 1984

THE FOUNTAIN OF AGE, by Betty Friedan. Simon & Schuster: 671 pages

Betty Friedan has a habit of writing a book about whatever is bothering her. In 1963, worried about being "just a housewife," she wrote *The Feminine Mystique.* Now, worried about growing old, she has, shall we say, entombed the age mystique.

Her latest project is the fruit of the same research techniques that she made infamous in her study of female brain-death: combing through back issues of magazines to find proof of what she has already decided to think, and running around the country interviewing everyone under the sun.

Her thesis is that denying age, however you do it, is bad. People who dye their hair and get facelifts are just as unliberated as those who give up and rock on the porch. They ought to celebrate age; they ought to be out there reveling in "the third stage," "affirming one's life as a branching tree," and getting geriatric counseling called "spiritual eldering."

Her case histories have the dreary gusto of public service announcements and television commemorative minutes. She sings the praises of a widow of eighty who swims fifty-five laps before breakfast, another who founded Senior Ballet, and an endless parade of hikers and bikers. She lets them talk as long as they want, faithfully reports every word they said, then jumps in and analyzes it, explaining what they meant, how much she agrees with it, and why.

A stranger to irony, she sees nothing wrong with the story of the old lady who had a heart attack while carrying her river-rafting gear through the airport. Nor does she spot the desperate denial in the sales pitch of a seniors-only mobile home park:

"People who really enjoy people come here. My husband who was a doctor said if you move to Florida, you add ten years to your life; if you move to this community, you add ten more years, because of all the activity, because of the community itself. You can't just stay home and feel sorry for yourself. There's something doing all the time." Indeed there is. The bulletin board of this hellish place contains a blizzard of notices for square dance lessons, Easter pageant rehearsals, Thursday Crafts, and horseshoe pitching, to list just a few. But Friedan lists them all, getting so caught up in the thrill of it all that she blithely includes an unintentional memento mori tacked up alongside the summonses to non-stop fun: a business card for the Bayshore Funeral Home.

Furthermore, her stereotypical images of porch rocking and plastic surgery constitute a false either-or. America's new stereotype of age is the very same frenetic activity that her subjects pursue and that she recommends without surcease. The old people we love and remember best—the imperious dowager and the crusty curmudgeon—were happy and respected precisely because they made no attempt to be "eighty years young," but Friedan is too much of a blinkered conformist to see it.

Her confusion is evident in her fuzzy sentences: "Older, we must move, and stay, and move again, to keep our life-giving ties alive, for this movement *is* our fountain of age. And there's a freedom in realizing this, a new freedom to move or stay, new necessities and possibilities of choice." This is vintage Friedan and the English language may not live to draw another breath if she keeps it up.

She alternates bouncy, whistling-in-the-dark phrases such as "the surprise adventure of age" with soporific seal barks about the importance of emerging, reaching, evolving, sustaining and affirming—instead of stagnating, denying, absenting, disempowering and forfeiting. She also has a phobia about declarative sentences, preferring to set up her arguments with a stream of rhetorical questions. On a single page we find eight in a row, and one contains fifty-five words. Coping with her literary style is like trying to get chewing gum off the sole of a shoe.

A timid soul since the feminists jumped all over her for backpedaling in her 1982 book, *The Second Stage,* she is now so afraid of offending that she manages to drone even when she's not droning. Carefully balanced statements such as, ''despite my own feminist suspicion of doctor-as-god, I respect many doctors, male and female, including some in my own family,'' have the plink-plonk of a tennis ball.

Occasionally her timidity makes for an excellent primer in logic. Striving for an inoffensive way to criticize aging baby boomers who obsess about menopause, she writes: ''I didn't exactly suspect a new conspiracy against women.'' This is a perfect paralepsis: saying something by saying that you don't intend to say it.

The book is spottily interesting when Friedan shuts up and quotes other writers. Like those thoughtful people who always enclose clippings in their letters, she has an eye for the good extract, so if you've missed anything, such as the *New York* cover story on facelifts or Gail Sheehy's *Vanity Fair* cover story on menopause, you can count on finding it tucked away somewhere in this otherwise wonky behemoth.

Richmond Times-Dispatch, September 26, 1993

NEW YORK DAYS, by Willie Morris. Little, Brown: 416 pages

Reading Willie Morris is like taking a child to the circus. A large, hyperactive child who points wildly to everything at once, talks in superlatives through a mouthful of cotton candy, and finds similes in his Cracker Jack.

An intellectual son of Yazoo City, Mississippi, Morris fled to New York in 1962 for a job as junior editor at *Harper's.* After publishing a memoir of his early life, *North Toward Home,* he was appointed editor-in-chief of the financially troubled magazine in 1967 at the age of thirty-two—the youngest man ever to take the helm.

Harper's was owned by the Cowles family of Minnesota and overseen by John Cowles, Jr., a mossbacked Wasp scion who thought that what the flagging magazine needed was a bully article on the finer points of bridge. Willie Morris, equally Wasp but bursting with the kind of blithe spirit that makes jacket-copy writers think "naked and unafraid," set out to drag *Harper's* into the tumultuous Sixties.

Ignoring the sibylline pronouncement of his friend, the poet Robert Lowell ("Your people won't allow it, how on earth could they?"), Morris positioned himself on the cutting edge of everything, seeking out controversial topics and writers and running book-length excerpts that took up whole issues.

William Styron's "Confessions of Nat Turner" was followed by Norman Mailer's 90,000-worder, "The Steps of the Pentagon," which became an even longer book, *Armies of the Night.* Morris lasted until the fateful March 1971 issue containing Mailer's "Prisoner of Sex." That did it; the magazine's owners flung down the gauntlet and Morris resigned amid one of the great furors in recent publishing history.

New York Days is the story of his years at *Harper's.* Some of it is vivid: Hedy Lamarr shoplifting candy, gum, and cigarette lighters from a coffee shop counter; Truman Capote's erratic driving; black novelist Ralph Ellison enduring the torments of owning a car in New York to avoid racist taxi drivers; the founding of Elaine's restaurant, where improvident writers were carried so long that there was talk of publishing a boxed daily count of their unpaid tabs in the *Wall Street Journal* next to the Dow-Jones.

Unfortunately, Morris confuses evocative with exhaustive. His imitation of Thomas Wolfe's frantic purple prose starts on page one with hosannas to New York. "I was exalted by it, exulted in it . . . my patron city, crux and apogee . . . matrix and pinnacle . . . stunning cosmos . . . majesty as epicenter . . . seething zenith." Raindrops are surreal, snowfalls are dervishing, mists are phantasmic, summer sidewalks are lush baking cauldrons, touches are gossamer, regret is miasmic, greenery is herbaceous, smells are olfactory sensations, sounds are farragos, whispers are lambent, something is halcyon, something else is onrushing, and Morris, like Wolfe, is inchoate and nocturnal. "Life pullulated for me," he confesses alarmingly.

He also quotes large chunks of the real Thomas Wolfe's rhapsodies about the "Fabulous Rock," as well as the voice-over description of New York from the opening scene of the movie *Laura.* The purpose of it all is to showcase his own adaptability; his Upper West Side neighborhood was "an environ that small-town and rural Anglo-Saxon Americans would have found nearly impossible to comprehend." But not, of course, Willie Morris.

He's perpetually agog. Imagining a party at George Plimpton's: "If I knocked on the door, would they let me in? Would I ever be part of all that?" Meeting Orson Welles: "I was in the presence of a man who had once been married to Rita Hayworth!" Coming upon a legendary writer: "There he was, sitting across from my desk: Upton Sinclair!"

He also jerks us around with Proustean flashbacks. His madeleine is the Dixie movie theater in Yazoo City, where he first saw many of the people he later met in the flesh as editor-in-chief of *Harper's*. Describing a luncheon with Svetlana Stalin, he tries to imagine "what my approximate response might have been if on watching a Movietone News in our frayed little theater on a wartime evening in 1944," his boyhood buddy had turned to him and said, "You'll be having lunch with that man's daughter in a restaurant called the Four Seasons in New York City one day a long time from now."

The aching wonder of it all never stops. During a one-night stand, a famous movie actress tells him, "You really can't believe you're with who you're with, can you?"

Despite Morris's vaunted liberalism, the book frequently lapses into testosteroniads reminiscent of first novels blurbed "All the Fine Young Men." After tossing off a cavalier tribute to "the secretaries, God bless them one and all!" he proudly describes how he and staffers David Halberstam and Larry L. King turned *Harper's* staid offices into an Ole Miss frat house; overflowing ashtrays, empty whiskey bottles, gnawed pizza crusts, spilled coffee, barefoot writers asleep on the floor, "the whole milieu pungent with the stale accumulated odor of coffee and cigarettes and whiskey and unwashed socks and nocturnal masculine sweat." This passage is pungent with the bogus machismo of English majors who carry razor blades to cut the pages of European paperbacks.

He can also be lip-biting hurt in the manner of our sensitive Prez. After resigning his job, "I never picked up a *Harper's* magazine again, sometimes even averting my gaze when I saw one on a newsstand." Describing his divorce, he actually says, "For the longest time I thought I could never love again." He did, however, stalk his wife's shrink with mayhem in his heart until he got close enough to see that "He is young! He looks innocent! He has red hair!"

I am tired! I feel like hell! I haven't seen "halcyon" in print since *Anthony Adverse*! Speaking to you out of a surrealistically dervishing alacrity of onrushing miasma, I say this book stinks.

Washington Times, August 29, 1993

THE FUNERAL MAKERS, by Cathie Pelletier. Macmillan: 247 pages

This hilarious first novel about the back of beyond is going to put its author out in front of the pack of American humorists. I haven't laughed so hard since *The Egg and I.*

All unpaved roads lead to Mattagash, Maine (pop. 457), an inescapable hamlet situated literally between a rock and a hard place on the cusp of the Canadian border, resembling in its possibilities for spiritual and fleshly temptation "a mousetrap where someone had taken the cheese years ago."

Unlike Peyton Place, which enjoyed a constant stream of fresh and delectable gossip, Mattagash is so dull that on the rare occasions when its goodwives have something worth telling, they drag it out to make it last ("Did you hear the news?". . ."What news?". . ."About the wreck?". . ."What wreck?"), "turning the words in their mouths like morsels of food, savoring them, for fear it might be the last food of their lifetimes."

Imagine the joy that leaps over the back fences when, in the course of a few weeks in 1959, the town is rocked by two seductions, an attempted rape, adultery, mysticism, campsite mayhem by an undertaker gone berserk, a blackmailing striptease dancer, housewives picketing with signs made from old Tide boxes, all topped off by the only recorded case of beri-beri on the North American continent.

The upheaval starts when Mattagash's first family, the McKinnons, gathers for the death watch of their spinster sister Marge, who has deliberately cultivated beri-beri by eating nothing but rice and tea for thirty years as a memorial to her missionary father who died in China of dum-dum fever.

Marge's older sister, Sicily, is married to an alcoholic elementary school principal. He's having an affair with a stripper, Violet La Forge, who lives in the bathroomless Albert Pinkham Family Motel. Violet is practicing her Dance of the Seven Veils when yet another McKinnon sister, Pearl, the undertaker's wife, pulls into the motel with her brood to wait for repairs on their trailer. It landed in a ditch when the children, who were traveling in the living quarters, signaled the occupants of the front seat with the wrong sign; instead of holding up WEE-WEE, they held up FIRE.

The antithesis of the McKinnons are the Giffords, a blend of Jukes and Kallikak whose outhouse has been declared a public health threat and whose sons are all in jail except Chester Lee, who masturbates over pictures of cars. He has vowed to take revenge on the snobbish McKinnons by impregnating and marrying Sicily's teenage daughter. He's making progress, but when all of the McKinnon females congregate in Mattagash to bury the beri-beri victim, Chester Lee conceives the idea of humping his way through all of them in a trial-by-phallus to establish some social bona fides for himself.

It works until he gets to Pearl's nervous wreck of a daughter-in-law. He slips through her bedroom window and starts caressing her, but when she realizes he isn't her husband she screams rape. What follows is a scene that Chaucer would envy:

" 'Rape! Rape! Rape!' she chanted, drawing from her experience as a cheerleader at South Portland High, where she had rattled pom-poms and shouted 'Go! Go! Go!' and 'Fight! Fight! Fight!' until her school-spirited throat became hoarse. She locked into the same rhythm now, using the word as a mantra."

The aroused Chester Lee must jump out of the window to escape this peppy houri, but when he hits the ground the sight of the Ivy Funeral Home's huge new Packard stops him in his tracks. Unable to distinguish between sex-lust and car-lust, he transfers his tumescence from human victim to metallic victim and steals the undertaker's pride and joy.

It is here, in the funniest part of the book, that the author deftly changes key and paints a brilliant portrait of the bleak interior life of a low-down, poor white trash, unsocialized stud. I can recall only one other scene like it: the drunken last moments of Raymond Cole as he freezes to death in his car in James Jones's *Some Came Running.*

It comes as no surprise that Jones could have written such a scene; he himself was a roughneck who caroused with such types, male-bonded with them, and shared many of their experiences. But Cathie Pelletier must use her imagination, and what a splendid imagination it is. Without once descending to Jones's *nostalgie de la boue,* she gets into the head of this detestable boy and turns him into a tragic hero.

I could not be more excited about this book if I had written it myself. Cathie Pelletier's talent is overwhelming.

Washington Post, March 13, 1986

DAPHNE DU MAURIER: THE SECRET LIFE OF THE RENOWNED STORYTELLER, by Margaret Forster. Doubleday: 457 pages

Margaret Forster, author of *Georgy Girl,* brings her sympathetic understanding of off-beat females to this highly readable biography of Daphne du Maurier.

Unlike the yearning, vulnerable Georgy, Daphne du Maurier did not need love. A loner whose personality was complemented by the bleak English weather she described so vividly in her novels, she loathed "the effort of talking . . . I don't know how people stand it."

A disastrous attitude for an army officer's wife to have, but it led to her finest novel. Stationed in Egypt in the Thirties, she began writing *Rebecca* as an antidote to the onerous social duties of a military post. There, in heat so intense that even her fingers sweated and slid off the typewriter keys, she escaped on paper to the blustery solitude of the Cornwall coast.

Irascible and easily exasperated, she disliked friendly people and was bemused by people with sunny and uncomplex natures, her sisters in particular. "The nurturing side of Daphne was almost non-existent," writes Forster, "and it horrified her to have any kind of care demanded of her."

She never should have married anyone, least of all Major (later General and Sir) Frederick Browning, an emotionally dependent hypochondriac with stomach trouble that he called "me tum," to Daphne's barely concealed contempt. Catering to sensitive digestions was not her bag. With a fine English scorn for finickiness, her idea of dinner was mopping up skillet grease with bread—never mind putting it on a plate—so that she could get back to her typewriter. (I love this woman.)

Blessed with an astonishing capacity for concentration and self-absorption, she wrote till all hours in the solitude of her isolated country house, unmindful of the rats that scurried across the beds of her sleeping children—motherhood was not to her tastes either. She claimed to adore her son (she tolerated her two daughters), but it sounds more as if she merely identified with his maleness. She had always wanted to be a boy, and spoke of her masculine side as "my boy in the box." He popped out three times, when her latent lesbianism (she called it "Venetian tendencies") drew her to women.

The first was a teacher at her French finishing school. The second was Ellen Doubleday, wife of her American publisher, who never permitted more than one kiss, which Daphne timed at precisely forty seconds. Later, she used Ellen as the model for the title character in *My Cousin Rachel* because she was "a source of great torment to others." Her most significant lesbian lover was Gertrude Lawrence, who went all the way.

Fortunately for the marriage, Frederick Browning was appointed Comptroller of Prince Philip's household and went to live in London, leaving Daphne happily buried at Menabilly, the Cornwall estate she leased but never bought. There she stayed, writing on, until the lease was up and she had to move—a loss that clearly devastated her more than her husband's death. She herself did not long survive the move, dying in her sleep in 1989 at the age of eighty-two.

This is not a literary biography in the strict sense, but Forster paints an engaging portrait of a woman who was a storyteller first and a writer second. "I don't know another author who *imagines* so hard all the time," said the reader's report on *Rebecca.* Plots sprang into her head full-blown, but writing itself—especially spelling—came hard: the fantasist was willing but the stylist was weak. Nonetheless, she had an awesome ability to buckle down and write fast, producing as much as 45,000 words in two weeks of six-hour days—children, rats, "me tum," and all.

MRS. DE WINTER, by Susan Hill. William Morrow: 349 pages

Daphne du Maurier's unforgettable *Rebecca* opened with a sentence that engraved itself on every reader's mind: "Last night I dreamt I went to Manderley again." In an obvious attempt to match these ingratiating rhythms, Susan Hill begins her sequelization with a sentence that is certain to stick in every reviewer's craw:

> The undertaker's men were like crows, stiff and black, and the cars were black, lined up beside the path that led to the church; and we, we too were black, as we stood in our pathetic, awkward group waiting for them to lift out the coffin and shoulder it, and for the clergyman to arrange himself; and he was another black crow, in his long cloak.

The story opens in 1949. Beatrice Lacey, Maxim de Winter's bluff, hearty sister, has died, and Maxim and his nameless second wife have returned to England for the funeral. They fled to the continent eleven years before, the night Manderley burned down, when Maxim simply turned the car around and drove to the Dover ferry without even stopping to view the damage or find out what happened. How he could legally have done this is never explained, nor is the couple's remarkable freedom of movement during World War II, which "sent us in search of another place, and then another," always hot and un-English but, like the heroine, never named.

She hasn't changed much. She still wears "mole-colored skirts," still says "It's all like a dream," and still stares in disbelief at the wedding ring on her finger and thinks "It's as if it were on some stranger's hand." All gothic suspense novels contain a lot of "as ifs" because nothing is ever as it seems, but this one has so many that it would make Kipling write "As If."

Trouble starts when she finds a floral tribute at Beatrice's funeral containing a card inscribed with a big black *"R"*. Rebecca! At this reminder of her predecessor, she starts running down corridors, tripping over things, scalding herself with tea, and saying "How stupid of me," just as she did as a new bride. She falls into a "dreadful, restless, haunted sleep," and soon every meal is "scarcely touched" because something fearful happens just before the dinner bell sounds.

The card is obviously the work of the still-living Mrs. Danvers, Rebecca's malignantly devoted maid, but the heroine can't be permitted to draw this logical conclusion right away lest it cut down on her beset-ness and reduce the number of rhetorical questions she asks herself. "How? Why? Why?" and "What? How? When?" make nice one-line paragraphs to take up space until we get to the red herring, Jack Favell, Rebecca's loutish cousin and former lover, who is now a raving street person.

He's not the only one who's raving. After reading this book, with its constant descriptions of dreams, fantasies, and "half-sleeps," and its seed-catalog recitals of every flower and shrub indigenous to England, my brain locked on two words and turned them into a Gilbert and Sullivan patter song that is still running through my head: "Woken in the bracken/as if bracken in the woken/and Rebecca went a-boatin' down at Man-der-ley."

Newsday, November 21, 1993

WHAT HAS SHE GOT?, by Cynthia S. Smith. Donald I. Fine: 225 pages

The only thing wrong with this surprisingly entertaining how-to book is its misleading title. It does not refer to diseases. The author means "what does he see in her?" or, to use a quip that passed for licentiousness in your reviewer's adolescence: "Whatever she's got, it's not showing." In other words, it's an examination of the nameless female quality known as "It."

Cynthia S. Smith, a seasoned author of burning-issues books *(Doctors' Wives: The Truth About Medical Marriages),* probes for the secrets of women who are not particularly sexy or beautiful but who nonetheless attract famous and powerful men.

How did Mia Farrow land Frank Sinatra, André Previn and Woody Allen even though she has, as David Susskind put it, "the sex appeal of Spam"?

She did it, says Smith, by being "the champion male-pleasing chameleon of all time." Truth, to Mia Farrow, is whatever a man is saying while she's listening to him: "She becomes instantly mesmerized by him and is transformed into a proselyte . . . she listens eagerly to his views on the world and mankind, becomes absolutely persuaded and joins into his activities like an intelligent, shared convert . . . she takes on a man's beliefs so easily that he feels Christlike."

This is the old trick called "hanging onto his every word," but according to the author, it can't be faked. A woman "has to start out with the conviction that she herself has no great value and thus her only possible path to great social heights is the derivative route." Self-effacement and sacrificed pride don't even enter into it; "her desire to please is so great that doing what he wants *is* what she wants."

So there. Women with strong egos need not apply. You really do have to be a tabula rasa no matter how many men write on you. One such woman is Pamela Digby Churchill Hayward Harriman, Washington's premier Democrat hostess. "When Pamela met a man she adored," said a friend, "she just unconsciously assumed his identity as if she were putting on a glove."

It also helps to have a boundless capacity for rationalization, like Françoise Gilot, Picasso's mistress, who convinced herself that his swinishness was a virtue that redounded to her credit. "She views intolerable behavior as a confirmation of a man's superiority," writes Smith. "The only quality she will not forgive is mediocrity. . . . In her view, emotional excesses are to be expected when one lives with brilliance."

Smith's chapter on "Trophy Wives"—the Fortune 500 man's second bride—is an ironic commentary on how feminism becomes its own backlash. By promoting no-fault divorce, feminists inadvertently revived the gold digger. She was supposed to go to graduate school and earn her own money in the brave new world of sexual equality, but she didn't.

"The new boardroom mentality that freed top execs to divorce without causing stock-shaking scandals has produced a vast, glittering supply of suddenly eligible men who are being picked off by this new class of predatory women. The guy's a prime candidate for an unfriendly takeover—and there's a whole new tribe of women out there who are looking for just such pigeons,'' the author explains.

Smith's Rules for Trophy Wifehood:

''You can't be too young, since that would make the elderly groom look like an undignified cradlerobber.''

''Appearance is everything. Crow's feet, sagging breasts and droopy tushes are definite no-no's; he had that already. . . . Stringent dieting, personal trainers and frequent liposuctions are part of your regular program.''

''Creativity and competence are needed to handle the needs of the faltering libido and sometimes dysfunctional equipment of the aging male and one must be cheerfully willing to administer—'' Enough said.

In essence this book is an extended version of the article called ''Are You a Man-Pleaser?'' that *Cosmopolitan* runs about every three years (I wrote one for them in the Seventies). What makes it stand out from the crowd, however, is Smith's unvarnished realism and her insightful recognition of the innate political conservatism of the ''man's woman.''

It comes through loudest and clearest in the philosophy of Slim Keith, the little nobody who bagged Howard Hawks. Never mind how she votes, listen to what she says.

''I subscribe to the conveyor-belt theory of life, which postulates that all people are presented with a stream of opportunities that continue to pass along during our lifetimes. Only some of us have the vision to recognize these opportunities, the brains to reach out and grab the right one and the guts to make it into something. All those less imaginative, timid bystanders enviously attribute the winner's success to luck, but luck is merely an alibi created by the losers of the world.''

There is no Social Darwinist like a woman determined to marry well.

Washington Times, August 21, 1991

REVOLUTION FROM WITHIN: A BOOK OF
SELF-ESTEEM, by Gloria Steinem. Little, Brown: 377 pages

N ow that "self-esteem" is the bee in every bonnet and the fork in
every tongue, it was only to be expected that Gloria Steinem, the
divine afflatus of feminism who has made a career of leading the
herd to trendy saltlicks, would take a crack at it.

She took two cracks. Her first draft was read by a friend who told
her it was too impersonal. "I think you have a self-esteem problem,"
said the friend. "You forgot to put yourself in."

Of course she forgot. She's been thinking of everyone but herself
for years. Hopping on planes the moment radical groups needed her,
soothing fevered caucuses, tucking in fretful taskforces, living in an
apartment with no furniture because she gives all her money away to
worthy causes. Her friends call her a "co-dependent with the world,"
but we of coarser fiber recognize Dickens' Mrs. Jellyby, who let her
own children go hungry in order to contribute to the African Children's Milk Fund.

Steinem claims she rewrote the manuscript to include herself, but
all we get are four discreet pages about her affair, at fifty, with a fabulously rich tycoon to whom she succumbed, she says, because her self-
esteem was at an all-time low (the feminist circumlocution for "last
fling"), plus a few scattered references to her mother's mental illness
that she covered thoroughly in a long essay, "Ruth's Song," published in 1984.

Several mass-circulation reviewers latched onto the eleventh-hour
affair, giving the impression that the present book is a tell-all confessional about the secret life of Gloria Steinem. It isn't. They fudged,
probably to make their task easier, because the book is practically un-
reviewable; a rambling, monomaniacal exercise in dimestore meta-
physics about finding one's "inner child" through meditation and
achieving cosmic self-esteem in oneness and universality with all
things.

She begins by telling us how to say "self-esteem" in other languages. Not content to stop at the French *amour-propre,* Steinem the
compulsive listmaker plows on through Russian, Hindi, classical

Greek, Hebrew, Yiddish, Anglo-Saxon *(soelf)*, and of course, Swahili *(kujistahi).* Next she reviews the synonyms in Roget's Thesaurus, then drags us on a usage trip through the OED, until the bloodied and beaten reader concludes that concern for self-esteem is not only ubiquitous, but that the world has talked of little else since time began.

Most books have an epigraph—a brief quotation stating the theme or a line of poetry containing the title. This book has fifty-four, drizzled over each chapter and sub-chapter in clumps of two or three—one chapter has five. The authors of these nuggets include everyone from Socrates to Susan Sontag, with pit stops at arcana like "Sufi Wisdom, from The Pleasantries of the Incredible Mulla Nasrudin."

Then there are the supporting quotations. "As Plato believed . . . as Margaret Mead observed . . . as J. Konrad Stettbacher illustrated . . . as Dorothy Dinnerstein explains . . . as Rilke wrote." One after another; Audré Lorde followed by Christopher Isherwood followed by Allison Stallibrass followed by Franz Kafka followed by Patti Davis, who explains why she used to slouch: "We wear our attitudes in our bodies, and I grew up looking like a question mark." Steinem must look like a colon from skidding to a stop to quote people.

Like the dirty-minded who can turn any topic around to sex, she finds her runic obsession everywhere. The revolt in Estonia was "fueled entirely by self-esteem." Economics? "I've noticed, too, that economists have begun to speak in terms of self-esteem . . . economic development without self-esteem is only another form of colonialism." Living under a white male-dominant society robbed the Cherokees of so much self-esteem that they abandoned their Council of Grandmothers. Women who dot their *i*'s with little hearts in obedience to "the smiling cheerful mask the patriarchy forces them to wear" eventually develop depression and eating problems—classic signs of low self-esteem. Saddam Hussein's brutal stepfather robbed him of his self-esteem; he got it back by brutalizing others until George Bush, whose "aristocratic, religious father" beat him with a belt buckle, salvaged *his* self-esteem by destroying Saddam's.

Acknowledging congenital differences is bad for self-esteem. The belief that some are blessed with creative talent while others are not is a hierarchical concept, so never admit that you can't draw or sing. That means "I can't meet some outside standard. I'm not acceptable as I am." Go ahead and sing like Roseanne Arnold. Go ahead and write like Diane Ackerman, a sample of whose prose Steinem provides: "Each night the sunset surged with purple pampas-grass plumes, and shot fuchsia rockets into the pink sky, then deepened through folded layers of peacock green to all the blues of India and a black across which clouds sometimes churned like alabaster dolls."

How to acquire self-esteem? Listen to the child within. Turn inward, journey backward in time, "re-parent" yourself. To invoke the You of sandboxes past she provides a mantra—"I am valuable," "I am well," or just "I am"—and includes a meditation guide: "Take some energizing breaths, inhaling more slowly than you exhale. Count to six as you breathe in, count to three as you breathe out. On the last count, open your eyes. Look at your hands and imagine that a child's hands are inside them. You are one and the same person—but different. You can protect and care for your inner child."

She even provides breathing instructions: "Just press one nostril closed while inhaling deeply through the other for one count, press both nostrils closed while holding that breath for four counts, and then press the other nostril closed while exhaling for two counts. . . . Yoga tells us this time of being full of breath, full of spirit, is a moment of feeling the true self; the soul."

Steinem went to a "time-travel therapist" to find her inner child. She also talks to her hands: "So I ask them what they have to say for themselves. 'A banner held in liver-spotted hands,' they reply. I get a title for a future article, plus my first inkling that liver spots have a sense of humor."

Do enough of this and you will become a "Universal I," as one with nature and ready to help the ravaged planet salvage its self-esteem, like "the Chipko movement that began in the Himalayan foothills, when women hugged local village trees to save them from the axe." Being as one with nature is essential, because people who have "dominion" over the beasts of the field lack self-esteem. To prove that species hierarchy destroys our inner peace she combs through nineteenth-century recipes and finds one that says—are you ready?— "Take a red cock that is not too old and beat him to death."

As a final fillip she recommends the development of Multiple Personality Disorder for positive purposes. "What if we could each gain access to the full range of human qualities that lie suppressed within us?" she asks. "People in different alters can change every body movement, perfect a musical or linguistic talent that is concealed to the host personality, have two or even three menstrual cycles in the same body, and handle social and physical tasks of which they literally do not think themselves capable.''

She promises to take us ''in concentric circles'' and she does. Like most feminist writers, her literary style consists of tossing a word into the water and letting it widen into a sentence. Start with communal, transforming, wholeness, burgeoning, nurturing, synthesizing, sensing, feeling, enhancing, intuiting, invoking, internalizing, seeking, or finding; and you will eventually get a sentence about circadian rhythms, hearing inner ''clicks,'' and looking inward or outward— through a prism, of course—to where the paradigms are.

Much of the book reads like the contents of a 1972 time capsule. Early Women's Lib themes such as Chinese bound feet continue to haunt her, and the clitoris remains the whistlestop between maidenhead and personhood on her train of thought. Clitoridectomy among the Bantu is still happening and Steinem is still against it. It's an ''excision of sexual will,'' which is bad for self-esteem, she says, and then quotes Adrienne Rich: ''The repossession by women of our bodies will bring far more essential change to human society than the seizing of the means of production by workers.''

Self-esteem takes many forms. I read this mewling, puking book but I'm still vertical and able to quote back. When Samuel Johnson was asked to comment on the plot of *Cymbeline,* he replied, ''It is impossible to criticize unresisting imbecility.'' My sentiments exactly.

National Review, March 2, 1992

REFLECTIONS IN A
JAUNDICED EYE

1989

Reflections in a Jaundiced Eye is the first book I wrote on a computer. It's also the first of my essay books. As such, it persuaded reviewers to stop calling me a Southern humorist and start calling me an essayist. That's fine with me; I never did feel entirely comfortable around the crackerbarrel.

There's another first involved here. Eye was my first post-menopausal book. I don't know why I'm telling you this, except that it's the sort of information Southern women volunteer. I was still menstruating—more or less—when Confessions of a Failed Southern Lady was published in January 1985. Then came a four-year hiatus when I was so busy reviewing other people's books that I had no time to write one of my own. I had my last menstrual period during my reviewing stint—in June 1986 to be exact. I started Eye sometime in 1988, so there.

Compulsive girltalk aside, the menopause really is a turning point, as Carolyn G. Heilbrun noted in "Women Writers: Coming of Age at Fifty." All of the women she quoted said the same thing. Some said it eloquently, like Isak Dinesen; others said it in the crunching drone of seminarese, but their observations were identical in spirit to what I wrote in my journal: "When a woman has the menopause she gets her real personality out of hock."

This is why Publishers Weekly said of Eye: "King leaves little room for backpedaling."

TWO KIDNEYS IN TRANSPLANT TIME

I am afraid of organs. Make that "organ-afraid" in honor of our hyphen-obsessed times. I am also transplant-afraid. In fact, I don't like anything about this whole switcheroo business.

Many people feel the same way but are loath to say so because organs are all tied up with America's twin gods, Compassion 'n' Humanitarianism. We're supposed to be organ-positive, but I am organ-negative and not at all loath to say so.

My fears are not triggered by the plethora of information about organs ("organ awareness") with which we are bombarded because I don't understand medical matters, but I understand all too well the

Orwellian phraseology the experts slip into when they get going on the subject.

Take, for example, that sentence we hear so often: "A donor heart was located and flown to the hospital." The rational part of my mind knows what this means: one set of doctors removed the heart of someone who just died and rushed it to the sick patient who needed it so that another set of doctors could perform a modern, miraculous transplant operation.

So much for the rational part of my mind. But what of the other part? The American part: that ghoul-haunted woodland of Weir, that dank tarn of Auber wherein dwell the spectral tendrils of egalitarian mist? This is the part that tells me George Orwell was right when he said that bad English is the beginning of the end.

Note the two passive verbs in our sentence: "was located" and "[was] flown." The passive voice is the voice of Sneaky Pete. Now look at the noun used as an adjective: "donor" heart. People who tailor words to suit their own needs will tailor anything to suit their own needs. The originator of that "donor heart" phrase *snatched* the noun out of its proper place and *put it in* where it was needed. See what I'm getting at?

At this point I should write that familiar qualifying sentence that begins: "Of course, I am not implying. . . ." But I am implying. Not only am I implying, I am saying flat out that I am worried (make that "concerned") that somebody out there in Democracyland is getting ready to render some of us organ-free for the benefit of the organ-deprived.

I keep a file of transplantese that I take out and read every now and then, the way a normal woman my age reads old love letters. Among my favorite clippings is one from the *Washington Times* dated June 18, 1982, headlined "MOUSE BRAIN TRANSPLANT SUCCESSFUL." It says:

SAN FRANCISCO—A piece of brain has been successfully transplanted from one mouse into another, where it not only survived but correctly hooked itself up and functioned near normally, a scientist reports. "This is what I call my science fiction experiment—except that it works," said Dr. Dorothy T. Krieger, chief of endocrinology at Mount Sinai Medical Center in New York City.

How do you like them droppings? I suppose the discrepancy between the San Francisco dateline and the New York (make that "New York-based") doctor is no cause for alarm. Perhaps Dr. Krieger was interviewed while attending a convention, or better yet, took a well-earned vacation from her tiny labors in the city of mislaid hearts.

Much more disturbing is what comes next:

> Although the partial brain transplant succeeded in seven out of eight tries with mice, Ms. [sic] Krieger said, "I will make no speculation as to any possible relation of this procedure to humans. I wouldn't touch that with a 10-foot pole. . . . This is only the first experiment."

Note the unclear slide from the writer's summation to the doctor's quotation in the sentence beginning "Although. . . ." Did the writer ask Dr. Krieger to speculate on the possibility of applying her procedure to humans, or did she bring up the subject herself? Somebody brought it up. And what do we make of her defensive reference to ten-foot poles? And what do those elliptic dots stand for? It all bodes ill in a country where "equality before the law" has been shortened to "equality."

Since experiments on mice are always done with human medicine in mind, we are justified in reflecting on Aulus Gellius's dictum, *Ex pede Herculem:* "From the foot alone we may infer Hercules."

The last paragraph of the mouse clipping says: "The research, the most dramatic ever done with such transplants, is to be described this month in the British journal *Nature.*" I don't subscribe to the British journal *Nature* but I do subscribe to the *Washington Post.* Imagine how urine-dead I felt on September 19, 1983, when I found myself staring at a five-column headline: "VA. DOCTOR PLANS COMPANY TO ARRANGE SALE OF HUMAN KIDNEYS."

The article is by *Post* staffer Margaret Engel, who really knows how to write a riveting lead:

> The growing demand for human body parts has prompted a maverick Virginia doctor to establish a company, believed to be the first of its kind, that would broker human kidneys for sale by arranging for donors throughout the world to sell one of their kidneys.

The colorful Wild West word *maverick* describes Dr. H. Barry Jacobs, "whose license to practice in Virginia was revoked after a 1977 mail-fraud conviction involving Medicare and Medicaid." While this is not cheering, it doesn't bother me too much because my fear awareness is not white-collar-criminal-oriented: con men can be fun. However, the article goes on to say: "Jacobs, who served 10 months in jail for his 1977 conviction, said he now works as a consultant in medical malpractice lawsuits." Check that phrasing. Not he *is* a consultant, but he *said* he is. This is turning into a fine kettle of fish on its way to becoming a fine kettle of kidneys.

The piece goes on to describe the medical and legal problems of Jacobs's projected plan. It is extremely long and involved but fascinating nonetheless, for tucked here and there amid the scientific and bureaucratic detail are certain buzzwords and convoluted euphemisms guaranteed to give the America-wise reader a jolt.

"It will be pure, free choice on their part," Jacobs said of the donors. Why did he feel it necessary to emphasize this? He goes on to say that the motivation to sell their body parts "would be whatever motivates someone to sell: greed, bills."

Can't you hear it? "Hi! This is Pam at Friendly Credit Bureau. I've worked out a debt-consolidation plan for you."

The colorful maverick continues: "There will be proper, written informed consent. Since many potential donors can't read, it [the informed consent conference] will be tape-recorded." Written, yet tape-recorded, you see?

Now we come to some exposition by reporter Margaret Engel:

> Other health professionals active in transplant activities say they had feared the creation of such a venture and supported a bill introduced in August by U.S. Rep. Albert Gore (D-Tenn.) to prohibit the sale of human organs.

Note the phrase: *"Other health professionals active in transplant activities. . . ."* This is a perfect example of how the search for euphemism destroys a writer's ear. Using "active" and "activities" that close together creates a discord. Such a lapse tells me that a writer is concentrating on *not* saying something. Exactly who are these "health professionals"—doctors, nurses, technicians, candy stripers, Burke and Hare?—and what is the difference between transplant operations and transplant "activities"? If it's anything like the "shower activity" so active in weather reports, I want to know the exact definition of rain.

Now comes something that will make you feel red, white, and blue all over. Explaining Medicare's role in reimbursing hospitals for removing a donor's kidney, a spokesman for the Health Care Financing Administration said: "The cost of harvesting" is covered.

Harvesting . . . what a soothing euphemism for the land of Thomas Jefferson, who said "Those who labor in the earth are the chosen people of God." Or as Thomas Cowper put it: "God made the country, man made the town." Americans believe wholeheartedly in these maxims. If it's country it must be cool, so apply the rustic word *harvesting* to what that city boy Jack the Ripper did, and no one will remember that Jack the Ripper did it.

Back to reporter Engel's exposition: "The problem of the great demand and low supply of human organs is one that the federal government itself is trying to solve. . . ."

Yes, indeed. Can't you see the civics textbooks of the future? *Duties of the federal government: print the money, deliver the mail, declare war, and harvest kidneys.*

Next we hear from Surgeon General C. Everett Koop, who wants to keep the government out of the organ business. To this end, he called a meeting of medical officials to set up a privately funded foundation to encourage people to donate organs. Said a spokesman for Dr. Koop: "We're hoping that a leader will emerge."

They needn't worry. If the American hyphen-harvesters keep churning out Germanic compounds, it won't be long before we have one nation, one leader, and lots of kidneys.

Back to reporter Engel:

> . . . worldwide demand for such operations is expected to further overwhelm the meager supply. This inequity could lead to some organ-selling companies who might not take the proper medical and legal precautions in obtaining organs, some worry.

Some had better worry; this tactful paragraph translates into visions of the Mafia going into the kidney business.

Always leave 'em laughing, so the article ends with a statement by Dr. Harold Meryman, past president of the American Association of Tissue Banks, who worries that the whole transplant movement will take an elitist turn: "Any millionaire with cirrhosis of the liver will gladly pay a half million dollars. That's not considered to be the American way."

Of course it's the American way, but that's not why I am organafraid. What worries me is that other American way, the one that is even more tempting than money. I have visions of a mad dash of Nice Guyism gone awry. The lugubrious pleas for a kidney here, a liver there, a heart in Sheboygan that descend like a sledgehammer on a neurotically friendly nation could easily inspire an organ Robin Hood to kill healthy people just to be able to arrive at the hospital in the nick of time with the needed part. When the melting imprimatur of Joan Lunden beckons, a line will form at the thorax.

Organ transplants have joined motherhood and apple pie on the list of things Americans must not be against. Well, tough titty—God knows whose—I'm against them. As Edgar Allan Poe said in the poem I ponied earlier: "But Psyche, uplifting her finger, said 'Sadly this star I mistrust.' "

The name of the poem is "Ulalume." You know what a *ulalume* is, don't you? It's the tiny gland that feeds the spleen, and I'm keeping mine.

UNSPORTIVE TRICKS

Junk mail used to look so obviously junky that we tossed it unopened into the trash or marked it "Return to Sender" and dropped it back in the box. But this cost the senders money—"dollars" in junk mailese—so they devised pitiless ways of tricking us into opening and reading it. Taking as their motto, "The only thing we have to use is fear itself," they decorated the front of their envelopes with messages calculated to scare us to death.

"URGENT! IMMEDIATE REPLY REQUESTED!" is on just about everything.

"OPEN THIS BEFORE YOU PULL OUT OF YOUR DRIVEWAY!" is from an auto insurance firm.

"WILL THIS BE OUR FINAL EPIDEMIC?" in rash-red letters next to your name is the inspiration of Physicians for Social Responsibility, who presumably decided to use the AIDS panic to get us to open their letters about nuclear war prevention.

"SUPPOSE SOLDIERS CAME AND TOOK YOUR SISTER AWAY IN A TRUCK?" asks Amnesty International. Not mother, not wife, not daughter, but that star boarder of the male id, the first virgin in his life, his sister—as in: "Would you want your sister to marry one?"

Junk mailers have also invented peekaboo greed. This is the window envelope containing a letter folded in such a way that an incomplete but intriguing sentence is visible above the recipient's name. Meant to look as if the letter was folded wrong by accident, the partial sentence reads: "Consideration and Compensation for Your Expense of Time and. . . ." No, it's not a check. The unfolded letter says that *if* we stay at one of the company's resorts, we will get discounts on items for sale there.

Then there is the official-looking envelope. This one is from the "Department of Verification" and has a Washington, D.C. return address and a seal of office. Have we inherited Montana or are we being billed for it? Neither. It's a letter verifying the recipient as an official buyer of discount items.

The smarmiest piece of junk mail—actually junque mail—comes in a starkly plain, pearl-gray envelope in whose lower left-hand corner sits a small but tasteful instruction.

OFFICIAL INVITATION
POSTMASTER: Please deliver as soon as possible.

It's from America's venerable secular abbey, the Smithsonian Institution. You've been invited to a party!

FLORENCE KING
You are one of a small group of
Purkins Corner Residents
invited to become National Associates
of the Smithsonian Institution.

They don't know that the only status symbol in Purkins Corner is buying whiskey by the fifth instead of by the pint. The accompanying letter says that membership includes generous discounts on "reproductions"—doubtless that graven image of the pre-Columbian Incan caught in an eternal squat—and on something never before offered in junk mail: a dulcimer. The Renaissance comes to K-Mart. Ben Jonson hits I-95. Just leave a kiss within the Slurpee glass and I'll not ask for a peel-away sweepstakes coaster.

Loneliness is good for business, so junk mailers have devised ways to trick us into thinking that a solicitation is really a personal letter. Their favorite ploy is the envelope addressed by hand. The staffer chosen for this sadistic ruse has a loopy, immature penmanship designed to trigger memories of long-lost daughters or old friends from P.S. 31.

Ms. magazine uses a combination of loneliness and celebrity worship. On one of their subscription pitches they leave off the name of the magazine in the return address and substitute a stamp of Gloria Steinem's signature like a congressional frank gone awry to make recipients think they have received a personal communication from one of America's leading egalitarian Junkers.

The manager of Shell Oil's merchandising department writes whole letters by hand, using a simulacrum of lined notebook paper to suggest an intimacy so mellowed by time that standing on the slightest ceremony would be an insult. "Just a quick note to tell you that I discovered some really super items for you in my recent travels around the country," he begins, and gushes on for two printed pages.

The *American Spectator* simply lies to the lonely, typing the word *Personal* on the envelope and highlighting it with a yellow Magic Marker. Inside is one of the most incredible pitch letters ever penned, a four-page threnody about mounting costs from editor-in-chief R. Emmett Tyrrell Jr., who turns into a Jewish mother in the opening paragraph: *"It is 9:15 P.M. and I am alone here in an almost totally dark office."*

Leftwingers do it, too. American Civil Liberties Union Director Ira Glasser begins his pitch: *"It is late at night. I'm tired and my burning eyes are telling me it's time to quit."* It is, Ira, it is. Thanks to you and your gremlins, the U.S. Constitution has turned into Mr. Nice Guy's hankie.

The flip side of sadism is masochism, so if you wish to play the dominant role in junk mail rape, simply neglect to renew a subscription to a national magazine. Some six weeks before your subscription is due to expire, you receive an expiration notice, a businesslike and unemotional statement of fact that gives no hint of the psychodrama to come.

Ignore the expiration notice and a few weeks later you will get an envelope marked "THERE'S STILL TIME."

Do nothing.

Next comes the fake mailgram with the first hint of desperation manfully concealed under a fake compliment: "KNOWING HOW BUSY YOU ARE WE HAVE MADE ARRANGEMENTS TO EXTEND YOUR SUBSCRIPTION RENEWAL PERIOD FOR TWO MORE WEEKS BECAUSE WE ARE CONFIDENT YOU STILL WISH TO RECEIVE OUR PUBLICATION."

Do nothing.

Next comes the fake telegram—thin, crinkly, Western Union yellow. It says: "WE'RE WAITING FOR YOU!"

Do nothing.

Once you ignore the fake telegram, the fun really starts. The magazine sends you pathetic gifts: an envelope containing a free stamp, and a peculiar ridge that turns out to be a tiny pencil for marking the *yes* block. Now you've got them on "tender hooks," as Alfalfa Bill Murray used to say. Here it is, the chance you've been waiting for. Your chance to frown in Smile Buttonland, your chance to slug a kid, your chance to park with the gimps, your chance to make Mario Cuomo's father's feet bleed some more.

Let bank tellers be warm and cuddly, let car salesmen give me free balloons, let official greeters hug me, let Ronald Reagan pull a one-eyed Navajo-Gypsy female West Point cadet out of his pocket and read her aloud. It doesn't matter, because I'm now the biggest little sonofabitch in Purkins Corner and it feels *great*.

Donning my green eyeshade, I sat under a twenty-five-watt bulb with all my junk mail spread out before me. All those coupons, RSVPs, check-a-blocks, and pledge cards, waiting to be mailed . . . to somebody or other. What to do?

I cackled, then said:

> "I am not shaped for sportive tricks.
>   And therefore, since I cannot prove a lover,
>   I am determined to prove a villain
>   And hate the idle printers of these days.

Plots have I laid, signatures dangerous,
By drunken mismailings, confusion and snafus
To set Amnesty International and Ira Glasser
In deadly hate the one against the other.
And if the *American Spectator* be as true and just
As I am subtle, false and treacherous,
This day should *Ms.* be mewed up
About a questionnaire that says that *F.K.*
Of *Time*'s heirs the subscriber shall be.
Dive, thoughts, down to my soul—
Here *Newsweek* comes.''

LUMP IT OR LEAVE IT

✝

1990

Lump It or Leave It is my second essay book. The dust jacket photo has caused me no end of trouble. In it I am holding a Ruger automatic and standing beside a vase of red roses, leading numerous people to conclude that I was sending some sort of hard-rock political message.

So help me, I had never even heard of "Guns 'N Roses" or Axl Rose. The picture was taken by the local paper for a feature on me. The day their photographer came I just happened to have a dozen red roses, sent me by a writer whose book I had raved. The photographer suggested using the roses in the picture, but the gun was my idea. When I produced it he said, "Ah, guns and roses," but I didn't get it. The paper headlined the feature "Guns and Roses" but I thought it referred to the picture: roses, a gun, and me.

It was a great photo, so when Lump *went into production and I needed a color picture for the jacket, I contacted the newspaper and got a copy of it. Everybody at St. Martin's must have assumed I knew what I was doing because my then-editor, Peter Ginna, said, "Ah, guns and roses," just like the photographer, but I still didn't get it.*

I didn't catch on until the reviews started coming in and one of them spelled out who "Guns 'N Roses" and Axl Rose were.

If you find this story hard to believe, consider my musical tastes. I like Irish tenors singing "The Rose of Tralee."

AS YE ROE, SO SHALL YE WADE

There was an abortion in my family that I found out about in my early teens. Sometime around 1910, my grandfather's sister was seduced—or something—and confided in Granny, then a young matron. Saying nothing to my grandfather, Granny took Aunt Jane to the family doctor, who performed an abortion.

According to my mother, the doctor was madly in love with Granny and willing to do anything she asked. It was an unrequited love, but still, the idea of Granny using sex to achieve her ends stunned me so thoroughly that I never did get around to feeling one way or the other about the abortion.

That this story was told—and stretched—so freely in our family circle says much about the atmosphere I grew up in. At no time during the many retellings did anyone raise the question of the morality of abortion, least of all Granny, whose ego would never permit her to spoil a starring role with a philosophical digression.

Instead she took bits and pieces of her favorite Gay Nineties ballads—"She's More to Be Pitied Than Censured" and "Take Back Your Gold!" are the most probable sources—and wove them into her story: Aunt Jane trudging through a snowstorm, midnight poundings on the door, the seducer publicly exposed as a cad. If even one of these things had really happened there was no way my grandfather could have remained unaware of his sister's plight. By the time Granny got through with the saga it had sprouted wings, but she never said a word about abortion per se.

I would still share my family's blasé attitude if times were normal, but lately a feeling has come over me that I cannot shake: Molly Yard is such a little old tennis shoe among ladies that anything she says has got to be wrong.

Anti-abortion women are always asked about their pelvic history, so here—ever so briefly—is mine.

I got my first diaphragm in 1957 by telling the doctor the then-necessary lie that I was engaged to be married. The lie was excellent training in resourcefulness and the diaphragm made further resourcefulness unnecessary. I used it correctly as the doctor had shown me, and I used it every time. I never got pregnant.

I never got married either, which is why the diaphragm served me so well. Diaphragms were ideal for Fifties affairs, especially adulterous affairs, when every occasion of delirious abandon was necessarily preceded by cryptic phone calls, passed notes, and the kind of precise syncronization of watches found in old RAF movies. Thanks to all this premeditation, no unmarried woman of my generation could possibly forget to insert her diaphragm.

Having no need for the spontaneity offered by the Pill, I never took it, nor used an intrauterine device. Moreover, whenever anything new—the Pill, IUDs, tubal ligation—came on the market, I always seemed to be having one of my lesbian interludes, so the question of exchanging the diaphragm for something more up-to-date was academic.

The four nagging questions of the anti-abortion stance are rape, incest, birth defects, and the life or health of the mother.

Putting myself in each of these positions, my feeling about the first would depend upon what kind of rape it was. Date or acquaintance rape is a phenomenon of the sexual revolution and so foreign to my experience that I can't think of anything to say about it. In my day, when a woman told a man to stop, he stopped. Teasing was not my bag; I never saw any reason to go out with a man unless I had already decided to go to bed with him, so except for one or two unusual occasions, I always finished what I started.

Violent rape by a stranger would make me feel that the baby was *his,* not mine. The alienation of the rape would extend to the baby: because I had nothing to do with the rape, the baby would have nothing to do with me. Yes, I would want an abortion, and if I didn't get it I would want to throw the baby over a cliff.

But as I contemplated infanticide, my tendency to intellectual cud-chewing would kick in and frame some cautionary hypothetical questions. Who among us is not a descendant of at least one violent rape? I once discussed this with a Jewish woman and our off-the-cuff, thumbnail histories of our respective mother countries produced some sobering reflections.

Did every single one of her ancestresses escape those centuries of drunken Cossacks? Surely not. This is probably the real reason why this dispersed and persecuted people developed a matrilinear legal system: the child of a Jewish woman must be considered Jewish because chances are good that the father might not have been.

And I? The English manage to keep a straight face when they boast that England has never been invaded, but I'm sure my ancestresses would beg to differ. Roman soldiers raped Celtic women, Saxons raped British women, Normans raped Saxon women, and Vikings raped a rock pile if they thought there was a snake under it. Somewhere in all this nefarious nation building I became *me* instead of somebody else.

So would I throw that baby off the cliff? I don't know.

The best way to keep women from having to abort rape-conceived babies is to increase the punishment for rape by placing much of it in the hands of women themselves.

All women should be allowed to own a gun simply by virtue of being female. A woman who prefers to conceal her gun in her handbag should be given a carry permit with no questions asked. A woman who is willing to wear her gun in a holster on the outermost layer of her clothing should be allowed to do so without having to bother with permits of any kind. In all cases it should be understood that an armed woman not only has a right to defend herself, but a responsibility to come to the aid of other women as well. The feminists want sisterhood? Sister, you've got it.

For the woman who gets raped despite these precautions, we should bring back the public whipping post and give her the option of flogging her rapist until . . . her arm gets tired. This would eliminate the need for garrulous rape counseling designed to restore a victim's self-esteem. As the Bible tells us, there is a sure-fire way to feel on top of the world: "Revenge is sweet, saith the Lord."

The question of pregnancy resulting from incest arouses my cynicism in this bicentennial year of the French Revolution, which produced the most famous false accusation of incest in history.

Louis Charles, Dauphin of France, had a character defect that was apparent from earliest childhood. A few years before the Revolution, his mother, Marie Antoinette, wrote in an oft-quoted letter to his governess: "He is very indiscreet and is apt to repeat whatever he has heard, and often, without actually wanting to lie, he adds according to his fantasy. It is his biggest fault and one which must be corrected."

In 1793 the revolutionary leaders took the eight-year-old Dauphin from the imprisoned Queen and sent him to live with a shoemaker named Simon, who caught the boy masturbating. To escape punishment, the Dauphin told Simon that his mother, and his aunt, Madame Elizabeth, had taught him to masturbate.

Knowing that the Tribunal was looking for evidence to ruin Marie Antoinette in the eyes of the people and thus justify her execution, Simon relayed the story to the Jacobin leaders, who grilled the child until he "confessed" to much more than masturbation. They found the Dauphin remarkably easy to coach. Joan Haslip, a recent biographer of Marie Antoinette, describes the scene:

Intimidated by their presence, not daring to contradict himself, the boy repeated the lie, and encouraged by Hébert, went so far as to say that his mother and his aunt had amused themselves by taking him into their beds and watching him perform. Royalist apologists would have us believe that the wretched child had been bullied and beaten by his tormentors who had forced him into telling that terrible lie. But unbiased witnesses claim that he appeared to be quite cheerful and unconcerned, and that he persisted in his lies, even when confronted with his sister and his aunt.

His aunt called him a "little monster," but Marie Antoinette, on the night before her execution, wrote in a letter to Madame Elizabeth: "I know how much my little boy must have made you suffer. Forgive him, my dear sister. Remember how young he is and how easy it is to make a child say whatever one wants, to put words into his mouth he does not understand."

In America, where anything can become a fad, the number of women now "remembering" incestuous incidents from their childhoods coincides suspiciously with the number of feminists now hammering on the theme. They have written so much about incest that it would fill an anthology called *The Uncle From M.A.N.*

In her 1976 book, *Of Woman Born,* Adrienne Rich wrote: "When a female child is passed from lap to lap so that all the males in the room (father, brother, acquaintance) can get a hard-on, it is the helpless mother standing there and looking on that creates the sense of shame and guilt in the child."

More recently, Kentucky newspaper heiress Sallie Bingham took up the cudgels in her 1989 memoir, *Passion and Prejudice.* A Southern gentlewoman before becoming a left-wing feminist, Bingham sidles up to the forbidden topic by means of sly, erudite hints about the awfulness of families in general and her own in particular. She slugs her father with a classical literary brickbat borrowed from the webby House of Atreus ("I remembered *Iphigenia in Aulis* and the sacrifice of the daughter"), and condemns her mother for voting against her in a Bingham corporate battle instead of coming to her rescue as Demeter came to the rescue of her daughter Persephone ("Perhaps no daughter is worth a descent into that Hades where women must oppose the men who support and love them").

These references to ancient Greek drama and mythology serve to keep the subject of incest in the reader's subconscious until anti-capitalist Sallie finally gets to the point with a lurid analogy linking Aeschylus and Marx: "No taboo has more dramatic meaning for the families of the very rich, who rarely find that outsiders 'measure up' and so turn, in secret, to their own kind."

Surpassing both Adrienne Rich and Sallie Bingham is a feminist so inimical to the Edenic arrangement that she recalls the old childhood rhyme that left the unwary in pain: "Adam and Eve and Pinch-Me-Tight/Went down to the river to have a fight/When Adam and Eve were swept out of sight/Who was left?"

Andrea Dworkin.

In her 1987 screed, *Intercourse,* she has this to say:

> Incestuous rape is becoming a central paradigm for intercourse in our time. Fathers, uncles, grandfathers, brothers, pimps, pornographers, and the good citizens who are the consumers; and men, who are, after all, just family, are supposed to slice us up the middle, leaving us in parts on the bed.

I don't deny that incest happens, but I don't believe it happens nearly so often as Dworkin & Company would have us think. They inject it into the abortion debate to paint Pro-Lifers into a corner and to give vindictive divorcing women the ultimate means of destroying their husbands. That no divorcing husband has accused a hated wife of incest with their son, and that aunts are going scot-free while uncles twist in the wind, says something about which sex has incest on the brain these days.

The feminist insistence that incest is already widespread could become a self-fulfilling prophecy. Considering what has happened to several other ancient taboos in recent years, it is naive to suppose that the incest taboo can survive in a liberation-crazed society that has made a taboo of "judgmental" thinking. There is already a group called the "North American Man-Boy Love Association" to promote acceptance of pedophilia. The incest revisionists are not far behind. Transsexual Jan (née James) Morris had this to say in her/his latest book, *Pleasures of a Tangled Life:*

"Actually all the best sex, in my view, aspires to the condition of incest."

"Particularly graceful, it seems to me, is the notion of love in all its forms between brother and sister."

Granted, Morris is an idiot, but idiots get a lot of respect in America.

Feminism's rush to expose and punish incest is on a collision course with its rush to create a new sexual order. With millions of working mothers leaving unsupervised brothers and sisters home alone together, we should not be surprised if some of the sibs take a notion to do what they saw on "I, Claudius," and then form a "Caligula and Drusilla Association." Nero and Agrippina will, of course, feel discriminated against and form their own association. Nor will it end there. Once, fathers used to yell "Put some clothes on!" whenever they saw their teenage daughters in anything less than a burnoose. But today's New Man fathers, fresh from sensitivity workshops, have been taught to be "accepting" of their daughters' sexuality. If they keep on "accepting" it we could end up with an association called "Daughters of Lot."

Since the inception of "sexist" and "racist," the dreaded suffix -ist has had the power to silence all objections in the land of the free and the home of the brave. Will incestist make it to the majors? Anything is possible in a madhouse, even a very small madhouse, and the one I'm talking about stretches from sea to shining sea.

I suspect that much of what is called incest by overwrought accusers is actually incestuous activity—fondling rather than intercourse. We could discourage such behavior if feminists would get their act together on the subject of male sensitivity. If they want men to hug and kiss their children, they should stop talking about incest; if they want to keep talking about incest, they should stop nagging men to hug and kiss their children. Our present age of enforced touchy-feely is so confused and confusing that a child could easily get the wrong idea and send a male relative to jail merely by telling what she *thought* was the truth.

We could reduce incestuous intercourse if we took bold steps. In a girl who has not attained her full physical growth, intercourse can tear and result in peritonitis. Therefore, intercourse or attempted intercourse with a girl under sixteen should be legally defined as attempted murder.

Meanwhile, what of the girl who claims to be an incest victim? We don't know whether it's true or not. Some day geneticists will devise an infallible test, and when that day comes, such an abortion should no longer be a subject of controversy.

Until then, we should let hypocrisy work in mysterious ways, its wonders to perform. Wait a week, or however long it takes the fertilized egg to enter the womb, or until just before the victim's next menstrual period is due, and clean her out with a D&C or a menstrual extraction.

If hospitals did this routinely for every incest claimant and rape victim, neither she nor anyone else would ever know whether conception had occurred or not. It would ease the minds of everyone concerned and satisfy all but the most fanatical Pro-Lifers. Long ago, a comparable moral dilemma was solved by putting a blank cartridge in one gun of a firing squad. True, the man with the blank can tell he has it because it makes a gun fire differently, but that does not alter the psychology: someone is allowed to be innocent, so all are permitted to hope.

Aborting a defective baby is hard to argue with unless you are a baseball fan. California Angels pitcher Jim Abbott was born with one hand; happily for the Angels, the ace hurler was allowed to live and become an inspiration for sports-minded handicapped youngsters. The sight of a drooling mental defective makes me recoil in disgust, but I am reverent when I watch Abbott switch his glove from stump to hand and back again in the blink of an eye. Where do we draw the line, and who shall draw it? Eleanor Smeal?

I also question the wisdom of basing such decisions on the up-to-date prenatal tests that supposedly reveal fetal handicaps. With all the "human error" around nowadays, how can we be sure that some worthy citizen of the land of E Pluribus Oops did not screw up? Take a sleep-starved lady doctor intent on Having It All, or a lab technician "working on his relationships" instead of paying attention to what he is doing, or a nurse fuming because her husband refuses to help with the housework, or a never-married records clerk with an "out of con-

trol'' teenage son—any of these people could do for prenatal testing
what has already been done for airline safety.

Abortion to save the life of the mother is a self-evident proposition:
first come, first served; she understands the finality of death but the
baby does not. She also may have a family, and it makes no sense to
create widowers and orphans.

Abortion to save the health of the mother ought to be self-evident,
used to be self-evident, but it is becoming less so as *health* is stretched
to its outermost definition to include the subjective area of mental
health. It has come to mean not whether having a baby would make a
woman go stark, raving mad, but that it might *upset* her to have one.

In the annals of unwanted pregnancies, Desiderius Erasmus's
mother got upset, William the Conqueror's mother got upset, Alexander Hamilton's mother got upset, but they all managed. So have countless other unwed mothers, and countless more married women who
got ''caught.'' My family, like yours, contains at least one of the latter, and wouldn't you know the unplanned, unwanted baby turned out
to be the pick of the litter?

''Health of the mother'' all too often means ''convenience of the
mother.'' This is the area of that fast-fading virtue, personal responsibility, whose advocates are now accused of ''blaming the victim.''
We have seen how this works. Some dumb sonofabitch decides to
clean his nails with a power screwdriver, ends up with an infected
hand that has to be amputated, sues the screwdriver company—and
wins! In today's atmosphere of neurotic compassion, not one person
in that courtroom, including the lawyer for the screwdriver company,
would dare say, ''As ye sow, so shall ye reap,'' but it still holds true,
never more than in the matter of abortion. As ye fuck, madam, as ye
fuck.

The debate over abortion has led to the feminization of our political
arena. It has gone on so long and grown so intense that it sometimes
seems as if we have never debated anything else. It is now impossible
to read American history without wondering if ''manifest destiny''
refers to the menstrual cycle, ''fifty-four-forty or fight'' has some-

thing to do with menopause, and "Oval Office" means pussy (actually it does).

The abortion debate also is destroying the legal profession as scientific "progress" forces it into the realm of the ridiculous. A nadir was reached in last year's embryo-custody case in Tennessee, land of the Scopes Monkey Trial, where a movie was born.

Snow White and the Seven Embryos stars W. C. Fields and Mae West. Fields, notorious for hating children, inherits a little jar containing seven very tiny bundles of joy that he must never let out of his sight. To get rid of them, he puts them in a jewel box and gets on a train that he knows is going to be robbed by Mexican bandits. His seatmate is a madam played by Mae. They get drunk together and he tells her what is really in the jewel box. In a sudden burst of regret over her sinful life, Mae saves the embryos from the Mexicans and leaves them on the steps of a convent with a note asking the nuns to give them a good home.

The next day, the now-sober Mae, reading in the newspaper that all seven embryos are female, promptly reverts to type. She devises a plan to stock her brothel with them, referring to them as her "farm team." Disguising herself as a worthy matron on a charity mission, she gains entrance to the convent and steals the jar containing the embryos, leaving an identical but barren jar in its place.

Meanwhile, to keep from going to jail for abandoning the embryos, Fields must find some way to con his way into the convent, where he thinks they still are. After he steals the wrong jar—

You finish it. I invariably reach a point in the abortion debate when I tune out, and it just happened. After all, the subject of fetuses is old-hat to one who heard the fetus story to end all fetus stories at the tender age of ten. . . .

Granny used to take me with her when she visited other old ladies in her set so I would learn how to make social calls and converse in a genteel ladylike manner on acceptable subjects of general interest.

The old ladies lived in narrow three-story row houses on those twisty sides streets of Washington, and held court in dark parlors crammed with fusty Victorian artifacts and faded photographs of grim relatives staring down from the walls. One such old lady was a sherry-drinking widow and Daughter of Everything named Mrs. Balderson.

Flaubert her no Flauberts, Bovary her no Bovarys, this is her story:

"Did I ever tell you about my sister-in-law's aunt's cousin's best friend Clara who had the tube baby that never got born? She didn't even know she was in the family way 'til one day she felt somethin' go *ping!* in her parts and she knew, *she just knew,* it was a baby that broke through her tube—tube babies ran in her family, you know. Well, she went to the doctor and he told her she wasn't in the family way and that it was all in her mind, but she could feel the poor little unborn baby movin' all through her body. It kept goin' *tap-tap!* here and *tap-tap!* there, like it was tryin' to get her attention, you know what I mean? Like it was tappin' out a message—'let me out, mama, let me out!'

"Well, the tappin' got worse and worse and Clara kept goin' to the doctor, and he kept tellin' her it was all in her mind. Finally, she got so frantic and beside herself that he said he would do an exploratory operation to soothe her fears. So she went to the hospital and they opened her up, and what . . . do . . . you . . . think . . . they . . . found?

"Two teeny-tiny little footprints on her liver! Just as plain as day, two iddy-biddy footprints! The doctor wasn't goin' to tell her about it but the nurse did—they say she got fired and drank herself to death. Well, poor Clara was just haunted after that. She knew, she just *knew* that the baby was floatin' around somewhere inside of her, so as soon as she got on her feet she went to a spiritualist to try to make contact with the poor little thing. There they sat, night after night, goin' *knock-knock!* on the table, but nothin' happened.

"Well, one day the spiritualist told somebody she knew from the carnival, and they asked Clara to be in a sideshow with the hairy lady and the sword swallower, and talk in a little iddy-biddy voice and call it 'The Livin' Unborn Baby!'

"Well, let me tell you! As soon as poor Clara heard that she just went to pieces and they had to put her away. But you know what? Her liver kept goin' *tap-tap!* 'til the day she died—she lived to be ninety-two—and when the undertaker opened her up to embalm her, *there* . . . just as plain as *day* . . . on her *liver* . . . after all those *years* . . . he saw two teeny-tiny little *footprints!*' "

EVERYBODY'S GOTTA
RIGHT TO BE FAMOUS

My first exposure to celebrity as we know it today occurred when I was six or seven and Frank Sinatra was singing on the radio. Walter Winchell aired regular reports about the behavior of Sinatra's screaming fans. They pulled buttons off his coat, grabbed his gloves off his hands, and invaded restaurants to salvage scraps from his plate.

As his fame grew, the gossip columns filled up with stories of his reaction to it all. He started slugging people, which landed him squarely on Granny's fighting side.

"That boy wasn't properly reared," she decreed. "When people admire and look up to you, it's your *duty* to be gracious and kind."

When I began getting fan mail, I heard Granny's voice in my head: *"If people are good enough to write to you. . . ."*

I answered every letter, and I answered them promptly—so promptly that I was embarrassed whenever my publishers dragged their feet, as publishers will, about forwarding mail. Afraid that someone would think that *I* had waited a month to answer, I made a point of explaining that I had just received the letter from New York.

Answering my mail was far from a grim duty, however, because I consider my readers sacred. To my added delight I found most of them to be intelligent and interesting. If they asked specific questions I answered them in as much detail as possible; if they simply said, "I loved your book," I sent a postcard saying, "Thank you so much for writing."

Several especially pleasant fan mail encounters stick in my mind:

When a certain national newsmagazine paraphrased me to the point of plagiarism, a reader whom I had heard from before wrote me again to say that I should sue them, and offered to sign a deposition for me.

A woman who read one of my *Cosmopolitan* articles picked up on a passing reference I made about the fourteenth-century romance between John of Gaunt and Lady Katherine Swynford. She had loved Anya Seton's novel, *Katherine,* and wanted to know if I had read it. I had—that's where I got the reference. A day or so later while browsing in a used-book store I came across a print of a medieval woman. I bought it and sent it to my correspondent, saying, "This looks just like Katherine." She wrote back to thank me and we exchanged a few more extremely enjoyable letters before losing touch.

The day after the publication of *Confessions of a Failed Southern Lady,* a young man who runs a rare book store called me immediately after finishing it. Because he was the first fan of a new book, I sent him an autographed copy. He responded with a beautiful edition of *The Letters of Henry Adams* with gilt-edged pages—the only really nice book I've ever had. We have been corresponding ever since, and I have a standing invitation to dinner whenever I'm in his city.

Experiences like these are one reason why I listed myself under my full name and address in the phone book. The other reason has to do with my version of democracy: ego, yes; conceit, no. Or: elitism, yes; status symbols, no. The unlisted number has gone the way of BMWs, Nike running shoes, and thirty-dollar jars of mustard and I want no part of any of them.

It was too good to last. My excellent track record ended last year with a nightmarish incident that says a little about me and a lot about America.

I got the following letter from two women:

Dear Florence:

We are writing this letter to you (assuming you are the famous authoress Florence King), to thank you for *Confessions of a Failed Southern Lady* and to confess that while we were on vacation we brazenly stole: 1.) *When Sisterhood Was in Flower,* 2.) *Southern Ladies and Gentlemen,* 3.) *Wasp, Where Is Thy Sting?* and 4.) first edition *Confessions* from a public library. We stole these books because after reading *Confessions* we both became Florence King fanatics, and being unable to locate these treasures from any bookstores in our town, were led to our current life of common library crime! (Note: *He: An Irreverent Look At the American Male* is missing from all the sources we have checked . . . got any ideas??)

Now Florence, it's only right that these stolen books go back to where they belong, but we refuse to return them unless you send us two signed copies of *Confessions.* If you meet our demands, we promise to return all of the stolen Florence King masterpieces to the libraries from which they came. (Our check for fifty hard-earned dollars is enclosed with a million thanks and the promise to be the two founding members of the Florence King Fan Club.)

With love and thanks we remain. . . .

Enclosed were photos of themselves holding the stolen library copies of my books.

I was a little put off by the first-naming, but what snagged my eye was the subtle note of threat in the line, *"If you meet our demands. . . ."* I procrastinated for two weeks, uncertain about whether to answer them. If I did not, it would be the first fan letter I ever ignored, and that bothered me as much as the threat line. I changed my mind several times before I finally decided to go ahead and do it, telling myself that the terrorist phrasing was simply a manifestation of something I had run into many times: when you're billed as a humorist, people feel challenged to try to make you laugh.

I also told myself—this is so Protestant—that the check they had enclosed was proof of their bona fides. It was more than enough to cover the cost of the books—much more than enough in view of my forty-percent author's discount. I decided that they had paid more than necessary to avoid the embarrassment of paying less—just the sort of thing I would do. This interpretation made me feel so relieved that I even debated sending them my check for the overpayment, but there's a line between Do Right and Miss Goody Two-Shoes so I let it go.

I signed two copies of *Confessions* in the standard fashion—"Especially for . . . with all best wishes"—and mailed them off.

I thought that would be the end of it, but a week or so later I got two effusive thank-you notes. One of them concluded: *"You may rightly read between the lines here and know that I would give anything to meet you. (I also travel a lot and would be in Fredericksburg in a second!)"*

Oh, Jesus. . . .

I ignored both notes. A month or so passed with no more word from them. I relaxed, figuring that it was really over now, but then I got a letter they had written together.

Dear Florence:
      We have read *Confessions* so many times and love it so much, we now yearn to have a picture of the people you brought to life

in the book. Would you *by any chance* have a picture that might include Herb, Louise, Granny, yourself, and possibly Jensy? We wouldn't dream of taking an original from you, but if you have a spare picture or one we could make a copy of, we would be thrilled. It would be truly wonderful to see the faces of these dear people. If this request causes the needle of your nuisance meter to go off the scale, please feel free to blatantly shun your most devoted fans!

Our gratitude endures. Love. . . .

The sadomasochistic dare in that last sly sentence made me mad. I knew I should ignore the letter but nobody was going to play head games with me. I wanted to have the last word and I wanted it to be a very curt last word. My father, like most Englishmen, could commit assault and battery with politeness, so I decided to use his technique.

I wrote back, addressing them formally as "Dear Miss_____ and Miss_____" and said: "My only family pictures are pasted in an album or framed and hung on the wall. Since you have expressed enjoyment of my writing, I suggest that a more interesting and constructive way to follow my fortunes is to subscribe to the Tuesday edition of *Newsday* and read my weekly book reviews." I closed with a cold "Sincerely" and signed my full name.

My most devoted fans, whom I had come to think of as "The Two," wrote back.

Dear Florence:

Thanks so much for your suggestion regarding the Tuesday *Newsday*. (How would you like to review *our* newest book: *Obsessions With a Failed Southern Lady*?!)

We have just learned that we are able to take mutual vacation time and would like very much to spend about four days in the D.C. and Virginia area. We thought it would be fun to take a self-guided tour of some of the following places.

—your birthplace at Park Road
—Meridian Hill Park
—the Mount Pleasant Branch Library
—Congressional Cemetery

—1020 Monroe Street
—Raymond Elementary School
—Powell Junior High School
—the house Granny inherited
—Fredericksburg

We will, of course, arrange for our own lodging and transportation. We are considering making our trip during one of the following time periods: [dates listed]. This tour that we are planning is not meant in any way to obligate you, Florence, although we would be delighted if you find that you would like to join us in our visit to any of these landmark locations! *It is never our intent to invade your privacy in any way,* and as your Fan Club representatives, it would indeed be a pleasure to, at the least, treat you to dinner.

Please let us know if any of the suggested dates sound convenient to you, or if an alternate time would suit your schedule better. Our real goal in all of this is to meet you, Florence. However, if, for any reason, you are unable to accept our dinner invitation, we will gladly postpone our trip until a better time unfolds. You've been so sweet to respond to us in your very personal way.

Bless your ever lovin' heart. . . .

I went into a panicky fury. The trite analogy about fighting mist or an unseen monster is too on-target for me to strive for anything more original to describe how I felt. Nothing is more frightening than being confronted by relentless contradiction. The repeated vows not to obligate me or invade my privacy, followed by stated intentions to do just that; the lavish adoration juxtaposed with arm-twisting hostility, seemed like an attack on rationality itself.

I began getting a lot of hang-up phone calls and suspected The Two were dialing my number just to hear my voice on the answering machine, though in view of their proven boldness it seemed more likely that they would say something . . . didn't it? I began sifting and weighing and analyzing everything, and actually used the dreadful phrase, "worst-case scenario," for the first time as I tried to anticipate what was going to happen next.

If I did not answer their letter they might take my silence for consent and go ahead with their trip. I would find them camped on my doorstep. Suppose they came to Fredericksburg and followed me around? Refused to leave? How would I get rid of them? Suppose they were crazy? They had already shown themselves to be precariously balanced between love and hate. Suppose they tilted hateside and pulled a gun on me? You don't have to be paranoid to think such things—just American.

Living through an extended period of mental tension affects different people in different ways. With me, release takes the form of giddy, cackling mischief. It occurred to me that if The Two carried out their plan to make a pilgrimage to my old D.C. neighborhood, my problem would be most efficaciously solved. I grew up in the section that was burned down during the Martin Luther King riots. The 14th Street of my childhood with its segregated dimestore lunch counters is now known as the Combat Zone; the Park Road of my birth is now lined with crack houses; and Meridian Hill Park, where Mama took me in my stroller, has been renamed for Malcolm X.

All I had to do was wait, and the Brothers would rescue me from my dilemma. Moreover, it would be the book-promotion coup of the century, the stuff that Jacqueline Susann's dreams were made of, something not even Irving Mansfield would dare try to arrange: two bodies found at 14th and Park Road with autographed copies of *Confessions of a Failed Southern Lady* clutched in their lifeless hands.

It was all but guaranteed that two lone white women roaming around such a neighborhood would get into serious trouble. When I thought more about it my mischief receded. Since they obviously knew nothing about Washington I felt it was my responsibility to warn them, but I couldn't do it without getting myself in deeper. They would interpret my warning as loving concern and be encouraged. For my own sake, I would have to stand by and do nothing while they walked into a trap.

That did it. . . .

Being thwarted of Doing Right (I can be *such* a shit) was the last straw. I detonated into a towering rage. Ignoring the possibility that I was dealing with psychopaths, I fired off what is known in certain quarters of the publishing world as "one of Florence's letters."

> Dear Miss_____ and Miss_____:
>
> I thought the formal tone of my reply to your request for family photos would be hint enough, but I see from your last letter that I shall have to be blunt.
>
> Unlike many writers, I have always made a point of answering my fan mail because I consider my readers sacred. You, however, have overstepped the bounds and taken advantage of my good manners.
>
> I find your familiarity offensive. I never address strangers by their first names and I don't permit them to so address me.
>
> I find your persistence childish and obtuse.
>
> I find what you call your "obsession" with me neurotic and repugnant.
>
> I leave you with a quotation from Raymond Chandler that you would do well to study: "If you loved a book, don't meet the author."

They replied in two separate notes. Both opened with "Dear Miss King." Each woman apologized in the most abject manner, with words like "humble" and "beg." Clearly I had won, but it was a pyrrhic victory. Aggression turned to supineness, boldness turned to timidity, presumption turned to deference were but the other side of the coin. I was still on the receiving end of behavioral extremes.

Spoiled by so many years of excellent relations with my readers, I had to figure out what went wrong this time. I watched Lauren Bacall as the beset Broadway star in *The Fan* and read a book about John Lennon, but they shed little light. I felt that they didn't apply to me; writers have always had a better class of fans than pop singers and sex symbols. It was performing artists who attracted the nuts. Writers were different.

"Not any more," said the writer friend I consulted. "This is the age of the book tour. We're all performing artists now."

I'm sure The Two had never seen me on television or they would have said so, but they doubtless had seen other writers. The studied folksiness of talk shows, with celebrities chatting off the cuff in a mock-up living room, permitted them to divest me of the writer's traditional remoteness and regard me as a performing artist who had "come into their homes." In sending the contradictory message that the famous are just plain folks from Mount Olympus, television has forged a relentless tension between loftiness and accessibility.

America's fame problem makes sense in light of one of my angel mother's inimitable phrases. When as a child I raised my voice in song, she would say, "You can't sing slop up a dark alley."

Mama was "supportive" (she called it backing me up) only to a certain point. That point was reality. I could read, I could write, I could spell "like a sonofabitch," as she proudly put it, but I couldn't sing and that was that.

Would that Mama and her vaudeville hook were with us still. Much of the ambivalence and hostility directed toward today's celebrities springs from the fact that a great many of them don't deserve to be celebrities. The country is full of famous people who can't sing slop up a dark alley, can't act slop up a dark alley, can't write slop up a dark alley, and they're all on television.

Having too many celebrities and not enough excellence makes it impossible to tell who deserves respect and who does not—hence the familiarity, presumption, and ambivalent adoration of The Two.

"THE MISANTHROPE'S CORNER"

✝

National Review

1 9 9 0 –

This column is an outgrowth of the old <u>National Review</u> standby, "The Gimlet Eye," written for years by Keith Mano. When he left at the end of 1990 to write a novel, <u>NR</u> decided to split the column between me and conservative commentator Andrew Ferguson. Andy kept "The Gimlet Eye" name and I chose "The Misanthrope's Corner" for mine, and we've been doing it that way ever since. <u>NR</u> is a fortnightly magazine so each of us is in once a month.

<u>NR</u> has succeeded where Granny failed: they have made a lady of me. Now when I want to call someone "the biggest asshole in town" I have to say "<u>anusissimus</u>." They also have some oddly formal stylistic rules that I have gotten used to, one of which caused me no end of confusion as I was copyediting the manuscript of this book. Most style books tell you to put names of radio and television shows in quotations, but <u>NR</u> puts them in italics. I debated with myself about making the entire manuscript consistent one way or the other, but that's such a pain in the <u>clunis</u>. If I went back and changed what I've already marked I would be sure to miss something and end up with inconsistency anyway, so I decided to do it <u>NR</u>'s way in this section and adhere to the more prevalent custom in the rest of the book.

<u>NR</u> lets me write my own heads, which is always nice. All of the columns included here carry the same titles I originally gave them, except one. I changed it just now because I realized I had stepped on my best line. See if you can guess which one it was.

HUGGEE

India's great tradition of immolation is called suttee. America's is called huggee.

Huggee is a lustless lust for flesh-on-flesh popularized by Jimmy Carter after he was grabbed by Leonid Brezhnev at a treaty signing. Nobody remembers the treaty but everybody remembers the batty, pole-axed grin that came over Mr. Peanut, like an old-maid librarian finally getting a taste of life, as the Russian crushed him in an ursine embrace.

Huggee got another boost from the "ethnic awareness" craze of the Carter Seventies, when Americans liberated themselves from what was then known as "our Anglo-Saxon heritage." Sexual restraint had to go, and it did. Now, Anglo-Saxon having metastasized into "white male," the axe has fallen on emotional restraint.

It has just about disappeared. Soon everyone will have hugged everyone else, and then it will be only a matter of time before one of Oprah's guests displays a jar containing a do-it-yourself extrauterine conception, and Oprah hugs the jar.

Huggee is a political form of *"pusillanimata,"* or "scrupulosity," the spiritual hypochondria of the Middle Ages wherein the sufferer was haunted by doubts about the strength of his piety. Americans are haunted by doubts about the strength of our squish. Are we caring enough? Loving enough? Spontaneous enough? Warm 'n' fuzzy enough?

George Bush is photographed with his arm slung around the shoulders of Illinois Governor Jim Edgar, who is holding hands with Mrs. Edgar as the three stroll through the state fair. A female caller on the Larry King show kicks off with, "I love you, Ross," and Perot replies, "I love you, too." Bill Clinton, remarking that he nearly dislocated his shoulder while shaking hands, suddenly realizes that he has registered a complaint and quickly adds: "I think it's important for us to touch as many of the American people as we can."

Of the two political conventions this summer, the Republican Huggee, I regret to say, was the more revolting. I expect Democrats to fling themselves about and emote like peasants because that's what they are, but the spectacle of maudlin Republicans insults the centuries-old conservative tradition of frostiness.

Seneca on health care: "Scorn pain; either it will go away or you will."

Talleyrand on family values: "A married man will do anything for money."

Ambrose Bierce's reply to the woman who asked his advice on childraising: "Study Herod, madam, study Herod."

Not a code word in the lot.

Nowadays the pyres of huggee burn everywhere. The Weather Channel features a "Pain Index" illustrated by a "respiratory distress map" with different colors for gasping, coughing and sneezing, as well as a Heat Index and a Wind-Chill Factor to make conditions sound worse than they are so we will have yet another excuse to comfort each other with hugs.

Just as the best-laid fires of suttee sometimes fizzle out, the lustless lust of huggee occasionally ignites, as D.C. Mayor Sharon Pratt Kelly discovered when Jack Kent Cooke patted her on the behind as they were hugging goodbye after a meeting about relocating the Redskins. As Kelly later explained at a press conference, the hug didn't bother her a bit; that was par for the course. "It was, you know, the way people hug each other," she said with a casual shrug. It was the pat she objected to.

If for some reason you can't hug, you can do the next best thing and slap high fives. This congratulatory fleshly contact, which started as a light tap between athletes who didn't have time for a formal handshake, has taken on a strange intensity lately. Even in once-staid golf, players rear back like dinosaurs and slam their palms together in a horrendous crash as if compelled to establish their bona fides as red-blooded touchers.

A few years ago a baseball player sprained a finger this way and ended up on the DL. Slapping high fives is now a tedious, touchy-feely ritual involving the whole dugout—not just for homers, but for routine things like tagging up and scoring from third after a fly. For that matter, the fan in the stands who catches a foul slaps high fives with every other fan within reach. Should he miss and accidentally slam somebody in the face, as I saw happen once, he can atone by reflecting that an unconscious stranger is a friend you haven't hugged yet, and smother him.

Huggee is but one aspect of a larger trend toward unrestrained behavior, which is why the orgasmic grunts of players in televised tennis matches are deliberately amplified. Like *"La Donna è Mobile"* in *Rigoletto,* it's "the good part."

Democracy breeds familiarity. The crowning glory of huggee was the indiscriminate *tutoyer* adopted during the French Revolution, when egalitarian Jacobins banned the formal *vous* and made everyone address everyone else with *tu.* We would be in the thick of this by now except for a linguistic quirk. English has an intimate form of "you" but we abandoned it long ago and now use it only when speaking to God. Most Americans are unaware of the grammatical connotation of "thee" and "thou." Let us pray that they don't figure it out. Meanwhile, you're nobody till somebody hugs you, so I'm worried. Suppose I, a spinster and an only child, decided to go into politics? Who would hug me? Mr. Buckley? Mr. O'Sullivan? Not on your tintype. That's what I like about this magazine: Nobody ever says a word about "the *National Review* family."

October 5, 1992

THE ETRUSCAN SMILE

Campaign '92 can't end soon enough for me. I am burned out in the manner of all print commentators who have watched too many talking heads on television. True, we can take half of our cable bills as a tax deduction, but it's not worth putting up with:

—Dan Rather, whose membership in the cultural elite proves that America really is a classless society.

—PBS shows in praise of the Year of the Woman that lead in and sign off with Renaissance chamber music to soothe the savage beastie in the tote-bag set.

—The Bobbsey twins of *Capital Gang,* Mona Charen and Margaret Anderson, cavorting in their hot beds of moderation and turning political commentary into a screen test for the Geraldine Fitzgerald part.

—Male liberals who ought to have *Born to Fax* tattooed on what passes for their biceps, who ooze so much unfettered guilt that they seem permanently trapped in that tragicomic dilemma of childhood: lying in bed idly peeling off the mattress tag, only to find that it says DO NOT REMOVE UNDER PENALTY OF LAW.

—The kind of feminist (Nina Totenberg comes to mind) who inadvertently promotes the ne plus ultra of choices: If a man went to bed with her, should he put the bag over her face or her personality?

To add to the torture, several must-watch public affairs shows have been running the same General Electric commercial for almost three years. In it we see all of Hungary being flooded with light as Lizst's Hungarian Rhapsody mounts to a frenzy and delirious Hungarians exclaim, "Everything is wonderful, I'm so happy. . . . It's like a dream, a beautiful dream."

GE's "new" ad, on for about a year now, is not calculated to soothe the nerves of anyone who writes for a living: "This is the man who turned on the light that lit up the room where he worked on the computer that was linked to. . . ." ad infinitum, a hideous run-on sentence that non-union teachers used to call "the house that Jack built."

I have watched these ads so many times that lately I have found myself singing "We Bring Good Things to Life!" I can also sing it in Japanese thanks to the one about flooding Tokyo with light.

Burn-out this severe leads to nightmares, and I had one—about, of all things, the art appreciation course I took as a college sophomore in 1954. . . .

I was sitting in the classroom taking notes on the lecture when suddenly the statue on the slide turned into a real statue. It got bigger and bigger, filling the room with stone until there was no space left. The air grew thin; I was walled in and starting to suffocate—

I woke up. Shaking, I lit a cigarette and tried to analyze the dream, but I had no associations to go on. We dream about things that matter to us, not things that make us shrug. I took the Art Ap course solely to fulfill the humanities requirement; art is the only area of high culture that bores me, so dreaming about it is like dreaming about the only vice that bores me. I've never dreamed about gambling, so why did I dream about art?

The answer came to me the next day while I was dutifully watching Bill Clinton on C-SPAN. Something about him stirred my memories of Art Ap.

It was a survey course, so relentlessly chronological that if you dropped your pencil you missed a hundred years in the time it took to lean down and pick it up. We went from Egyptian tomb paintings to Assyrian ziggurats in jig time, then we hit the sculpture of the Archaic Age, specifically, the *kouros* or *kouroi,* male statues with bodies still locked in the rigid Egyptian manner, but with faces containing a hint of the glorious triumph of the human spirit that was destined to flower in the golden age of classicism.

The hint was a tip-tilted little smile, as if the sculptor had made a vee of his fingers and pushed up the corners of the mouth while it was still wet, or still soft, or whatever, and let it set into the Great Stone Simper. Or maybe he gave it two final whacks with his chisel, one at each corner, to create a monolithic moue to last through eternity.

However they were made, the simple-minded expression they all bore had a name. It was called, said my professor, the "Etruscan smile."

Regression had struck. There I was in the autumn of 1992, still looking at the same thing I had been looking at in the autumn of 1954: Bill Clinton.

I was planning to sit out Election '92 but my nightmare gave me that elusive "reason to vote for Bush" that conservatives spent the summer looking for. Never, ever trust a candidate with an Etruscan smile. All politicians smile, but the Etruscan smile has a special warning behind it. A century ago it often was seen on the face of another public figure, and having taken a lot more history courses than art courses, I know who it was.

Crown Prince Rudolf of Hapsburg, of whom the historian Betty Kelen wrote: "That such doubts of himself occurred habitually to him is written plainly on his face, in the quivering, imploring glance of his eye."

November 2, 1992

THE HIGH-STRUNG CLASS

In all the incessant babble about the suddenly noble middle class, no one has mentioned the subdivision of it that has done so much to wreck America: the High-Strung Class.

Mind you, I'm "high strung" in the lower-case sense. All writers are, so are all artists and musicians, but we have an excuse: we're *supposed* to have sensitive nerves. If we didn't, we couldn't do what we do. Known as "creativity" or "artistic temperament," it has ever been the despair of those foolish enough to fall in love with us and demand our undivided attention. But while we may hurt those closest to us, we don't hurt the whole country, and in the final analysis we give more than we take.

The High-Strung Class is something else altogether. It is composed of thin-skinned pseudo-intellectuals who make their living second-guessing people completely different from themselves.

America's leading Strungleur was Henry David Thoreau, who took it for granted that "the mass of men lead lives of quiet desperation" because the mere thought of holding down a steady job set his teeth on edge. Our own era produced Betty Friedan, an unhappy Smith graduate who polled other unhappy Smith graduates and concluded that all American housewives were clamoring to leave their "comfortable concentration camps" for careers.

The High-Strung Class crawled out from under the rocks during the New Deal and never went back. The original Strungleurs were often the first members of their families to go to college; they are now second- and third-generation college graduates, but fear of the lunchbucket and the time clock dies hard.

Laboring now as government planners and think-tank philosophers, they have turned "I couldn't stand it" into public policy. By "it" they mean everything they have escaped: factory jobs, housewifery, "overcrowded" homes (i.e., each kid doesn't have his own room), or living, like Dorothy Parker, in shabby residence hotels where even dishes and cutlery are furnished and the management discourages what Strungleurs call "individual touches" and bona fide intellectuals call "clutter."

Strungleurs are too dense to grasp a simple fact: we who work with our minds could not function without a plodding working class and traditional housewives. These are the people who produce the strong families that make for a disciplined, orderly society—what Strungleurs call a "productive environment" and I call "peace and quiet."

Because Strungleurs work in the kind of places where neurotic rivals destroy each other's research notes, they are walking spider webs of sensitivity who quiver at the slightest movement. Unable to conceive of having the kind of job you can forget about after work, they assume that brawny machinists need stress-management workshops and transcendental-meditation breaks, too. The "human potential" movement of the Seventies, when companies trained managers to "relate" to employees and place blissful concepts of selfhood over production schedules, is a typical Strungleur contribution to the economy.

Florence Nightingale had no patience with Victorian England's High-Strung Class, whose passion for improving the lot of society's dregs she dismissed as "poor-peopling." In this area, our Strungleurs have killed the thing they claim to love by their pursuit of social leveling.

High civilization needs seedy poets and artists in garrets. The intellectual pretensions of the High-Strung Class make them logical champions of bohemianism, yet the poverty programs they conceive and administer have destroyed its natural milieu.

One of life's intriguing paradoxes is that a hierarchical social order makes cheap rents and outré artists' colonies possible. Raffish bohemian neighborhoods flourished in the days of racial segregation; under integration the artistic poor have no safe places in which to create. The urban intellectual enclaves once so hospitable to ethereal dreamers are gone with the windy blessings of egalitarian Strungleurs. If America lacks a vigorous culture it is partly because studios and ateliers have become crack houses.

The mass of mankind like their lives the way they are and ask only that sensitive thinkers leave them alone. As James Gould Cozzens wrote: "When Thoreau judged that most men lived lives of quiet desperation I think he failed to consider the fact that, by a merciful provision of Providence, most men have little or no more imagination than an animal. Good reasons for despair may be all around the average man, but he won't see them."

If that sounds cruel, it is less cruel than telling women their homes are comfortable concentration camps and then "helping" them escape by shredding the social fabric of an entire country as the feminists have done. Less cruel, too, than the incredible statement by labor leader Samuel Gompers, who must have been a closet Strungleur: "The promise of America for the laboring man is the promise of someday no longer having to work with his hands."

The High-Strung Class would do well to study an anonymous bit of verse about how workmanship leads to self-esteem without need of government meddling:

> If I were a tailor I'd make it my pride
> The best of all tailors to be;
> If I were a tinker, no other tinker
> Should mend an old kettle like me.

March 16, 1992

GIRLTALK

t's no longer fashionable to admit it—it's no longer fashionable to admit anything—but I loved "girltalk." I use the past tense because girltalk is dead.

It died around 1970 when feminists, convinced that women never talked about anything important, established "consciousness-raising" groups based on techniques used in Communist Chinese political reeducation camps. Early Women's Lib CR was the granddaddy, so to speak, of the support-group/task force/problem-solving craze presently filling the land with endless dreary talk, so the wonky din you hear is essentially a product of feminism.

Women no longer need girltalk to gossip privately about men-the-beasts and female trouble. Now that the secrets of the bedchamber are aired on television along with every conceivable gynecological problem, we have lost one of the most richly satisfying sentences ever to fall from female lips. I first heard it in 1939 while watching Garbo in *Camille,* when my grandmother leaned across me and whispered to my mother: "The doctor ought to tell him not to *bother* her."

Girltalk is thought to be rambling and repetitive, but it pales beside the speech code concocted by Donna Shalala when she was chancellor of the University of Wisconsin. Sounding like a Roget rolling brakeless downhill, she barred insensitive speech about "race, color, national origin, ancestry, religion, creed, sex, sexual orientation, disability, and age." She forgot "personal appearance," but then she's such a humanitarian that she never thinks of herself. (Oh, Lord, stop me from being catty, but not yet.)

Recently, a woman worried about her teenage daughter told me, "I know she's sexually active." It sounded cold and detached. The girltalk phrase, "I just know she's having things to do with him," expressed real concern: euphemisms have passion. They also develop the imagination; as a child overhearing gossip about a man and a woman "running around together," I visualized them tearing down the street hand-in-hand, like François Villon and Catherine de Vaucelles fleeing the Burgundians.

Girltalk had ingratiating rhythms. Inserting that theatrical "just" in front of verbs gave female voices a pleasing springiness, but now women avoid such speech habits for fear of not being taken seriously. The susurrant tones of female speech have flattened out; women now talk in the "caucus voice," metallic, grinding, scourging, the voice that filled the French Foreign Legion.

Feminism creates boring women the way democracy creates bad-tempered artists. Under the patronage of an absolute monarch who could do no wrong, artists were emotionally as well as financially secure, free to be openly elitist in the aristocratic manner instead of covertly elitist in the democratic manner. The system produced charming courtiers like Jean Racine, instead of surly snobs like NEA chief John Frohmayer.

Many otherwise charming women lapse into Femspeak whenever someone hits the right button. I got a fan letter from an obviously intelligent, well-bred woman who lives in a town I was thinking of moving to, so I asked her to tell me about it. Her letter describing housing and shopping was thorough and helpful, as well as witty and colorful, but suddenly, à propos of nothing, Femspeak squirted out of her like ink from a squid: "I would not stand living here in the provincial, white-male dominant society if it were not for the liberating and liberal influence of the colleges and for the respect I have for what my husband does within this particular setting."

I no longer enjoy talking to women because I know that sooner or later they're going to say "the operative word is *choose*." Some other verbal dental drills are "career move," "glass ceiling," "institute" as a verb, "educate" meaning propagandize, "perception" meaning any non-feminist point of view, and "passive-aggressive." That last is Femspeak for "Patient Griselda, always spinning," a literary allusion now lost in the mudslide of multicultural ignorance. Today's Patient Griseldas are always wonking, especially if they went to law school, where normal, intelligent women without speech defects are turned into rolling balls of tangled wool.

I especially avoid married career women because they always want to talk about how boring their husbands are. Flaubert could describe Emma Bovary's boredom without becoming boring himself, but feminist matrons induce the sleep that knits the ravell'd sleeve of dress-for-success suits.

Above all, I avoid lesbians. It's impossible to enjoy a martini when someone keeps saying, "I'm tired of being invisible."

The sorry state of female conversation is but one aspect of a larger problem. To explain, let me tell you a story I heard in one of my most interesting girltalks.

Once upon a time, a woman was so hounded and pestered by a man that she nearly went mad. Shrewdly recognizing him as the kind of persistent suitor who, once he gets a woman, loses all interest in her, she realized that there was only one way out of her problem. ''I married him,'' she explained, ''to get rid of him.''

Now, a perpetually hoarse new president has taken office in tandem with his lawyer-wife. As the Billary wonk and crunch their way through what remains of the English language, we just might get so glazed and numb that we will let them do anything they want if only they will shut up.

In other words, we will marry them to get rid of them.

February 1, 1993

SHE DIES IN THE END

I get the distinct impression that feminists don't like strong healthy specimens of womanhood. They're forever ransacking history in search of role models, but they always seem to ignore the fine strapping girls and focus on those who fit my grandmother's definition of a good movie: ''She dies in the end.''

Take, for example, their virtual blackout of Eleanor of Acquitaine (1122–1204), Queen of France and England, who lived to be eighty-two in the twelfth century, sans mammograms, sans Pap smears, sans everything. You would think such an indestructible old rip would do feminists proud, but they have avoided her like the plagues and poxes she never caught. With the stated aim of making women ''feel better about themselves,'' they obsess instead over the welts and weals of Fredegund of Thuringia, dead at seventeen, a victim of medieval diaper rash whose chastity belt killed her.

The same thing has happened in the realm of mental health. The women's studies crowd has snubbed Charlotte Corday, the slip of a girl with nerves of steel who singlehandedly conceived and carried out the assassination of Jean-Paul Marat during the French Revolution.

What do feminists want? Charlotte stabbed a white male in his bathtub, for God's sake, and afterwards behaved like such a brick on the scaffold that the executioner, infuriated by her unfeminine stoicism, slapped the face of her severed head.

But bricks don't sit well with feminists. They much prefer nervous wrecks like Alice James, or those frayed women writers like Jean Stafford who, in the words of one critic, "read her glowing reviews behind locked doors at Payne Whitney."

Woman as picture of health had a brief day in the sun during the early years of feminism, when Ashley Montague's *The Natural Superiority of Women* was still in vogue and there was no one else to quote. For a while feminists crowed that women live longer than men, are less susceptible to color blindness and dyslexia, and withstand cold temperatures better, but they soon began to sound hollow and dispirited, if not downright bored. This was not the stuff of girltalk.

They were rescued by the abortion debate, the crisis over the side effects of the Pill, the crisis over the dangers of IUDs, and the crisis over the dangers of synthetic estrogen. This was more like it. The chance to describe their aches and pains at congressional hearings opened up a heretofore unimaginable world of pelvic politics; instead of laying a guilt trip on one man in the privacy of their homes, they could wear down a whole tableful of men on television.

It took the Los Angeles riots to dislodge silicone implants as the lead story on the evening news. Night after night we watched rubber-gloved hands squeezing liquid beanbags and performing blood-drenched open-breast surgery during what Sam Donaldson calls "the dinner hour." In televised congressional hearings, as women recited the history of their lumps and described in detail how it feels to be a vessel of leaking, seeping, dripping silicone, the faces of the trapped congressmen left little doubt that they were secretly thinking what Hemingway boldly stated: "It's being sick that makes them act so bloody awful and it's because they're sick that you can't treat them as you should. You can always trade one healthy woman in on another. But start with a sick woman and see where you get."

As a final fillip, Sam's Dinner Hour carried a story that Berengaria of Westphalia and Elfrida of Northumbria would be hard put to match: the Texas woman who was in such silicone agony that she slashed her breasts and threatened to yank out her implants herself unless her insurance company agreed to pay for the operation.

Los Angeles burned down the same week this story broke. Remember that the next time somebody starts talking about "root causes." If South-Central had to be incinerated to get Gundrun of East Anglia off the tube, then so be it.

Female invalidism, real or simulated, has had a much too long and successful history to pick up its chaise longue and go quietly into the feminist night. When the Victorian woman pretended to be sick to avoid sex, illness as female metaphor took root in the male mind. Woman's physical weakness came to denote spiritual strength, as if a compensating Nature had drained all the health from her body and transferred it to her soul, making her morally superior to the sturdy male—an idea that came to full flower in the character of Melanie Wilkes: "She never had any strength, she never had anything but heart."

This kind of quasi-sainthood is looking better and better in today's sexually savage world, where the warning Margaret Mead issued in 1970—"Women's liberation has to be terribly conscious of the danger of provoking men to kill women. You have quite literally driven them mad"—has come true.

Illness is to women what "fear-grinning" is to baboons: a way to disarm dangerous Alpha males. If women are once again instinctively using illness as protective coloration, it is a subconscious way of saying that they want their moral superiority back. That they seem to be placing special emphasis on pelvic and mammary disorders should come as no surprise. After all, when you think about it, there is nothing more feminine than female trouble.

July 6, 1992

THE LOVELY PERSON

We've heard much about "Bubba" recently, but in the vast storied realms of Southern antonomasia, Bubba is not terribly important. What Americans need to contemplate now is the South's sobriquet for a certain type of woman.

We call her a "luhvly puhson."

Southerners don't go in much for gender-free language, but we have had to make an exception in this case. "Lovely person" and "lovely woman" are *not* synonymous. The latter has sensual connotations, but the Lovely Person has finished with that, if she ever started, and acquired a more rarefied image. Calling her a "person" signifies the complimentary kind of indeterminate gender traditionally associated with awesome mythological figures and angels.

Nobody ever sat me down and explained what a Lovely Person is, but somewhere along the line Southern osmosis kicked in and I *just knew,* the way I *just knew* the difference between a good ole boy and a redneck, or the subtle social gradations of ordinary, common, and trash. Thus, when I read *Gone With the Wind* at the age of eight, I understood that Scarlett O'Hara's mother was a Lovely Person: "To Ellen, mares never foaled nor cows calved. In fact, hens almost didn't lay eggs. Ellen ignored these matters completely."

There are nicey-nice women everywhere, but in the South, where firebells in the night ring a little louder, the Lovely Person is Lord Chesterfield in Depends. Life is a post-menopausal bladder and she will see to it that not a drop seeps out.

The Lovely Person has a signature sentence that she uses to stop people before they get to the juiciest part of the latest gossip, or whenever any conversation gets too interesting. Probe a subject that fascinates the vast majority of humankind—Jack the Ripper, Lizzie Borden, the Donner Party—and the Lovely Person will flutter her fingers delicately in the air as though fanning an unpleasant odor, and murmur with gentle reproachfulness, "I don't *want* to know."

She follows that with, "Let's talk about something pleasant." No wonder the baroque bloodthirstiness of Arab political rhetoric upsets her so. There isn't a Luhvly Puhson in the entire Middle East. It was bad enough when Saddam Hussein predicted, "Everyone who conspired against Iraq is moving toward a black end, to the hell of oblivion, ruin of present and future," but what really made Arabs non-puhsons in her eyes was the Iraqi mother's vow: "I will cut off the head of my baby and swallow it if it would make Bush lose."

The Lovely Person prefers news stories like the one I recently clipped for my files: "The Bonding Power of Andrew; Hurricane's Rampage Added Strength to Family Ties." Chances are a Lovely Person wrote it, because it is no longer necessary to be a rarefied Southern female to qualify for the sobriquet.

Americans are turning into Lovely Persons quicker than you—or even I—can say ''sonofabitch.'' As soon as the election was over, pundits began flagellating themselves over the way they had covered it, coming up with peer ratings that sounded just like the Lovely Person tamping down her dinner table. Fred Barnes displayed ''chilling hostility'' to Eleanor Clift on *The McLaughlin Group.* Sam Donaldson was ''snarlingly rude'' to Cokie Roberts on *This Week With David Brinkley.* I found both of these exchanges to be merely vigorous, but in Lovely Person America the operative words are *flay, icy, savage,* and that stepfather of all television images: *threatening.*

Lovely Personhood is the driving force of our age. The uproar over negative campaigning is Lovely Personhood. Self-defeating guff about a ''kinder, gentler'' America is Lovely Personhood. The moral collapse known as ''growing in office'' is Lovely Personhood. The paralysis known as ''preserving one's place in history'' is Lovely Personhood. As for political correctness, it's such a replication of Lovely Personhood that we ought to call it LP.

A country that thinks Andy Rooney is a curmudgeon can't take too much unpleasantness. Even speaking in a manner described as ''crisp'' is cause for alarm in Lovely Person America, where ''demanding'' means punctual, ''cold'' means efficient, and ''obsessive-compulsive'' means neat. The most reassuring thing an American can be is ''vulnerable.'' If I'm vulnerable and you're vulnerable we're all okay, which is why the words ''human error'' make any crash or explosion somehow acceptable, especially when Dan Rather brings them out in that gulpy voice he uses to make himself sound large of soul.

Lovely Persons stalk the land. Some merely say nice things as the easiest way out, like the husky young Marine interviewed by CBS after Hurricane Andrew. Asked if he was surprised to find himself helping hurricane victims instead of fighting, he replied that he had joined the Marines ''to travel and to be part of humanitarian relief.''

Other Lovely Persons are motivated by narcissistic challenge—like Oxford's Bill Clinton, who, reports the *Washington Times,* ''befriended the curmudgeonly former sergeant major of artillery who was the British school's porter.''

I know all about this trick, having become a goal of ''threatened'' professional extroverts since my misanthrope book came out. I can just see First Bubba homing in, extending himself and going out of his way, all the while thinking: ''If I can crack *this* nut I must really be a Luhvly Puhson.''

December 28, 1992

THE MATCHBOOK MAN

To liberals he is the ''blue-collar, white-male, racist, sexist, homophobe.'' To feminists he is ''unsocialized'' because he continues to elude their gelding shears. I call him the Matchbook Man because he was the target of self-improvement ads in the matchbooks of my childhood.

Having had a mother who smoked four packs a day, I saw a lot of matchbooks and practiced my reading with them. On the inside of the cover were tiny gray coupons with ads that said: ''Finish High School at Home in Your Spare Time!'' or ''Learn Locksmithing'' or ''Study Radio Repair'' or ''Be a Private Detective''—always at home in your spare time.

A few such ads can still be found in gun magazines or on late-night local television, but today's dwindling supply of matchbooks has been classed up. Now the inside is blank and the cover contains embossed pictures of exclusive hotels and restaurants that the Matchbook Man never enters.

He frequents places like the pool hall where I have my midday beer after finishing my errands. I like it because they have no talkative waiters named Bruce, just chainsmoking waitresses, and because the clientele neither know nor care who I am. No one interrupts my reverie to talk about ''wanting to write.''

It was the day of the House budget vote and several young workingmen were watching the noon news. When the announcer said, ''Congressman Timothy Penny has resigned,'' the tee-shirted, tattooed viewers exchanged eager glances, their eyes lighting up with an energizing spark that seemed to bounce from face to face, linking them all in a circuitry of joy. There was something profoundly touching about it, and also something familiar. I had seen this raw masculine pride before.

It was during the 1962 Cuban missile crisis, when Adlai Stevenson cornered the Soviet representative at the UN and demanded the truth, vowing, "I'll stand here till hell freezes over!"

The next day, some tree pruners were working outside my apartment building and I heard one of them say, "Boy, old Stevenson really told 'em, dint he?" His face was lit with the same glow that I saw on the faces of the boys in the pool hall. It's a look that never comes over a woman even though she may share the opinion that brings it on. Epiphanies composed of bellicose swagger and a purity having nothing to do with sexuality are the exclusive property of the Matchbook Man.

It's just about all he has left. He used to be "the man who found a home in the army," but now he must look hard to find the army amid the welter of homemaking missions on which it has embarked. Craving an arena of Spartan hardness in which to prove himself, he gets instead Operation Restore Hope in Somalia, made glorious, said Dick Cheney, by "the interaction we're accustomed to seeing between American troops and people we help"; or Operation Provide Comfort on the Iraqi border where, wrote Mary McGrory, "Americans thrilled to the sight of U.S. soldiers changing babies."

While liberals form taskforce after taskforce to cure alienation in their beloved urban underclass, the Matchbook Man is being driven crazy by the growing primacy of warm feeling over cold justice in American life. His own moral center has the bleak unequivocal beauty of a January dawn, but let him display it and it will be dismissed as an "inappropriate response."

When he watches news reports about "Iron John" manhood-weekend outings he sees the same whey-faced academics who condemn him during the week, who know nothing about a carburetor except how to spell it. If he changes channels he very likely will find Weekend Man's feminist wife in a panel discussion about "the myth of masculinity." And should he leaf through a magazine he will come across one of those nasty little editorial asides that politically correct journalists take pains to insert in their copy—like *Time*'s Richard Corliss and his gratuitous description of Mike Tyson as ''an exemplar of all those sad studs who are prisoners of manhood.''

When the Matchbook Man objects to Betty Boop congresspersons like Pat Schroeder or an attorney general with the mean mouth of a social worker on the rampage, it merely proves that ''he just doesn't get it.'' What he does get all too well are our new definitions. An honorable man is one who doesn't cave until the last minute, a maverick is an unpredictable hysteric, and ''dashing'' is no longer a male adjective, just a descriptive participle for bureaucrats who schedule too many meetings. Every time he ''gets it'' the Matchbook Man dies a little, but no, he's not alienated.

For him, every week is the Week That Was. He recoiled when California Highway patrolperson Melanie Singer burst into tears on the witness stand and wrecked the defense in the second LAPD trial. Now he has a brand-new crazymaker: the majestically ditzy Marjorie Margolies-Mezvinsky, a dead ringer for Zasu Pitts, who changed her mind at the last minute to put the Clinton budget over the top, then spent the following day on the tube wondering whether she had ''fallen on her sword.'' Another noble Roman concept bites the dust.

Feminists will find my response to the Matchbook Man inappropriate, but I'm sure Mae West would back me up:

I like a man who just doesn't get it.

September 20, 1993

ON TENDER HOOKS

If love means never having to say you're sorry, America is on tender hooks. Somebody is always apologizing.

Country club memberships, baseball ''necessities,'' Confederate flags, water buffalo, Madame Butterfly, speaking English, being male, roasting people at roasts, belittling the flexed-arm hang, Hiroshima, oil spills, babies without fathers, swimmers without buoyancy, Columbus, ''you people,'' Tammy Wynette, the tomahawk chop, and the 1916 popular song, ''Where Did Robinson Crusoe Go with Friday on Saturday Night?''

I threw in that last one just to see if you were paying attention. It hasn't become a cause célèbre because few people now alive know the lyrics, but it's a real fan hitter ("Did they dine out with wild mens on cannibal trimmins? / Where there are wild mens there must be wild wimmens") and a twofer besides.

The vocabulary of apology grates on the nerves like chalk squeaking across an African-American board. The moment we hear "to any and all" we know an apology is coming, so we bite down hard and wait for "inappropriate," "regrettable," and "perceived" (the last means that white feminists can jump to conclusions). The jaws start to relax at "let us put it behind us and go forward," a signal that the agony is over until the next time.

"Never apologize, never explain," said Immanuel Kant. This maxim has so many versions that it qualifies as received truth. From the Frenchman who said, *"Qui s'excuse, s'accuse,"* to John Wayne's signature line in *She Wore a Yellow Ribbon,* "Never apologize, mister, it's a sign of weakness," the wisdom of taking your knocks, thumbing your nose, and leaving well enough alone was universally acknowledged.

No more. Now we eat our way down a Baskin-Robbins menu of apologies with something for every craving. "The buck stops here" is the apology of choice for anyone in the throes of a calm, firm, manly panic. VMI's contention that single-sex schools "celebrate diversity" is the steadfast cave-in sundae: when you defend yourself with your enemy's language you are apologizing whether you know it or not. Claiming "humanitarian" reasons for government policy is how to apologize for having a national interest. And if you believe that cringing actions speak louder than craven words you can savor the gesture-as-apology and voluntarily turn in your guns at community drives.

On it goes. The only way to say what you really think is to talk into an open mike and then apologize for not knowing it was open.

Tender Hooks originated in the nursery and the sewing room. Hurt feelings and apologies have always been the purlieu of women and children, who conduct interminable, maniacally detailed investigations of the finer points of emotional affronts the instant someone wails "Johnny talked mean to me!" Having been designated as the umpires of these disputes, women developed a third ear for subtle tones, trenchant pauses, and vocal syncopation that only a connoisseur of bad vibes can catch.

"But what did I say?" asks the luckless male.

"It was *how* you said it," is her tremulous reply.

Welcome to the Zeitgeist. America, no longer a man's country, is now rigged for the exquisite sensibilities of women and children—the same people who gave us "if you can't say something nice, don't say anything at all," and "take that back or I'll never speak to you again as long as I live!"

I don't care what people do to each other but I care passionately what they do to English. Tender Hooks makes crisp, concise language an object of fear and loathing. I don't mean just clumsy vagaries like "native American." Far more serious are the current trends of using words to mean what we wish them to mean, and banishing outright any word whose definition fails to satisfy our emotions.

A case in point is the distinction between *sympathy* and *empathy,* now deliberately ignored even by people who know better, like the editors of *Time.*

Sympathy, the ability to commiserate with someone different from ourselves, always includes the element of pity. Empathy, the ability to commiserate with someone like ourselves, always includes the element of identification.

Obviously, sympathy requires more effort and hence is the greater virtue, but we have cast it into outer darkness, choosing instead to "empathize" with everyone under the sun. In our rush to gild the lily of apology we have convinced ourselves that "empathy" sounds more sympathetic, but in truth we are afraid of having to apologize for the implied insult in sympathy. Mary McCarthy put it best. "Pity," she wrote, "signifies a conquered repugnance."

The whole country has a bone in the throat—the real cause of the "stress" we hear so much about. As Boris Pasternak noted in *Dr. Zhivago:* "Health is ruined by the systematic duplicity forced on people if you say the opposite of what you feel, if you grovel before what you dislike and rejoice at what brings you nothing but misfortune."

Anyone who thinks that Tender Hooks will keep America's fragile peace should think again. "Why are you always saying you're sorry?" is, after all, the signature line of the wife beater.

June 21, 1993

When I sent this column in I attached a note: "tender hooks is a deliberate error, please don't change it to tenterhooks."

My editor, Geoffrey Morris, saw to it that no one changed it, but I did not anticipate the reader response. I was inundated with letters, most of which started out "imagine my despair. . . ." Several people sent me photocopies of the dictionary page containing the proper spelling of "tenterhooks," and one man wrote a disquisition on the textile industry, explaining that a "tenter" is the frame on which fabric is stretched to dry, and the "hook" is the nail driven into the frame to hold the fabric while it dries; the fabric is thus in a state of suspended tension, etc. etc.

The Richmond Times-Dispatch reprints my NR column. When I faxed them a tear sheet of "On Tender Hooks" I was so worn out from answering all the NR mail that I forgot to repeat my editorial warning. Virginia being a textile state, you know what happened: someone at the Times-Dispatch carefully changed every "tender hook" to "tenterhook."

As I plan to say in my forthcoming address to Congress, the State of the Punnybone is not good. [STET the P!]

EX PEDE HERCULEM

ogic ought to be sacred. That's why I have been on the alert ever since Yamaha named a motorcycle "Virago" and Shakespeare's symbol of unreliability ("false, false, false Cressid!") inspired a car.

How on earth did it happen? We can't blame it on "cultural differences." The companies are Japanese but their advertising and PR firms are geared to the Western world. It is impossible to believe that these wildly wrong names could slip past the panoply of research and development, market testing, and "creative" meetings that go into such decisions. We can bet the connotations were known and discussed, but in the end someone probably said it won't hurt sales because the slobs don't know the difference and the eggheads will just write us snotty letters about the Trojan War.

The latest assault on logic is the opera-backed commercial. In the one for a recreational vehicle, we first see the product covered with mud, then a titanic inundation of water comes out of nowhere and washes it clean while a soprano voice sings *"Un bel di"* from *Madame Butterfly*. The same aria is used in another ad for athletic shoes, sung to visuals of stouthearted runners straining heroically toward a finish line. What is the connection here? The aria is about a girl who's been jilted and is too dumb to realize it.

Another one, for a luxury car or an aftershave, I forget which, shows a woman in a slinky black evening dress running across the lawn of a palatial estate at sunrise while a soprano voice sings *"O Mio Babbino Caro"* from Puccini's *Gianni Schicchi*. This aria has the melting quality of romantic passion but it isn't that at all. The title character of this one-act comic opera is a wily Tuscan peasant who fakes a will; the aria, sung by his worried daughter, means "Oh, My Dearest Daddy."

Don't assume Madison Avenue is full of philistines: it isn't. They knew, all right, but they didn't care. Opera is perceived as classy, therefore products advertised with opera are perceived as classy, so don't worry about which opera or aria you use as long as it "soars."

This might sound like a minor point in a country where millions can't even read, but remember that little things mean a lot, or as the logician Aulus Gellius put it: *Ex pede Herculem,* "From the foot alone we may infer Hercules."

Contempt for logic grows daily. Nobody has "ideas" anymore, just shattering mental jolts known as "wake-up calls." Books with titles like *You Just Don't Understand* and the daily crowing over people who "don't get it" betray an undeniable pride in flux and chaos. In *Earth in the Balance,* Al Gore condemns "the Cartesian model of the disembodied intellect," and the majority have accepted the feminist canard that logic is masculine (bad) and emotion is feminine (good). The new literary criticism demonstrates, point by unraveling point, that nothing means anything because every book now has a "subtext," and our kneejerk characterization of any utterance that makes no sense whatsoever is "thoughtful."

Americans have gotten the message that life is easier if they don't think straight. Aware that logic demolishes political correctness, they conclude that meaninglessness is the better part of wisdom and eagerly embrace fuzzy thinking as a refuge against charges of -ist, -ite, -phobe. Thus we have letters to the editor like this one from the *Washington Post:* ''Mr. Maguire has a right to question the fairness of affirmative action, but his reference to a specific group's test scores was an unwarranted and malicious act.''

The only time we even hear the L-word nowadays is when voters lie to exit polls and pundits sigh, ''There's no logic behind it.''

Post hocky ergo propter hocky has hit the fan. Need an objection to the law barring HIV-positive persons from entering the United States? Just say, as one activist did, ''Travel doesn't cause HIV.''

Need to make sure the whole world knows there is no connection whatsoever between you and your mind? Just go on *Nightline* and say, as Lani Guinier did: ''Most important, I think, is not what I wrote but who I am.''

Need to destroy your own argument? Object to the implications of the politically correct language now used in Lamaze classes, where instructors now speak of ''partners'' or ''moms and coaches'' instead of ''husbands'' and ''wives,'' and then write, as Mona Charen did: ''Now, I do not disparage the sentiments expressed at all, merely the terminology.''

In America, when Birnam Wood moves to Dunsinane it brings along its own developers. Is it any wonder we got the Clintons? This gang says military ''mission'' when they mean up the creek without a paddle, and ''moving deadline'' for a date that will live in infamy just as soon as they decide what it is.

Significantly, after Billy Boop had his ''spirited'' bipartisan meeting about Somalia with congressional leaders, an aide describing the fray to reporters took eerie liberties with a name CBS recently bestowed on a regular segment of its evening news show. The meeting, said the aide, was ''a good reality check.''

Need an operatic aria for Hillary's health-care commercials? How about *''Che Gelida Manina''* from *La Bohème?* It means ''What a cold hand.''

November 15, 1993

TIME CAPSULE

They say a drowning person sees his whole life flash before him as he goes down for the third time. The feminization of America is having the same effect on me.

The chain of reasoning in date rape cases brings back my grandmother's lecture on the proper way for a lady to walk past a barbershop.

"Always look straight ahead. If you look in, the men will think you're looking in."

"But if I looked in, I *would* be looking in."

"Yes, but not really."

In debates about women in combat, I hurtle through time the moment a worried general utters the words "male bonding" and "unit cohesion." The brass had better worry; every veteran of girls' gym has heard a snippy little voice say, "I'm not going to throw the ball to *her*," even though *her* is standing directly under the basket without a guard in sight.

Dee Dee Myers' disjointed press briefings find me back in a Fifties dorm, listening to a panicky coed trying to figure out when her last period started.

"It's my middle, but it isn't really my middle because it's February, and that messes everything up because it's so short. I think it was the day you traded that green sack dress you hated for Flo's blue shrug—no, no, wait a minute, it was before that, because Flo wore the shrug to the movies the night I had cramps. What movie did we see? If I knew that, I could call the theater and find out when it played. Oh, I know! It was the one where Deborah Kerr saved the boy from being a sissy—no, no, wait! I take that back. It was the one where Charlton Heston was Andrew Jackson, and Yul Brynner did . . . um, something, I forget what, and there was this big battle."

Just about everything brings back memories of how I got started in writing. The 2,476th feature on mammograms, the 4,728th segment on unwed mothers, the eternal "special" hosted by Connie Chung, Meryl Streep's soulful face as she discusses her "films"—expose me to any one of these and I will start reciting verbatim from the 1958 *Writer's Market:*

True-confessions stories must be about subjects of interest to women: marital discord, adultery, problem children, alcoholism, insecurity, anxiety, depression, nervous breakdowns, accidents, illness, surgery, and sudden death. Upbeat ending essential. No humor; our readers take life seriously. Length 3,000 to 5,000; payment 5 cents per word. Enclose SASE.

The first story I sold was called "I Committed Adultery in a Diabetic Coma." I think of it every time a Women's Health Special Supplement falls out of the newspaper.

The feminization of America has progressed so far that sometimes I have a hard time telling whether I'm watching the news on CNN or a three-hankie weeper on American Movie Classics. Barry Goldwater's sudden espousal of gay rights, or Barbara Stanwyck yearning for social approval? George Bush sabotaging himself to preserve his "place in history," or Lana Turner agonizing over What People Will Think? The scandal-tainted politician who decides to retire "to spend more time with my family," or Joan Crawford growling "I'll do anything for those kids, you hear me, anything"?

It's especially confusing to watch old movies in the era of apologies. A nation so nice-nellied that it sees nothing odd about apologizing for homeless gypsies has only one apology left, and we just used it. In October, the Senate passed a resolution apologizing to Hawaii for overthrowing Queen Liliuokalani in 1893. It finally happened: we apologized to ourselves. Is that Joan Fontaine cringing through *Rebecca* or not?

I hopped on another time capsule when the Houston Oilers fined football star David Williams for skipping out on a game in order to attend the birth of his child. The Sensitivity Patrol led by Anna Quindlen flew into the usual hysterical rage, but I flew back to the 1940s and sat once again on the floor beside our huge Philco console, my ear pressed against the brocaded vent so as not to miss a word of *Abbott & Costello.*

This particular show was as wonderfully wacky as all the others. Not once did Lou Costello give any indication that anything was wrong. It was not until the next day that we learned he had gone on the air only hours after receiving word that his son had drowned. No one called him "insensitive" for leaving his wife alone while he made the whole country laugh; in the flood of admiring editorials that followed, one word stood out: "trouper."

The feminization of America has made emotions sacrosanct while condemning as cold and unfeeling rigorous concepts such as duty and honor. Propelled by incessant hosannas to woman's "finer" this and "softer" that, we make emotional decisions instead of ethical ones and then congratulate ourselves for having "heart."

We need to get a grip on ourselves while there's still time. A bracing antidote to feminization is Mary Wollstonecraft, the Ur-feminist of the rational eighteenth century, who knew that political correctness is nothing more than female touchiness writ large. Said she:

"I wish to persuade women to endeavor to acquire strength, both of mind and body, and to convince them that the soft phrases, susceptibility of heart, delicacy of sentiment, and refinement of taste, are almost synonymous with epithets of weakness."

December 13, 1993

THE NEW HYPOCHONDRIACS

I am the opposite of a hypochondriac, whatever that is. I consulted the thesaurus for an antonym but hypochondria has no entry of its own. It is listed under Dejection, along with typical Roget synonyms like "infestivity." The antonyms are listed under Cheerfulness and include "canty."

My vocabulary problem arises from the fact that hypochondriacs have cornered both sides of the neurosis. They are obsessed with being sick, but they are also obsessed with being well, so it is impossible to be the opposite of a hypochondriac. All I can do is state my philosophy: If whiskey or salt won't cure it, then to hell with it. I worry about important things. I'll sit up all night nursing an ailing paragraph, but I refuse to bow down before the latest sacred udder. I never had a mammogram and never hope to get one, and far from dreading mastectomy, the subject makes me positively canty: I could get a better fit in a shoulder holster.

American hypochondria has undergone an interesting change in recent years. The classic or "normal" hypochondriac simply wanted to be sick so that he could want to get well. He did not want others to be sick lest they steal his thunder, and he did not harbor any hostility to healthy people; indeed, he was very fond of them and liked having them around because they made him seem sicker.

The New Hypochondria throbs with the morbid narcissism of liberalism. New Hypochondriacs don't really want to be either sick or well, but rather "information receptive" and "medically aware"—code words for intelligent and educated and thus a delineator of class, a way of separating the people who read "The Forgotten Spleen" in the *Washington Post's* Health section from the people who don't. To the New Hypochondriacs, the fun lies not in the croupe kettles and mustard plasters of times past; they want to skip both illness and health so they can get to prevention and recovery, co-dependency and enabling, and have vanity plates that say SUVIVR.

The hypochondria of education and awareness is why we have commercials for medicines whose purpose is never revealed. These spots invariably sound like snide academics sitting on the floor playing Scrabble.

"Like many people, you're probably curious about Rogaine," the shill begins. He goes on in that vein, with teasers like "Of course you want to know more about Rogaine," but he never says what Rogaine is or what it's for. "Ask your doctor about Rogaine," he concludes, adding in an offensively high-handed tone: "Go on, what are you waiting for?"

Then there's the colloquy between the pharmacist and the customer. The customer hands over a prescription for "Cardizem SR" and the pharmacist asks, "Have you tried Cardizem CD?"

"No, can you give me Cardizem CD?" asks the customer.

"Only your doctor can prescribe Cardizem CD," chides the pharmacist.

"Cardizem CD? Okay, I'll ask my doctor."

We never find out what Cardizem SR is, much less Cardizem CD, but we don't really want to know. The human spirit needs tantalizing mysteries but our supply has run out. Now that femmes fatales practice total honesty, medicine is the only thing left that keeps us guessing.

As New Hypochondriacs convince themselves that the only thing they have to fear is food itself, a bitter resentment against the French is peeping out of the lucubrations of the politically correct. France, long the nirvana of alienated intellectuals who want to escape crass America, is the land of the pig-out. Butter, lard, goose liver pâté, and two packs of Gauloises a day, and still France lives. Our medically aware elite is hurt by this picture of health, but they are incapable of grasping—or admitting—the reasons for it.

The French are a secure, adult people who are proud of their language and culture and never apologize for being French (quite the contrary). They are also a homogeneous people, and thus never come down with Americanoma Diversititis Democratosis, which kills with kindness. Above all, although they are not religious, they are Catholic, a seeming conflict which they understand perfectly and which gives them a stress-defying spiritual ease that few Americans know. You couldn't clog a French artery if you injected it with silicone.

We are living in ironic times and I relish the coming spectacle. The New Hypochondriacs are all pumped up from exposure to shows like The Learning Channel's week-long series, "The Operation," which features complete surgical procedures, a different one for each day, like a teenage girl's underpants. What happens when they get hit with socialized medicine? Hypochondriacs need complete medical freedom to do their stuff, but the same government that made them medically aware is now promising two bureaucrats in every pot and Hillary in the garage.

The Nanny State soon will need a cautionary tale, so I have written one for them:

When they came for the smokers I kept silent because I don't smoke. When they came for the meat eaters I kept silent because I'm a vegetarian. When they came for the gun owners I kept silent because I'm a pacifist. When they came for the drivers I kept silent because I'm a bicyclist.

They never did come for me. I'm still here because there's nobody left in the secret police except sissies with rickets.

July 11, 1994

THE DECLINE AND FALL OF THE HUSSY

Thank God I'm over the hill. The only heat I have left comes from hot flashes, my promiscuity is confined to the words "one size fits all," and I buy my white cotton unmentionables at Boadicea's Retreat, not Victoria's Secret. None of the things men do to women could possibly happen to me now unless the U.S. is invaded by one of those new Russian republics whose soldiers aren't fussy.

I'm glad my desirability is a thing of the past because the heyday of the hussy is over. I like to do things well; if I were young again and embarking on the primrose path, I would want to be what Ross Perot would call a world-class hussy, but current standards of dissoluteness have fallen so low that nobody would know the difference.

The hierarchy of female ruin has collapsed along with all the other hierarchies that once made life colorful and provocative. World-class hussies have gone the way of courtesans and back-street wives, lost in the mudslide of interchangeable bimbos like Rita Jenrette, Jessica Hahn, Donna Rice, and Gennifer Flowers, and garrulous "victims" like Palm Beach date-rapee Patricia Bowman.

To illustrate, take what Bowman kept calling "an interesting conversation." The most telling moment in her testimony was when she said that she never misses a chance to discuss her daughter's medical problems whenever she meets a doctor socially. She elaborated on this with a snooty, pathetic pride in her ability to meet doctors as equals and talk their language, leaving no doubt that she actually believed this made her irresistible to William Kennedy Smith and all the other hapless medicos she corners at parties.

Is there a doctor alive who doesn't dread such females? They do the same thing when they meet lawyers at parties. Trying frantically to be what women's magazines and self-help books call "interesting," they babble on about asthma and torts, sublimely unaware that they are dragging their captive professional men on a busman's holiday.

Egalitarianism has replaced the arch wordplay of sexual tension with the soporific drone of equal partners. Nowhere in Bowman's reams of testimony do we find the slightest hint of clever repartee on the night in question, which is why her story sounded so sordid.

Risqué banter elevates squalid situations, as when satyrish Napoleon III asked, "What is the way to your heart?" and Eugénie replied, "Through the chapel, Sire."

Scintillating verbal foreplay is the way to a man's mind, the fortress a woman must breach if she wants to make him aware of her "as a person," but Patricia Bowman just didn't get it. Stuffed with propaganda about professional equality and sexual freedom, she droned on about acute mycoplasmal tularemia and then started digging in his pants.

This is not Madame Récamier trading bons mots with Talleyrand, nor even Hepburn trading bons mots with Tracy. It's Messalina with a master's degree.

The English duchess who reputedly said "Sex is too good for the common people" was on to something. Today's pseudo-hussies are nothing more than updated versions of that put-upon figure of Victorian melodrama, the "little shop girl." There are millions of them in every age and they invariably get caught in sexual tragedies because they lack the personality trait that identifies a bona fide hussy: a bandit streak.

Falling somewhere between eccentric and sociopath, the female bandit is tough, but it's not the slutty toughness of Madonna or the desperate, doomed toughness of *Thelma and Louise*. It's the kind that used to be called "stouthearted." She also has a flair, a style, a whiplash outrageousness found only in aristocrats—either the real kind, or the kind our Founding Fathers called "natural."

Nell Gwynne, mistress of Charles II, showed her bandit streak when she stepped out of her carriage into the howling anti-Catholic mob surrounding it and said, "Calm yourselves, my good people, I'm the Protestant whore." Edwardian actress Stella Campbell showed hers when George Bernard Shaw asked her what her new husband was like and she replied: "Six-foot-four and everything in proportion."

For female banditry on the witness stand we can do no better than Caroline of Brunswick, consort of George IV, who was called to testify in the House of Lords when the King, who was secretly married to his mistress, Maria Fitzherbert, tried to divorce her. Asked whether she had ever committed adultery, Caroline shot back: "Only when I slept with Mrs. Fitzherbert's husband." Patricia Bowman could have used a rapier thrust like that. Caroline also could have punched up the

the droning seminar on stained intimate garments with her famous boast: "I change my drawers once a year whether they're dirty or not."

Hussydom, by definition an elite sisterhood, has been relentlessly democratized. The worst leveler is *Cosmopolitan* magazine, which stands in relation to true seductiveness as Robespierre to the ancien régime. Today's victim-bimbos must devour every issue. Listening to their pedestrian testimony and banal press conferences, we hear not the hiss of the serpent of the Nile, but Helen Gurley Brown's deathless exhortation to the daughters of the Common Man: "If you're a little mouseburger, come with me. I was a mouseburger and I will help you."

The American Dream strikes again: Everybody's gotta right to be a hussy.

February 17, 1992

Did you catch what I told you to watch for in the introduction to this section? This is the column whose title I changed when I realized I had stepped on my best line. The original title was "Messalina with a Master's Degree."

"THE OPEN BOOK"

†

Literary Columns

RALEIGH NEWS & OBSERVER

1 9 9 3

Nothing irritates a writer more than those people who ask us, "Have you ever had a real job?"

It so happens I have. From 1964 to 1967 I worked as a feature writer on the woman's page of the Raleigh News & Observer. *The woman's editor was Marion Gregory, whom I nicknamed "Torb" for "the Old Rugged Boss." The woman's page is long gone but Marion is still there. She's the managing editor now, High Torb of the whole shebang. Her richly deserved elevation is one of the two results of feminism that I approve of (the other is pants suits).*

About a year ago she called me and said that their book editor having left, the Sunday editor's column was open and she wanted to try out a new idea. Instead of the same person writing the column every week, she thought it would be interesting to have a variety of "voices" and asked me if I would like to be one of four revolving book-page columnists.

I said yes. The deal calls for me to write approximately nine hundred words on a "literary subject." That can cover a multitude of sins—and I did.

MY SAVIOR, FANNIE HURST

The trouble with censorship is that the people who do the censoring are always so shortsighted, especially when they set out to protect "Our Children." Instead of taking certain books out of school libraries, we should make a point of putting them in—one in particular.

If I had a teenage daughter I would make her read *Back Street,* Fannie Hurst's 1931 bestseller about a kept woman. It's a better aid to chastity than a dorm full of housemothers, a palace guard of eunuchs, and a posse of Southern brothers all rolled into one.

It was made into a movie in 1932 starring Irene Dunne, and again in 1941 starring Margaret Sullavan, but both versions used only the first two-thirds of the book.

Ray Schmidt is a German-American girl in Gay Nineties Cincinnati who manages her father's dry-goods store. She meets Walter Saxel while he is engaged to the niece of a rich banker. They fall in love, but when Ray inadvertently stands him up, the disappointed Walter puts her out of his mind and goes through with his marriage to the rich girl.

Six years later, Ray and Walter accidentally run into each other in New York, where she has a promising career in fashion design. He is now a Wall Street financier and solid family man. Chemistry strikes again and she agrees to be his mistress. He establishes her in a shabby-genteel flat and makes her quit her job so that she can devote herself to the job of making him happy. "But I've been a business girl all my life," she protests weakly. "From now on," he tells her, "your business is me."

Thus begins her life of waiting—for the phone to ring, for the mail to come, for Walter to show up. Over the years, as he becomes a prominent international banker, she does much of her waiting in Europe, where he stays in luxury hotels and stashes her in crummy ones so nobody will find out about her.

Walter has a sudden massive stroke on a business trip and the isolated Ray learns of it from the newspaper. He tries to speak to her on the phone from his deathbed but dies before he can say anything. His son offers to continue her financial support, but a short time later Ray also dies, presumably of a broken heart, and the movie ends.

This is not how the book ends, nor is it a love story.

Fannie Hurst's Ray Schmidt is a feminist's nightmare, so eager to please everyone but herself that she gets a reputation for being "easy" without quite knowing how it happened. "It's so hard for me to dislike people or get huffy," she muses. "I've never learned to say no without its hurting me a whole lot more than the person I've said it to. . . . Many a time I've felt sorry for a fellow while he was insulting me."

The rich Walter is so tight with money that Ray has to paint china to make ends meet, but she is helpless to stand up to him; "just as surely as the blood was locked in her veins, so was her inertia to clear herself of this octopus of circumstance locked in her temperament."

She embroiders portraits of the presidents for his children, taking the cost of the materials out of her meager house money, but he never thinks to reimburse her, and complains that the close work is giving her an unattractive squint.

Sometimes when his peevishness provokes her, "forbidden rages crept out like poisonous little mice from their corners," but her unassertiveness always holds her back; ''her words lay unspoken between two lips that were splinters of wood that would not open.'' Walter's idea of an apology—''When a woman is as wonderful as you are, a man knows he's not worthy and stops trying''—makes ''the knowing slants of her mind dance in the heat lightning of anger.'' But instead of getting mad, she ends up apologizing for making him apologize.

Walter continues to keep her after her youth has gone, not because he loves her but because he needs his punching bag; ''the passion of her surrender to his every conviction, wish, desire, spoken and unspoken, continued to lash and dominate her unabated through the years—a slavery that was precious to her, a subservience that exalted while it abased.''

Walter's furious son confronts her and demands that she leave his father alone, but she is too whipped down to tell him to mind his own business. Wearily, hopelessly, she sees herself through his eyes:

> One of those frowsy kept women, who live indoors too much, and who, as the hair begins to streak, the neck to thin, and the veins to bulge, take on that plucked look of old eagles. . . . If only the floor, yawning, would swallow you up, in your red challis wrapper and slapped heart, before the merciless, unhurt, disgusted eyes of this perfect-shouldered, lean-thighed polo player, sitting there on his high horse, to whom easy women without youth were horrible.

Shortly after this humiliating scene, Walter suddenly drops dead—of acute indigestion, not a dramatic stroke, and without a deathbed phone call. His Will leaves millions to charity but makes no mention of Ray, whose only money has been the two hundred dollars he left in a flower pot each month.

His son, chastened now, promises to set up a trust fund for her but he never gets the chance. Instead of Ray dying of a broken heart as she does in the movie, the son is killed in a polo accident and the aging Ray is left penniless.

I won't tell you what happens to her—and you wouldn't believe it if I did. You're too used to contemporary feminist definitions of tragedy, like the fate of the heroine in *The Women's Room,* who is reduced to teaching English in a community college after attending Harvard on alimony. Ray's fate is unbearable and unbelievable, except that Fan-

nie Hurst makes us believe it; I started crying while I was reading it—
the only time in my life I've ever done that.

Suffice to say that *Back Street* scared the daylights out of me. I read
it when I was twenty-six and sex was never quite the same afterwards.
If we put a copy in every high school we would soon have a nation of
virgins.

ROCK 'EM, SOCK 'EM FEMINISM

There is nothing wrong with "women's studies" that studying the
right women can't cure, but feminist literary scholars have a penchant for dragging the rivers of deserved obscurity for third-rate
neurotics.

The worst of these has to be Anais Nin, she of the endless introspective diaries, of whom one feminist critic wrote numbingly: "The inter-
play of the powerful forces within Nin molded her into a woman of
inner and outer beauty who danced, laughed, sighed, wept, breathed as
she stilled the flowing, limited the infinite, personified the amorphous,
and decanted her images in structured feelings and translucent ara-
besques."

Ethereal stuff like this gives all women writers a bad name and
bores the daylights out of the luckless students who have to read it. It's
time feminists paid attention to a red-blooded American gal who is
languishing in *un*deserved obscurity: Kathleen Winsor.

She's the author of the fabulously popular *Forever Amber,* a novel
about a seventeenth-century English vixen who climbed up a ladder of
men until she reached the bed of Charles II. When it was published in
1944, Kathleen Winsor was only twenty-six, and so breathtakingly
beautiful that she could have played her own heroine in the movie that
was soon made. But women endowed with both beauty and brains are
a double-barreled threat, and she was made to pay.

Critics poked fun at her excellent writing and dismissed her meticulous historical research; decency societies demanded her head on a
platter, and gossip columnists distorted everything she said and did.
When she divorced her first husband and married band leader Artie

Shaw, who collected wives, she was accused of collecting men like Amber.

Her tormentors waited eagerly for her next book, but instead of another bodice-ripper, she wrote a contemporary novel called *Star Money* about a Navy wife named Shireen Delaney who writes a best-selling historical novel while her husband is serving in World War II.

Clearly autobiographical, *Star Money* is Kathleen Winsor's revenge on a sexist world. It came out in 1950 when I was fourteen; I read it then and I've been rereading it ever since. For sheer no-holds-barred, rock 'em, sock 'em feminism, it can't be beat.

The heroine, Shireen Delaney, is so honest that she frequently seems to be suffering from Tourette's syndrome. When a pregnant war wife sobs that if her husband is killed, she will at least have his child, Shireen blurts, ''I'd rather have another husband.'' Advised to see a psychiatrist to get over her dislike of children, she replies, ''I don't want to get over disliking children. Because if I got over it I might want to have some—and I don't want to.''

Basking in fame and fortune in New York, she goes through men like a hot knife through butter but she refuses to play the submissive role. Told that she could have ruled empires through the men who loved her, she replies, ''I'll do the ruling myself.'' When another man says she reminds him of a predator surrounded by the bones of her victims, she reflects, ''At least they were someone else's bones—not hers.'' Spurning feminine tact, she asks a man for her love letters back, explaining, ''They might be useful someday if I ever decide to write another book.''

On sexual equality: ''I've always thought that men were superior to women—except me.''

On pleasing men: ''Why should I change—for you or anyone else? Everyone else in my life comes and goes, but I stay here with me.''

On the battle of the sexes: ''Men and women haven't got much business together except when they're in bed.''

On constancy: ''I always burn my bridges before I come to them.''

On creativity: ''Most people haven't got enough imagination even to imagine that anyone else has.''

On careers: ''When the sense of having somehow expressed yourself is left out, sooner or later there's a realization of complete waste. Nothing will make up for it.''

On self-knowledge: ''More people would be like me if they could get away with it.''

On her personality: ''In her opinion, megalomania was an interesting and enviable symptom. Everyone should have it. If they ever expected to amount to anything in life.''

A brutal sensualist, Shireen nonetheless has a Spartan nobility that we admire, as when she loses patience with an hysterical Navy wife: ''Why doesn't she get a grip on herself? That's no way to send a man off to war.''

We also like her for her rigid honor in the literary cocktail party scene, when she overhears a pretentious guest: ''She was quoting the latest issue of *Vogue* and Shireen recognized the quote and was a little shocked that the woman did not give her source.'' By no stretch of the imagination could Shireen Delaney be called a lady, but at her best she's a gentleman.

Predictably, *Star Money* was panned by the critics—with one glorious exception. In his introduction to the French edition, André Maurois, member of the French Academy, wrote: ''This is a novel one cannot put down,'' and suggested somewhat ruefully that Kathleen Winsor was born in the wrong country; ''the author's remarkable gift, her art, the realistic portrayal of her characters, the straight-forward frankness of her observation—all were not recognized as readily as they should have been by a Flaubert or a de Maupassant. . . . But here is that one matchless quality: Truth.''

Women's studies departments—*please* read this book.

CARPE BOOPSONIC

like to visualize words as craftsmen's tools, all hung up in shining rows on a wall rack, ready for any task. If I were asked to name the perfect pleasurable experience, it would be sitting up all night with another logophiliac, talking about words—not about writing, but about words per se.

Unfortunately that's hard to arrange, but I came close when I served on the Usage Panel of the *American Heritage Dictionary*. The panelists never got together in a group, but the monthly ballots we received in the mail contained the seeds of many a good nocturnal discussion.

We had to check "Approve" or "Disapprove" beside the usage examples they gave us, and sometimes we had to write brief opinions on matters in dispute. One of these was about the use of foreign words and phrases in English. Should you or shouldn't you? What foreign words are acceptable? Not acceptable? Where do you draw the line?

I could go on for days about this, and probably would have if the AHD had given us more room on the ballot. I was tempted to give the nod to my all-time favorite, *Kinderfeindlichkeit,* an immensely satisfying compound noun meaning "an intense dislike and disregard for children." There simply is no substitute for it in American English, for obvious reasons: people don't have words they don't need, which is why this one makes me want to move to Germany.

I confined my ballot discussion to Matthew Arnold's lovely observation: "The word *curiosity* has lost, in English, that sense of delight in the free play of the intellect without ulterior motive which it possesses in French."

Yes, indeed. As I just got through saying, people don't have words they don't need. The American intellect, such as it is, never plays.

An author who uses too many foreign words for my taste is Mary McCarthy, and I'm not alone in my opinion. She once used so much Latin in a *New Yorker* essay that the normally rarefied editor lost his cool and sent it back with a curt note asking her to translate it.

In one of her novels, describing two very different women, she called their respective personalities *posse* and *esse.* This, I think, is going too far. The contrast between a "having" woman and a "being" woman is too interesting to obscure with Latin. McCarthy, like so many intellectuals, had a whopping case of *libido sciendi*—lust for knowledge—which the Middle Ages considered a crime punishable by burning at the stake.

I object strongly to the use of foreign phrases that can be translated directly into English with no trouble. Why say *"viva voce"* when you can say "aloud"; or *"sotto voce"* when you can use a vivid English idiom like "under his breath"? On the other hand, *"habitué"* saves us the trouble of explaining whether we mean "a steady customer" or "a regular visitor" or a "long-time resident."

Even more irritating, as well as dangerous, is trying to pun in a foreign language. I once reviewed a supposedly sexy women's novel containing the line: "She carped the diem by making love with Tom." *"Carpe diem,"* from a poem by Horace, means "seize the day," but I've often wondered what That Cosmopolitan Girl thought the lovers did.

Why the hell am I writing all this? Linguistic preciosities don't matter any more. The most important form of communication nowadays is the Customer Support fax.

C.S. Lewis coined the term "verbicide" to describe the murder of a word by those who latch onto it for a party banner, or to sell something. The Customer Support fax begins with the name of the company—always something like BOOPSONIC. The company is located—or "headquartered," as they put it—at a typical computer-age address: 139248729 Industrial Tech Highway Extended. Does that sound soul-shriveling or not? No wonder their user manuals make no sense.

> Gentlemen:
>
> I have some questions about my BOOPUPS fax surge protector. On page 2 of your user's manual you mention only one phone cord, the one you provide, but as I understand the diagram, *two* phone cords are required. One runs from the fax machine to the left-hand jack on the BOOPUPS. The other runs from the wall jack to the right-hand jack on the BOOPUPS, so that the BOOPUPS takes the place of the wall jack. Is this right?
>
> You're probably presuming the existence of another phone cord already in use on the fax, but a complete illustration showing a fax properly hooked up to the BOOPUPS would be helpful.
>
> Second, your manual says "See Specification section" for the battery number and type, but there is no Specification section.
>
> Third, it says, in red: "DO NOT use the BOOPUPS for pure inductive or capacitive loads!" What does this mean?

A badly written user's manual can cause literal accidents, but when it creates frustration and makes people feel stupid, it can also cause figurative accidents, harder to define but just as damaging.

Clumsy language, bad grammar, and misplaced punctuation are more important than techies think. Atlanta lawyers used to say that it was impossible to misinterpret a Will written by Eugene Mitchell, Margaret Mitchell's father. ''In drawing a Will,'' he always advised, ''just look after the grammar, and the law will look after itself.''

Techies, take note.

HOW I BECAME A SONGWRITER

Permissions. . . .

The word, a pesky plural in the publishing world, is all it takes to make a writer feel like Sisyphus pushing a rock up the hill, only to lose it at the summit and have to go back down and start all over.

Permissions are (is?) the last thing you have to take care of before your editor releases your manuscript to the printer. True, you can take care of it earlier, but it's such a mess that many writers tend to put it off till the last minute, or else we develop a mental block about it and actually forget to do it until the last minute. Even if you're an obsessive-compulsive like me and do everything early, something awful always happens and drags on until the last minute. The writer, already exhausted from having just finished a book, must deal with a spiraling crisis when he is least able to cope.

''Permissions'' is about quoting copyrighted material, which means locking horns with ASCAP, the Library of Congress, and literary widows. On my blacklist, the last shall always be the first.

Literary widows are in the last stage of handmaidenhood, known as ''keeper of the flame.'' Because they know nothing about writing except how to marry a writer, they hate women writers with a special passion.

My nemesis was the late Mme Vladimir Nabokov. I needed to quote one sentence by the great man in my novel, *When Sisterhood Was in Flower.* Had it been a non-fiction book I could have quoted him without permission, but novels are different. Using the form letter provided by my publisher, I wrote to Mme N., giving her the sentence I wished to quote.

Weeks passed. Finally she wrote back asking for a copy of the manuscript page on which the quote was to appear. I sent it to her. More weeks passed before she broke silence, this time demanding a copy of the entire chapter. I sent it to her and the waiting game recommenced. Meanwhile, the book was scheduled and the production department was going wild. A week before the printing deadline, Viking sent her a cable and she cabled back—collect—"Permission denied." Fortunately, I managed to find another quotation in the same vein by Sir Francis Bacon, whose wife was good and dead.

Never quote song lyrics unless you want someone from ASCAP to break down your door in the middle of the night. They're a rough bunch, which is why novelist Ann Beatty uses only the titles of songs when she wants to evoke her beloved Sixties: titles can't be copyrighted.

Music copyright rules apply just as strictly to non-fiction, but the lyrics I wanted to use in my memoir, *Confessions of a Failed Southern Lady,* were so old that I didn't think I needed permission.

The book is about my grandmother's efforts to make a lady of me. Among the weapons she used were the songs of her youth, all about fallen women. Granny turned twenty-one in 1900 so I figured her musical heroines were in the public domain in more ways than one. I wanted to quote the lyrics of "She's More to Be Pitied Than Censured," "The Picture That's Turned Toward the Wall," and "The Mansion of Aching Hearts" (that's a brothel), but my publisher cautioned me to write to the Library of Congress first. It seems that old songs can still be under copyright if someone records new arrangements (as Julie Andrews did with several Gay Nineties songs).

I dutifully wrote to the Library of Congress and they sent me a stack of copyright laws. One look at this impenetrable bureaucratic mess was all it took. Remembering Mme Nabokov, I dumped the whole business in the trash can.

Loath to go through another permissions wrangle, I decided to write my own Gay Nineties lyrics and let readers think they were real ones. Who would know the difference in this day and age? Who would care? Besides, they were so easy to write; all you needed was a bad girl and a snowstorm.

Most of Granny's songs were about farm girls from the middle west, probably because Theodore Dreiser's songwriter brother, Paul Dresser, wrote so many of them. You can't beat the banks of the Wabash for a good girl gone wrong, so I settled on my location and began:

Fallen and forgotten,
Without a good man's name,
She dreams of Indiana
As she walks the streets of shame.

After that I really got into it in a big way. Granny's favorite song was called "The Fatal Wedding," wherein the bride's former lover rushes up to the altar and stabs the couple and himself after the preacher says "Speak now or forever hold your peace." I didn't want to duplicate the plot too closely, so I combined it with "Just Tell Them That You Saw Me" by Paul Dresser and came up with my own fatal wedding:

Just then the church door opened,
The wedding guests turned round,
And seeing the intruder,
They dared not make a sound.
"Stop!" the ragged woman cried.
"My story must be told!
The bridegroom is the father
Of this dead child that I hold!"

I hope this sent ASCAP and the Library of Congress searching madly through their files to find the "real" songs. I hope they're still looking.

FIRST, WE KILL ALL THE FACT CHECKERS

Ask any randomly chosen group of writers for a list of their pet peeves and you will get remarkably similar replies. No matter how different we are in literary style and philosophy, we all tend to bear the same crosses in the everyday business of writing and publishing.

My own list of pet peeves begins with fact checkers. These are the people who write *source?* beside sentences like "Joan Fontaine starred in *Letter from an Unknown Woman* in 1948." Source? I remember it, damn it. I was twelve when it came out and I saw it. But that's not good enough; fact checkers are frequently sweet young things just out of college and the dew is still on the footnote. They won't believe you until you copy the proper page from *Popcorn Venus* and fax it to them. You emerge from these frays feeling that your word has been doubted and that you have been suspected of senility—which fact checkers always change to Alzheimer's.

Sometimes their political correctness is downright scary, especially when they don't even bother to consult with the writer and simply go ahead and change something. I recently wrote a piece for the *Los Angeles Times Magazine* in which I referred to Belle Watling, the madam in *Gone With the Wind*. When I got the galleys, my correct spelling had been changed to "Bell." I called and spoke to one of the editors, who rather nervously explained, "They said that was right."

Who was this sinister "they" and what was going on? How could anybody reference GWTW and come up with Bell for Belle? After giving it some thought I was pretty sure I knew what had happened. In *Roots* Kunte Kinte's wife is named Bell, and currently a black feminist scholar named Bell Hooks is making news. I suspect that some fact checker either made a fashionable but honest mistake—or worse, decided that Belle "ought" to be Bell in the name of spelling reparations.

I copied a page from GWTW on which Belle is mentioned several times and faxed it to L.A. The name appeared correctly in the published article but the whole needless episode was one of nervewracking alarm for me.

Even when there is no question of ulterior motives or political agendas, the average fact checker is maddeningly literal-minded. They don't catch jokes, particularly puns, so I end up *explaining* why something is funny. They also tend to ask for the surnames of people who don't use surnames ("Anastasia Who?"). Above all, they love to wreck historical anecdotes by inserting needless documentation: "Caroline of Brunswick (1768–1821) boasted that she changed her underdrawers once a year whether they were dirty or not."

Even good fact checkers drive writers to distraction. When James M. Cain was asked to write for the *New Yorker,* where the legendary Mrs. White thought nothing of attaching sixty or seventy flags to the average article, he replied, "On the whole, I'd rather be dead."

The time-honored literary conventions of artistic license and suspension of disbelief are anathema to fact checkers, probably because these conventions contain the seeds of their own unemployment. James M. Cain ran into this mindset when he wrote *Galatea,* a novel about the love affair between an enormously fat woman and a fight trainer who knows how to get weight off boxers.

When the trainer goes into the woman's bathroom he finds two sets of scales. Reflecting that the average bathroom scale goes up only to two hundred pounds, he concludes that she must weigh herself with a foot on each scale, which would put her weight at somewhere between three and four hundred pounds.

The reader accepts this because Cain deftly plays on the universal human fascination with the grotesque to make us suspend our disbelief—we want to believe it, and so we do. We know from the title that the trainer is going to slim the woman down and fall in love with her, so the fatter she is, the better the plot. We don't *care* about the details; as long as the author gives us a good story we will grant him the right of artistic license.

But fact checkers don't think this way. Cain found himself buried under a blizzard of challenges that could occur only to a mind locked in tunnel vision:

"Possible to get accurate weight using two scales at once?"

"Druggist supply-house catalog lists models up to 250 pounds."

"How does she see dial? Magnified? Pls. specify."

"Suggest change to hospital scale."

The best fact-checker story I ever heard concerns a woman who worked at *Harper's* twenty years ago. One very minor point in an article about Ralph Nader had eluded her, and she just couldn't stand it. Although they were already late going to press, she did everything short of holding the production staff at gunpoint while she ransacked the entire country to find out the color of Nader's briefcase.

The author had said it was black but a little voice in her steel-trap mind said brown. Unable to get hold of Nader himself, she called everybody who might know him well, including the FBI, until at last she found an alienated hippie who had been one of the original "Nader's Raiders."

Ralph's briefcase? Sure, he remembered. It was brown.

ASK ME NO QUESTIONS

nterviews have always bothered me regardless of which side of the notebook or microphone I have been on.

When I worked for the *News & Observer* in the Sixties, as the only opera fan on the woman's page I got to interview Risë Stevens and Dorothy Kirsten. It was a thrill to meet them but an agony to interview them because I don't like to question people. I just don't. I think it's rude. The journalist's rationale, "I'm just doing my job," was no comfort. Asking one question after another made me feel like a nosy neighbor or a pesky child and I found it embarrassing.

I thought being the interviewee would be different, and at first it was. I put myself on automatic pilot and sailed along, but after a couple of book tours I got irritated and stripped the gears.

I stopped touring but continued granting interviews at home, thinking maybe it would be different, but it wasn't. In fact, it was worse. An intimate setting inspires more, not fewer, questions; interviewers can ask to see family pictures and old report cards, opening up several new avenues of inquiry, and once you produce them, they want to borrow them.

The home interview also brings out the amateur shrink in many interviewers. What does the arrangement of the furniture signify? What does it symbolize? Did she place the sofa there because she subconsciously wants to shut people out?

Listen, it doesn't mean a damn thing. Employed people have a hard time understanding that an office-in-the-home quickly degenerates into a home-in-the-office; writers never put things in suitable places because we can't. It's that simple, and it has nothing to do with whether my father loved me enough.

The "in-depth" question I've been asked over and over, the one that seemed to fascinate everybody, is why I lived in Seattle for ten years. The spin that interviewers have tried to put on this makes me sound like Gauguin running off to Tahiti. Moreover, because it was exactly ten years—1972 to 1982—they assume it indicates some sort of compulsion, a ritual of measured flight within a contained psychic framework, etc. etc.

The truth, believed by no one, says more about the writer's psychic framework than anything my inquisitors dreamed up. In 1949 when I was thirteen I read *Annie Jordan* by Mary Brinker Post, a novel set in Seattle at the turn of the century. I loved that book, so at the age of thirty-six I decided, on the spur of the moment, to move to Seattle—just like that.

That I stayed ten years has an even simpler explanation. A Southerner who discovers what it's like to sleep under a blanket in July tends to linger a while. (Now I wish I had never left.)

When I drew the line on home interviews my publisher persuaded me to grant telephone interviews, and I foolishly consented. Most Americans feel more relaxed and comfortable on the phone than anywhere else, but I, who don't, nearly went mad.

If questions are synonymous with rudeness, telephones are synonymous with dishonesty. Whenever I use one I can hear my grandmother saying, "Look people straight in the eye when you talk to them." Unlike my in-person interviews, of which a few were quite good, all of my telephone interviews have been terrible. I am just not myself on the phone, not even with people I've known for years, so I drew the final line. Now I am out of the interview-granting business entirely.

In my experience, the biggest mistake interviewers make is conducting the interview as a conversation. Equipped now with high-tech electronics instead of the old pen and pad, they end up with far too many notes. Unable to pull them together, they go the cafeteria route and pick out the tastiest morsels to use in their copy, making for non sequiturs, bad transitions, and being quoted "out of context" (except that there is no context).

I still haven't drawn the line at "commenting." This is the print version of a soundbite and every bit as dangerous. A writer doing a piece about the Dorothy Parker centennial for *Vanity Fair* recently asked me how I felt about being compared to Parker by so many reviewers.

Here is what I said: "I'm tired of being called 'the second Dorothy Parker.' I'd rather be the first Florence King. I've decided there's only one way to stop it. Parker left all her money to Martin Luther King, so if I leave mine to David Duke, the comparisons are sure to end."

Here is what will probably end up in *Vanity Fair:* "I'm going to leave my money to David Duke."

Group interviews at college symposia are the safest in that there are plenty of witnesses, but troubled young people can ask rocky questions, and I have a tendency to blurt truthful but strange answers.

"If you could be someone else," asked an intense coed, "who would you want to be, and why?"

"Jack the Ripper, so I could find out who I was."

I simply meant that I am a true-crime buff who would go to any lengths to solve the true-crime buff's favorite mystery. But afterwards, as the panel was breaking up, a feminist reporter from the student newspaper rushed up and asked if she could interview me about repressed rage, cross-dressing, and female misogyny.

UNCOLLECTED
ARTICLES

✝

1992 – 1993

PRIVATELY EYEING
G W T W

A longer version of this essay appeared originally in The Oxford American, *a literary quarterly published in Oxford, Mississippi. After it came out, I wrote a short version of it (nine hundred words) for my* Raleigh News & Observer *column. On rereading both to decide which to include here, I decided that I didn't like either one, so I wrote the following medium-sized version especially for this volume.*

I could make life a lot easier on myself, but old maids are picky.

*G*one With the Wind and I both came out in 1936, so perhaps that explains my affinity for it.

Scarlett would understand. *"Atlanta had always interested her more than any other town because when she was a child Gerald had told her that she and Atlanta were exactly the same age."* She later discovered that Gerald had stretched the truth; the city was founded as Terminus and later renamed Marthasville, but in 1845, the year of her birth, it was christened Atlanta.

I'm often asked how many times I've read the book. I don't know. I was eight the first time, and I've been rereading it ever since. Not once a year, from cover to cover, as some people read the Bible; but here and there, this part and that, wherever it happens to fall open. I'm now fifty-eight, so you figure it out.

On the fiftieth anniversary of its publication, I compiled for *The Washington Post Book World* a page of quizzes and puzzles (Ashley's real first name, Rhett's middle initial, etc.) off the top of my head, without having to check the text. And when I needed to find the passages I quote in this essay, I knew exactly where they were and turned right to them.

Whenever I've shopped for a new typewriter or computer, I always test it with the opening paragraph. As soon as the salespeople see *"Scarlett O'Hara was not beautiful . . ."* they start looking over my shoulder and remain transfixed until I get to the end. I never consciously memorized it, nor any of the other passages I know by heart; they simply engraved themselves on my mind over countless rereadings.

People always assume that I identify with Scarlett but I never have. How could I? *"Large numbers of books always depressed her, as did people who liked to read large numbers of books."* As a child I had a tomboyish crush on the Tarleton twins, and today I empathize with the spinsterish rigidity of India Wilkes, but I've never really identified with any of the characters. Why, then, do I love this book?

If you like playing literary detective as much as I do, GWTW is a feast.

A novelist never invents a character who serves no dramatic purpose, but Margaret Mitchell did. If you look closely, you will find a loose thread that she neglected to snip off.

In chapter forty-three, Scarlett asks Rhett why he goes to New Orleans so often, saying that Atlanta gossips believe he has a sweetheart there. He replies: *"It isn't a sweetheart that takes me to New Orleans. It's a child, a little boy . . . he is my legal ward and I am responsible for him. He's in school in New Orleans. I go there frequently to see him."*

In chapter forty-five, when Melanie and Belle Watling converse in Belle's carriage, Belle compliments Melanie's son and says: *"I got a boy myself. . . . He ain't here in Atlanta. He ain't never been here. He's off at school."*

Obviously, Belle had a son by Rhett. No further mention is made of him, but an illegitimate child is such a standard plot complication that we can be fairly certain Mitchell originally planned to make use of this boy and later changed her mind, probably for reasons of length, but forgot to delete the references to him.

Equally intriguing is her fixation on hair color. The book is oversupplied with brunettes; Scarlett, Ellen O'Hara, Rhett, and Bonnie all have black hair, but Mitchell went even further and flouted the historical novelist's convention of making the sweet girl a blonde.

In the barbecue scene Melanie's hair is called simply "a dark mass," but we get a specific description in chapter nine: *"Melanie rustled in from her room, a worried frown puckering her forehead, a brush in her hands, her usually tidy black hair, freed of its net, fluffing about her face in a mass of tiny curls and waves."*

All of the admirable characters who do not have black hair are redheads. The red-haired Tarleton twins are introduced on page one, and soon thereafter we meet their mother, *"so white of skin that her flam-*

ing hair seemed to have drawn all the color from her face into its vital burnished mass . . . she had borne eight children, as red of hair and full of life as she.''

We begin to scent obsession when Mitchell describes the Tarleton girls in their carriage on the way to the barbecue: *''All shades of red hair were represented beneath these hats, Hetty's plain red hair, Camilla's strawberry blonde, Randa's coppery auburn and small Betsy's carrot top.''*

Finally, Belle Watling is a dyed redhead, as Mammy reminds us the first time she sees her: *''Ah ain' never seed ha'r dat color in mah life. Not even in de Tarleton fambly.''*

Mitchell herself had black hair, so vanity may have gotten the best of her when she colored in her main characters, but why so much red hair for the minor ones?

Her first husband, Berrian Kinnard Upshaw of Raleigh, was nicknamed "Red." She divorced him but apparently never forgot him because the tonal similarity between "Red Upshaw" and "Rhett Butler" is striking.

Even more striking is Rhett's middle initial. When Belle Watling gives Melanie a contribution for the hospital, the gold coins are wrapped in a man's handkerchief that Scarlett immediately recognizes. *''There was a monogram in the corner in which were the initials R.K.B. In her top drawer was a handkerchief just like this, one that Rhett Butler had lent her only yesterday to wrap about the stems of wild flowers they had picked.''*

The same scene in the movie used just two initials, "R.B." We never find out what Rhett's middle name is, but the "K," mentioned only once, is clearly a tribute to the red-haired man in Mitchell's life.

Her second husband, John Marsh, was a blond, and since he was also her proofreader he must have been the first to discover that there is something wrong with every blond in the book. Either they are weak and doomed like Ashley; or unattractive and unpopular like his sisters, the "washed-out Wilkes girls"; or else they are social inferiors like Emmie Slattery, "the dirty tow-headed slut," and Will Benteen, who had *"the sallow malarial face of the south Georgia Cracker, pale pinkish hair and washed-out blue eyes. . . ."*

Scarlett's youngest sister, the fragile, wishy-washy Carreen, is not even described until chapter thirty, as if Mitchell either forgot to describe her earlier, or was putting it off as long as possible. When we finally get a good look at her, we learn that she, too, has the mark of Cain: *"The day came when his pale blue eyes, perfectly cognizant of his surroundings, fell upon Carreen sitting beside him, telling her rosary beads, the morning sun shining through her fair hair."*

Mitchell's aversion to blonds extends gratuitously and sometimes comically to very minor characters. Seeing the Atlanta belle Maybelle Merriwether in an apple-green dress at the bazaar, Scarlett thinks: *"That green is just my color and it would make my eyes look—Why will blondes try to wear that color? Her skin looks as green as an old cheese."*

The most tragic figure in the book is Cathleen Calvert, daughter of a Clayton County planter, who is introduced in the barbecue scene as a "dashing blonde." Cathleen's dramatic purpose in this early scene is to tell Scarlett the gossip about Rhett's Charleston scandal. That done, she vanishes from the book until chapter twenty-nine, when she turns up at war-ravaged Tara to tell Scarlett and Melanie that she is going to marry her family's Yankee overseer. Her appearance raises questions about blondes having more fun:

"Her sidesaddle was strapped on as sorry a mule as Scarlett had ever seen, a flop-eared lame brute, and Cathleen was almost as sorry looking as the animal she rode. Her dress was of faded gingham of the type once worn only by house servants, and her sunbonnet was secured under her chin by a piece of twine."

Scarlett and Melanie can't believe the dashing Cathleen has sunk so low, but worse is still to come. From this point on, Mitchell uses Cathleen as the symbol of people who lack "gumption," who can't come back after defeat. Cathleen Calvert, even more than Ashley, is a human testament to Mitchell's Social Darwinism.

When we see Cathleen for the last time at Gerald's funeral, her degeneration is complete and the mystery of Mitchell's hair-color prejudice is solved:

"Scarlett saw with amazement that her percale dress had grease spots on it and her hands were freckled and unclean. There were even black crescents under her fingernails. There was nothing of quality folks about Cathleen now. She looked Cracker, even worse. She looked poor white, shiftless, slovenly, trifling."

It's a class thing, and Margaret Mitchell understood it. Blond hair reminded her of Appalachia, the "South's South." Katherine Anne Porter made the same point in *Old Mortality:* "First, a beauty must be tall; whatever color the eyes, the hair must be dark, the darker the better. . . ."

So much for the glories of the "Anglo-Saxon South."

Shortly after the 1993 Inauguration the <u>Los Angeles Times Magazine</u> asked me to do an opinion piece on Bill Clinton. This is not as strange as it sounds. Liberal publications offer me assignments from time to time to prove how balanced they are.

My original title was "A Wonk. A Dither. A She." It was supposed to be a parody of Maya Angelou's Inaugural poem, "A Rock. A River. A Tree," but it fell flat. The editors had either forgotten the poem or else had a mental block against it (both being entirely possible).

They chose to call it "Jus' What Kind of Good Ole Boy is President Billy?" That doesn't do a thing for me, so I have given it another title here.

The piece caused an uproar, generating sixty letters to the editor— three faves and fifty-seven epileptic fits. One of the latter accused me of dissing the President and stereotyping Southerners by giving my article a title like "Jus' What Kind of Good Ole Boy is President Billy?"

BILL CLINTON: MASOBEAR

Southerners are the only Anglo-Saxon Protestants who have to worry about "the ones who give us a bad name."

In the old days, our worries centered around three-hundred-pound sheriffs named Vonnie or Beverly who split heads and infinitives. Later, we were saddled with Jimmy Carter, the "nukier" scientist with lust in his heart who made luncheon speeches about diarrhea.

Now, Bill Clinton, the divine afflatus of co-dependency, is President of the United States 'R' Us, but to my vast relief he doesn't seem very Southern. In fact, I can detect only two regional characteristics. The first is his fondness for food.

As he eats his way into William Howard Taft's custom-made bathtub, visions of him dropping dead in the prime of nice will send alarmed pundits scurrying for Freudian theories and Rabelaisian parallels to explain his appetite. The truth is very simple. To a Southern Baptist, eating is the only sensual pleasure that is not a sin. Gluttony may be one of the Seven Deadly Sins, but that's Catholic. Baptists have replaced the high-church groaning bed with the low-church groaning board and every good ole boy knows the path to righteousness.

The South's other oral tradition is talking. As Clinton continues to lose his voice, going hoarser and hoarser at closer and closer intervals until it's completely and permanently gone and we really *need* the manic sign-language lady that Democrats always include on the dais, remember that Southern men routinely talk the hind legs off a mule. They always have an encyclopedic knowledge of something or other—guns, cars, Civil War cavalry strategy—and hold forth on it until there isn't an unglazed eye in the house. They are compulsive talkers because they have spent three hundred years explaining the South to the rest of the country. Slavery, states' rights, segregation, poll taxes, literacy tests, integration, busing, redistricting; and finally, after losing all of these, backpedaling former firebrands have had to explain what it means to "mellow." History has made Southern men America's original policy wonks.

Other than what he does with his mouth, our New Age tribune is a Southern anomaly. For one thing, he believes in "getting in touch with your feelings"—middle-aged spreadese for the hippie credo of "let it all hang out" that shaped his youth. But Bubba don't hug men; he greets his friends by punching them in the heart. To Clinton's oft-repeated campaign priority, "I think it's important to touch as many of the American people as we can," Bubba replies, "Sheesh."

There is something oddly rootless about the whole Clinton family; their *from* is on a par with Oakland's *there*. Mama Virginia Kelley *ought* to look like Belle Watling, *could* look like Belle Watling, and on good days *almost* looks like Belle Watling, but in the final analysis she looks like Everymadam.

Brother Roger is a dead cert to make Billy Carter look like Lord Byron, but Roger's final disgrace, whatever it is, will happen in a nightclub, not a gas station: he is a creature of rooms without clocks.

The heart of a true Southern ne'er-do-well beats under the bib of his overalls, but Roger's beats under a cover charge.

Hillary, of course, is from Chicago, which may explain what really drives her—not Yuppie careerism, but the knowledge that she's a Yankee wife. Knowing that people are saying "why couldn't he have married one of our girls?" has been known to do terrible things to Northern women.

Time's Margaret Carlson effused that when the Billary were in law school together, Clinton "couldn't keep his mind—or his eyes—from wandering over to the smart girl in the flannel shirt and thick glasses." He is reported to have told his mother, "I won't marry a beauty queen," which is another way of saying, "I won't marry a Southern girl." Why?

Maybe, thinking ahead to his presidential bid, he wanted to balance his domestic ticket with a wife from another part of the country (Cook County has a lot of votes). Or maybe he wanted to be the adorable half of the marriage and knew a Southern girl would be too much competition. Or maybe he felt he could not spare the time and energy it takes to be married to a human candy store. The Southern wife strives to be a hot Melanie; so good in bed that she seems insatiable, yet at the same time, sweet and submissive and eager to be dominated. Elsewhere, women who are good in bed are not sweet and submissive, and women who are sweet and submissive are not good in bed, but in the South they are. This can get eerie. One way to avoid the rigors of Southern matrimony is to marry a Yankee, particularly one in flannel shirts and thick glasses.

Certain things about Clinton are not only un-Southern but *non*-Southern. Incredibly, he does not even know what his name is. He may have found his inner child but neither he nor his mother can say for sure whether it was christened William Jefferson Blythe III or William Jefferson Blythe IV. Mama was quoted as saying she *thinks* Bill was the IV, though she *might* have made a mistake. In other words, she isn't sure if his father was William Jr. or William III.

This is anthropologically impossible. Southerners are so devoted to genealogy that we see a family tree under every bush. Historical societies, quiet enough places in other parts of the country, do a land-office business in Dixie, where dusty-fingered women looking for still more ancestors stand in line to read rare pamphlets with titles like "The

Pathetick Historie of Sir Guillaume de Fornays, Who Was Hangèd, Drawèd, ynd Quarterèd, With a Commentarie on his Colonial Descendants in the Carolinas, by Bishop Fornay of Pluckley.''

Our little old ladies get locked in the courthouse overnight because it's hard to see matchstick widows crouched in the stacks behind huge black-bound public records. They research things like the maiden name of the wife of Thomas Jefferson's overseer's grandfather's cousin—and they find it, too, because they have been practicing shintoism for so long that they are expert self-taught archivists. Even our baton-twirling airheads can manage history class because they know how to read genealogical charts and keep all the kings and queens straight.

The typical Southerner has no trouble rattling off the name, rank, and serial number of antecedents all the way back to the seventeenth century. That the Clintons forgot a numeral in the preceding generation is strange enough, but what really astonishes is whose numeral it was.

Tennessee Williams did not exaggerate. The South is Big Daddy country. Ole Colonel Portnoy, who seduces with bourbon instead of chicken soup, is the reason why so many Southern men well into middle age still talk in whining voices about "what my Daddy said." Daughters are equally susceptible to our drawling Agamemnons. Margaret Mitchell could not keep her fingers off those magic keys, f-a-t-h-e-r, giving us not one but two Electra-fying father-daughter relationships: Gerald and Scarlett O'Hara and Rhett and Bonnie Butler.

Southern boys grow up hearing "if you're half the man your Daddy is you'll be all right," but it's a dubious compliment. The halving imagery can be deleterious even under the best conditions, but Bill Clinton was not born under the best conditions. He was a posthumous son, saddled with the knowledge that his father vanished from the face of the earth before his own existence began: he *wasn't* before I *was*. It's the difference between desertion and bereftness, and growing up in Big Daddy country can only make it worse.

Name changes are not undertaken casually in the South. Fifteen-year-old Billy Blythe's decision to become Bill Clinton would have been regarded as a betrayal of his dead father, but he did it anyway. According to the White House version of the story, this noble adolescent made a conscious decision to surrender his patronym to placate stepfather Roger Clinton and bring unity to a troubled household.

A drunken stepfather makes a convenient villain, but the name-change petition Billy Blythe filed in 1962 tells a different story: "[He] assumed the name of William Jefferson Clinton and has used the name for almost 12 years and his school records and his friends all know him by the surname Clinton."

What no one seems to remember is that Roger Clinton was a Southerner, too. No matter how irascible he was, he would have said, "You keep your Daddy's name, Bill. He was a fine man. If you're half the man your Daddy was you'll be all right." He would have said it drunk or sober, whether he meant it or not, because these are the words that roll unbidden off Southern tongues when we speak of fathers.

But Billy Jeff, who has the inner resources of a cruise ship social director, could not cope with the anxiety of being half of a ghost. Letting others define him, he oozed gradually into his Clinton identity and then made official what was already a fait accompli.

But his anxiety remained because the subject of name changes simply would not go away. When Hillary refused to give up *her* father's name, the words "you're half the man your wife is" must surely have crossed his mind. Next, when Arkansans objected to her feminist habit of calling herself Rodham, she gave in and changed it to Clinton— *exactly what Bill did in high school*—forcing him to relive the whole traumatic experience and turning him into a man who could not stop thinking about tomorrow's name change.

Now she's calling herself Hillary Rodham Clinton, which puts him one misprint away from an identity crisis. Sooner or later, she's going to acquire a hyphen. Once she becomes Hillary Rodham-Clinton, Bill will be in nomenclatural bedlam with Harry Thomason and Linda Bloodworth-Thomason. You can't call them Mr. and Mrs. Bloodworth-Thomason because he's not a Bloodworth and she's more than a Thomason. Nor can you call them Mr. and Mrs. Thomason because there is no Mrs. Thomason. If Hillary takes on a hyphen, there will no Mrs. Clinton, and if there is no Mrs. Clinton. . . .

If the U.S. Constitution is all sail and no anchor, Bill Clinton is all therapy and no insight. His lumbering, endomorphic exterior makes him seem like an easygoing good ole boy with his chair tilted back against the gas station wall, but when his mask slips he displays the querulousness of a neurasthenic on the sun porch of a Swiss sanitarium.

His grandiloquent vow to "force the spring" is designed to suggest the idealism of Woodrow Wilson at Versailles, but his demeanor and behavior suggest the hysteria of Sally Field at the Academy Awards, blinking back tears and gasping, "You like me, you really *like* me."

As long as Clinton is campaigning he can reassure himself that people like him, but when the campaign stops, so does the reassurance. Ensconced at last in the White House, but painfully aware that fifty-seven percent of the electorate had voted for somebody else, he needed another kissy-fix right away. Did we like him, really *like* him? He had to find out somehow, and so he set out to test our love.

It took Jimmy Carter a couple of years to make people wonder if he had a screw loose, but Clinton took only a week. His headlong plunge into the issue of gays in the military was described in the media as "puzzling," "baffling," "reckless," "obsessive," and "self-destructive." Next, he tackled the deficit issue by floating the idea of cuts in Social Security, which Sen. Daniel Patrick Moynihan called a "death wish." Then he risked a national panic by attempting to lift the ban on immigrants infected with the AIDS virus, which the Senate defeated. And now he is threatening, via his supine relationship with Sin Tax Hillary, to force forty-five million smokers into nicotine-withdrawal fits to see if they love him enough not to storm the White House and stick his head on a pike.

Natalie Shainess analyzes this kind of behavior in her 1984 study of masochism, *Sweet Suffering:* "Few human beings find ambiguity comfortable, but for the masochistic person it is nearly unbearable. She would rather transfer her inner discomfort into a sure loss than to remain in a limbo of uncertainty. She experiences a release upon ending the suspense."

Bill Clinton is not Panderbear, he's Masobear. If you want to read a devastatingly accurate fictional portrayal of his psychological type, look up the old British suspense novel, *Before the Fact* by Francis Iles, on which Alfred Hitchcock based his movie *Suspicion.*

The movie, as you recall, ends happily when Cary Grant saves Joan Fontaine's life, thereby proving that he wasn't trying to murder her as she had suspected. But in the book, the husband really does intend to murder the wife, and she knows it. The strain of wondering when and how he will do it becomes too much for her, so she lets him kill her to relieve the tension.

This sounds like Masobear's now-famous ROTC letter to Col. Eugene J. Holmes thanking him for his help in evading the draft. He didn't have to write it; he had gotten what he wanted out of Holmes, and he must have known that muzzy soul-searching would not sit well with a soldier. But he was compelled to write it to make sure that Holmes still liked him, really *liked* him.

But Holmes hated him, really *hated* him—that's why he released the letter.

It's going to be an interesting four years. Our hoarse saxophone player's insubstantial personality and almost palpable insecurity recall what the wag said about Frédéric Chopin: "The only constant thing about him was his cough."

Los Angeles Times Magazine, April 4, 1993

EVE FATIGUE

The Marine Corps's bachelor party was over almost as soon as it began. First came the news that Commandant Carl E. Mundy, Jr. had issued a directive barring married recruits. Then, the very next day, Defense Secretary Les Aspin reversed it, whereupon the chastised Mundy apologized with the usual sports analogy—he had "kicked one into the grandstand."

At first it sounded like just another Clinton administration foul-up, but then we learned that Mundy had acted behind the administration's back—"blindsided" them, as he put it. Aspin actually was surprised. As for President Clinton, he was "astonished." As much as this administration lies, these reactions somehow have the ring of truth.

Pat Schroeder, as always, was "outraged," and came up with her best non sequitur yet: "Even the Pope allows his Swiss Guards to be married." She twittered on in her usual Betty Boop way, calling the Marines "the least family-friendly" of the services and recommending still more supportive programs for military families, but then even she said something that rang true. She wondered aloud whether Mundy had "taken leave of his senses."

Think about that. A man with obedience in his blood simply doesn't do such things. He must have known it would cause a furor but he did it anyway. Why?

I think he's suffering from what I call Eve Fatigue, a mental aberration that afflicts people who have had all they can stand of America's out-of-control gynocracy.

Unlike mere anti-feminism, which is a sane stance amenable to logical debate, Eve Fatigue is touched with madness. Its victims are suddenly overcome by an instinctive revulsion against our present unnatural state of female dominance. They feel compelled to strike a blow against it, even if means destroying themselves in the bargain.

A probable case of Eve Fatigue occurred two years ago in Northern Virginia when an orthopedic surgeon, Dr. Geraldine Richter, was charged with drunk driving and assaulting an officer. Dr. Richter pleaded PMS—premenstrual syndrome—and Judge Robert J. Smith accepted it and let her off.

Dr. Richter walked out of court a free, if bloated, woman and returned to her medical practice, seemingly unconcerned that her patients might henceforth be leery of receiving her ministrations at the wrong time of the month. Indeed, if such a thought had ever crossed her mind she never would have pleaded PMS in the first place. Taking a guilty rap and being known as a doctor who got drunk *once* would have been far less damaging than painting herself as a helpless victim of a recurrent affliction rooted in nature.

Why did Dr. Richter risk her professional reputation? And why did Judge Smith help her do it? Because juris without prudence works in mysterious ways, its subconscious wonders to perform. What better way to shaft feminism than to restore ''lady's complaint'' to its former glory?

That's Eve Fatigue for you. People do wild, crazy, suicidal things when they're all shrewed out. General Mundy probably saw one nurturing gunnery sergeant too many—and cracked. Then, his mind swirling with visions of a barracks filled with long rows of chaste Spartan cots, he issued his fatal directive.

USA Today, August 17, 1993

THE EDGE OF THE BED

The belief that liberals are funnier, smarter, and sexier than conservatives will not die, but it's wrong on all three counts.

Funny? Let's just say that a computerized search of people described in the media as "enraged" would result in an enormous printout of liberal names.

Smart? Liberals think they alone can appreciate irony because it's tied up with literary criticism, quirked eyebrows, and that one-sided media smirk called a "twisted smile." In truth, political correctness has given them an irony deficiency. They went berserk when the new talking Barbie Doll dared to say, "Math class is tough," yet they missed a delicious admission in *The Autobiography of Malcolm X:* "I'm sorry to say that the subject I most disliked was mathematics. I think the reason was that mathematics leaves no room for argument. If you made a mistake, that was all there was to it."

Diffidence is the liberal's anemia. Steeped in white wine, brie, and chamber music, they like to think of themselves as "civilized," offering as proof their tolerance for single motherhood, yet they never carry the argument back far enough to see that manless females and their offspring replicate animal life.

Sex? Don't even think about it. The liberal male has bad nerves because his politics keep him in a perpetual state of guilt and his passivity keeps him in a perpetual state of sexual anxiety. Consequently, his fear of nervous breakdown is very real and always on his mind—which is to say, his mind is always on his mind.

As the pressure mounts, he feels compelled to collect his thoughts on the perils of thinking. A classic of this genre is "A Crisis in my Mental History" by the nineteenth-century feminist, John Stuart Mill.

"Analysis," Mill declared, "is a perpetual worm at the root both of the passions and of the virtues; and above all, fearfully undermines all desires and all pleasures." He vowed to quit thinking, or as he put it: "The cultivation of the feelings became one of the cardinal points in my ethical and philosophical creed."

He turned to music, but instead of letting it wash over him, he analyzed it. Reflecting that the octave consists only of five tones and two semitones which can be put together in only a limited number of ways, he went into a snit: "It seemed to me that most of these tones must have been already discovered and there could not be room for a long succession of Mozarts and Webers. . . . I was seriously tormented by the thought of the exhaustibility of musical combinations.''

In desperation, he renewed his vow to quit thinking and sought the peace and simplicity of nature, but then it happened again. Lured into an argument by a friend who hated Wordsworth's rustic poems, Mill agreed "to have the fight out at our Debating Society, where we accordingly discussed for two evenings the comparative merits of Byron and Wordsworth, propounding and illustrating by long recitations our respective theories of poetry.''

Al Gore displays the same mind-body conflict in *Earth in the Balance.* Finding the "neocortex" of the brain too over-evolved for his tastes, he asks, with a Mill-like rhetorical wail: "How can we concentrate purely on abstract thinking when the rest of our brain floods our awareness with feelings, emotions and instincts?''

Give me a "simplistic" conservative every time. Liberal lovers sit on the edge of the bed with their heads in their hands, moaning, "I shouldn't come here on the days that I see my analyst.'' The only thing they deliver is sweet savage supportiveness.

USA Today, October 20, 1993

A WASP LOOKS AT LIZZIE BORDEN: A CENTENNIAL APPRECIATION

f you want to understand Anglo-Saxon Americans, study the Lizzie Borden case. No ethnologist could ask for a better control group; except for Bridget Sullivan, the Bordens' maid, the zany tragedy of August 4, 1892 had an all-Wasp cast.

Lizzie was born in Fall River, Massachusetts on July 19, 1860, and immediately given the Wasp family's favorite substitute for open affection: a nickname. Thirty-two years later at her inquest she stated her full legal name: Lizzie Andrew Borden. "You were so christened?'' asked the district attorney. "I was so christened,'' she replied.

Lizzie's mother died in 1862. Left with two daughters to raise, her father, Andrew Borden, soon married a chubby spinster of thirty-eight named Abby Durfee Gray. Three-year-old Lizzie obediently called the new wife Mother but twelve-year-old Emma called her Abby.

Andrew Borden was a prosperous but miserly undertaker whose sole interest in life was money. His operations expanded to include banking, cotton mills, and real estate, but no matter how rich he became he never stopped peddling eggs from his farms to his downtown business associates; wicker basket in hand, he would set out for corporate board meetings in anticipation of yet a few more pennies.

Although he was worth $500,000 in pre-IRS, gold-standard dollars, he was so tightfisted that he refused to install running water in his home. There was a latrine in the cellar and a pump in the kitchen; the bedrooms were fitted out with water pitchers, wash bowls, chamber pots, and slop pails.

Marriage with this paragon of Yankee thrift evidently drove Abby to seek compensatory emotional satisfaction in eating. Only five feet tall, she ballooned up to more than two hundred pounds and seldom left the house except to visit her half-sister, Mrs. Whitehead, who lived nearby.

Emma Borden, Lizzie's older sister, was forty-two at the time of the murders. Mouselike in all respects, she was one of those spinsters who scurries. Other than doing the marketing, she rarely went anywhere except around the corner to visit her friend, another spinster named Alice Russell.

Compared to the rest of her family, Lizzie comes through as a prom queen. Never known to go out with men, at least she went out. Most of her sorties were missions of mercy. A member of Central Congregational, she taught Sunday school, served as secretary-treasurer of the Christian Endeavor Society, belonged to the Ladies Fruit and Flower Mission, and was a card-carrying member of the Women's Christian Temperance Union.

What did she look like? Like everyone else in that inbred Wasp town. *New York Sun* reporter Julian Ralph wrote during the trial:

> By the way, the strangers who are here begin to notice that Lizzie Borden's face is of a type quite common in New Bedford. They meet Lizzie Borden every day and everywhere about town. Some are fairer,

some are younger, some are coarser, but all have the same general cast of features—heavy in the lower face, high in the cheekbones, wide at the eyes, and with heavy lips and a deep line on each side of the mouth.

Plump by our standards, she had what her self-confident era called a good figure. She also had blue eyes, and like all blue-eyed women, she had a lot of blue dresses—handy for changing clothes without appearing to have done so. The case is a vortex of dark blue dresses, light blue dresses, dark blue dresses with light blue dots, light blue dresses with dark blue dots, blue summer dresses, blue winter dresses, clean blue dresses, paint-stained blue dresses, blood-stained blue dresses, and an all-male jury struggling to tell one from the other.

Five years before the murders, the Bordens had what passes in Waspland for a family fight. Abby persuaded Andrew to put one of his rental houses in her name. Lizzie and Emma were furious, so they said politely, "What you do for her, you must do for us." That's a Wasp conniption fit and Andrew knew it, so he took refuge in fair play and gave his daughters houses of exactly the same value ($1,500) as the one he had given his wife.

What could be fairer? Now they were all even-steven and everything was settled—except it wasn't. Having failed to clear the air, everyone started smoldering and brooding. Emma and Lizzie stopped eating with the elder Bordens, requiring the maid to set and serve each meal twice. They never reached that pinnacle of Wasp rage called Not Speaking—"We always *spoke*," Emma emphasized at the trial—but she and Lizzie eliminated "Abby" and "Mother" from their respective vocabularies and started calling their stepmother "Mrs. Borden." What a cathartic release that must have been.

Lizzie ticked away for four years until 1891, when she committed a family robbery. Entering the master bedroom through a door in her own room (it was a "shotgun" house with no hallways), she stole her stepmother's jewelry, her father's loose cash, and a book of horsecar tickets.

Andrew and Abby knew that Lizzie was the culprit, and Lizzie knew that they knew, but rather than "have words," Andrew called in the police and let them go through an investigation to catch the person the whole family carefully referred to as "the unknown thief."

The robbery launched a field day of Silent Gestures. Everybody quietly bought lots of locks. There were locks everywhere, three on the front door alone and at least one on every bedroom door. To supplement the key locks there were bolts, hooks, chains, and padlocks.

Abby's Silent Gesture consisted of locking and bolting her side of the door that led into Lizzie's room. Lizzie responded with her Silent Gesture, putting a hook on her side of the door and shoving a huge claw-footed secretary in front of it.

The best Silent Gesture was Andrew's. He put the strongest available lock on the master bedroom, but kept the key on the sitting-room mantelpiece in full view of everyone, where Lizzie could get at it if she decided to rob the master bedroom again. Lizzie knew she was being tempted, and she also knew that if the key disappeared, she would be the prime suspect. In one fell swoop, Andrew made it clear that he was simultaneously trusting her and distrusting her, and warning her without saying a word. Wasps call this war of nerves the honor system.

Since Emma Borden *was* a Silent Gesture, there was no need for her to do anything except keep on scurrying, so she did.

The Borden house must have been a peaceful place. There is nothing on record to show that the family ever raised their voices to each other. "Never a word," Bridget Sullivan testified at the trial, with obvious sincerity and not a little awe.

Bridget, twenty-six and pretty in a big-boned, countrified way, had been in the Bordens' service for almost three years at the time of the murders. A recent immigrant, she had such a thick brogue that she referred to the Silent Gesture on the mantelpiece as the "kay."

Bridget adored Lizzie. Victoria Lincoln, the late novelist and Fall River native whose parents were neighbors of the Bordens, wrote in her study of the case: "*De haut en bas,* Lizzie was always kind." Stories abound about the affection Lizzie inspired in her social inferiors, especially servants. Her habit of calling Bridget "Maggie" has been attributed to laziness (Maggie was the name of a former maid), but I think it was an extremity of tact. In that time and place, the name Bridget was synonymous with "Irish maid." Like Rastus in minstrel-show jokes, it was derisory, so Lizzie substituted another. Whatever else she did, she never forgot her noblesse oblige.

Anyone who studies the Borden case grows to like Lizzie, or at least admire her, for her rigid sense of herself as a gentlewoman. It would have been so easy for her to cast suspicion on Bridget, or to accuse her outright. Bridget was the only other person in the house when Andrew and Abby were killed. The Irish were disliked in turn-of-the-century Massachusetts; a Yankee jury would have bought the idea of Bridget's guilt very easily. Yet Lizzie never once tried to shift the blame, and she never named Bridget as a suspect. "A cramped, false world made Lizzie Borden, but she had her code," wrote Victoria Lincoln.

A week before the murders, Emma did something incredible: she went to Fairhaven. Fifteen miles is a long way to scurry, but scurry she did, to visit an elderly friend and escape the heat wave that had descended on Fall River.

That same week, Lizzie shared a beach house on Buzzards Bay with five friends: Mary Holmes, Anna Holmes, Elizabeth Johnson, Isabel Frazer, and Louise Remington. At a press conference after the murders, this quintet showered Lizzie with compliments.

"She always was self-contained, self-reliant, and very composed. Her conduct since her arrest is exactly what I should have expected. Lizzie and her father were, without being demonstrative, very fond of each other."

They got so caught up in Wasp priorities that they inadvertently sowed a dangerous seed when the reporter asked them if they thought Lizzie was guilty. No, they said firmly, because she had pleaded *not* guilty: "It is more likely that Lizzie would commit a murder than that she would lie about it afterwards." She had always been, they said, "a monument of straightforwardness."

She certainly was. A few days before she was due at the beach house she tried to buy prussic acid in her neighborhood drugstore.

The most puzzling aspect of the case has always been Lizzie's choice of weapons. Ladies don't chop up difficult relatives but they do poison them. The jury did not hear about Lizzie's drugstore caper because the druggist's testimony was excluded on a legal technicality, but it establishes her as a monument of straightforwardness.

Picture it: In broad daylight in the middle of a heat wave, she marched into the drugstore carrying a fur cape, announced that there were moths in it, and asked for ten cents' worth of prussic acid to kill them.

The druggist was stunned. Even in the casual Nineties, when arsenic was sold over the counter, it was illegal to sell prussic acid. "But I've bought it many times before," Lizzie protested. Doubtless she looked him straight in the eye when she said it.

The druggist's astonishment mounted in the face of this stout-hearted lie.

"Well, my good lady," he said, "it is something we don't sell except by prescription, as it is a very dangerous thing to handle."

Lizzie left, never dreaming that she might have called attention to herself.

At the beach, her friends noticed that she seemed despondent and preoccupied. They were puzzled when she suddenly cut short her vacation, giving as her excuse some church work, and returned to Fall River.

Back home in the stifling city heat, she sat in her room and brooded. Somehow she had found out that Abby was about to acquire some more real estate: Andrew was planning to put a farm in his wife's name and install his brother-in-law, John Morse, as caretaker. This last was especially infuriating, for Lizzie and Emma were Not Speaking to Uncle John. He had been involved, so they thought, in the other real estate transfer five years before, when Andrew gave Abby a house. Now he was back, plotting with their father and stepmother to do her and Emma out of their rightful inheritance.

Something had to be done, but what? Lacking ladylike poison, Lizzie did what every overcivilized, understated Wasp is entirely capable of doing once we finally admit we're mad as hell and aren't going to take it any more: She went from Anglo to Saxon in a trice.

On the day before the murders, Lizzie joined Abby and Andrew for lunch for the first time in five years—an air-tight alibi, for who would do murder after doing lunch?

That evening, she paid a call on Alice Russell and craftily planted some red herrings. If Machiavelli had been present at this demonstration of the fine Wasp hand he would have gone into cardiac arrest.

"I have a feeling that something is going to happen," she told Alice. "A feeling that somebody is going to do something."

To make sure Alice got the point, she hammered it home with stories about her father's "enemies," prowlers seen in the yard, attempts to break into the barn, and her suspicion that "someone" had poisoned the milk as it sat on the steps. Her father was such a ruthless businessman, she said, that "they" all hated him, and she would not put it past "them" to burn down the house.

When she returned home, Uncle John had arrived with plans to spend the night, but since she was Not Speaking to him, she went directly to her room.

The next day, August 4, 1892, the temperature was already in the eighties at sunrise but that didn't change the Bordens' breakfast menu. Destined to be the most famous breakfast in America, it was printed in newspapers everywhere and discussed by aficionados of the case for years to come: Alexander Woollcott always claimed it was the motive.

If Lizzie had only waited, Abby and Andrew probably would have died *anyway,* for their breakfast consisted of mutton soup, sliced mutton, pancakes, bananas, pears, cookies, and coffee. Here we recognize the English concept of breakfast-as-weapon designed to overwhelm French tourists and other effete types.

Bridget was the first up, followed by Andrew, who came downstairs with the connubial slop pail and emptied it on the grass in the back yard near the pear trees. That done, he gathered the pears that had fallen to the ground. These were the breakfast pears.

After breakfast, Andrew saw Uncle John out and then brushed his teeth at the kitchen sink where Bridget was washing dishes. Moments later, she rushed out to the back yard and vomited. Whether it was the mutton or the toothbrushing or something she had seen clinging to a pear we shall never know, but when she returned to the house, Abby was waiting with an uncharacteristic order. She wanted the windows washed, all of them, inside and out, *now.*

Here is one of the strangest aspects of the case. Victoria Lincoln writes of Abby: "Encased in fat and self-pity, she was the kind who make indifferent housekeepers everywhere." Moreover, the Wasp woman is too socially secure to need accolades like "you could eat off her floor." Why then would Abby order a sick Bridget to wash the windows on a blistering hot day?

Because, says Lincoln, she was getting ready to go to the bank to sign the deed for the farm, and she feared a scene with Lizzie who, knowing Abby's hermitlike ways, would immediately suspect the truth. The mere thought of "having words" in front of a servant struck horror in Abby's Wasp heart, so she invented a task that would take Bridget outside.

That left Lizzie inside.

Around nine o'clock, Abby was tomahawked in the guest room while making Uncle John's bed. Andrew was to meet the same fate around eleven. Lizzie's behavior during that two-hour entr'acte was a model of Battle-of-Britain calm. She ironed handkerchiefs, sewed a button loop on a blouse, chatted with Bridget about a dress goods sale, and read *Harper's Weekly*.

Andrew came home at ten-thirty and took a nap on the sitting-room sofa. Shortly before eleven, Bridget went up to her attic room to rest. At eleven-fifteen she heard Lizzie cry out.

"Maggie! Come down quick! Father's dead. Somebody came in and killed him."

Somebody certainly had. Murdered while asleep, the entire left side of his face and head was a bloody pulp; the eye had been severed and hung down his cheek, and one of the blows had bisected a jaw tooth.

Lizzie sent Bridget for Alice Russell and Dr. Bowen, then sat on the back steps. Seeing her there, the Bordens' nextdoor neighbor, Mrs. Adelaide Churchill, called over to her and got a priceless reply.

"Oh, Mrs. Churchill, do come over. Someone has killed Father."

Mrs. Churchill came over, took a quick look at Andrew, and asked, "Where is your stepmother, Lizzie?"

The safe thing to say was "I don't know," but the people who invented the honor system are sticklers for the truth.

"I don't know but what she's been killed, too, for I thought I heard her come in," Lizzie blurted.

Bridget returned with Alice Russell and Dr. Bowen, who examined Andrew and asked for a sheet to cover the body. Lizzie told Bridget to get it. Whether she said anything else is in dispute; no one present testified to it, but the legend persists that our monument of straightforwardness added "better get two."

Bridget and Mrs. Churchill decided to search the house for Abby. They were not gone long. When they returned, a white-faced but contained Mrs. Churchill nodded at Alice.

"There is another?" asked Alice.

"Yes, she is upstairs," said Mrs. Churchill.

The only excited person present was Bridget.

By noon, when Uncle John returned for lunch, the house and yard were full of cops and a crowd of onlookers had formed in the street. There is no way Uncle John could have missed them. Aware of the hatred between Lizzie and Abby, he must have guessed the truth, but he chose to exhibit so much Wasp nonchalance that he became the first suspect. Instead of rushing into the house yelling "What's the matter?" he ambled into the back yard, picked up some pears, and stood eating them in the shade of the tree.

Meanwhile, the police were questioning Lizzie, who claimed that she had gone to the barn and returned to find her father dead. And what had she gone to the barn for?

"To get a piece of lead for a fishing sinker."

It was the first thing that popped into her head, less a conscious deception than an ink-blot association triggered by her aborted seaside vacation with her friends. She was playing it by ear. It never occurred to her that she could have stalled for time by pretending to faint. Women often fainted in those tightly corseted days, but she even rejected the detective's gallant offer to come back and question her later when she felt better.

"No," she said stoutly. "I can tell you all I know now as well as at any other time."

A moment later, when the detective referred to Abby as her mother, she drew herself up and said stiffly, "She is not my mother, sir, she is my stepmother. My mother died when I was a child."

Before you start diagnosing "self-destructive tendencies," remember that the English novelist's favorite character is the plucky orphan, and she had just become one.

Alice Russell and Dr. Bowen took her upstairs to lie down. Lizzie asked the doctor to send a telegram to Emma in Fairhaven, adding, "Be sure to put it gently, as there is an old person there who might be disturbed." It's all right to disturb your sister as long as you don't disturb strangers; Wasps haven't kithed our kin since the Anglo-Saxon invaders wiped out the Celtic clan system.

Dr. Bowen must have sent the gentlest wire on record, because Emma did not catch the next train, nor the one after that, nor the one after *that*. She didn't return until after seven that night.

When Dr. Bowen returned from the telegraph office, Lizzie confided to him that she had torn up a certain note and put the pieces in the kitchen trash can. He hurried downstairs and found them, and was putting them together when a detective walked in. Seeing the name "Emma" on one of the pieces, he asked Dr. Bowen what it was. "Oh, it is nothing," Dr. Bowen said nonchalantly. "It is something, I think, about my daughter going through somewhere." Before the detective could react to this bizarre answer, Dr. Bowen, nonchalant as ever, tossed the pieces into the kitchen fire. As he lifted the stove lid, the detective saw a foot-long cylindrical stick lying on top of the flames. Later, in the cellar, he found a hatchet head that had been washed and rolled while wet in furnace ash to simulate the dust of long disuse.

Lizzie had been in the barn, but not to look for sinkers. The barn contained a vise, blacksmithing tools, and a water pump. Blood can be washed from metal but not from porous wood. She knew she had to separate the hatchet head from the handle and burn the latter very quickly. She did all of this in a very brief time, and without giving way to panic.

Victoria Lincoln believes that because she really had been in the barn, her compulsive honesty forced her to admit it to the police. Then, having placed herself in the barn, she had to think of an innocent reason for going there, and came up with the story about looking for sinkers. "She lied about *why* and *when* she had done things, but she never denied having done them," writes Lincoln.

Alice Russell displayed the same tic: "Alice's conscience forced her to *mention* things at the trial, but not to *stress* them." The Wasp gift for making everything sound trivial, as when we introduce momentous subjects with "oh, by the way," enabled Alice to testify about a highly incriminating fact in such a way that the prosecution missed its significance entirely.

On one of Alice's trips upstairs on the murder day, she saw Lizzie coming out of *Emma's* room, and a bundled-up blanket on the floor of *Emma's* closet. What was Lizzie doing in Emma's room? What was in the blanket? Victoria Lincoln thinks it contained blood-stained stockings, but the prosecution never tried to find out because Alice made it all sound so matter-of-fact that they didn't even cross-examine her on it. The same technique worked for Dr. Bowen in the matter of the note; we happy few don't destroy evidence, we just tut-tut it into oblivion.

Everyone who saw Lizzie after the murders testified that there wasn't a drop of blood on her. How did she wash the blood off her skin and hair in a house that had no running water? What trait is cherished by the people who distrust intellectuals? *Common sense* told her to sponge herself off with the diaperlike cloths Victorian women used for sanitary napkins and then put them in her slop pail, which was already full of bloody cloths because she was menstruating that week.

Now we come to the dress she wore when she murdered Abby. Where did she hide it after she changed into a fresh one? Some students of the crime think she committed both murders in the nude, but Victoria Lincoln disagrees and so do I. Murder is one thing, but. . . .

Where would any honest Wasp hide a dress? In the dress closet, of course. It's so forthrightly sneaky. Like most women, Lizzie had more clothes than hangers so she knew how easy it is to "lose" a garment by hanging another one on top of it. Victoria Lincoln thinks she hung the blood-stained summer cotton underneath a heavy winter woolen, and then banked on the either-or male mind: the police were looking for a *summer* dress, and men never run out of hangers.

She got no blood at all on the second dress. Her tall father's Prince Albert coat reached to her ankles, and common sense decrees that blood on a *victim's* clothing is only to be expected.

After her arrest Lizzie became America's Wasp Princess. People couldn't say enough nice things about her icy calm, even the Fall River police chief: "She is a remarkable woman and possessed of a wonderful power of fortitude."

A Providence reporter and Civil War veteran: "Most women would faint at seeing her father dead, for I never saw a more horrible sight and I have walked over battlefields where thousands were dead and mangled. She is a woman of remarkable nerve and self-control."

Julian Ralph, *New York Sun:* "It was plain to see that she had complete mastery of herself, and could make her sensations and emotions invisible to an impertinent public."

To ward off a backlash, Lizzie gave an interview to the *New York Recorder* in which she managed to have her bona fides and eat them too: "They say I don't show any grief. Certainly I don't in public. I never did reveal my feelings and I cannot change my nature now."

I find this very refreshing in an age that equates self-control with elitism. If Lizzie were around today she would be reviled as the Phantom of the Oprah.

Wasp emotional repression also gave us the marvelous fight between Lizzie and Emma that took place in her jail cell while she was awaiting trial. Described by Mrs. Hannah Reagan, the police matron, it went like this:

"Emma, you have given me away, haven't you?"

"No, Lizzie, I have not."

"You have, and I will let you see I won't give in one inch."

Finis. Lizzie turned over on her cot and lay with her back to Emma, who remained in her chair. They stayed like that for two hours and twenty minutes, neither of them saying a word, until visiting time was up and Emma left.

When Mrs. Reagan spilled this sensational colloquy to the press, Lizzie's lawyers said it was a lie and demanded she sign a retraction. Doubts arose, but Victoria Lincoln believes Mrs. Reagan: "That terse exchange followed by a two-hour-and-twenty-minute sulking silence sounds more like a typical Borden family fight than the sort of quarrel an Irish police matron would dream up from her own experience."

After her acquittal, Lizzie bought a mansion for herself and Emma in Fall River's best neighborhood. Social acceptance was another matter. When she returned to Central Congregational, everyone was very polite to her, so she took the hint and stopped going.

She lived quietly until 1897, when she got pinched for shoplifting in Providence. This is what really made her an outcast. Murder is one thing, but. . . .

In 1904, Emma suddenly moved out and never spoke to Lizzie again. Nobody knows what happened. Maybe Lizzie finally admitted to the murders, but I doubt it; the Protestant conscience is not programmed for pointless confession. It sounds more as if Emma found out that her sister had a sex life.

An enthusiastic theater goer, Lizzie was a great fan of an actress named Nance O'Neill. They met in a hotel and developed an intense friendship; Lizzie threw lavish parties for Nance and her troupe and paid Nance's legal expenses in contractual disputes with theater owners. Nance was probably the intended recipient of the unmailed letter Lizzie wrote beginning "Dear Friend," and going on to juicier sentiments: "I dreamed of you the other night but I do not dare to put my dreams on paper." If Emma discovered the two were lesbian lovers, it's no wonder she moved out so precipitously. Murder is one thing, but. . . .

Lizzie had enough money to live anywhere but she chose to stay in Fall River and brave it out; refusing, as she had once sworn to Emma, to give an inch. She lived on alone in her mansion, dying of pneumonia in 1927 at the age of sixty-six.

Emma, living in New Hampshire, read of Lizzie's death in the paper but did not attend the funeral or send flowers. Ten days later, Emma died from a bad fall. Both sisters left the bulk of their fortunes to the Animal Rescue League. Nothing could be Waspier, except the explanation little Victoria Lincoln got when she asked her elders why no one ever spoke to their neighbor, Miss Borden.

"Well, dear, she was very unkind to her mother and father."

National Review, August 17, 1992

WITH CHARITY TOWARD NONE

✝

A Fond Look at Misanthropy

1992

*Choosing the excerpts from this book presented a problem that I
analyzed in the following letter to Cal:*

Salvo Calvo:
*I was browsing through CHARITY to pick out the chapters to use in
FKR when something occurred to me. As my most recent book, it's
still fresh in people's minds. Photocopying two or three chapters and
tossing them in verbatim strikes me as uncricket, so I've decided to
give them their money's worth by rewriting the book as a précis of the
original.*

*Don't worry, it won't take as long as it sounds. It's all on disk so it's
just a matter of cutting, and as you know, I'm the Lorena Bobbitt of the
manuscript. "Polish, repolish, every color lay; sometimes add, but
oftener take away." I wonder if Lorena has read Boileau?*

*I'm going to do "A Gallery of Misanthropes," concentrating on the
ones that say something about the contemporary American scene:
Timon of Athens, Fisher Ames, Rousseau, Flaubert, Nixon, Dian Fossey, and Florence King.*

*You heard me, Florence King. I'm putting myself in the line-up be-
cause it's the only way I can get all the me-stories in one place. I've
pulled them from wherever they appeared, beginning with the Author's Note, and written connecting tissue to make it all segue into a
biographical portrait.*

*FYI: Since I'm using Timon of Athens I omitted Coriolanus—too
much Shakespeare already. I omitted the Ambrose Bierce chapter (too
many quotes in it) but I bring in the most important fact about him in
my own section. I'm also omitting the Gordon Liddy/Cyrano de Ber-
gerac section because that goddamn Washington Post reviewer accused me of being in love with Liddy.*

*Along the way, I tighten and fine-tune—you know me, never satis-
fied. I also updated some stuff, so it's actually a new-old book.*

Bestissimus,

Florence

TIMON OF ATHENS

A misanthrope's fondest dream is carving "Go Away" on his tombstone. One who actually did it was a citizen of ancient Athens who makes a brief appearance in Plutarch's *Lives,* the source for Shakespeare's *Timon of Athens.*

As the play opens, the rich, neurotically nice Timon is practicing the "untirable and continuate goodness" for which he is famed. He adds to a girl's dowry so her beloved's father will consent to the match, sends his servants hither and yon with cash gifts to people who have touched him for loans, and pays a friend's debts to get him out of debtors' prison. Believing that "we are born to do benefits," he throws regular banquets for the deadbeats of Athens, who are steadily eating him out of house and home.

His only real friend is Apemantus, a cheerful cynic with an unvarnished opinion of human nature that comes through in the table grace he recites as a warning at one of Timon's banquets.

> *Immortal gods, I crave no pelf;*
> *I pray for no man but myself;*
> *Grant I may never prove so fond*
> *To trust man on his oath or bond,*
> *Or a harlot for her weeping,*
> *Or a dog that seems a-sleeping,*
> *Or a keeper with my freedom,*
> *Or my friends if I should need 'em.*
> *Amen. So fall to it.*

Timon ignores this shrewd advice. When the man he rescued from debtors' prison tries to repay him, he refuses to hear of it, saying, "I gave it freely ever." Taking their cue, the rest of his debtors tear up their IOUs. At last, when the inevitable happens and Timon himself goes bankrupt, no one lifts a finger to help him.

Furious over their ingratitude, he throws one last banquet for them. Thinking that he has somehow recouped his fortunes, the freeloaders all show up in their usual expectant mood, but this night they are greeted by the New Timon.

"You knot of mouth-friends!" he screams, and then uncovers the platters. Dinner is warm water and stones.

"Live loathèd and long," he tells them, calling them "smiling, smooth, detested parasites, courteous destroyers, affable wolves, meek bears, trencher-friends and minute-jacks." Then he really lets loose:

> *Burn house! sink Athens! henceforth hated be*
> *Of Timon man and all humanity!*

He takes up a vigil outside the walls of Athens and there enumerates the calamities he hopes will strike the city: adulterous wives, disobedient children, thieving servants, slave uprisings, "itches, blains, and leprosy," and sons who "pluck the lined crutch from thy old limping sire, and with it beat out his brains." He himself won't be there to see it, because:

> *Timon will to the woods, where he shall find*
> *The unkindest beast more kinder than mankind. . . .*
> *And grant, as Timon grows, his hate may grow*
> *To the whole race of mankind, high and low.*

He becomes a hermit. His still-loyal steward comes to visit, but Timon advises him:

> *Hate all, curse all, show charity to none,*
> *But let the famished flesh slide from the bone*
> *Ere thou relieve the beggar. Give to dogs*
> *What thou deniest to men. Let prisons swallow 'em.*

Alcibiades also visits him, with no better luck. "I am Misanthropos, and hate mankind," Timon tells him. "For thy part, I do wish thou wert a dog."

Apemantus the Cynic makes the trek out to the hermitage and tries to talk some sense into him. "The middle of humanity thou never knewest, but the extremity of both ends," the wise old man says, but it does no good.

Next comes a delegation of senators. With seeming hospitality Timon gives them a tour of his hermitage and asks them to take a message back to the citizens of Athens. The senators assume he's feeling better, but this, according to Plutarch, is what he said:

"I have a little yard where there grows a fig tree on which many citizens have hanged themselves. And, because I mean to make some building on the place, I thought it good to let you all understand that, before the tree be cut down, if any of you be desperate, you may there go hang yourselves."

Shortly afterwards Timon himself dies and is laid to rest under his notorious tombstone.

> *Here lie I, Timon, who alive all living men did hate;*
> *Pass by and curse thy fill, but pass,*
> *And stay not here thy gait.*

Knowing that the curious will ignore the inscription and come anyway, he spent his last days landscaping the spot so that the weight of the crowd will cause it to sink into the sea.

Timon of Athens is universally acknowledged as Shakespeare's worst play—"two plays, casually joined at the middle," according to Mark Van Doren. Its dramatic fault is lack of foreshadowing. Timon's swing from an extreme of niceness to an extreme of hatred happens so fast that audiences can't believe in it.

American audiences could. It's called "compassion fatigue."

JEAN-JACQUES ROUSSEAU

In his monumental work, *Rousseau and Romanticism,* literary critic Irving Babbitt defined two types of misanthropy. One, "misanthropy of the naked intellect," has its origins in honesty and its basis in logic. The other, emotionally based and essentially dishonest, motivates left-wingers to destroy society in order to save it. Babbitt called this type "tender misanthropy."

The quintessential tender misanthrope was Jean-Jacques Rousseau, who urged people to be "noble savages."

Rousseau's *Discourse on the Origins of Inequality* praised "natural man" over his civilized counterpart, who, he believed, had been ruined by knowledge, culture, luxury, and "insincere" good manners. As a corrective, he recommended tearing down civilization and abolishing all laws so that everybody could be happy like the simple peasants who placed heart over head, emotion over logic, nature over culture, soul over all.

He sent a copy of the *Discourse* to Voltaire but the grand old cynic, who was a bona fide liberal, saw through Rousseau's misanthropic liberalism and took a dig at him in his thank-you note: "I have received, sir, your new book against the human species, and I thank you for it. No one has ever been so witty as you are in trying to turn us into brutes; to read your book makes one long to go on all fours. As, however, it is now some sixty years since I gave up the practice, I feel that it is unfortunately impossible for me to resume it."

Rousseau was born in Geneva in 1712 to a forty-year-old mother who died two days later. His father, a watchmaker with aristocratic pretensions, wore a sword and kept it on the equivalent of hair trigger, resulting in several incarcerations for public brawling.

Jean-Jacques also had aristocratic pretensions but they went beyond his father's simpleminded pleasure in swashbuckling. "What was hardest to destroy in me," he wrote later, "was a proud misanthropy, a certain acrimony against the rich and happy of the world as though they were so at my expense, as though their alleged happiness had been usurped from mine."

Apprenticed to an engraver, he hated the common atmosphere of the workshop so much that he ran away, becoming a nomadic Jack-of-all-trades and, whenever possible, an older woman's kept boy.

The ad hoc quality of Rousseau's mind and the hysteria that lay just under the surface of his personality emerge in the story he told of how he came to be a writer. In 1749 as he was walking along the Vincennes road on his way to visit a friend in prison, he happened to buy a newspaper in which he happened to see a notice that the Dijon Academy was holding an essay contest on the influence of formal manners on French culture.

"All at once I felt myself dazzled by a thousand sparkling lights; crowds of vivid ideas thronged into my head with a force and confusion that threw me into unspeakable agitation; I felt my head whirling in a giddiness like that of intoxication.'' He sat down under a tree, ideas surging through his fevered brain. When he finally pulled himself together, he saw that his shirtfront was wet with tears but could not remember having shed them.

He wrote the essay, won the prize, and wormed his way into the society of bored French aristocrats, becoming the last word in radical chic.

Scribbling away in his unselective fashion, Rousseau turned out a plethora of how-to and self-help treatises on subjects ranging from botany to solitary hikes to breastfeeding. He was notoriously a tit man, but instead of admitting it and accepting it as one of life's more pleasurable hang-ups, he intellectualized it, writing and talking so much about primitive scenes, mother's milk, and peasant warmth that breastfeeding became a national fad, even among women of the nobility who had always used wet nurses.

His concern did not extend to his mistress, a scullery maid named Thérèse Vasseur, by whom he had five children. Having gained entrée into Parisian society, he was loath to advertise his connection with the common Thérèse, so he dumped all five little ads in a foundling home and then wrote a book on how to raise children. *Emile,* as it was called, laid out a program of ''natural'' behavior over rigid discipline, ''natural'' environments over artificial ones, and ''freedom'' from stifling rules.

In quick succession came a romantic novel, *La Nouvelle Héloïse,* equating sincerity of feeling with manic depression (''I love you as one must love, with excess, madness, rapture and despair''), and a political treatise, *The Social Contract* (''Man is born free but he is everywhere in chains''). After that the Establishment had had enough; Rousseau's books were condemned by church and state and their author exiled.

He lived for a while in England where he met David Hume, soon breaking with him over some imagined offense, and young James Boswell, who visited him at his next place of exile in Switzerland. They had dinner in Rousseau's kitchen, served by the long-suffering Thérèse Vasseur, who had stuck with him despite the disappearing act he performed with their children. The visit ended abruptly when Rousseau snapped at Boswell, ''You are irksome to me. I cannot help it, it's my nature. Go away.''

Boswell was the last man to see him before he went completely round the bend. Two weeks later, Voltaire published a pamphlet poking fun at *La Nouvelle Héloïse* and spilling the story of the five abandoned bastards. Thereafter a broken man, Rousseau suffered regular delusions of persecution until his death in 1778.

He was buried on the estate of one of his hard-core fans, the Marquis de Girardin, a forerunner of today's limousine liberals, who planted him on the "Isle of Poplars" in the middle of a lake, the gravesite surmounted by an imposing tomb and surrounded by benches reserved for nursing mothers. His death triggered a new round of sentimental hysteria as thousands of pilgrims, including Marie Antoinette, flocked to his grave, and rumors of Elvis-like sightings filled the press. Fifteen years later during the Reign of Terror, the Jacobins, who rode to power on the primitivism he had unleashed, reburied him in the Panthéon, where he still lies.

Rousseau's philosophy can be summed up by the buzzword of his day: *sensibilité*—what our age calls "getting in touch with your feelings." His methodology was crying.

Rousseauian tears, says Simon Schama in *Citizens,* were regarded as "the soul directly irrigating the countenance. More important, a good fit of crying indicated that the child had been miraculously preserved within the man or woman. So Rousseau's heroes and heroines, beginning with himself, sob, weep and blubber at the slightest provocation."

According to Rousseau, the best place to cry was in the woods. Nature was particularly well-suited to his overwrought vocabulary. The woods were *wild, untamed, primitive, lush.* The woods were full of *nooks, copses, verdant canopies, umbrageous illusions.* They were also full of sobbing Rousseau fans but never mind that, you could be *alone with nature* in the woods, *lose yourself* in their beauty, *let it wash over you,* sleep *naked* in a *bower* and *become as one* with nature's *torrents.* Afterwards, you could write about your sylvan crying jag and claim to be *drunk with* emotion, a cliché that is with us still.

The *sensibilité* craze spread to other arts. The "philosopher," Diderot, also endorsed coming apart: "Move me, astonish me, unnerve me, make me tremble, weep, shudder and rage." Jean-Baptiste Greuze, the Rousseau of the palette, had all of Paris in a sodden mess with his painting, "Girl Weeping Over Her Dead Canary." An art critic wrote that he went back again and again to gaze at it and cry some more: ''I have passed whole hours in attentive contemplation so that I became drunk with a sweet and tender sadness.''

To understand why eighteenth-century France succumbed to Rousseau's glorification of unbuttoned hysteria, we must understand what France was like in the seventeenth century. Called the Age of Reason, it was a neoclassical period that modeled its behavior on the stern virtues of Early Rome: honor, duty, courage, and especially *gravitas,* that dignified stoicism in the face of personal pain considered the mark of an aristocrat.

In literature and drama, these virtues were transmuted into logical plots faithful to the Aristotelian model, pithy epigrams after Martial, a reverence for linguistic precision as dictated by the Académie Française, a lofty formalism requiring actors to declaim rather than emote, and a ''curtain of charity'' prohibiting scenes of lust and violence from the stage.

In life as in art, the watchwords were self-control and decorum, with manners based on the precision etiquette that prevailed at the court of Louis XIV. Rigid perhaps, but the seventeenth century had a high opinion of human nature and a limitless faith in Man's capacity for rational behavior. We get from people what we demand of them and the French neoclassicists demanded much.

It was not that the Age of Reason denied the existence of subjective feelings; one of its leading lights, Blaise Pascal, penned the famous line, ''the heart has its reasons of which reason knows nothing,'' but he said it and got out, leaving posterity an exquisitely balanced epigram. Rousseau said it and kept on saying it over and over in purple prose until his followers were as conditioned as Pavlov's dogs. If he did not actually cause the French Revolution, he certainly set it up. His message of *I feel, therefore I am* ushered in a self-indulgent emotionalism that spilled over into political anarchy and became the rationale for the Reign of Terror.

Jean-Jacques Rousseau would feel right at home in America. The words *pursuit of happiness* have a suspiciously Rousseauian ring, as well they might. The well-read Thomas Jefferson was his contemporary, and served as Minister to France in the period just after his death.

Environmentalists would welcome him as one of their own—tender misanthropes, wrote Irving Babbitt, hate humanity through an "Arcadian haze." He could run around talking up the woods and bask in the discovery that Greenpeace has seen fit to replicate his literary style in their junk mail: "Listening to 500 dolphins shrieking in panic as they fight and gasp for air . . . standing by helplessly as living dolphins were dragged aloft thrashing and flailing in terror. . . ."

He would be a fixture on "Nightline," popping up whenever they needed a self-proclaimed expert on this or that to comment on the latest crisis in entitlements or civil liberties. Does a fireperson have the right to breastfeed her baby at the station house? Should the judge take the child away from the mother who puts it in day care and give it to the father who's home all day because he's on welfare? "Bear with me a moment, Jean-Jacques, but didn't you abandon five children of your own?" Then on to "Crossfire" for a discussion of Michael Fay's buttocks. "Now, look here, Jean-Jacques, weren't you ever belted as a kid?" And finally, the nirvana of talking head-dom. "Welcome, Jean-Jacques, glad to see you again, it's good to have you, thank you for coming."

He would have a ball hanging out with Jesse Jackson. The various self-realization and human-potential movements that have shredded our social fabric in the name of self-esteem and feeling good about oneself are outgrowths of the oxymoronic mass individualism that Rousseau promoted in his posthumously published *Confessions,* which contains the Western world's first mantra: "I am not made like anyone I have seen; I dare believe that I am not made like anyone in existence. If I am not better, at least I am different."

Those who truly love people do not encourage them to revert to barbarism. Humanity never has regained the loftiness that Rousseau destroyed. His glorification of "natural" behavior is with us still, the driving force behind the coarsening influences of "let it all hang out," "if it feels good do it," and "getting down and dirty."

The noble savages, simple peasants, and wailing hysterics Rousseau enshrined are now the dominant force in American life—hugging each other, finding their inner child, and letting unleashed emotions wash over them in today's version of the verdant canopy: the confessional talk show. The cheapness, tawdriness, and utter lack of class that ooze out of Oprah, Donahue, Geraldo and Sally Jessy are nothing more than the recycled *sensibilité* of Jean-Jacques Rousseau, the tender misanthrope who dumped human dignity in a foundling home.

FISHER AMES

Fisher Ames (1758–1808) is our forgotten Founding Father. His name never appears in schoolbooks and only rarely in college texts. His misanthropy has earned him a virtual blackout.

He was a member of the First Congress and the author of the final version of the First Amendment. Later, as leader of the Federalists, he delivered a speech on Jay's Treaty that was called the finest example of American oratory by Abraham Lincoln and Daniel Webster, who memorized passages from it to train themselves in the art.

Ames's contemporaries called him a "sweet" man. His earliest biographer spoke of "the charms of his conversation and manners [that] won affection" and "the delicacy, the ardor, and constancy with which he cherished his friends. . . . He had a perfect command of his temper; his anger never proceeded to passion, nor his sense of injury to revenge."

Ames was a devoted husband and father whose seven children received large chunks of paternal quality time thanks to the pleasure he took in inventing and playing educational games. He even got along well with his in-laws; his letters to brother-in-law Thomas Dwight are as warm as they are voluminous.

How can such a man have been a misanthrope? It's not always a matter of congenital temperament. Ames's loathing of mankind was caused by a political event: It is no exaggeration to say that he was goaded into misanthropy by the French Revolution.

He was not alone; Burke in England reacted the same way. The French Revolution probably created more misanthropes than any other event in history. In other bloodbaths the evildoers have been exotic foreign marauders or nations within nations—Huns, Bolsheviks, Nazis, Khmer Rouge—but in the France of the Terror they were *the People,* humanity's upper-case whole.

When the newly created United States learned of the excesses of the Terror—summary executions, blood drinking, cannibalism, massacres of nuns, the sexual dismemberment of the Princess de Lamballe—all done in the name of "the People," Ames coined the word "mobocracy" and questioned the wisdom of representative government.

"What other form of civil rule so irresistibly tends to free vice from restraint and to subject virtue to persecution?" he asked. "Our mistake is in supposing men better than they are. They are bad, and will act their character out."

Ames grew to loathe Thomas Jefferson, whom he considered a dupe of the French Enlightenment's naive optimistic faith in the essential goodness of human nature. Whenever anyone quoted Jefferson's "all men are created equal," Ames shot back: "but differ greatly in the sequel."

The "Jeffs," as he called the democratic republicans, moved him to savage eloquence:

> They learn to throw their eyes beyond the gulf of revolution, confusion, and civil war, which yawns at their feet, to behold an Eden of primitive innocence, equality, and liberty. . . . The rights of man are to be established by being solemnly proclaimed, and printed, so that every citizen shall have a copy. Avarice, ambition, revenge, and rage will be disenchanted from all hearts and die there; man will be regenerated . . . and the glorious work of that perfectibility of the species, foretold by Condorcet, will begin.

When the Jeffs insisted that anarchy could be avoided by giving the people so much freedom that they would have nothing to rebel against, Ames countered that human nature being what it is, people will always find something to rebel against; if nothing else, envy will make them crave "the power to make others wretched." He predicted the rise of what he called "factions" and we call pressure groups:

> A combination of a very small minority can effectually defeat the authority of the national will. . . . Suppose at first their numbers to be exceedingly few, their efforts will for that reason be so much the greater. They will call themselves the People; they will in their name arraign every act of government as wicked and weak; they will oblige the rulers to stand forever on the defensive. . . . With a venal press at

their command, concealing their number and their infamy, is it to be doubted that the ignorant will soon or late unite with the vicious?

But, the Jeffs argued, the majority rules! No, said Ames, it doesn't. The price of liberty is eternal vigilance and most people are unwilling to pay it: "The virtuous, who do not wish to control the society, but quietly to enjoy its protection; the enterprising merchant, the thriving tradesman, the careful farmer, will be engrossed by the toils of their business, and will have little time or inclination for the unprofitable and disquieting pursuit of politics."

The only eternally vigilant citizens in a democracy, he warned, will be members of factions whose ceaseless demands will cause "a state of agitation that is justly terrible to all who love their ease . . . it tries and wears out the strength of the government and the temper of the people. It is a game which the factious will never be weary of playing, for conquering parties never content themselves with half the fruits of victory."

As time went on and his health failed, Ames's bitterness increased. When Jefferson became president he said, "We are in the hands of the philosophers of Lilliput." As for the Louisiana Purchase, it was "a Gallo-Hispano-Indian Omnium Gatherum."

He continued to pound away at democracy with unequivocal statements that would guarantee his absence from our school books.

"Our disease is democracy. Democracy is a troubled spirit, fated never to rest, and whose dreams, if it sleeps, present only visions of hell."

"There is universally a presumption in democracy that promises everything, and at the same time an imbecility that can accomplish nothing, not even preserve itself."

"We are sliding down into the mire of a democracy, which pollutes the morals of the citizens before it swallows up their liberties."

Five years before his death he wrote Thomas Dwight: "Our country is too big for union, too sordid for patriotism, too democratic for liberty."

In the end, he seemed to adopt a broader misanthropy extending beyond American politics to the entire race of mankind: "Indeed I consider the whole civilized world as metal thrown back into the furnace, to be melted over again."

Most people know that John Adams and Thomas Jefferson both died at a ripe age on the same day: July 4, 1826. Given the superstitious weight of the number *three,* a study of the life of Fisher Ames concludes with a chill down the spine, for Ames died of tuberculosis at age fifty on July 4, 1808.

The Grim Reaper's unhealthy interest in America's birthday takes on ominous significance when we examine our present national mood in the light of Fisher Ames's warnings about factionalism. "Diversity" and its handmaidens, affirmative action and political correctness, are our French Revolution, goading us into misanthropy as surely as the excesses of the Terror goaded Ames. There's so much pluribus in the unum that everybody is somebody's "them."

GUSTAVE FLAUBERT

Unlike the tender misanthrope, the misanthrope of the naked intellect hates people straight down the line with no exceptions and no regrets.

Having no wish to liberate the repressions of a species he already finds intolerable, he scorns such categories as "noble savages." If he must share the world with people, he wants them to be as decorous and self-controlled as possible. Holding humanity to the highest standards of behavior for purely selfish reasons, the misanthrope of the naked intellect ironically emerges as the true friend of mankind.

"I detest my fellow-beings and do not feel that I am their fellow at all," wrote Gustave Flaubert.

He was born in Rouen in 1821 at the height of the Romantic Movement spawned by Rousseau, an era of palmy neuroticism when the affliction of choice was *Sturm und Drang* and the beau ideal was a dead poet, preferably under thirty.

Next to suicide, the spectacle of insanity exerted the most fervent pull on the Romantic imagination. Disdaining rational cause-and-effect, Romantic writers resolved their plots with delirium and brain fever and upped the ante on Rousseau's woods, stocking them with *stygian mists* and *melancholy penumbra.* Above all, the Romantics were round-the-clock free spirits who enshrined impulse and held in contempt such bourgeois habits as planning ahead and thinking things through.

None of this suited Gustave Flaubert's practical, easily irritated Norman soul. He was quintessentially middle class, a doctor's son who set out to be a lawyer. When he gave up law for writing there was no question of starving in a cold garret *à la bohème*. He lived in his family's spacious country home near Rouen with his doting widowed mother, waited on hand and foot by her and a devoted female servant who arranged the household to accommodate his need for solitude and silence.

Visits to Paris to partake of literary ambience left him overwrought. "Contact with the world, with which I have been steadily rubbing shoulders now for fourteen months, makes me feel more and more like returning to my shell," he wrote his mother. "I hate the crowd, the herd. It seems to me always atrociously stupid or vile."

But life back home also presented problems. "I took a walk in Rouen this afternoon and met three or four Rouennais," he confided to his journal. "The sight of their vulgarity and of their very hats and overcoats, the things they said and the sound of their voices made me feel like vomiting and weeping all at once. Never since I have been in this world have I felt so suffocated by a disgust for mankind!"

He had a mistress, Louise Colet, but she got on his nerves so he saw her only when the demands of the flesh gave him no choice. The rest of the time she had to be content with the only kind of human contact misanthropes are good at. "The most successful love affairs are conducted entirely by post," said George Bernard Shaw. And so Flaubert wrote letter after letter to poor Louise who, incapable of understanding him, assumed that the voluminous correspondence meant that he could not live without her.

She got a taste of the misanthropic point of view when she wrote him that she thought she was pregnant.

"The idea of giving birth to someone fills me with horror," he wrote back, and threatened to throw himself into the Seine. He enlarged upon the point after her fears had proved false. "This paternity would have made me fall into the ordinary conditions of life. My virginity, with respect to the world, would have been wiped out, and I would have sunk into the abyss of common misery."

That misanthropes are literary classicists is axiomatic, but Flaubert didn't know it yet. Determined to master the Romantic style and able to afford leisurely travel, he took an extended trip to the Near East to soak up some Oriental exoticism. After visiting Early Christian sites in North Africa, he returned to Rouen and wrote *The Temptation of St. Anthony,* a long, lush, lyrical fantasia full of demons, meditations, and visions.

It came to six hundred pages. He read the entire manuscript aloud to a captive audience of two friends. It took four days, and by the time it was over they were in worse shape than St. Anthony, who was a psychotic hermit. The novel was crammed with vivid descriptions and meticulous detail but it did not "move"; the plotless story was as flat and static as its protagonist.

At this Maalox moment in literary history, one of Flaubert's friends suddenly remembered a recent local scandal. "Throw it in the fire," he said of St. Anthony, "and write a novel about that doctor's wife who killed herself."

Flaubert resisted the idea at first, but he soon realized that this stark domestic tragedy was a perfect vehicle for a misanthropic author. The story of a woman enslaved by cheap sentiment and puerile romantic dreams, *Madame Bovary* demanded a writer able to remain aloof from the emotions he had to describe. To "identify" with Emma Bovary, to weep and wallow with her in Rousseauian fashion, would have dragged both author and story down to the level of tasteless melodrama and unfastidious pity.

"One must write coldly," Flaubert pronounced. "It is not with the heart that one writes but with the head." He wrote *Madame Bovary* like a bookkeeper looking for a penny, yet it was an act of mercy that only a frosty soul could have performed. His detachment, his objectivity, his emotional restraint, his pitiless insight and savage realism gave Emma Bovary the importance she craved and put her in a class with Phaedra.

He was equally kind to his readers. Unlike the Romantics, who believed that a writer should forget about grammar and spelling and "just let it come," Flaubert was too rigid to confuse writing with vomiting. He spent whole days searching for *"le mot juste,"* the right word, the perfect word, the *only* word that would express exactly what he wanted to say.

He always cut more than he saved. The misanthrope's abruptness finds a friend in the classicist's economy of expression. It is easy to imagine how Rousseau would have written the arsenic scene; by contrast, Flaubert's laconic sentences twist like short-bladed knives: "She opened the jar and began to eat it" and "Still there was the taste of ink."

There is no such thing as a bad translation of *Madame Bovary* because it is so clear and concise that no translator could possibly go off the rails. The language is so simple, the sentences are so direct, the scenes are so logically arranged around unifying points, that anyone with a few years of French under his belt can read it with ease in the original, even when schooldays are long in the past.

Madame Bovary, the work of a man who hated people, is the most user-friendly novel ever written. Job counselors who emphasize image and voters who succumb to smiles can learn much from Flaubert and his masterpiece. If you want something done right, don't hire a Nice Guy.

RICHARD NIXON

Ask any American his opinion of Richard Nixon and you will get an answer as complex and contorted as Nixon himself. The French, on the other hand, respond with childlike simplicity: they're crazy about him. Small wonder, since they know him so well. The "real Nixon" has been a fixture at the Comédie Française since 1666. His name is Alceste, and he's the protagonist of Molière's play, *Le Misanthrope.*

In the Paris of Louis XIV, where style and form are everything, Alceste is notorious for his charmlessness and gaucherie.

> *The soul God gave me isn't of the sort*
> *That prospers in the weather of a court.*
> *It's all too obvious that I don't possess*
> *The virtues necessary for success.*
> *My one great talent is for speaking plain;*
> *I've never learned to flatter or to feign;*
> *And anyone so stupidly sincere*
> *Had best not seek a courtier's career.*

In 1948, Congressman Alceste Nixon was a member of the House Un-American Activities Committee. When that body called a witness named Alger Hiss, Alceste came face to face with the kind of man he hated.

"Hiss," Alceste later wrote, "was a striking representative of the fashionable Eastern establishment—a graduate of Harvard Law School, clerk to a Supreme Court Justice, an aide to Franklin D. Roosevelt at the Yalta conference and one of the major organizers of the United Nations conference in San Francisco. He had impeccable social and intellectual qualifications, and the list of people who he said would vouch for his character ranged from Adlai E. Stevenson to John Foster Dulles. He, in effect, pleaded innocence by association."

And when there's any honor that can be got
By pulling strings, he'll get, like as not.

Hiss had been accused of membership in the Communist Party by Whittaker Chambers. When Chambers appeared before the committee, the press reacted like Versailles courtiers presented with a country bumpkin.

"Although he was a senior editor of *Time* magazine, Chambers was poorly dressed, pudgy, undistinguished in appearance and in background," Alceste wrote. "Most of the reporters covering the Hiss case were obsessed with style. They were so dazzled by Hiss's background and his brilliant conduct on the witness stand that they failed to see that beneath the unimpressive exterior, Chambers was a stronger, more intelligent man."

Hiss was shown a photo of Whittaker Chambers and asked if he had ever known him. At this point, it was simply a matter of one man's word against another's; he could have extricated himself with a charmless *no*, but the stylish Hiss made the mistake of showing off.

"If this is a picture of Mr. Chambers," he purred, "he is not particularly unusual looking. He looks like a lot of people. I might even mistake him for the Chairman of this Committee."

Hiss's studied urbanity and supercilious sarcasm got Alceste Nixon's goat: "Hiss's friends from the State Department, other government agencies, and the Washington social community sitting in the front rows of the spectator section broke into a titter of delighted laughter. Hiss acknowledged this reaction to his sally by turning his back on the Committee, tilting his head in a courtly bow, and smiling graciously at his supporters.''

> *Notice how tolerant people choose to be*
> *Toward that bold rascal who's at law with me.*
> *His social polish can't conceal his nature;*
> *One sees at once that he's a treacherous creature.*

Continuing to gild the lily, Hiss asked if Whittaker Chambers were present in the hearing room. ''He then looked from side to side, giving the impression that he did not have the slightest idea who this mysterious character might be and that he was anxious to see him in the flesh.'' Told that Chambers was not present, Hiss assumed a theatrical air of disappointment that roused Alceste Nixon's deepest suspicions.

> *This artificial style, that's all the fashion,*
> *Has neither taste, nor honesty, nor passion.*

Alceste's instinctive distrust paid off. Thanks to his dogged pursuit, Alger Hiss was exposed as a Communist and sent to jail for perjury. From that moment on, the media courtiers hated Alceste and he hated them in return.

Alceste ran for president in 1960 but came up short in looks and style in the first televised debates with John F. Kennedy.

> *No one could possibly be taken in*
> *By those soft speeches and that sugary grin.*
> *The whole world knows the shady means by which*
> *The low-brow's grown so powerful and rich. . . .*
> *Are you in love with his embroidered hose?*
> *Do you adore his ribbons and his bows?*

The answer was yes. Two years after losing the presidency, Alceste ran for governor of California and lost that election, too. Calling in the media courtiers, he announced that they would no longer have Alceste to kick around; he was leaving politics.

> *Come then: man's villainy is too much to bear;*
> *Let's leave this jungle and this jackal's lair.*
> *Yes! Treacherous and savage race of men,*
> *You shall not look upon my face again.*

It was his finest hour, but he didn't know it.

Alceste Nixon went into retirement and wrote *Six Crises,* a political autobiography about the Hiss case and other landmarks of his career. Meanwhile, America had several crises of her own, and so Alceste ran for president again in 1968.

To conceal his misanthropy, he concocted an image called the "New Alceste" and took "Bring Us Together" as his campaign slogan. He tried his best to be warm and friendly, but his cold, anomalous black eyes shone with obsidian flatness, betraying his scornful opinion of political campaigning.

> *I see you almost hug a man to death,*
> *Exclaim for joy until you're out of breath,*
> *How I despise the frenzied operations*
> *Of all these barterers of protestations,*
> *These lavishers of meaningless embraces,*
> *These utterers of obliging commonplaces.*

Under normal conditions he would have lost, but 1968 was a strange year. He won, which sealed his fate because it meant that he would have to run again. The American electorate, who assuage their insecurity by demanding Nice Guyism of their leaders, have no idea what years of spurious warmth can do to someone like Alceste Nixon. Nothing is more stressful for a misanthrope than trying to be nice with no end in sight. It's hard enough on the people who must witness it, but it just about kills the misanthrope. If it goes on too long, paranoia normally kept under control suddenly explodes and the misanthrope starts doing things he would not ordinarily do.

> *Ah, this is what my sad heart prophesied;*
> *Now all my anxious fears are verified;*
> *My dark suspicion and my gloomy doubt*
> *Divined the truth, and now the truth is out.*

Yes, now I have no pity, not a shred;
My temper's out of hand; I've lost my head.
A righteous wrath deprives me of my senses,
And I won't answer for the consequences.

Alceste Nixon got into some trouble that he could have gotten out of very easily, but he let it go on and build up out of an unconscious need to justify the misanthropy he had denied all his life.

I'll discover by this case
Whether or not men are sufficiently base
And impudent and villainous and perverse
To do me wrong before the universe.

They are.

The misanthrope who tries to hide his misanthropy is invariably despised. This is what people sensed but could not pin down when they said, ''There's something about Nixon I don't like.''

The unabashed misanthrope, on the other hand, evokes a surprisingly different response, as Robert Lewis Taylor notes in his biography of W.C. Fields: ''Fields' defiance of civilization, over a period of sixty-seven years, became an institution in which the public took pride. . . . Most persons, as a scholar has noted, harbor a secret affection for anybody with a low opinion of humanity.''

This secret affection springs from a universal familiarity with the grind of daily life. For the meek majority, who never say what they really think and never get even with the people who do them wrong, the misanthrope is a stand-in whom they can cheer from the safety of the sidelines. He has little to offer victims of crushing evil, but he is the nemesis of mankind's little meannesses, the ones that hurt most of the people most of the time. By his withering contempt for all things human, the ostensibly uncharitable misanthrope ironically becomes a warrior for the shat-upon.

A politician could benefit from such a stance, but Nixon would not risk it. In denying his misanthropy and trying futilely to bend himself into the requisite American shape, he missed his chance to be an indomitable prince of darkness and became instead a vulnerable Gloomy Gus.

The universal fascination for what-might-have-been is used to clever effect in the vegetable-juice commercial featuring people who gulp down candy bars and ice cream for quick-energy snacks, and then, too late, slap themselves on the forehead and say, "I coulda had a V-8!"

But for our sweet tooth, America coulda had a Richelieu.

DIAN FOSSEY

The ranks of female misanthropy are thin, but one shining exception has walked this earth and she makes me look like Little Bo Peep.

A six-foot-one, gun-toting virago whose sobriquet was "the gorilla lady" was not a woman to cross, but somebody finally did. On December 27, 1985, Dian Fossey was butchered at the Karisoke Centre for Mountain Gorilla Research in Rwanda where she had spent eighteen tumultuous years.

She was found in bed, her head split in two by a machete left nearby. The murderer had entered her cabin through a hole cut out of the tin wall. The most puzzling aspect of the macabre scene was the hair clutched in her stiff hands: it was her own.

Solving Fossey's murder was not the purpose of the late Harold Hayes, who died in 1989 just as he was completing his engrossing biography, *The Dark Romance of Dian Fossey.* Whodunit interests him less than whydunit, and here he hits pay dirt, for there were very few people in Dian Fossey's life who did *not* have a motive for murdering her.

Poachers, cattle herders, park officials, Western conservationists, members of her staff, a couple dozen researchers—the parade of possible suspects extended far back into the past. . . . Fossey had shot at her enemies, kidnapped their children, whipped them about the genitals, smeared them with ape dung, killed their cattle, burned their property, and sent them to jail. Anyone who dared to threaten her gorillas, or even to challenge her methods, set her off, and the force of her malevolence was difficult to imagine.

Born in the Bay Area in 1932, Fossey attended San Jose State College and worked as a physical therapist at a Louisville, Kentucky hospital. Refusing to live in nursing quarters, she insisted on renting a remote cabin deep in the woods miles outside of town. The landlord, who had advertised the place for a couple, refused at first to rent it to her, saying it was too isolated for a woman alone and that he would not be responsible for her safety. She threatened to return to California if she could not have the cabin, so her supervisor at the hospital called the landlord and explained that Fossey's position had been hard to fill and they could not risk losing her.

The landlord relented and Fossey moved into the cottage, where she lived alone for ten years, collecting stray dogs instead of boyfriends. Eventually she moved to an even more remote house when she returned from a vacation and found that the landlord had put a mobile home for his aunts too near her place.

The consensus among her co-workers was that she liked animals better than people. When they gathered for coffee, she refused to join them and took her breaks alone. In what was probably a subconscious decision to insure that others kept their distance, she was less than fastidious in her grooming and often gave off body odor.

A fervent desire to see exotic animals led her to borrow $8,000 to go to Africa. Her articles on the trip attracted the attention of the famous prehistorian Louis Leakey, who preferred female assistants for his ape studies because "women were more patient, more sensitive to mother-infant relations, and less likely to arouse aggression in males." Little did he know that his latest Galatea would nearly start a civil war.

Fossey arrived in East Africa in the Sixties "when just to be white was to risk your life." Much of what happened during this time of Communist-inspired Simba incursions was not reported by a press eager to put a good face on newly emerging nations, but Hayes fills in the blanks with some riveting passages:

> Led by witch doctors, the Simbas believed themselves impervious to bullets. They stoked their courage on hashish, and dressed themselves

in monkey skins and whatever else might be at hand—lamp shades, women's panties, chicken feathers. . . . Many [of their victims] died by being forced to drink gasoline, then their stomachs were cut open and set on fire. One specially prized victim, a moderate politician named Sylvere Bondekwe, saw his liver cut out and eaten while he was still alive. . . . In their extended siege of Stanleyville years earlier, the Simbas had held 1,100 Belgians and Americans hostage. "We shall cut out the hearts of the Americans and Belgians and wear them as fetishes," the Simbas had announced. "We shall dress ourselves in the skins of the Americans and Belgians."

Joseph Mobutu, financed by the United States for his anti-Communist resistance, swore to put down the Simbas. Knowing the limitations of his own army—"In a crisis, Congolese soldiers tended to drop their guns, take off their shoes, and run"—he hired white soldiers of fortune to protect his position. When the white mercenaries, many of whom held Nazi-style racial views, turned against Mobutu and began killing their black comrades-in-arms, Mobutu announced that Europeans were trying to take over the country and ordered all whites killed.

It was at this time that Fossey claimed she was held for two days in a cage and "raped and raped and raped" by black African soldiers. No one knows what actually happened. One story has it that she was urinated on and otherwise humiliated, but that she escaped actual rape by defying her tormentors with the force of her rage, screaming, "You don't have the balls to rape me!"

It has the ring of truth given Fossey's hell-for-leather personality, and it might have worked for a woman over six feet tall. Leakey believed her rape story, but the son of Congo colonialists did not: "If any African raped a European in that part of the world," he told the author, "you might as well forget that European's existence. . . . You don't get out of those kinds of camps."

This same ex-colonialist, on discovering that Fossey intended to stay and study gorillas come hell or high water, gave her some practical advice:

"The only option you've got to stay alive is to make yourself into some sort of spiritual witch. You've got to do this with such effectiveness and create such a sense of terror about you, people will give you a wide berth. All over Africa, there have been European women who lived on farms by themselves while their husbands went to war—my mother was one of them. The only way they survived was to become known as some sort of banshee. All Africans, you know, live in a spook land. They believe almost everything is invested with spiritual meaning. . . . I suggested she should make herself into someone no one would want to go *near*—that she should get wailing systems, smoke bombs, false faces, that sort of thing.

"At the same time, I told her she should beat the bejesus out of anybody she felt like beating the bejesus out of. And then they would get the feeling there was a woman up there who was behaving totally unwomanly."

This is precisely what Fossey did. To stop farmers from grazing their herds on the gorilla preserve, she shot a cow and vowed to shoot one a month: the grazing stopped. When farmers kidnapped her dog, she kidnapped eight of their cattle and spread the word that she would shoot one cow a day until she got her dog back: she got it back by nightfall. Tracking the killers of a water buffalo, she opened fire on them; spotting one of their children hiding behind a tree, she kidnapped the child and offered to exchange him for his father's spear: she got the spear. "Naturally I returned the brat," she wrote to Leakey.

Word of her incredible courage began to spread. The Africans had never seen a woman like Fossey:

In a country where women were subservient to men, this giant female *mzungu* [European]—looming over the pint-sized Hutu and Batwa—was subservient to no one. . . . So effective were her techniques of terrorizing the Africans that some members of her staff believed she had supernatural powers. One day, a tracker brought the body of a small child into her camp. He asked her to cure it, to bring the child back to life. He had no doubt that the white witch could do this.

Rwanda became her only home. After her affair with Robert Campbell ended in 1972, she sloughed off the few friendships she had ever made back in America and burned the bridges connecting her to her earlier life in her native land. Her social life in Africa was minimal; she endured the occasional company of the embassy people, who had to endure hers for political reasons even though she called the wife of one official a cunt.

The "Malthusian nightmare" of densely populated Rwanda drove her to fury as she watched the native peoples overwhelm the preserve, their only source of food and water, crowding her beloved gorillas out of existence. In an extreme reaction to the encroachment of her own species, Fossey became a surrogate mother to infant gorillas, "tending them night and day as though they were her own babies, feeding them, cuddling them, sleeping with them in her cabin, covered with their diarrhea."

She flew into a rage if people interrupted her work. When a group of Chicago tourists showed up unannounced, she fired bullets over their heads and sent them scrambling back down the mountain in fear of their lives. Her own scientific staff felt her iron hand. "The person who runs a field station sets its style. Fossey's was hermitic. She stayed in her cabin all day and all night, and expected the researchers to stay in theirs when they weren't in the field. They all ate their meals alone. If they wanted to say something to somebody, they sent a note."

A National Geographic producer saw her beat four African porters with her walking stick. Another saw her threaten a captured poacher with castration. "She would approach the poacher, holding pliers or machete, looking at that part of their anatomy.... All during the brutal ritual, Fossey shouted obscenities at the prisoner, a mixture of words that came into her head—English, French, German, Swahili, communicating a feeling of absolute outrage."

State Department cables flew when she asked the Rwandan government for permission to kill poachers on sight. But somebody killed her first. She was buried in the gorilla graveyard she started when her special pet, Digit, was mysteriously slaughtered. The Rwandan government tried and convicted her African tracker, who allegedly committed suicide in his cell. Her American assistant, Wayne McGuire, whom she had bawled out two days before her death, was also convicted in absentia after he returned to the United States, but Rwanda has never tried to extradite him.

* * *

All the reviews of Hayes's book that I've read stopped short of calling Fossey a misanthrope. Most concluded that she had "gone bushy"—the African version of cabin fever—a stretch implying that it's better to be insane than unfriendly. Others, especially women reviewers, piously insisted that Fossey's hatred of people proved that she really "hated herself"—the leading cliché in American discussions of misanthropy.

The reviewers either missed or chose to ignore a passage indicating that gorilla ladies do things differently. Speaking on condition of anonymity, another female primatologist told the author: "I didn't like humans. The monkeys allowed me to opt out, to get my need for social interaction and social closeness, so I didn't have to pay the price of human interaction."

So it was with Dian Fossey, a blip on the radar screen of Smile Button America. She was a Mean Green, as wacky and brutal as the anti-"speciesism" crowd who believe in civil rights for spotted owls, but the resemblance ends there. Ready and willing to go it alone, she committed all her outrages without the help of screaming minions on college break, and unlike the tree spikers of Oregon, there was nothing sneaky about her: she had guts.

In an America drowning in Happy Talk, a woman who refuses a rabies shot with "I'm no more rabid than usual" has my undying admiration, but what I really identify with is her fixation on that isolated Kentucky cabin and what she went through to get it.

I know the panic she must have felt when the landlord refused to rent it to her. I know the blind rage she must have felt when she threatened to quit her new job if she could not live alone. I know the emotional exhaustion she must have felt when she had to run around making phone calls and explaining herself to people so they would intercede for her. I know the crumple of relief she must have felt when she got the cabin after all. And I know the shame that surely came over her when involuntary gratitude crept into the relief and she found herself saying "thank you" to the landlord for letting her be a loner.

That cabin—and those coffee breaks—are all I need to know to understand why she ended up in Africa beating the bejesus out of anybody who got in her way.

FLORENCE KING

mericans are supposed to be nice all the time. American women are supposed to be nice even more of all the time. In other countries, congenital introverts simply remain introverts all their lives, neither advancing nor retreating, but America's commitment to extroversion as a national art form can abrade some naturally aloof personalities until they flower into deadly nightshade.

I am such a personality. This is my story.

I landed in the wrong place, in the wrong sex, at the wrong time. History must contain some dawn when bliss it was to be a misanthrope, but I was born in 1936 when Shirley Temple was turning tricks. It was the Age of the Darling Little Girl.

My debut as a misanthrope occurred shortly after I learned to talk. I was being wheeled through a store in my stroller when a child-loving woman exclaimed, "What a darling little girl!" and squatted down in front of me.

"Hello, you sweet thing," she cooed.

"I doan yike you," I replied.

Thereafter I latched onto the sentence as children will, and said it to every stranger who crossed my path. My extroverted grandmother always hastened to explain, "She's just shy"—one of America's many rationalizations for misanthropy which I was destined to hear time and time again.

I have always maintained that I was not all that unusual. Children are admirably gimlet-eyed before adults put them through the American make-over program. When *Snow White and the Seven Dwarfs* came out in 1940, my favorite dwarf was Grumpy, and for once I conformed. Grumpy was the overwhelming favorite of children, and Grumpy dolls outsold all the others. (As children of the Depression we had to choose *one* doll; today's children would get the whole set and this valuable statistic would be unavailable.)

Unfortunately, a malignant institution exists for the sole purpose of changing children from baleful realists to people who love people. It's called school. "Much may be made of a Scotchman if he be caught young," said Samuel Johnson, and he was right.

As the enforced extroversion and other-directedness of the American education system closed in on me, I felt compelled to remain Scotch, as it were. I invented a game called "making it night"—closing the blinds and curtains and turning on all the lights during the day. It was, I know now, my way of banishing the Little Mary Sunshine that school, my first American institution, expected me to be.

In the second grade I was profoundly inspired by Veronica Lake's famous scene in *So Proudly We Hail,* the World War II movie about Bataan nurses, when she walks into a Japanese barracks with a grenade tucked in her bra. The lustful grinning soldiers surround her, and then. . . . Thereafter, whenever teachers nagged me about being antisocial, I thought about Veronica Lake and wondered if my undershirts were up to the task. *They want me to have extracurricular activities, huh? They want me to join clubs, huh? They want me to go to group functions, huh? Okey-dokey. . . .*

Time passed and so did Shirley Temple, but her shoes were quickly filled by another nemesis from America's apostolic succession of sunbeams.

"Why can't you be sweet and nice like June Allyson?" Granny asked quizzically.

To be both a female and a misanthrope is to be a carnival sideshow billed "the Human Oxymoron." Women are philanthropists in the original sense of the word, before money got involved in it, always hurling salvos of bigger and better niceness and meeting hostility with warnings of "there's more niceness where that came from." Despite a quarter century of feminism, everyone from counselors of battered wives to teachers of karate report that women still say, "I can't get angry enough."

I can. Feminists are always talking about "choices" and I have made one. Life for a woman is such a minefield of conflicts that misanthropy, at least in the figurative sense of "everybody buzz off," is the only thing that really works. Yet when women talk about "privacy" they mean abortion rights, and the millions of words feminists have written about "a room of one's own" refer to psychological space, rarely to physical solitude. For most women, being alone is tantamount to being deserted.

What is it like being a misanthrope on a daily basis? Not too bad most of the time. I can go on automatic pilot when I have to; in the South, a properly inflected "Ha yew?" covers a multitude of sins.

Much depends upon the kind of people I'm called upon to deal with. They fall into two categories: those who know what *misanthrope* means and those who don't.

The cognoscenti always ask the same question in properly shocked American tones.

"How can you hate *people*?"

"Who else is there to hate?"

The others are like the persistent president of a Southern women's club that wanted to take a literary tour of Europe and offered me a free trip in exchange for being their guide. I put her off politely the first two times she called, but the third time I was blunt.

"I'm sorry, I'm a misanthrope."

"Oh, honey, you don't have to let it cramp your style! My sister-in-law's a diabetic and she can go anywhere she wants as long as she takes her little kit with her."

People have stopped saying "She's just shy," but they persist in rationalizing my misanthropy with other clichés. Usually it's "She's been deeply hurt," often pieced out for greater adverbial effect with "somewhere, sometime, by someone."

I often get this from reviewers who, as citizens of the Republic of Nice, feel guilty about liking my books. A male reviewer, after placing me "in the first rank of American wits," added, "but like Dorothy Parker, King's success might well have been purchased with the coin of personal happiness."

If Dorothy Parker had been a misanthrope she would be in this book. I left her out because she was a romantic masquerading as a cynic, who hated to be alone and attempted suicide several times after broken romances. Misanthropes love to be alone, and the only emotion we feel after broken romances is relief. If we embroidered samplers they would say: "A Lover Is a Stranger You Haven't Met Yet."

Female reviewers are even more determined to find hidden tragedy: "Despite the wisdom and clear, clever observations King makes, the reader can't help but wonder if this woman's acid wit is the result of a lifelong feeling of rejection cushioned by books, which, if true, is very sad."

Bull, madam, bull. I do the rejecting. As for books, you should be as happy as I am when I'm reading. One time in particular sticks in my mind. It was November 1957 and the book was *The Prodigal Women* by Nancy Hale. The day was wet and cold, with a blustery wind. Whenever I got up to get another cup of coffee, I leaned on the kitchen windowsill waiting for the water to boil and gazed out at the gray afternoon with intense pleasure, my mind savoring John Donne's line, "In Heaven, it's always autumn."

Another rationalization I hear a lot is, "Oh, you're just kidding." It goes like this:

"Why don't you go on the 'Today Show'?"

"I'd rather corner them in a dungeon and pull the caps off their teeth. The only thing I have in common with those people is a sofa."

"Oh, you're just kidding."

Oh, no I'm not. My hero is the man who died on the Dick Cavett show. I forget his name but it doesn't matter; to a veteran of book-promotion tours who has walked through the valley of the shadow of Happy Talk, he will go down in history as the Man Who Got Even. Having no wish to emulate him just yet, I told my publisher that I am through touring books. I went to college with Willard Scott so I was already half dead in 1955; I refuse to let him and his ilk finish me off now.

Book tours aside, writing offers the best professional milieu a misanthrope could hope for. Writers stay home alone, so I get along fine with everybody I work with. Dian Fossey had her gorillas and I have my fax machine. As an enthusiastic letter writer I can savor the warmth of human contact without leaving the house or talking. I can even practice my version of Southern hospitality: standing in front of the fax and watching the paper appear over the edge is like standing at the window watching for company, except I don't have to say "Oh, God, here they come."

The publishing world presents certain problems, such as the word *upbeat*. Some years ago I had an editor who had done so many books on finding love and getting cancer that he used it constantly. He was without a doubt the most relentlessly cheerful person I have ever met, and seemed to take my temperament as a personal challenge. During the course of our project he enclosed a "Love Is . . ." cartoon in every letter. He also sent me a Norman Cousins roundup, a profile of Marjorie Holmes, a syndicated filler called "Heartstrings," and a *National Enquirer* clipping about a poll which found that the most popular television shows were those on which married couples sang love songs to each other.

I stood it as long as I could. Finally one day I told him that if he had been the editor on *Anna Karenina,* he would have said, "Leo, please, take out the train."

If there is no psychiatric literature on classic misanthropy, it is not solely because psychiatrists are people too. It's simply that misanthropes don't need to "seek help."

If we define a misanthrope as "someone who does not suffer fools and likes to see fools suffer," we have described a person with something to look forward to. Anticipating the spectacle of seeing fools suffer makes us wake up in the morning with a song in our hearts: in short, we are happy. We may be cynics and fatalists but we are not nihilists or existentialists (not the least because they tend to be bohemians and bohemians run in packs: if you go around saying "nothing matters," you need someone to say it to).

There is, however, a small amount of psychiatric literature on a trait connected to misanthropy. Known colloquially as "itchy feet," its clinical name is *dromomania,* from the Greek *dromos,* "to run."

The dislike of commitment that links misanthropy and dromomania is pinpointed by Kathleen Winsor in her novel, *Star Money:*

> What a relief it was to have anything done, finished, over with for good. So you could throw it out of your life and forget it and go on to something new. Some of her happiest moments had been spent cleaning out closets or drawers, throwing things away, knowing that whatever the symbolism they had had for her, she was destroying it. Each time she finished with something or someone and knew that she had finished forever, it gave her in some sense the illusion of having been granted a new beginning to life. . . .

I've been a dromomaniac for years. Although I hate to travel, I love to move. As a child I collected road maps and gazed contentedly at them by the hour, sounding out the names of strange new places and fantasizing about living in them. When I grew up, I did it. Since graduating from college I have had some forty addresses in various parts of the country, most for a few months and none for more than three years, until moving to my present apartment, where I've lived for ten years.

For some time now I have been planning to move to the mountains of western Virginia. My object is to live in a place that does not call itself "the community with a heart." I want one of those godforsaken towns where all the young people leave and the rest sit on the porch with a rifle across their knees.

I would have moved by now, but I had to wait for the 1991 Census figures to find out which towns are losing population, then I got involved in a book and didn't want to move in the middle of it. Meanwhile, to make myself feel that I was doing something to hasten the day, I cleaned out my closets and drawers with the same absorbing pleasure described by Kathleen Winsor. (Clutter symbolizes a life filled with people so misanthropes tend to be excellent housekeepers.)

When I finished, my apartment looked like a Spartan barracks but the mood was still on me, so I had the back seat taken out of my car— ostensibly to make more packing space, but really for the sheer thrill of shedding something else. After the surgery, I looked back at all that beautiful emptiness (I'm an agora*phil*iac) and toyed with the idea of having the buddy seat taken out as well. Having had only two passengers in the last ten years, I didn't need it, and I'm so used to driving alone that it makes me nervous to have someone with me. Best of all, I thought hungrily, if my car had nothing but a driver's seat it would be a bona fide misanthrope's car.

The only trouble was, other people might not see it that way. The cops might pull me over and ask me what I was planning to transport, and if I should move to another state and have to take another driving test, where would the examiner sit?

I didn't do it. But I still relish the thought of a would-be carjacker yanking open the door while I'm stopped at a light. . . .

By all rights, a misanthrope should be a Luddite. Championing advanced technology is a progressive stance and progressive people are notorious lovers of mankind. But technology is also "cold," and therein lies its charm for me.

In one of my battles with local feminists in the letters column of the Fredericksburg paper, a NOW cow latched onto an article of mine in *Ms.* in which I said that I had fallen in love with my computer. Taking it literally as feminists will, she wrote: "Erich Fromm described the most disturbing and extreme form of necrophilia as a fascination for machines rather than people. Can this explain Flo?"

When will feminists learn to think before they write? The most disturbing and extreme form of necrophilia is *necrophilia.* Nonetheless, she had a point. After vowing that I would never give up my typewriter; that, indeed, I would use a quill or even a stone tablet and a chisel rather than yield to "word processing," I was forced to buy a computer when a reviewing contract with *Newsday* stipulated that I had to send in my copy via modem.

My new "system" was delivered on the day of the 1987 stock market crash. Computers were being blamed for the calamity so I began to think better of them, and by the end of the first week I was hooked. If my favorite dwarf was Grumpy, my favorite key is Escape.

Now that high tech has created the growing trend of working at home, the day of the misanthrope is at hand. A bevy of psychological counselors has sprung up to advise newly minted homeworkers on how to "answer the needs" of family members who "place demands" upon the worker's time and "invade his space." Suggestions abound, including drawing little pictures of computers on the children's calendar, but it will do no good. The handwriting is already on the wall, right up there with the children's crayon scrawls.

The best way to handle invading family members is not to have any. In lieu of that, you must feel comfortable practicing the dying art of yelling "goddamnit!" But that's *inappropriate,* so most attempts to work at home will founder on the shoals of the Republic of Nice, leaving the way open for misanthropes to corner the market.

Misanthropes have some admirable if paradoxical virtues. It is no exaggeration to say that we are among the nicest people you are likely to meet. Good manners build strong walls; our distaste for intimacy makes us exceedingly cordial "ships that pass in the night." As long as you remain a stranger we will be your friend forever.

We are law-abiding in the extreme, not because we are plaster saints, but because criminals must deal with people constantly. Most crimes require a gift of gab and an ability to inspire trust in the victim, so we do not become con artists. We do not take hostages because once you take them you can't let them out of your sight. We do not commit serial murder because we recoil in moral revulsion at the very word: *serial.* As for child molestation, in order to molest a child you must first be in the same room with a child, and I don't know how perverts stand it.

Nor will you find us among "affectless" psychopaths. Misanthropes were sensitive back when sensitive wasn't cool; to us, life is a Chinese water torture and every drop is a tidal wave. We may be psychopaths in our own fashion, but we behave because we know that prison life is communal. If ever you meet someone who cannot understand why solitary confinement is considered punishment, you have met a misanthrope.

Do not make the mistake of attributing misanthropy to the great monsters of history. Caligula and Ivan the Terrible were insane, but Hitler, Mussolini, and Stalin exuded a certain heavy-handed bonhomie (Saddam Hussein appears to belong in this category) that suggests normal conviviality. As leaders of great masses of people, monsters must be able to use their personalities to mesmerize their followers and forge primal bonds with them by becoming father figures. Whatever this gift is called—heart, the common touch, public relations—no misanthrope could hold such a pose for more than five minutes, and then only on a good day.

If you think misanthropes have "nothing to contribute" to society, think again. Youth-obsessed America can learn much from us.

Jonathan Swift: "No wise man ever wished to be younger."

"A hatred of youth and of being young" was Ambrose Bierce's definition of misanthropy. "Youth, it seemed to him, was something to be gotten over as quickly as possible, with adulthood the only goal worthwhile," according to a Bierce biographer.

Ayn Rand felt the same way. "Childhood was an overture," writes Barbara Branden, "a preparation for the future, with no significance in itself."

It was not simply that Bierce and Rand came as adults to dislike children, but that they disliked children while they were children themselves, and resented *being* children. I know the feeling well: it's hard to be a misanthrope when you're that short.

It's also hard to be one when the optimism and energy of youth press in on you from all sides. Call it what you like—salad days, *jeunesse dorée,* or twentysomething—we're against it. Middle age, when temperament and chronology become a matched set at last, is the misanthrope's finest hour.

Richard Nixon's "deep-in-the-gut loathing for the sixties" was not only political but "an integral part of his personality," write Dan Rather and Gary Paul Gates in *The Palace Guard.* "As a young Congressman, Nixon gave the impression of being older than he was—a man, say, in his middle to late forties. In an eerie sort of way, he has remained frozen in that bracket into his sixties, as though he had made some kind of Faustian bargain to give up the spark of youth in exchange for becoming forever forty-seven."

That misanthropes actually look forward to the aging process makes us the luckiest people in Oil of America. The latest testimonial to our Biercean calendar comes from Rush Limbaugh. He likes to call himself "a harmless little fuzzball," but the ruminative remarks he made on his radio show on his forty-third birthday (January 12) suggest otherwise. "When you're young, nobody respects you, nobody pays you any money," he reflected. "My parents used to worry about me because when I was sixteen I wanted to be forty."

Hmmm. . . . I detect the mother of all attitudes. Welcome to the club, Rush.

Like any other personality trait, misanthropy is a matter of degree. Taken in the literal sense, the obvious problem is one of logistics: hating the entire human race is hard to do—though not, of course, impossible.

In the figurative sense, however, misanthropy is a realistic attitude toward human nature for Americans who do not necessarily hate everybody, but are tired of compulsory gregariousness, fevered friendliness, we-never-close compassion, goo-goo humanitarianism, sensitivity that never sleeps, and politicians paralyzed by a hunger to be loved.

The advantage in being a misanthrope in the age of political correctness cannot be overstated:

It is extremely hard to accuse a person of being an *-ist,* an *-ite,* or a *-phobe* when he has already established himself as a *-thrope.*

If some inflamed zealot does it anyway, I always reply, "Don't think small."

THE END